"I'm sorry," she said. She gestured at the badlands behind her. "My brother has sent for me. I have to go to him."

Lonal drew away the coverings from his face. He was still as handsome, but he was no longer the unmarked youth she had met on her arrival in the desert. He held out his right hand. He had a scar there, on his wrist. It matched the one on hers.

"You have come far among the Zyraii," he said. "Don't lose your honor now."

"There's no time to waste. Something has happened. I can't risk the wait."

"By law, I am required to stop you."

She nodded. "I know that. Will you?"

"Yes," he whispered.

She sighed, and slid her rapier out of its sheath.

He drew his scimitar....

DAVE SMEDS

THE SORCERY WITHIN

ACE FANTASY BOOKS
NEW YORK

AUTHOR'S NOTE

A prelude to this novel, entitled "Dragon Touched," was included in the Ace anthology DRAGONS OF LIGHT, edited by Orson Scott Card. While it is by no means necessary to read the short story in order to follow the novel, those who prefer things in chronological order may wish to seek it out. For those who've already read the short story, you should be aware that the character Alemar in "Dragon Touched" is not the same as the one introduced on the first page of this book.

THE SORCERY WITHIN

An Ace Fantasy Book/published by arrangement with the author

PRINTING HISTORY
Ace edition/August 1985

All rights reserved.
Copyright © 1985 by Dave Smeds
Cover art by Kevin Johnson
Maps by Dave Smeds
This book may not be reproduced in whole or in part, by mimeograph or any other means, without permission.
For information address: The Berkley Publishing Group, 200 Madison Avenue, New York, New York 10016.

ISBN: 0-441-77557-8

Ace Fantasy Books are published by The Berkley Publishing Group, 200 Madison Avenue, New York, New York 10016.
PRINTED IN THE UNITED STATES OF AMERICA

ACKNOWLEDGMENTS

The following people contributed the financial and material support without which this novel would never have seen print before 1995: Connie Willeford Smeds, Alfred and Josephine Smeds, Bob Fleming and Cherie Kushner.

The following people contributed comments on the manuscript-in-progress that ultimately sharpened and clarified the final version: Connie Willeford Smeds, Deborah L. Sweitzer, Lucy Buss, Bob Fleming, Paul Avellar, Becky Priest, Jim Musto, Shirley Johnston, Steve Swenston, Peter Fablé, Cherie Kushner, Margaret Silvestri, Sally Margolit, Beth Egan, Jim Hershey, Diana Hershey, James Ellison, Yves de Cargouet, Dee Doyle, Brian Crist, Dinene McClure, Teresa Bippert, Ben Pivnick, Ken Macklin, Coleeta Morris, Brett Morgan, Walter Sauers, Jonathan Sachs, Marian Gibbons.

The map and many of the place names are taken from original cartography by John Gast.

And thanks to Susan Allison and Terri Windling of Ace/Berkley, as well as Drew Mendelson, LOCUS, and Orson Scott Card, for weaving the web that resulted in the sale of *The Sorcery Within*.

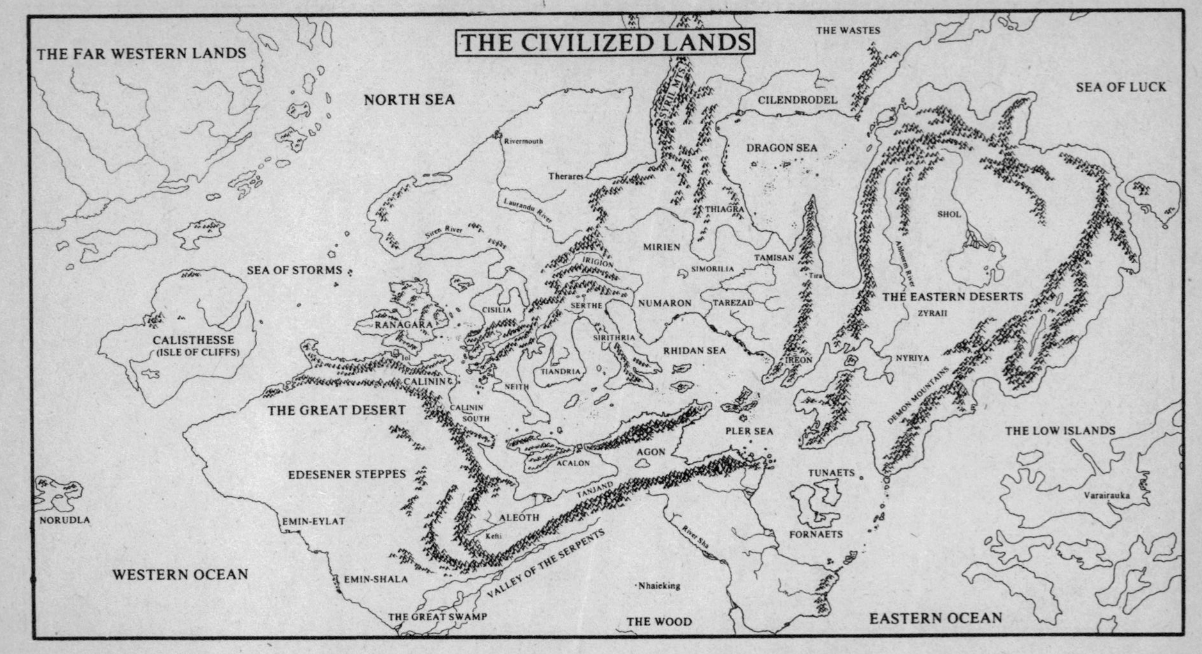
THE CIVILIZED LANDS
THE FAR WESTERN LANDS
NORTH SEA
THE WASTES
SEA OF LUCK
CILENDRODEL
SYRIL MTS.
DRAGON SEA
Rivermouth
Therares
Laurandu River
THIAGRA
SHOL
Siren River
MIRIEN
TAMISAN
Ahloorm River
SEA OF STORMS
IRIGION
SIMORILIA
Tira
THE EASTERN DESERTS
CISILIA
SERTHE
NUMARON
TAREZAD
ZYRAII
RANAGARA
CALISTHESSE
(ISLE OF CLIFFS)
SIRITHRIA
RHIDAN SEA
IREON
NYRIYA
Iol
TIANDRIA
CALININ
NEITH
DEMON MOUNTAINS
THE GREAT DESERT
CALININ SOUTH
PLER SEA
THE LOW ISLANDS
AGON
ACALON
EDESENER STEPPES
TUNAETS
TANJAND
Varairauka
NORUDLA
ALEOTH
EMIN-EYLAT
Kefti
FORNAETS
River Sha
VALLEY OF THE SERPENTS
WESTERN OCEAN
EMIN-SHALA
Nhaieking
THE GREAT SWAMP
THE WOOD
EASTERN OCEAN

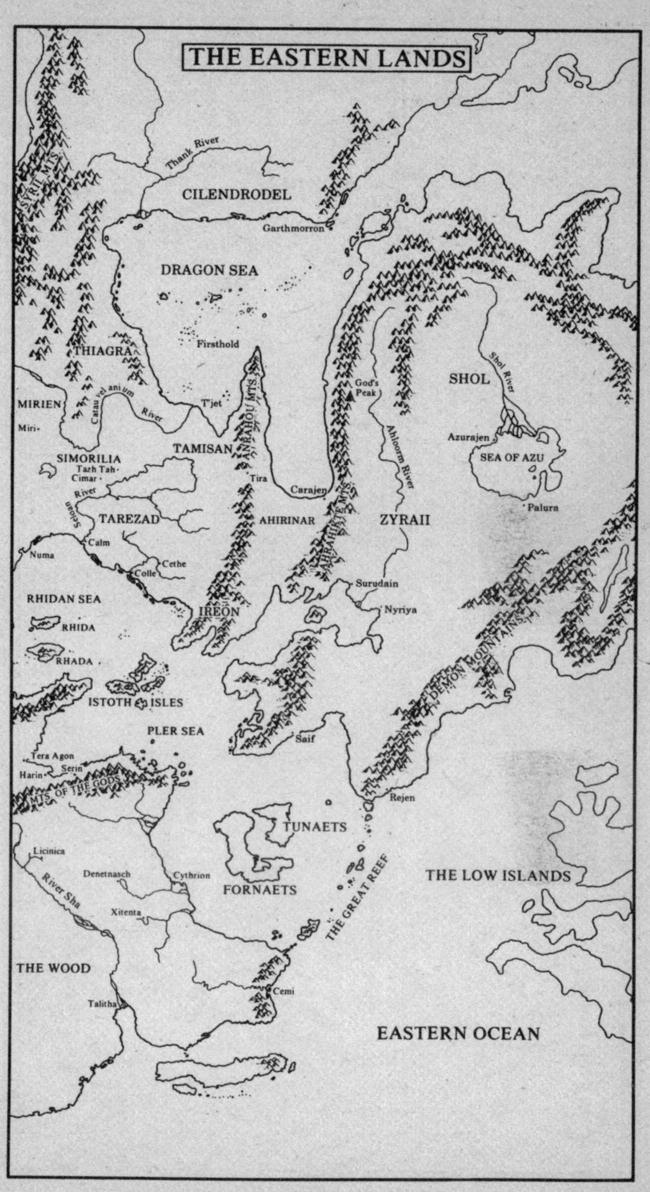

THE EASTERN LANDS
SYRIL MTS.
Thank River
CILENDRODEL
Garthmorron
DRAGON SEA
Firsthold
THIAGRA
MIRIEN
Miri
Catau vel ani um River
T'jet
ANAHAOU MTS.
God's Peak
SHOL
Shol River
Azurajen
SEA OF AZU
Palura
Ahloorm River
TAMISAN
SIMORILIA
Tazh Tah
Cimar
Scloan River
Tira
Carajen
TAREZAD
AHIRINAR
AHRAHIKTE MTS.
ZYRAII
Calm
Numa
Cethe
Colle
Surudain
Nyriya
RHIDAN SEA
RHIDA
RHADA
IREON
DEMON MOUNTAINS
ISTOTH ISLES
PLER SEA
Saif
Tera Agon
Serin
Harin
MTS. OF THE GODS
Rejen
TUNAETS
Licinica
Denetnasch
Cythrion
FORNAETS
River Sha
Xitenta
THE GREAT REEF
THE LOW ISLANDS
THE WOOD
Cemi
Talitha
EASTERN OCEAN

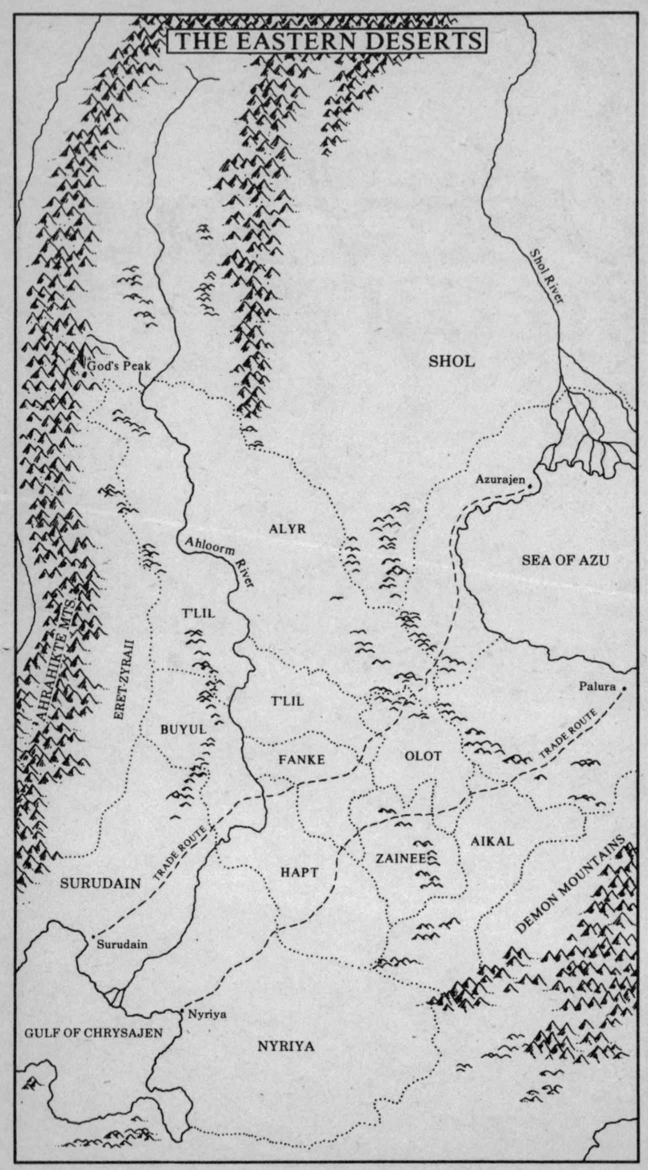
THE EASTERN DESERTS
God's Peak
SHOL
Sho1 River
Azurajen
ALYR
Ahloorm River
SEA OF AZU
T'LIL
AHRAHIKTE MTS.
ERET-ZYRAII
T'LIL
Palura
BUYUL
TRADE ROUTE
FANKE
OLOT
TRADE ROUTE
AIKAL
ZAINEE
HAPT
SURUDAIN
DEMON MOUNTAINS
Surudain
Nyriya
GULF OF CHRYSAJEN
NYRIYA

THE SORCERY WITHIN

I

The water hole was a tiny pool virtually hidden in the rocks, an unexpected blessing in the middle of tracts of scoured hardpan and powder-dry arroyos. The lichen growing on the stone at the water's edge was the only green growth they had seen for two days. In the far west, barely visible as early morning sun illuminated their slopes, the Ahrahikte Mountains lay across their rearward trail.

Alemar dipped his fingers into the water and brushed them tentatively against his lips. The feel of liquid was almost alien, a cool, soft sensation that vanished almost immediately, absorbed into the cracks and dust on his skin. He took a small sip. It was gone within moments, without ever reaching his throat.

"It's good," he said hoarsely.

Elenya stooped beside her brother, away from her sentry position. Leaning to the water's surface, she relieved her swollen lips. Alemar sprinkled drops on his face and stayed back, as there was no room for two. Anywhere else, the water would have been brackish and unworthy of consuming. As it was, he didn't complain. Elenya filled her mouth once, held it, and sat back. She pulled the cowl and veil around her face again, blocking out the glare.

They drank by turns, relearning how to swallow. After a small amount, Alemar felt dizzy, and lay back against the rock that shadowed the pool. As his head settled onto the rough surface, he felt vibrations.

Hoofbeats.

He rolled to the side as two daggers landed heavily on the spot he had just vacated. Elenya flipped over the water hole, already reaching for her rapier. Another knife narrowly missed her.

The attackers were three desert riders, clad in loose white robes and veils much the same as the twins' own, mounted on oeikani. They bore down on the twins at full speed, drawing long, slightly curved blades.

Alemar flung himself flat. A blade snipped a seam in his cowl, just touching his hair. A second rider was on him before he could draw a weapon. He sprang to the balls of his feet, and as the scimitar came down, he sidestepped it, grabbed the man's wrist, and pulled down. The oeikani galloped past, while its surprised rider plunged headlong into the rock, uttering a sharp expletive in an unfamiliar tongue. Alemar kept his grip on the arm through the tumble, hearing and feeling it splinter. He took the weapon.

He glanced to the side. Elenya was ducking the third rider. The man sliced viciously, contemptuous of her thin blade. The cut would have killed a slower opponent, but it missed her entirely, and Alemar saw the glint of metal from her return blow. The rider continued on for several paces, and abruptly fell from the oeikani. A dark stain spread across his midsection. He didn't move again.

The first rider had circled, and plunged toward Alemar in a slightly less headlong fashion. He pulled up, parried Alemar's thrust, and harassed him from his superior position. As Elenya turned toward them, the rider passed, hoping for a quick victory. Alemar avoided the oeikani's hooves, slipped his dagger out of his belt with his left hand, and flung it. The rider blocked the dagger with a small shield bound to his empty hand, but wasn't fast enough to catch the thrust that followed. He fell from his mount, partially disembowelled.

The moaning of the man with the broken arm turned their attention toward the east. There, twenty riders waited at a standstill only fifty paces away, where moments before there had been none. Their robes and the markings on their oeikani were the same as the three attackers. As a group, they raised their scimitars and lifted reins to whip their animals forward. One man in the center held back.

"Na tet," he shouted. Abruptly, the other men lowered their weapons. He gave a few more terse commands, and the group rode quickly forward to surround the twins.

When the circle was complete, well within range of the

throwing daggers that all the warriors bore, the leader spoke again. *"Ai natt dor kem?"*

"We use the High Speech," Alemar answered.

The man regarded them. He was taller than most of the group, a bronzed, handsome forehead showing above the veil. He bore himself like a man accustomed to authority.

"The tongue of the Calinin is seldom spoken here," he said. His inflection was wrong, but his construction was excellent. "Who are you, and what are you doing here?"

"I am Tebec."

"And your brother?"

Before Elenya could answer, Alemar said, "He is Yetem. We come from Cilendrodel on our father's business."

"You have come a long way." The leader pointed to the water hole. "Here, among Zyraii lands, the penalty for stealing water is death."

"We are not dead."

To Alemar's surprise, the leader smiled, the expression visible in the creases around his eyes. "That is true. And you say you came from the west?"

"Yes."

"God has indeed been merciful to bring you through the eret-Zyraii. *We* do not go there." He pointed to the wasteland.

The last two days had not seemed merciful to Alemar.

"Foreigners are rare in the steppes. Where are you bound?"

"Setan."

An animated murmur spread immediately through the riders. The leader laughed momentarily without amusement. "You and every bastard child of ten nations. At least you're honest about it."

Alemar hesitated.

The leader said, "I am Lonal, and these are my brothers. We are of the T'lil tribe. You have taken our water without permission." He toyed with his knife hilt, but his expression seemed to soften, the aggressiveness replaced by curiosity. "Nevertheless, I offer you an alternative to death."

He gestured toward the dead and wounded. "I have never seen anyone deal with mounted attackers quite so efficiently."

Alemar inclined his head at the compliment, for he could see that this was the appropriate response. Lonal did not seem overtly angry that his men had suffered. He pointed to the two riderless oeikanki that had been rounded up during the conversation. The man from whom Alemar had stolen the scimitar was being shoved onto his saddle, arm tucked in front of him. "The laws of the So-de'es allow me to use my discretion in certain cases. You have taken our water"—he shrugged—"but the rains have been good this year. The T'lil need all our fighting men, and you have deprived us. If you will take their places, and become our brothers, holy law may yet be observed without requiring your deaths."

Alemar searched the leader's face three times over, wishing the veil didn't hide half of it. He had already begun to detach himself, preparing to die, and it was difficult to shake the mood. He hadn't expected this. There were hidden motives at work, but if it were a trap, Alemar couldn't fathom it—their lives were already in the hands of the desert men.

"How many of them understand the High Speech?" Alemar asked of Lonal's companions. "Do they know what you propose?"

"I am Lonal," the leader said simply. "They will do as I say."

"And what of Setan?"

Lonal scowled. "Does greed dull your wits? You were rational enough to wear Zyraii robes as you tried to pass our borders." He fingered his own garment. "Foreigners are not allowed in Setan."

"It's not treasure we're after."

"Now you mock me. Are you going to accept my offer or not? The sun climbs. . . ." Already since the fight, the temperature had increased noticeably.

Abruptly Elenya slipped her rapier into its scabbard and climbed into the saddle of one of the oeikani. Alemar paused a moment longer. He was not angry at her impulsiveness; it merely meant that she had already thought of what he was just realizing—in their circumstances, they shouldn't question luck.

Lonal traded words with his companions after Alemar had mounted. Two of them asked short questions, which the leader answered even more briefly. He told the twins, "Forget whatever life you had in the world that is outside Zyraii. This land will never let you live unless you are committed to it, and to its people. The sooner you accept this, the sooner you profit." It was hard to tell if this were advice, or a command. He ordered them to the middle of a double column, and the group set out.

As soon as they were away, carrion birds began circling the bodies of the two dead men. Alemar looked back at one point. Lonal noticed the hesitation.

"Those who die in battle need no ceremony," he said. "God will care for them."

II

The forest of Cilendrodel stretched entirely across the northern edge of the Dragon Sea. The village of Eruth hid within the silent giants that made up the wood, buildings interspersed between the boles of the largest trees, the underbrush and smaller trunks removed to make way for the community. Even then the forest attempted to reclaim its own; many of the house yards were swamped in berry bushes and decorated with vines that sometimes concealed all but the windows and doors. The late hour had doused the lights of all but a few houses, but lantern glow paraded out of the larger of the town's two taverns, full of belly laughs and the scent of rich woodland ale.

The main room contained heavy beams of wood set high and many rough-hewn tables and chairs. Approximately half were occupied by villagers wearing brightly colored clothing made of the durable quarn silk for which this part of Cilendrodel was famous. They took little notice of Keron as he entered, dressed as he was in an identical manner. Eruth was on the main thoroughfare and accustomed to newcomers. He strode to the bar, and the barkeeper recognized him.

"Hello, Ampet," Keron said.

If the man was surprised, he hid it. He gestured toward a door just to the side of the bar. "Wait in there. Have you eaten?"

"Not recently."

"I'll see that something is sent in. He'll be with you when we close—it shouldn't be very long."

Keron did as he was told. The room behind the bar was a small chamber containing a table, four chairs, and a narrow bed. A rear door led to the compost pile, outhouse, and forest. A stairway from the inn on the second story ended just to the left. Even next to the building, the overhead foliage was thick, and stole the starlight.

Keron stood in the rear portal and whistled—a single, quick note. Soon the same note, sounded twice, came from somewhere in the nearby underbrush. Satisfied, Keron reentered and secured the door with a heavy bar.

The decor was wooden—extremely so. Except for a small carpet near the bed and the straw tick mattress, everything was hard and uninviting. A large cask of ale stood in one corner, and every wall contained shelves or racks of steins, bowls, and other utensils. Keron lifted the carpet and inspected the planks of the floor to be certain they were immobile.

A boy brought a slab of cold meat, vegetables, and a loaf of bread. The bread was stale, and the vegetables had simmered to the point of formlessness, but it hardly mattered. As soon as he was sure that the boy would not return, Keron disposed of the entire meal on the compost pile, leaving only enough scraps to make it seem as if he had eaten it. Then he drew a stein of ale and sipped tiny amounts to pass the time.

Presently the noise of the drinking room stilled. Not long after, an obese man wearing an evening suit embroidered with silver walked in, alone, and closed the door behind him. Their gazes met, the straightforward glances of men who had learned to lie.

"Good evening, Master Luo," Keron said.

"I've been expecting you, Captain."

"I'll wager you have."

"It was a fine trick, capturing the Dragon's frigate like that." He drew himself an ale and sat down across from his guest.

"One gets inspired when one's own ship is sinking out from beneath one's feet."

"Indeed."

Keron leaned forward. "I don't like losing my ship, Luo."

"Is that an accusation?"

"Let's just say I'm suspicious that it happened so soon after we had last done business."

Luo cleared his throat. "I am the biggest silk producer in this province, and you Elandri royalists are my best customers. What motive would I have to betray you to the Dragon?"

"I haven't solved that one yet. Yet there was a betrayal."

"If you think I'm the one responsible, why are you here?"

"My people need silk. The last shipment is feeding crabs and octopi off the reef." Keron stroked his close-cropped beard. "And that's a problem. I can't let the smuggling be hamstrung, but I can't proceed blindly, either. We both know it wasn't likely that the Frog's ship was there by coincidence. Either you or your men gave me away, or one of my own men has turned traitor."

Luo folded his hands firmly around his stein. "Agreed," he said presently. "But may I point out that I didn't know the drop point until that very night?"

"I've taken that into account."

"And what have you decided?"

Keron shrugged. "I've decided to buy some silk."

Luo sipped his ale, feigning disinterest. He cleared his throat. "I'm not sure I dare, Captain. If your security has been breached, my own is endangered."

Keron frowned. "How much to soothe your fears?"

Luo shrugged. "Sixty-six droels per bolt."

"That's expensive insurance."

"The Dragon's blockade is becoming tighter all the time. I would have had to ask for an increase soon anyway."

"Sixty-four droels."

"Captain . . ."

Keron drew out a small pouch, and poured several large pearls out on the table. Luo picked one up and examined it, a hungry look in his stare.

"Currency is a problem. These will have to do. I'm sure you'll be satisfied with the quality."

"These are amath, aren't they?" Luo said reverently.

"Yes."

"Sixty-four, then." With the blockade in force, amath pearls were hard to come by in Cilendrodel. The exchange rate improved almost weekly against gold and oyster pearls. If he maneuvered correctly, Luo could realize a substantial gain simply by holding them for a short time. "But two more for the violet."

"Eh?"

"You know we make violet dyes from wendruil root. We import that from the Syril Mountains. Either we pay the Dragon his new tariff or pay more for overland shipment."

"Very well. Can you have it ready by the fourth of Three Moons?"

Luo calculated absently with his fingertips. "Yes. The green and blue are being dyed now, but it should be no problem. I'll expect your man at the usual time."

"Done."

Luo rose, well aware of the intimidation value of the movement of so much weight, and set his stein back on its perch. He clutched the pouch of jewels tightly in his palm. "I am sad that it came to this, Captain. Perhaps, if the Dragon allows it, we won't have such . . . strained times . . . in the future." He glanced toward the rear of the room. "You'll be leaving immediately, I trust."

"Yes. It's best."

"True. Good night, sir. Pleasant journey." Luo reached for the door back into the tavern.

"A moment," Keron called.

"Hmmm?"

"The password is *faernak.*"

Luo grunted. "Ah. Of course. May the rythni keep you well."

"Good night," Keron said.

As Keron listened to Luo's footsteps recede, the uneasiness that had possessed him ever since arriving at the tavern intensified. Luo was not a forgetful person. But the conversation had revealed nothing untoward. Keron stepped over to the outer door and whistled as he had before.

Two long heartbeats later, a double whistle came from just on the other side of the wall.

The signal was correct. Keron lifted the bar off its cradles and began to open the door. Only then did he remember that his men were supposed to remain in the forest, not next to the building.

Too late.

The door slammed inward, knocking him to the floor before he could let go of the bar. Three men surged inside. A heavy blue glint reflected off the steel in their hands.

Keron kicked, catching the first man in the groin, sending him crashing into the ceiling. A rafter cracked open the man's skull. The body, however, landed on Keron, thwarting his attempt to rise. The other two assassins closed in.

Keron felt the knives pierce him. One peeled loose a section of his scalp; another slid along his ribs; he took a stab in the thigh. Only the interference of the corpse prevented a fatal blow.

By then, Keron had a grip on the ankle of one of his attackers. He yanked, pulling the man's knee out of its socket.

The man screamed and fell to the side. The effort had left Keron exposed. It cost him a knife in the back, close to the heart. He nearly fainted from the pain. He struck blindly. His elbow connected with something that caved in like a melon.

After that, neither of the assassins lasted very long.

Keron collapsed against a wall. He could sense the blood spurting from the wound in his back. He tried to control his breathing, staving off the shock that would doom him. A few seconds. If he could just last long enough . . .

He felt sorcery kiss him, soothing and strong. It worked quickly. The river in his back was stemmed. He felt his tissues begin to knit.

As suddenly as it had come, it left. The magic, as he had feared, had its limit. His distant doctor had done what he could. He had a reprieve, but only the most severe damage had been dealt with. He might still die. The pain was still intense. For a time, he could only shake, and would have made a passive victim for a fourth assassin.

He looked at the lithe, dark-cloaked figures of the men he had killed. He recognized the insignia on their vests. The Claw. Frog's men.

They were good. The Dragon's best. They had almost been good enough.

While he still could, he roused and stumbled outside, toward the underbrush, searching. Soon he saw the crumpled bodies.

Both had been stabbed from behind. Faces that he had shared the decks with on long sea voyages stared up empty, already losing the heat of life. But he had expected no better from the moment he had been attacked.

"Good wind and clear sky," he murmured, and closed their eyes.

The brawling of oeikani disrupted his mourning. It came from the stables next to the tavern. Spurred with a final reserve of energy, he limped around the perimeter of the building, arriving at the stable doors just as they swung open.

Luo whipped his animal when he saw Keron, but the Elandri stepped aside, grasped an antler in his good hand, and yanked downard. The oeikani squealed and plunged into the dirt, flipping its rider to a landing so heavy as to dent the roadway. Luo emitted the sick wheeze of someone who had lost all the air his lungs have ever possessed.

"Going somewhere?" Keron asked.

"How?" the silk trader squeaked, when he could breathe.

"I'm strong," Keron replied.

"It wasn't my doing! They forced me!" Luo whined.

"Who forced you? Give me names!"

"I don't know." Luo managed to roll on his side, lifting one hand in supplication.

Keron walked unsteadily forward and picked up the sword that had broken free of Luo's belt on impact. Clothing soaked with blood, skin an unhealthy pallor, he moved toward Luo.

"Listen, Elandri! We can bargain!"

Keron chopped through Luo's neck like an executioner. He wiped the steel off on the fine quarn suit of the deceased.

"The best bargain we've ever struck," Keron muttered. He paused only long enough to search the body. He found the pearls he had given Luo earlier, along with another small sack. It contained only five objects. Four were gems of the highest quality. The fifth was another amath pearl. Had the latter not contained a flaw, it would have been fit for a king. As it was, it was still extremely valuable. Keron had rarely seen specimens this large.

Shouts came from the inn above. Keron glanced up and saw Ampet silhouetted in a window frame. He heard running feet. His ravaged body threatened to buckle, but he had to find safety, a place to heal. The neck of the beast he had downed was broken, so he seized another from the stables, not stopping to look for a saddle. He knocked an oil lamp into straw fodder on his way out, and left Eruth blazing with two kinds of fire.

III

Alemar and Elenya spent the heat of the day resting in one of the arroyos common to the region. The banks of the ancient streambed cut deeply and suddenly into the plain, invisible from only a short distance away, a trick characteristic of the land and one that had allowed the T'lil to appear so suddenly at the water hole. The desert riders used canopies to augment the natural shade. It was shocking to the twins to be suddenly free of the burden of sunlight.

The group stretched out on either side of them, a long row of individuals and clusters. The oeikani were gathered together at a spot where the stream's course widened, where they could be easily guarded. The twins scooted into a shallow fissure, left to themselves, but not enough so that they couldn't be seen at all times. Elenya barely managed to smooth the sand beneath her before she fell asleep.

When she awoke, the sun occupied the opposite quarter of the sky. High above, a huge black bird circled, probably a carrion vulture. For a moment, still half dreaming, she pictured it as a dragon, waiting to dive upon her, flame spouting from its throat. An unlikely fantasy—Gloroc, the Dragon of Elandris, was the only living example of his race within the civilized world, and he wasn't old enough to fly yet.

She heard the snores of napping Zyraii. Other members of the tribe were engaged in games of chance played with three twelve-sided dice. One or two honed their weapons. She uncurled herself, groaned, and noticed that Alemar was awake.

"Haven't you slept?"

"No. Couldn't."

"If you fall off your animal later, don't expect me to pick you up," she said, noting his bloodshot eyes and the heaviness of his lids. She didn't need to ask how he felt; they had been through the eret-Zyraii together.

"Have some salt," he said, handing her their precious supply. She sprinkled some on her tongue and followed it with several swallows of water.

"What now?" She spoke quietly, and used the Low Speech of the Cilendri for extra measure, but none of the strangers gave any sign that they were interested in the twins' conversation.

"They know where Setan is. We don't."

"That doesn't help us much if we're prisoners."

They both felt the alert eyes that pretended not to look at them and noted the smooth, feline gait of a warrior walking by. In their state of exhaustion they couldn't even think to escape. The fight at the water hole had taken what scant reserves they had left.

Not far away, a Zyraii relieved himself. Elenya felt no longings from her own bladder, despite the time since she'd last emptied it, but she began thinking.

"Do I look like a man?" she asked, gesturing down at her body. Like her brother, she was small and slender. Although fair-skinned, the sun had tanned them almost to the swarthiness of the Zyraii, and shoulder-length, jet-black hair occasionally peeked out of either of their cowls. The clothing hung so loosely as to completely conceal her small breasts unless she pressed the cloth against herself, and the veil hid the fact that she had no beard.

Alemar squinted at her, as if trying to place himself in an objective viewpoint. "No. But neither do you appear not to be. One would see what one expected to see."

"They made the mistake very easily."

"I know. That's why I didn't correct Lonal. Maybe there's a good reason why you should be a man."

"But they'll know I'm a woman before very long, one way or another."

He frowned. "What happens when they find out we've lied?"

"I don't know."

They rested a while longer. More and more of the party stirred as the heat began to wane. They felt caresses from the faithful afternoon breeze. A half dozen Zyraii began practicing knife throwing. Elenya had recognized the short daggers carried by all of the riders. They performed demonblade. The name was taken from the Demon Steppes, a label Zyraii territory was known by outside the Eastern Deserts. Legend had it that Zyraii boys learned to throw knives before they could hold the weapons with one hand. The twins carried knives of their own, weighted for throwing, and knew how to use them, but they had never before had the opportunity to watch the skill performed by its traditional masters.

The men aimed at a wooden shield, the same type that could be found strapped to each rider's nonthrowing hand. Like the demonblades, the shields were cherished articles, wood oiled for protection from the weather, leather straps sewn tight. Wood, not metal. Metal became too hot in the sun. Likewise, wood slowed a blade's momentum in cases where metal only deflected.

The target piece, however, was worn and cracked, and covered with several layers of hide to protect the points of the knives that struck it. Though it was barely wider across than the span of an adult's thumb and middle finger, the throwers rarely missed.

"They're good," Elenya said.

"Yes," Alemar answered. "Better than we."

"Better than you," Elenya said. Alemar didn't dispute her.

"The good ones aren't practicing," she continued. "Like the two on the left there. I can smell others. And isn't it funny how our view is seldom blocked?" Feigning disinterest, members of the tribe stole glances in the direction of the twins. Elenya stared them down.

Eventually she pointed to Lonal. "*He* is the best. He's not even on the same scale." The war-leader scarcely watched the proceedings. Even at rest, he broadcast confidence. When he did move, each action had its place, nothing wasted.

"Better than you?" Alemar asked.

She paused. "I would like to spar with him someday."

At dusk, they mounted their oeikani and proceeded swiftly toward the east. The terrain became more varied. Desert flowers, cacti, and sparse brush appeared. After so long in utter desert, Alemar smelled the increase of water in the air. He shrugged this off as fantasy, born of exhaustion and the intellectual knowledge that as they travelled east they approached the Ahloorm, Zyraii's only major river.

The sun's stifling brilliance gave way to the cool, muted

light of Motherworld. The Sister had already climbed high in the sky, her glow no longer dwarfed by the day. Shadows diffused and broadened. Hints of life scurried next to the path. Occasionally a rider would swing out from the group, small bow in hand, to return with a sagecrawler or a small mammal. Tiny feral sounds increased as the darkness deepened. It wouldn't grow beyond twilight until near morning, as Motherworld was in a gibbous phase, bold with her bands of ochre and beige.

At last, the land seemed to live. In the west, the eret-Zyraii, the best that could be hoped for was the rare water hole such as the twins had found that morning. Nature was a bad enemy. It was better here, among human adversaries. People were vulnerable.

They reached the Zyraii camp during midevening. It was a substantial settlement—three concentric rings of goat-hide tents, the largest and best toward the center. A small ritual fire burned at the hub, an area that also contained a spacious, undecorated tent of actual cloth, as well as a smith's forge and the livestock corrals. The first thing Alemar noticed about the place was the scarcity of fire—only the central flame and a few scattered oil cooking braziers. He saw figures bustling to and fro. Sentries had alerted the inhabitants, and children rushed out to greet the incoming warriors. Women hurried in other directions to prepare the reception.

The group rode immediately to the oeikani corral, through a twisting aisle between the tents just wide enough to accommodate their double file. Alemar deduced at once the significance of placing the corrals in the center—the valuable oeikani, sheep, and goats stood less chance of being lost in a raid. Boys came forward to tend to the mounts, including one who trotted up without hesitation to take those of Alemar and Elenya. He stopped short as soon as he saw them closely. The twins read his surprise as they dismounted but, handicapped as they were by lack of language, could only stare back with equal perplexity.

"Rol, yil ta wakani!" Lonal told the boy, who blanched.

The oeikani shuffled impatiently, awaiting their feeding. The boy turned and quieted them by name, glanced back at the twins one more time, and hurried away with his charges.

Alemar felt the blood on his hands.

Lonal ignored the questioning glances, and led them through the tents. As they passed, women and children stared at the twins in a manner that the warriors had not, open-mouthed and shrinking back, making ritual signs. They wore no veils. The women dressed mainly in loose, flowing skirts with multi-layered wraparound tops, seldom exposing more than head, hands, ankles, and feet. A few wore leather sandals; most were barefoot. Infants and small children ran naked. Fabrics boasted many colors and patterns, some quite plain, others intricate in both the design and weaving. Only grown men, and not all of these, displayed the white robes of the group that they had ridden with. Eventually, Alemar noticed that those who wore white were the only ones who bore weapons.

Lonal spoke to them as they ferreted their way through the walls of hide. "These are the tents of my clan, the T'krt, largest of all the T'lil. We journey to the Ahloorm Basin. For tonight, you will be shown your tent and introduced to the elders. We will decide what to do with you tomorrow. Your adoption must be recognized, and you will have to be educated in our ways."

Lonal seemed completely unperturbed that he was declaring the long-term fate of two people with a handful of words. He drew off his veil as he spoke, and flipped back the cowl, revealing a handsome, hawk-nosed face, much younger than Alemar had expected. There was energy in that face.

He instructed them to wait where they were for a few moments, and disappeared into a tent. Soon they could hear him conversing with another man in the Zyraii language. When he returned, a short, lame tribesman followed him.

"This is Fumlok," Lonal said. Fumlok walked with a limp and stood slightly bent. He was thin and leathery, a gaunt face drawn with distinct contours along the bone. His eyes seldom lit on any one spot for long, and he smiled for no apparent reason at regular intervals. Unlike the warriors, he wore trousers and a loose shirt reminiscent of the city dwellers to the south, though his features were unmistakably native.

"Few of my tribe speak Calinin. Fumlok will be your mouth until you learn Zyraii. I will leave you in his hands for the moment. You are to stay near him at all times. He will show you your holdings, while I consult with the elders."

"Our holdings?"

Lonal nodded. "I told you that you were to replace Am and Roel, whom you killed today. They were cousins, the last adult males of their family. What was theirs is yours." He gestured to Fumlok and said firmly, "He will answer your questions now." He marched away, soon to be obscured behind the tents.

Alemar turned and found Fumlok smiling at him. When the twins failed to respond, the translator's happiness vanished.

"So you know the High Speech?" Alemar asked.

"I speak many tongues," Fumlok said awkwardly. His eyes darted from Elenya to Alemar to the ground. "It's what I'm good for."

Alemar wasn't sure if Fumlok literally meant to judge himself that way or not; the man stressed his syllables oddly and clearly was no master of the language. But perhaps it was true. The nomads might not tolerate a cripple among them if he couldn't be of some use. Alemar didn't like the little man. Fumlok reminded him of fawning courtiers. But if keeping him near would allow them to communicate, they would put up with him. The sooner they gathered some knowledge, the better.

"Come, come," Fumlok said, leading them toward a modest-sized tent in the second ring. As they walked, observers began to gather, including warriors who had not been on the excursion. Three or four well-armed, well-dressed men followed most closely of all, keeping a distance barely casual.

Five people came out of the tent as the twins approached. All of them prostrated themselves, touching noses to the ground, and waited on their knees with eyes downcast. Four were women; one was the boy who had taken their oeikani from them at the corral, and thereby drew their attention first. He was strong-featured, alert, just short of puberty. There had been members in the party with whom they had ridden who had been only slightly older. Alemar saw a little of himself seven or eight years gone.

The two plain, thirtyish women lifted hands, palms down and fingers limp, heads still tilted toward the earth. "These are your wives," Fumlok said. "They are called Omi and Peyri."

"Wives?"

Fumlok nodded, smiling. "Lonal tell you about it already. Am and Roel are dead. Now Omi and Peyri are yours."

"You mean they're property?"

"What is property?" Fumlok asked.

Alemar wasn't sure whether Fumlok didn't know the word or didn't know the concept. "Like slaves?"

Fumlok recoiled. "No! Only foreign women are slaves! A man must look after the women of his own tribe. It is his duty to God."

Alemar looked at the strange women's faces, and at the home behind them, which they had shared with the men he and Elenya had killed. Peyri glanced up at him, met his eyes, and quickly looked back down, trembling at her own audacity. Alemar sickened—both at the sheer wretchedness of the women and at the guilt they inspired.

"What if we don't want them?" Alemar suggested.

Fumlok's small eyes went round. "Not want?" He stepped over to Omi and slapped her belly, and made her open her mouth to show her teeth. She had most of them. "They both young. Healthy. Still bear good sons." He continued on toward Peyri.

"I was raised by different customs," Alemar explained. It was alarming enough to have been involuntarily adopted into the clan. To be suddenly burdened with a family compounded the disaster. "Ask them if they want us."

"It doesn't matter," Fumlok said. "What they think not important."

"Ask it anyway."

Fumlok muttered a few words to the women. They, as well as the two younger girls behind them, suddenly cowered and prostrated themselves again. The boy scowled.

Alemar was confused. "What exactly did you tell them?"

"I say you don't want wives, maybe."

"Why are they afraid?"

Fumlok shuffled nervously away from the gradually increasing group of spectators. "Women who are not wives, not daughters, not mothers, not sisters—they are . . ."

He struggled to find the right word, as if the one he would have used were inappropriate. "They are what?" Alemar demanded.

"Available."

Fumlok shrugged, eyes darting meaninglessly back at the men standing not far away. Absent of veils, too many of the faces betrayed the hard lives behind them. Alemar grimaced. Now he understood. The offer of wives was not a reward for victory in combat; it assured that Am and Roel's widows would continue to have a source of physical protection and provender.

"We'll keep them," he told Fumlok.

"Are you crazy?" Elenya whispered.

"I won't let them be turned into whores," he argued.

As soon as Fumlok translated Alemar's acceptance, the women tried to crawl forward and kiss the twins' feet. Elenya danced away. "Ask them to go inside and prepare a meal," Alemar said, merely to free himself of the embarrassment. He needed a moment to meditate on this state of affairs. The incident had shaken him more than the attack at the water hole. He could understand laws requiring death for stealing water. This custom was insidious.

Omi and Peyri complied immediately, but Alemar had the younger women wait long enough to be introduced. Sesheer was an unappealing, somewhat pudgy teenager, timorous and ungainly. Meyr was about the same age as the boy, Rol, in the midst of her growth spurt. She was slender, sharp-featured, with plenty of nervous energy.

"Where are the small children?" Alemar asked. "I thought you said Omi and Peyri were still good childbearers."

Fumlok shrugged. "The desert is not kind to them. Omi lose last young one two seasons ago." His manner was offhand. Alemar sensed that it was not entirely callousness. To lose several children was simply the way of the desert. Although infant mortality was common enough in his homeland, Alemar preferred not to think of it as inevitable.

"Don't you have healers here?" he asked.

Fumlok seemed surprised. "The Hab-no-ken are rare. Sometimes they visit a clan only once or twice a year."

"The Hab-no-ken?"

Fumlok paused. "There are four ken. You learn when you are taught the laws of the So-de'es." He wouldn't elaborate.

The two girls slipped inside the flaps, but the boy stayed. He stood stiffly, and shook when the twins turned toward him.

"Elique pertoh va nagt Po-no-pha!" the boy said. *"Oi soh."* He spun on his heel and ducked into the tent.

"Why is he angry?" Alemar asked, though, in truth, he understood the reaction better than he had those of the women.

"He say that in one year he rides with the Po-no-pha, the warriors. Then this tent is his. But you kill Am and Roel too soon. Now Rol must listen to you. If he disobeys, you can throw him out."

Abruptly, Alemar heard a deep voice speaking to him in Zyraii. The words meant nothing, but the tone implied a great deal. He turned around to face a burly, barrel-chested man.

Elenya shifted her stance meaningfully. Alemar tensed. Their training would serve them again, if need be, but after the disorientation and physical trials of the day, he wanted only to lie down for a very long time.

"Translate," Alemar ordered Fumlok.

"Shigmur say that it not polite to wear veil among your brothers, inside the camp. He say take it off." Fumlok's demeanor hinted that the suggestion was a good one.

Alemar could tell Shigmur was going to press the matter. But weary as he was, he couldn't submit so simply.

"What if we don't want to take them off?" Alemar asked. Fumlok gulped and translated.

Shigmur's reply sounded both calm and ominous.

"Shigmur say no reason to cover the head and face among one's brothers. It is insult. Shigmur does not like it. Of course, a very great warrior do as he please, if he beat ones who disagree. He say you are being a very great fighter to insult so openly."

Alemar considered things for a few moments. Then he flipped back his cowl and dropped the veil. Shigmur frowned.

"My brother is better," Alemar said softly.

Alemar stepped back, and Elenya replaced him. "Do as you will," he told her. "I've had enough of customs and laws for one day."

Elenya stood where she was.

Shigmur said something gruff.

"Take off your veil," Fumlok repeated.

"No," she said.

"Na," Fumlok told Shigmur.

The crowd immediately began to clear away from the front of the tent. Fumlok pressed Alemar back. Soon Elenya and Shigmur were in the center of a ring some ten paces wide.

"Shigmur duels you. The loser admits he is wrong," Fumlok said.

"What are the rules?" Elenya asked.

Fumlok blinked. It was the first time Elenya had spoken clearly, betraying her throat's high pitch. After a moment's hesitation, he said, "First blood or surrender." Hastily he added, "Killing is not permitted in the camp."

Alemar was relieved. On the other hand, his sister was often only hampered by rules. She was best in an all-out fight.

"Your choice of weapons, or none," Fumlok said.

She drew her rapier.

Shigmur stared at the insubstantiality of the blade and furrowed his eyebrows. He spoke to Fumlok.

"We have no swords like that here," Fumlok said.

"Let him use his scimitar," she said. She motioned to Alemar, who loaned her his saber. Though less curved than the Zyraii weapon, it was similar in weight and length.

Shigmur nodded and drew his weapon.

"This is very bad for your brother," Fumlok told Alemar under his breath.

It was, Alemar decided. Shigmur towered over Elenya, so wide that he appeared overweight, though his grace denied it. His bulk hinted at endurance, rather than ponderousness. As did the other warriors, Shigmur wore only white, but in contrast to many of the clan, the workmanship of the clothing and the material was superior. The other members of the crowd gave him a clear berth.

Shigmur didn't smile as Elenya assumed her stance. That, too, was bad. Apparently, he had more sense than to scoff at unknown antagonists.

He made the first move, a sudden thrust. Elenya shifted her hips abruptly, turning her torso away. The point jabbed empty space just in front of her breasts. She held her own weapon upright in front of herself, so that the man's sword edge brushed her own, but it was only a precautionary measure. Her body movement had been enough.

The spectators murmured, impressed, as Elenya wove from side to side. She slashed three times, an irregular rhythm aimed at three different points. The man countered easily, the last time opening a tiny slit in her sleeve above the left elbow.

He tested her again. Elenya parried his blow, but lost ground. Though more than twice her weight, he was light on his feet.

The crowd noise grew stronger off to one side. People made room for Lonal and an authoritative group of men, older than most of the warriors. The duelists were oblivious, and the newcomers did not attempt to interrupt. They took places in the forefront of the spectators.

Elenya had clipped a shoulder seam on Shigmur's robe, but it had been a wild stroke. She was forced back another step. Alemar wiped his palms dry. Shigmur was neither impulsive nor unskilled, as the attackers at the water hole had been. The crowd's opinion of him was clear in the way they anticipated his victory each time he moved.

He thrust again. Elenya twisted away, but less gracefully than the previous time. Alemar noted the tenor of the thrust—aimed precisely at her shoulder, where the muscle was thick and risk of a fatal injury smaller, and pulled so that penetration would not be deep if the strike succeeded. Shigmur's control was superb.

Not so Elenya. Wheezing, she made another reckless swipe. Alemar began to worry. She was exhausted from the trip through the eret-Zyraii, and though she knew the saber almost as well as the rapier, her skill could be just deficient enough to make her question herself. She was getting impulsive.

Don't kill him, sister, he thought. The humiliation was written in her posture, and he knew what she was capable of in such a state.

The duelists continued to circle and feint. They had engaged eight times now, far more often than an ordinary contest—certainly much longer than a fight to the death. It was a challenge to be able to score against a well-matched opponent without causing serious harm. A definitive move eluded them. Alemar had to consciously remember to breathe.

Elenya's veil quivered from the action of her lungs. Worn, as well as unused to the climate, she had no stamina. She faltered slightly. Immediately, Shigmur rushed forward with a series of power slashes that kept her backing up as fast as she could, each impact threatening to snap her saber. His movements were stunning, most of them hidden within a blur. All eyes seemed riveted to his scimitar.

Alemar, however, watched his sister, and stopped worrying.

And abruptly, the man's sword flew through the air, flipped out of his hand by a tiny but accurate movement of Elenya's wrist.

Children's eyes bulged. The men in the foreground grunted in surprise. Shigmur wielded his imaginary weapon for a split moment after he had been disarmed. He cried out and stared disbelieving at his own hand.

The sword splashed into the sand behind him.

Alemar sighed. Shigmur had pressed too soon. Thanks to her size, Elenya had rarely trained with anyone weaker than herself. As long as she had any strength left, she was capable of tricking a power fencer.

Elenya stretched her sword point forward and made a tiny scratch on the back of her challenger's hand, which he offered to her, his expression a mixture of surprise and respect. He didn't seem angry.

A flood of words poured through the crowd, cut short by an elder's sharp command. Another order followed, and Shigmur bowed deferentially to the source and walked back to his original companions. Elenya remained in the center of a circle of highly intrigued Zyraii.

Fumlok was called to the elders and questioned briefly. The cripple was especially meek, blending into the audience as soon as permitted. The elders traded a few comments among themselves, and Lonal came forward into the circle.

Elenya waited, saber lowered but still drawn. Lonal stopped a few paces away.

"You are a good fighter, which I had already seen. This morning you had cause to fight. But this is too small a thing," and he flicked the cloth of his own lowered veil. "You do insult to all present by refusing to reveal your face. I cannot demand it of you by law, but if you persist, you will duel every warrior in this camp, one by one."

Something in his tone told Alemar that Lonal would be the first one Elenya would have to battle. He saw her fingers twitch. If Lonal had physically threatened her, she would have dealt with it. But he had approached with undrawn weapon, so close that he could not have escaped a critical wound should she care to deliver one. He stood within her power, yet told her what to do.

Alemar knew that part of his sister would have been glad to fight every man of the tribe. She would have known her measure against such a task. She was not defeated, yet she had won little beyond passing admiration. And in order to have her way, she would have to go through Lonal. They both knew that her victory over Shigmur had been a combination of surprise and luck.

The war-leader remained as he was, supple arms lax at his sides, breath easy and regular.

Elenya took off the veil.

The crowd was silent. She shook loose the thick black hair framing her delicate features. The children of the clan were the first to express their astonishment.

"Reimi!" a small boy shouted.

The tribe chattered. The stern, stultified visages of the elders melted in shock. And Lonal, after having so tranquilly dealt with the situation, suddenly looked very young and, so it seemed to Alemar, a bit frightened.

Lonal stared at Elenya's chest and crotch. "Is it true? Are you a female?"

"Of course."

Lonal looked as if he had been betrayed. He turned to Alemar, as if to double-check that he were, in fact, a male.

"Fumlok!" he yelled.

Fumlok limped forward.

Lonal didn't look at the cripple, but said fiercely, "Explain to these two what this means after I leave." To the twins he added, "Go to your tent, and do not come out until bidden." To Elenya he said, "You have destroyed me."

The war-leader, no longer the confident figure they had known up to that point, strode off, the block of elders in his wake. The twins were left to the stares of women and children, and soon slipped into their tent to escape them.

"What happened?" Alemar asked Fumlok.

The little man kept gulping and opening his mouth like a fish. At first, Alemar worried that the man's discomfiture concerned Elenya's gender; then he realized that Fumlok had been terrified to have been so close to Lonal's anger. When he could finally speak, his answer was tentative.

"It is a religious question. Toltac, most high of the Bo-noken, must judge."

"I don't understand."

Fumlok pointed to Elenya. "She wears white. She plays the *ju-moh-kai,* the duel. And she kills a man in combat. Women cannot do this."

"Why not?" Elenya demanded.

When Fumlok replied, he spoke only to Alemar. "Because women have no souls."

IV

Lerina plunged into the water, feeling the tug of the singlet against her body. The warmth of the Dragon Sea enveloped her, familiar as a lover. She surfaced, flung the salt water from her hair, and waded, waist-deep, toward one of the many small islets that dotted this section of Cilendrodel's coast. Fishermen and smugglers feared the reef offshore, providing Lerina with a privacy broken only rarely by visitors searching the shallows for shellfish. The solitude pleased her, the beach and the islets a refuge to which she would escape whenever possible, often spending entire days sunbathing, swimming, or hunting in the tidepools. Her favorite place of all was a thin snout of land about a hundred lengths out. From the coastal side it appeared to be steep and rocky—inhospitable—but the far side had been worn by the ages into a slender beach, a special place she had never shown even to her lovers. As now, she went to it when she needed relief from the uninspired existence of Garthmorron Hold.

The water deepened; she swam the last of the way. The sun and the Sister both shone in a cloudless sky. Lerina slipped off her singlet and left it on an eroded chunk of stone above tide level to dry. As she stretched out on the sand, she sighed at the warmth striking her skin. Her jet-black hair curled into random patterns as it dried; her nipples, enlivened by the swim, flattened with the effects of the sunshine. She was a petite woman, flushed with youth. As she created patterns with the salt crusting on her abdomen, she wondered how her figure compared to those of the fine ladies of the Calinin courts.

Lost in reverie, she almost didn't notice the first moan.

The rising surf lapped at her ankles, eroding her drowsiness. She sat bolt upright. Faint sounds of suffering came from the cave at the head of the beach, ordinarily her ultimate retreat. Heart racing, she inched her way toward the rock on which she had laid her garment.

As she put it on, she discovered a small bloodstain on its front. Not hers. She heard another moan. Holding the wet spot away from her breasts with one hand, she examined her surroundings.

Blood on the rock had soaked into the fabric. It was fresh. She saw another drop on the sand nearer the cave. The spoor of dragging footsteps was clear now that she was paying attention.

Abruptly she rushed forward, pausing briefly at the cave entrance to allow her pupils to adjust to the shadows. Now that the thunder of the surf no longer muted her hearing, she distinctly detected strained breathing.

He sat, body leaning against the far wall of the cave, eyes open and glazed. Sickly anemic skin peeked through the rents in his clothing, coughed blood spotting older, darker stains on the front of his jacket, clotted areas on his scalp and thigh betraying recent seepage. His hair hung in disarrayed, fevered strands.

"Oh, no . . . ," she whispered.

He didn't respond when she squatted beside him. She brushed him on the cheek.

"Who are you? How did you get here?"

His eyes focused briefly on her hand. A small croak emerged from his throat.

"What?" she coaxed, leaning her ear to his mouth.

"Water . . ."

He closed his eyelids. "I'll get help," she said, gently squeezing his unwounded shoulder. She rose.

"No," he said, and tried to lean forward. He made it only the width of a finger, and sagged back.

"But . . ." His expression contained a plea she didn't understand. "You'll die without care."

He didn't speak again, but continued to stare at her. She was transfixed. The fear and helplessness on the surface couldn't hide the life of challenge and courage beneath. No such man as this lived in Garthmorron.

Finally he closed his lids and slumped into unconsciousness. She had to do something. She arranged him more comfortably, leaving his upper body against the cave wall to ease his breathing. He would be dead by the time she returned. But then, he should have been dead already.

She ran, she swam, and she climbed. By the time she had gained the mainland, mounted the bluff, and navigated the forest trails between the shore and the hold, the wind of her passage had dried her clothing once again. She used the back entrance, through the vegetable gardens, and entered the central grounds without being seen.

Cooking smells wafted from the kitchens near the main house, stablemen groomed oeikani, and Lerina's great-uncle conversed with two serious-faced townsmen in the courtyard. She stole into her father's cottage and cast off the singlet. She chose a light tunic to replace it. She also found a watertight satchel into which she stuffed tights, leggings, blankets, a small cape, and sundry articles.

Next she slipped into the pantry while Brienna, the old cook, was busy in the kitchen. Lerina grabbed a large wicker basket and filled it with food, particularly that easy to consume in a weakened condition. Then she hid both basket and satchel behind a dilapidated, abandoned outhouse.

No longer concerned about concealment, she removed two large flasks from the tack room and filled them at the well in the middle of the courtyard. The stablemaster greeted her.

"Good morning, young mistress," he said.

"Morning, Rictane."

Rictane limped to the other side of the oeikani he was grooming and reapplied the brush. "You must be very thirsty today."

She smiled. "I'm planning on staying at the beach all day. I thought I'd make sure I had enough."

Rictane waved an aged hand toward the main house. "Best ask your uncle about that. There's been some trouble in Eruth. He may want you close to home, especially with your father gone with Lord Dran."

"Trouble? What kind?"

"Can't say. Two riders pulled up a short time ago. They're talking with the chamberlain now. I don't like to repeat rumors until I've had the story straight."

"I see," she said thoughtfully. "All right. I'll wait."

The old man winked. She smiled and went to visit her favorite oeikani in his stall. The stallion snorted and lowered his head so that she could scratch the bases of his knobby antlers. She patted him, checked his mane for burrs and the gap between his cloven hooves for lodged gravel. Rictane or a stableboy had beaten her to it. He shuffled impatiently.

"I'm sorry," she whispered into one of its ears. "We won't be riding today, much as I'd like to."

She returned to the tack room and its familiar, leathery smell. The shelves lost a quantity of bandages, needle and thread, ointments, cotton, and alcohol. Not so large an amount, however, that it would be missed among the supply needed to maintain a lord's stable.

A loose board at the rear of the stable permitted Lerina to squeeze out. She made it to the old outhouse and added her new booty to the satchel.

With the satchel looped over head and left shoulder, the flasks on the opposite side, and the basket cradled in arms, she almost bore more than she could manage. She had wanted to carry them on a saddle, but didn't dare risk taking an animal now. Even burdened so, she knew the grounds and made it to the forest without being discovered.

She had to stop frequently to rest her arms. Once, a gamekeeper happened along the path; she hid in the undergrowth until he had passed. The scent of salt spray increased. Her journey down the bluff was the slowest leg of all. With the extra weight, she didn't want to develop dangerous momentum.

She checked for observers before venturing into the ocean. The current dug away sand from beneath her feet, but she kept her balance. She set the basket on her head as the water deepened. The tide was near its lowest ebb, allowing her to keep touching the entire way, though she had to hold her breath for the final distance.

She emerged soaked, but the basket stayed dry, and the other items were sealed. Gratefully she lowered the basket to the sand, dropped the satchel, and entered the cave.

He lived.

He opened his eyes, and she saw recognition there, though he didn't attempt to speak. Without preamble, she uncorked one of the flasks and brought it to his lips. He drank one sip only, waited for it to flow down his throat, then sipped again. He stopped after a few swallows, but Lerina left the cork out, patient.

"Thou art the queen of all women," he said softly.

Something in the way he used the High Speech told her it was his native language. Of all the lands where the Calinin had ruled, only the Elandri used the pure form. Lerina knew it from her childhood tutors, though she, like most Cilendri, tended to use the lower form.

"You're a smuggler," she said.

He nodded, and gestured for more water. She gave it to him.

"What were you after in Cilendrodel?"

"Silk."

Of course. "How did you get through the Dragon's blockade?"

"I swam under it."

He seemed serious. She scoffed. "I suppose you intend to swim back with bolts of silk tied to your belt, through the reef?"

He smiled, tilting his head seaward, and spoke haltingly. "My ship is out there. A boat was waiting for me. I'm afraid I've missed it."

"What happened to you?"

"I was ambushed by Dragon's men in Eruth."

"Is there any way to contact your people?"

"No. I can't reach the rendezvous point. If I live, the boat will be there next month, or the one after."

Talking appeared to exhaust him. She let him have more water, then retrieved the other supplies from the beach. When she returned, he had lost consciousness.

She examined his wounds briefly. Withdrawing a rag from the basket, she applied antiseptic to the gash in his scalp.

He groaned, and woke up.

"The oeikani don't like this either," she said. "But it's the strongest there is, and you need it. It numbs after a while."

"I wouldn't have guessed you were a healer."

"My lord's stablemaster made me learn everything about caring for my animal. I know how to clean and stitch wounds."

"Who are you?"

"I am Lerina Elb-Aratule. My father is head gamekeeper of Garthmorron Hold."

"Thy presence honors me."

She started to retort, but considered his condition. Certainly her father was worth the pride, but perhaps she had spoken too vainly, as her elders frequently accused.

"Who are you?" she asked.

"Call me Ethmurl," he said.

"Is that your name?"

"Does it matter?"

She shrugged. "I suppose you have your reasons."

He allowed her to finish working on his head. The injury there was not critical, but Lerina needed to compose herself before she could face the prospect of the more serious spots. As long as they weren't bleeding, she would postpone it momentarily.

"I'm afraid this will leave a scar," she said.

"I know."

"Why haven't you bled to death yet?"

He coughed. "A spell cast upon me slows my blood loss."

She looked at him oddly. "I'm going to get my thread."

He didn't wince as the needle went in. By that time it must have been only a small agony on top of many large ones, she imagined. He fainted before she completed stitching, but she guessed that this was fatigue and wondered how he could remain awake even for the short periods he managed. She moved to his chest. The cloth had adhered to the open flesh, despite the dunking in the ocean he must have taken in order to reach the islet. She had to peel it carefully free.

She sucked in her breath. The stabbing had been worse than she thought. He shouldn't be alive. She cleaned the long gash that ran along his ribs and got out the needle again. He woke at the first stroke.

"I'm sorry."

"No, it's not your fault. You have a gentle touch." Still, tears welled in his eyes.

"I've never seen wounds this size stop bleeding by themselves. I've heard of this spell you mentioned. It's supposed to be beyond the reach of most magicians. The kings of the Calinin nations pay dearly for the service."

"You're well educated."

"I can read and write. Don't change the subject. The spell we're talking about is even harder to maintain from a distance—how is it that your life is worth so much?"

"I'm the king of Elandris."

She tugged the thread harder than she had to. "You have a great deal of nerve for someone whose life is being saved."

He lost the smile. He said evenly, "Lerina, it's best that you don't know who I am, for both our sakes." His expression softened. "I don't mean to seem ungrateful. I'd rather my enemies not know how I died."

She started. "What about the spell?"

"Spells can only do so much. You can only do so much. . . ."

"You aren't going to die," she said strongly. "And you don't believe it either, or you wouldn't have lasted this long."

"I came here to die." Abruptly, he contorted in pain. Lerina hesitated.

"Am I doing this wrong?"

"No, it comes and goes. . . ." His eyelids cemented shut. Quickly Lerina crawled to the basket and withdrew a small vial. She placed it directly in front of his nostrils and uncorked it.

"Breathe this," she said.

He obeyed. Within moments, he slumped. He would sleep for several hours. She recapped the vial and put it away. She had wanted to get more food and water into him before she did that, not to mention her reluctance to move him by herself to get at the wound in his back, but perhaps it was better this way.

She had stitched and bandaged all of his injuries by midday, but he still rested tranquilly. She created an acceptable bed out of sand with some of the blankets she'd brought, to which she gingerly moved him. She also removed his weapons and the remnants of his upper-body clothing, and swabbed away the crusted blood from his skin. For the first time, she was able to tell what he actually looked like. He was younger than she had guessed—no more than thirty. He was short of stature, but lean and powerful, black-haired, deeply tanned. She stroked his beard idly. His face contained a peace that hid when he was awake. He was a handsome man.

Who was he? The king of Elandris? King Pranter, she knew, had reigned for almost fifty years and was now over eighty years of age. His son couldn't be under fifty. But whoever Ethmurl might be, he was important.

She checked his pulse, found it stable, and covered him with a blanket. Would he die and leave her with the mystery? She went outside. The tide was higher, leaving a sliver of beach between herself and the limit of the strongest breakers. The noise from the reef almost drowned her thoughts as she stared southward, toward Elandris.

Later she returned to the cave and lay down beside her patient. What did it matter who he was? she wondered, and began to doze.

The chill of late afternoon fog violated her slumber. A mass of formidable gray billows boiled slightly offshore, preparing to envelop the coast.

Ethmurl was watching her. She felt it and turned his way. He shook.

"You have a fever," she said, touching his neck. It was damp.

"Yes."

"I have to go. The fog will be in soon. You should let me bring back help."

"They would hang me. I killed one of your countrymen."

She remembered the townsmen at the hold. "Did he deserve it?"

He seemed surprised by the question. "Yes."

"Then that may save you," she said.

He smiled kindly. "You are young, after all. I was beginning to wonder."

"You're too used to war, Elandri," she answered stiffly.

"Yes," he admitted. She let the matter drop.

They said nothing as she fed him in small bits. He had little appetite. She didn't force it, trusting the body's wisdom. Before long, the grayness crept forward.

"I have to leave before I'm missed," she repeated. "I'll return tomorrow." She laid the water and anything else he might require within reach, worried again by his trembling, and rose.

"Lerina?"

"Yes?"

"Why are you doing this? Why help me?"

She smiled gently. "Because I want to." Then she turned and left the cave.

"Thank you," she heard him say.

As it often did, the fog clung to the land with honeylike tenacity. Lerina ascended into it as she climbed the bluff, immediately losing sight of the tree she had passed ten paces earlier. As she reached level ground, she heard the crunch of snails being squashed underfoot somewhere behind her.

She listened. The ground murmured under the impact of foot steps. Heavy ones. She walked faster. A stream of fog flowed just above the mulch of the forest, hiding potholes and roots. Tendrils thrust out of the earth every other step to snatch at her. By the third stumble, she could taste the bile of panic on her tongue. The footsteps behind her quickened.

Not far ahead, two great trees stood adjacent to each other, so closely placed that some of their upper branches, fifty feet higher, had united. The gap between the trunks permitted a small person such as Lerina to fit through without difficulty, but would block the passage of anyone larger. She plunged into the space. Chill sweat stained her tunic. She ducked down, trying to quiet the heavy panting of her lungs.

A man hurried past, an opaque outline. She waited several moments, as his footsteps faded, and began to catch her breath.

Two hands closed on her shoulders.

Her heart leapt into her throat.

"Mistress Lerina," a familiar voice said. "What are you doing here?"

She turned and recognized the ruddy face of Barr, a gamekeeper, one of her father's men. The pounding of her heart eased.

The sounds on the path returned.

"Ascot!" Barr shouted.

"Ho?"

"I've found her."

Soon the heavy figure of Barr's son emerged out of the fog and Lerina recognized the shape of her pursuer.

"Thank the rythni you're safe, miss. Your uncle has been very worried."

"Come," Barr said, squeezing through the trees onto the path. "Let's be on to the hold."

The bearlike form of Ossatch Elb-Aratule loomed above her. Though Lerina had long since reached her full height, she still felt child-size when confronted by him, especially when he assumed a mood of disapproval or anger, which was most of the time. As her family's eldest male, he was accustomed to obedience. She tried to draw herself up tall, earnestly missing the presence of her father, her first, and best, ally. An ember cracked loudly in the fireplace of Garthmorron Hold's great hall, where Barr and Ascot had escorted her as soon as they had arrived. Ossatch was the chamberlain, and virtual lord of the manor when Lord Dran was absent.

Her great-uncle held forward her singlet. The drenching in the ocean hadn't quite washed out the bloodstain. "Where did this come from?"

"What were you doing in my room?"

"Don't be impertinent. If your mother were alive, she would have been frantic with worry—you gone all day with a murderer on the loose. You are my kin—I should know where you are at such times."

"I pricked my breast this morning with a kitchen knife. Would you like to see?"

Ossatch's expression blackened. "Answer my question. Where were you?"

"At the beach. I'm old enough to look after myself, Uncle." They had had arguments like this before.

"The oeikani the man rode was found not far from the hold. I'll not have my niece about until I'm convinced it's safe. You'll remain in the cottage tomorrow."

"But—"

"No, Lerina. I have spoken." He turned and stalked off, the echo of his footsteps measuring the sinking of her heart.

V

Omi and Peyri served the twins a porridge made principally of millet and goat's milk, together with a small platter of dates; to drink, a choice of very strong coffee or either of two wines, one of the grape, the other of the pomegranate. The meal seemed strangely soft—the dates were the only genuinely solid food—but the twins did not complain. They were grateful not to have to deal with heavy foods yet. They ate only a little of the porridge, but over a long period of time made generous use of the liquids. Plain water, for some reason, was totally absent.

"Maybe tomorrow an animal is slaughtered to honor new husbands," Fumlok suggested, as if to excuse the fare. "No time tonight. And to butcher is man's job."

The wives served the meal and remained unobtrusive, usually concealed behind a cloth purdah that segregated the tent into rough halves. The younger members of the family appeared not at all. For the moment, this social distance comforted the twins. The language barrier preserved them from the embarrassment of communication.

Fumlok stayed with them, but didn't eat. Alemar suspected sharing food would create some sort of social debt the translator was reluctant to incur. Fumlok utilized the time to explain the implications of Elenya's lack of soul, a process hampered once again by his difficulty with the High Speech. He seemed unable to apply the subjunctive case, impeding his ability to convey abstract concepts. He tended to use the present tense regardless of what the context required. After most of an hour, however, the twins managed to distill out a rudimentary understanding of Zyraii mythology.

For as long as the tribe remembered, their highest religious order, the Bo-no-ken, had taught that God created men and gave them souls as stakes in the Bu, the great game of life. A man sharpened and advanced his soul by conducting himself with honor, by contributing to the tribe's welfare, and/or using his wisdom effectively. If he played the game well enough, after death his soul would pass to a new body to play the game again. If he dishonored or wasted a lifetime, he would return as a worm, animal, or other creature, and endure whatever punishment in these forms that God willed, until he could become a man again. Warriors who died in battle, before they had lived enough of their lives for fair judgment, would automatically be reincarnated into a newborn of the same social status and similar physical abilities.

As for women, they were created merely to produce more men, and to raise the children so that men, the players in the Bu, would be spared this burden, which might distract them from the real tasks. Females had no souls, and it was not appropriate that women should participate in any activities that would interfere in the Bu, and inadvertently lessen a man's chance for a good incarnation.

Thus, the Ah-no-ken, the religious order responsible for the daily affairs and conduct of the people, forbade to women the teachings of history, the pursuit of theology, and professional crafts not associated with homemaking. Most of all, they were forbidden to be warriors.

"So, a male spider has a soul, but I do not," Elenya stated wryly.

"I always thought something was missing," Alemar said.

She poked him in the ribs.

Rubbing his side, Alemar asked Fumlok, "What happens to a woman if she does kill a man in combat?"

Fumlok licked his lips. "Such a thing never happen before. But . . . they think of something."

"I'm sure they will," Alemar said, preferring not to dwell on it. "But I don't understand the reasoning. Why should a man be any less a warrior because his sister carries a sword?"

Fumlok scratched his ear as if he couldn't believe what he had heard. He attempted to answer the question from a different angle. "Men are given a great challenge by God, but He also provides us with gifts to help us. For sake of man, woman is created—to soothe, to feed, to propagate. Women are given only the one life. They are not knowing the completeness of being. Men must remember this and be grateful to Him. A woman's life must not be wasted—she is the seed of more life and the measure of a man's success. To let a woman die before her time is to spit at God. Zyraii know that women are sacred, so women do not need to carry weapons to protect themselves. This cannot change. Women must not be endangered in raids." For Fumlok, the speech was eloquent; Alemar suspected he was paraphrasing.

Alemar sighed. "This is not what people in my homeland believe."

"Your people are wrong," Fumlok replied. It was the first time the little man had seemed certain of anything. "They know it in their hearts. Do you make soldiers of your women?"

"Not often," Alemar admitted. "But they are permitted to protect themselves. My sister would have died before now otherwise—today, in fact."

"That was a mistake. If she dress as a woman, she is not attacked."

"What does it matter who's right?" Elenya said sharply. "We're in trouble, and it's too late to do a thing about it."

"No, you are safe, maybe."

Eyebrows raised on both twins' faces. "What do you mean?" Elenya asked. The comment had seemed all the more intriguing because, at last, Fumlok had addressed Elenya to her person.

"This morning, Lonal save you by invoking *niutap*. It is adoption ritual. War-leaders have right to do this. If a widow is made in battle, the killer should take care of her. *Niutap* also brings new blood to T'lil."

"How can you trust us?" Elenya interjected.

Fumlok held his finger up. "War-leader takes risk. He is responsible until elders accept his choice. Later, you are educated, and you are blamed if you disobey. For now, Lonal is embarrassed if you offend the laws of the So-de'es. His honor is smirched. This is bad to happen at this time."

Alemar sucked a contemplative mouthful of wine. "Are you saying that Lonal will be punished for Elenya being a woman? And that she won't be?"

Fumlok gave one of his nervous smiles. "If Lonal is punished, she is punished, too. Both. But . . . maybe Lonal is not punished. Maybe his honor is saved."

"How?"

A cloud covered the Zyraii's expression. "I don't know."

The twins tried to draw him out, but Fumlok wouldn't say more. If anything, he seemed anxious that he had spoken in the first place. Wine and dates bridged the awkward moments until Alemar thought of more questions.

"We're not really members of the tribe yet," Alemar stated.

Fumlok drew his glance back from the corrugations of the tent walls. "No. You must learn laws and rituals. And you must endure the rite of manhood. Then you are T'lil warriors. And if you prove your honor, then maybe you are *hai-Zyraii.*"

"If we did all this, could my sister and I go to Setan?"

Fumlok stared back. "No. I don't think so."

"Why not?"

"Setan is holy. It is sacred ground reserved for the training of the ken. The Bo-no-ken, the Zee-no-ken, and the Hab-no-ken go there to be tested. Warriors must have a special reason to visit, and must get permission."

"How are the ken tested?" Elenya said suddenly.

"That is for the ken to know. I only know that those with weak wills do not survive."

More he would not reveal. His demeanor turned morose, and shortly thereafter he left them for the night, warning them that they must not leave the tent.

"We should have come to the country dressed as priests," Alemar said glumly, after their interpreter had gone.

"We should have come as bustards," Elenya suggested. "Then we could have flown above these madmen." She rose and opened the flaps of the entrance. A heavyset Zyraii warrior stood a few paces away. Elenya didn't bother to step out. "We could have flown out of this camp, too."

Omi entered to remove the clay bowls, timorous face constantly pointed toward the ground, except for an instant when she met Elenya's gaze and looked away immediately. She hurried off, as if stung.

Elenya shuddered. "If I have to become like her to live among these people, I won't live among these people."

"I have a feeling we may be lucky if we're allowed to live at all. We seem to be committing all sorts of mortal sins just by existing."

"We're trapped," she murmured. She drew a rapier, as if to skewer her invisible captor. Omi glanced out around the partition and ducked away again, eyes wide. "I feel like trying to escape now, and damn the chances."

Wistfully she sheathed her weapon. She was more impulsive

than her brother, but she liked realistic challenges. Time might be the only thing on their side.

"Tell me, is this what *you* expected?" she asked.

"No."

Further conversation was equally pointless. Soon Alemar was sagging, eyelids helpless against the tug of gravity. The hard days in the eret-Zyraii, and now this evening, had exhausted his reserves. She sat behind him, placing his head on her lap. He fell asleep rapidly, and would not wake, she guessed, until the night died. She stroked his hair pensively.

Eventually, Peyri emerged with a goatskin flask and gestured inquisitively to Elenya, who shook her head. Alemar had started to snore softly. Peyri disappeared, to return a moment later, taper in hand, and cross the room to open curtains Elenya had not previously seen past, revealing sleeping compartments. It took little imagination to realize whose they had been, and whose they were now.

Peyri returned to the women's side of the tent. This was a section forbidden to men, as the twins had discovered when Alemar tried to enter. The boy shared that side. Soon the glow of the lamps through the wooden drapes was extinguished, and not long after the rustle of waking activity faded away.

Elenya ignored the offer of the bed. Not only did her skin crawl to think of sleeping in those blankets, but the woven straw mats that served as mattresses for the Zyraii seemed much too luxurious to her, after the desert's bosom.

She was listening to Alemar's serene breathing when she heard a deep, threatening boom. She felt it through the sand under the hides. It set her heart to pumping loudly. But no noise came from the women's side, and the camp beyond the walls raised no alarm. Gradually her uneasy meditation resumed.

She imagined islands and coastlines, a warm, shallow, beckoning sea. Ships plied its waters, buildings rose around its harbors, and beneath the surface, men lived. Majestic edifices and an empire without peer stood in homage to one man's power and dream.

And in the sky above, a dragon hovered, patient and amused.

"Oh, my father, we have failed you," Elenya murmured.

VI

The tribesmen overflowed the great tent even before all of those permitted to enter had done so, and many had to be content to listen at the flaps. In the inner circle, the clan's ten Ah-no-ken ringed the traditional silver brazier, which glowed with a low, almost heatless flame of ibsinthe oil. Toltac and Jathmir, the two Bo-no-ken, conducted the gathering. Lonal stood across the brazier from them. At the tent walls, several dozen Po-no-pha had managed to crowd within. The body odor in the air was like a solid wall.

Lonal's second, R'lar, had just finished recounting the story of how they had found Alemar and Elenya. The crowd maintained utter silence, not daring to murmur in front of the two high priests. A nod from Jathmir allowed R'lar to sit.

A long pause followed. The Bo-no-ken sat impassively, their austerity and authority settling over each person in the room. Lonal waited obediently, feeling the cloth under his arms grow damp.

Eventually Jathmir spoke, his voice soft yet easily audible throughout the tent. "Simple matters first. You agree with R'lar that Am, Roel, and Quom acted upon their own decision?"

"They were on point, yes, and chose to attack by themselves, rather than wait for the support of the entire patrol."

Jathmir frowned. "The desert breeds both smart men and dead men. So be it. These strangers—Tebec and Yetem—shall not be blamed for the casualties."

Lonal bowed his head, not to Jathmir, but to Toltac. Though the former acted as spokesman, the latter had the final authority. Toltac was the opsib, high priest not simply of the clan but the entire tribe, and deferred only to the High Scholar at Setan.

"I am puzzled, war-leader," Jathmir continued almost conversationally. "It is obvious that the kin of Am and Roel needed to be cared for, but why invoke the *niutap?* These were waterstealers, trespassers who admitted they sought Setan. What inspired you to spare them?"

"I was impressed."

The Bo-no-ken stared back. Jathmir had asked his question not only to satisfy the curiosity of those assembled, but to fulfill the requirements of law. By that time, the Bo-no-ken might already have made their decision to support or deny the adoption, but ritual demanded that the war-leader be asked, and be given the opportunity to formally explain, why he had exercised his privilege. They waited.

Lonal wondered, if he were to stop there, whether these men, with their austere view of the world, could understand his feeling. He was Po-no-pha, and war and its preparation defined his existence. If he were not appreciative—no, even awed—at the performance of the strangers that morning, he would be no more than one of his common riders.

"I was moved by their mastery of the sword. I prevented their deaths to ask their names and country, so that, should I kill them, perhaps one day their family would know that they had died as warriors. I liked the boldness of their answers. Furthermore, they had come across the eret-Zyraii."

The audience mumbled. A few hadn't heard this yet. The priests deliberately assumed unastonished poses. They had, of course, learned this information soon after the riders returned to camp. Raised hands signalled quiet.

"You weren't concerned for the holy grounds?" Jathmir asked.

"No. If they had known where the citadel stood, they would have since turned north. I considered it, and it seemed we had little to lose. They were good warriors, certainly better than Am or Roel. Why not add them to our ranks? We will be needing fighters of exceptional caliber soon."

Jathmir nodded gradually. "True, but it is rare that the *niutap* is invoked upon individuals not of the Eastern Deserts. They may not understand the irrevocability of the ritual. We can't waste men continually guarding them."

"No," Lonal conceded. "We'll watch them only a few days, until the march to Ahloorm begins. I believe I can convince them by then of the wisdom of staying. And if they try to escape, where in the desert could we of the T'lil not track them? If they are too much trouble, they can be dealt with at the time."

When no further comment arose, Toltac and Jathmir leaned

closer to each other and exchanged a handful of words that none but they two could hear. Jathmir straightened up and announced, "In that case, son of Joren, the *niutap* is confirmed. It is up to you to do as you've promised."

The mood of the crowd grew more intense. A bead of sweat formed at the end of Lonal's nose. The first matter of the night, really no more than a formality, had been resolved. No one there had seriously believed the priesthood would embarrass their war-leader by failing to support him in a matter traditionally within his prerogative. Not so the next matter.

Toltac himself spoke. "War-leader, when you adopted these persons, did you suspect that one of them . . . might not be a man?"

"No," Lonal said.

Toltac lowered his head, shadows thick under his brow. "I understand that they gave you male names, and to be sure, one would not guess that someone wearing the white would be female. Still, if this is the case, the laws of the So-de'es are explicit." The aged Bo-no-ken's eyes fixed on Lonal. On his countenance the lines of desert wind and many years were prominent.

Despite himself, Lonal trembled.

Jathmir's voice dominated a somber tent. "The Po-no-pha and its leader will retire from these walls. The ken must deliberate privately."

Slowly the warriors filed out, leaving only the circle of the priesthood. The holy men all looked like workers preparing for hard labor.

Lonal wandered to the central firepit, glad to be out under the open sky. As he stared at the embers, several of the Po-no-pha, mostly those whose ranks were only slightly below his, began to mill next to him. A low babble of voices travelled across the camp.

"Well, what are the chances?" Lonal asked.

R'lar, a lanky, desert-worn individual, and, as it happened, one of Lonal's uncles, said, "Females are always trouble."

This brought more laughter than it deserved, but it broke the tension.

"True," Lonal said dryly.

An imposing form shifted to the forefront. "I'm sorry, war-leader," Shigmur said.

Lonal shrugged and draped an arm about the shoulders of

his huskiest second. "No, my friend, you only compounded the disaster. You will lose face, but I have offended God."

Shigmur stooped to stir the coals and toss more oeikani dung on the fire. "It's ironic. After the duel, I told myself, 'So now Lonal's not the only man of the T'krt who can best me with a sword.' Then she dropped the veil."

Lonal chuckled. "She used a trick. It wouldn't have worked again. Nor would you have been so polite."

"I only meant to discipline, not humiliate," Shigmur said. "I was afraid she would fall over if I breathed too hard."

"Now it's all the worse," R'lar said. "Our war-leader has adopted a woman, and one of our best has been beaten by her. The men of the Alyr will laugh at us. Such a loss of *haiya* as could have been arranged by our enemies."

"Now there's an idea," said Granyet, a young Po-no-pha. "Do you suppose?"

"No," Lonal answered. "Even the Buyul and the Fanke would not conceive of it. It would offend the laws of God even more than what I have done."

"Holy law could be wiser," R'lar said forcefully, though not so loudly that those in the great tent would have any chance of hearing.

"Ah, but, Uncle, the other tribes will judge us by those laws, just as we judge them. We are Zyraii, the noble of God. If we are to ask the tribes to rally behind me in battle, I must be known as a righteous man. I must be *hai-Zyraii*. But now, my honor is besmirched. I cannot be opsha without the sanction of the ken any more than without the respect of the common people."

"But you must be opsha. You are the son of Joren. You're the only one who could manage it. Even the Alyr concede that fact in their hearts."

"The legend of an opsha could be only another mirage of the desert. Perhaps our people are meant to lose command of the trade routes."

"To *city-dwellers?*" R'lar spat.

While Lonal stayed to himself, R'lar, Shigmur, and Granyet continued to debate, not so much because they disagreed, but out of frustration. They didn't like feeling helpless. Like the majority of adult males, they were Po-no-pha. They herded, they raided, they conducted commerce. But on moral issues, they relinquished all authority. The Bo-no-ken dictated what was right, the Ah-no-ken spread the word and saw that it was heeded; and that was the way life was among the Zyraii.

"Priests and women—fah!" R'lar muttered.

The ken did not call the Po-no-pha back into the great tent until nearly dawn. The time had passed slowly, and Lonal walked into the circle red-eyed and stiff-kneed. The expressions of the priests mirrored his own.

Toltac's words were metered and precise. They were more than an announcement; they were a command.

"The laws of the So-de'es state that a woman may not wear white or carry weapons, nor shall any Zyraii sanction such behavior upon peril of exile. And it has been seen by this clan that the strangers who call themselves Tebec and Yetem have done these things. Therefore, both are men, whatever the appearances may be, and from this day forth, no member of the tribe will say otherwise."

Toltac's voice echoed slightly before the reaction arrived. The war-leader had been saved. At the same time, it was difficult to believe what the price had been.

When the crowd had calmed themselves enough to listen again, the opsib continued, "Every member of the tribe is called upon to assist in the education of this pair. They will learn our language, be inducted into the rituals of manhood and ordeal of the Po-no-pha. When they have completed these, the adoption will be finalized and, should they later earn it, they may be admitted to the rites of the *hai-Zyraii*. I have spoken."

Lonal and Toltac exchanged stares, and the war-leader saw the revolution that had taken place within the opsib to have permitted the decision. Toltac knew that without Lonal, he risked becoming opsib of a defeated people. The word of God had been swayed by practical necessity. But the message was blatant: No man, however important to the welfare and future of the tribe, would manage such a feat again. At this moment, if they were all to look up with the proper sort of vision, no doubt they would see the foundations of Heaven trembling.

VII

King's Ransom lolled in the calm waters off the Cilendri coast, sails slack. At some distance to the west, a ketch and a sloop of its fleet tacked lazily, nets out. The fine weather invited the men to indulge in a swim, but despite the grime of shipboard life, none did so. Some sunned; still more slept; none strayed far from their posts. The lookout was vigilant in the crow's nest, and unease wandered from face to face among the crew.

Three figures occupied the smallest of the four cabins at the stern. A man about forty-five years of age, and a woman near thirty, stood watching a much older man seated at a small, finely wrought hardwood table.

An unadorned pewter bowl rested in the center of the table, containing what appeared to be fresh blood. The seated man's attention, like those of his companions, was riveted to it. At random intervals, a swirl or a ripple appeared on the surface of the liquid. Once, it geysered, and the woman sucked in a sudden breath.

As she bit her lip, the geyser subsided. In a moment, the blood resumed a glassy-smooth texture, affected only by the slight yaw of the ship. The man wiped off his balding head and sighed, but never took his gaze away from the bowl. Sweat dripped off his chin and had already stained the underarms of his garment down to the waist. His eyes were red.

"Come, milady," the other man said, "we're doing no good here."

Reluctantly the woman allowed herself to be led from the little cabin to her own stateroom, where she wandered across the chamber and stared out the broad grillworked windows at the ship's wake. Windless, the vessel's passage hardly disturbed the water's surface. Her escort waited just inside the portal.

"Will he live?" she asked, afraid to speak up.

The man strode to her, while she kept her glance away, and lifted hands as if to embrace her, but he stopped, close enough to have dreamed he felt the lace of her blouse.

"Obo is trying, Lady Nanth."

"Obo has been without food or sleep for two days. If Keron is so badly hurt as to require such an effort, how can it be possible that he will live?" She bowed her head, bringing out her tendency for a double chin, one of the slight flaws that chipped at her noble vanity.

"If we could find him . . ." she murmured. "How many men did you send?"

"Five from the ship. Another five of our agents near Garthmorron will be joining them."

"You could send ten—twenty . . ." She turned and paced, looking everywhere but at her listener, though his eyes never left her.

"I could not," he said firmly. "An army of ours in the vicinity would only antagonize the Cilendri, if not draw in the Dragon's forces."

"You can't abandon him, Admiral Warnyre," she said.

The man's jaw tightened. "Lady Nanth, the only reason this ship remains near the coast is so Obo can manage to work his spell. And once he is done—whatever the outcome—we must sail south to open waters. I am doing all I can. Your husband would agree—he wouldn't endanger the fleet for one man."

She pressed a hand against the grillwork and knotted it into a fist. "I hate this sea," she said through tears.

Warnyre shifted uncomfortably, feeling the stiffness of muscles no longer honed to a military edge. "You should sleep."

Her fist uncoiled; her shoulders drooped. "No. Obo needs my attention. He endangers himself with this effort."

Out of her sight, he frowned. "I will send Lady Heormaphta and her maid to look after him, as will I myself when duties allow."

Nanth shook her head. "This is the critical time. I must stay with Obo. In fact, I shouldn't have left now. I took this upon myself when I married an ambitious man. We could have lived out our days at court, in safety. But Keron wanted the chance to distinguish himself, and I will be the first to know if he has failed. Thank you for your consideration, Admiral."

"Yes, milady. As you wish," Warnyre said tersely. He stood such that, when she passed by, he could catch the scent of her hair, then followed her out. As they parted ways, he muttered to himself.

Lady Nanth's thoughts were filled with visions of the civilized comforts of life in the capital, where feminine companionship consisted of more than a handful of other officers' wives and maids. Once, when she was single, a noted diplomat had asked for her hand—but she had wanted better. When she had caught Keron, she'd assumed, from his heritage, that she had obtained her goal.

Obo still stared at the bowl, eyelids half-closed. Small shudders coursed over his wizened body. Without disturbing the wizard's concentration, Nanth filled a dipper from the barrel near the hull and raised it to his lips. He gave no sign that he noticed her, other than to gradually suck up a mouthful.

After several sips, he seemed calmer. He spoke for the first time in days—not to her, but to verbalize his thoughts.

"Take off the belt, you idiot."

VIII

Alemar coughed as a cloud of dust hit him in the face. He wished for dunes again; the sand slowed them down, but spared the lungs. He envied those at the front of the line. The caravan transformed the road to powder long before the twins and those in their position passed by.

It was a crepuscular existence—up and moving before dawn, resting for several hours at midday, active well into the night. They moved slowly, the entire clan travelling as a group. The men rode oeikani, if they had them to spare. The women and children walked, carrying tent poles and household goods that could not be loaded onto pack animals. Elder boys ranged to either side, allowing the livestock to graze. The pace never exceeded a common walk, and if forage were relatively abundant, it slowed or stopped altogether.

Elenya rode just ahead, and slightly apart, from her brother and "their" family. She had left her face cowled, but her upper body was bare. She held her chest out, nipples forward, covering them only incidentally when she brushed the grit off her breasts and shoulders. She stared straight ahead and spoke to no one, not even Alemar.

Occasionally, one of the women in the caravan, but more often one of the small children, would stare in her direction, only to turn away suddenly if noticed. But no one spoke. Only once, when she had first opened her robes earlier in the day, had Fumlok tried.

"Is there a Law against it?" she asked.

The scenery shifted gradually, but filled the senses. The region was high plateau. Though their road on the average remained at one elevation, the terrain frequently dipped into sudden, severely eroded gullies, rose into scarred mesas thousands of feet above the valley floor, and in odd, unexpected places, supported life. A low-lying landmark could vanish behind them in less than an hour's walk, while ahead a particularly prominent mountain had not changed during two days of travel. They followed wadis that opened out onto dry plains crusted with salts and minerals, but never to bodies of water.

The T'lil consisted of five clans—the T'krt, the T'lan, the Kol, the Ena, and the Hysic. At first it astonished Alemar to learn how much territory these five families owned, until he understood the relativity involved. It took prodigious amounts of the sere land to support an individual. The T'krt numbered less than a thousand, the entire T'lil nation less than three thousand, counting in Zyraii fashion: adult males only. For the most part, they strung out over the land in small knots of immediate kin, often no more than three or four adults, only to such density as could support their animals. They gathered for migration and raids on neighbors. At the moment, the cause was the annual trek to the Ahloorm Basin, the broad plain split by the only continuously running stream in the nation, the Ahloorm, which meant simply "the river." The Zyraii controlled its upper portion, while the city-states of Surudain and Nyriya held the coast.

"Is it like this all the way to the Demon Mountains?" Alemar asked.

"One part of Zyraii is never the same as the rest," Fumlok said, avoiding the challenge of describing his country using the High Speech.

The twins had lived among the Zyraii for ten days, long enough that the curious no longer wandered in their direction. Already teachers had taken them through myriad lessons on history, geology, weather, theology, desertcraft, martial training, and most of all, obedience. People had started to converse with Alemar, encouraging, in their taciturn way, his stumbling attempts to speak Zyraii. Knowledge threatened to ooze out of their pores. But they had only touched the surface. For the moment, the instructors concentrated upon the language.

Elenya noticed a tent-maker observing her, so she deliberately scratched the bottom of one of her breasts. The man looked away.

Fumlok occasionally tried to reason with her, but to no effect. It had also been he who had originally tried to explain to her that she was really a man. It had taken a substantial amount of time, considering that his entire argument stemmed from one thesis—the laws of the So-de'es must be obeyed.

"Who makes the laws?" she had demanded.

"God, of course." It had astonished Fumlok that in other countries, men had the audacity to decide their own laws.

"What happens when a law is no longer needed? What if one needs to be changed?"

"God's laws do not need to be changed."

"What would happen if a law were not clear? Who would interpret it?"

"We must ask God."

She had made rude noises. "How does one talk to God?"

"The Zee-no-ken talk to God," he had answered matter-of-factly. "They sit alone in the hills and meditate. If they are true of spirit and do not falter, they hear God's voice. In this way God passes down His word. If the need is urgent, we call upon the High Scholar at Setan, and he journeys to God's Peak."

"Then I'd like a word with God," she had announced.

Fumlok had sighed. It was clear that Elenya was not going to make a very good man.

The first cricket of evening chirped, and in the west the earth swallowed the sun. The front end of the caravan looped around and coupled with the rear, forming a protective circle. The animals flowed to the inside, sheep bleating, while the people moved to the edges. Soon boys took small clusters of pack animals, freed from their burdens, out to brief grazing.

Lonal weaved casually through the throng, occasionally offering suggestions to the camp-makers that would increase the impregnability of the defenses. He approached the twins.

"Nannon abat se," he said.

"Se, gomo," Alemar answered. Elenya looked the other way.

Lonal regarded her in a friendly manner, staring frankly at her bust. "You'll get sunburned that way," he said.

"I'm trying to wither them so I'll look like a proper male."

He nodded. "That's a good idea. I hadn't thought of that." He nudged his oeikani with his knees and resumed his tour.

Elenya stared after him with a gaze too cold to suit the climate.

"Tonight," she told Alemar.

They slept in the open, under a canopy of moons. Small tents and partially erected larger ones surrounded them, whatever was necessary to screen private activities. The tribe wouldn't remain more than one night here.

Sentries paced the perimeter. Insects and small creatures of the night became bolder, encouraged by lack of human noise. The stars of the arid, clear sky daunted illusions of significance.

Elenya turned toward Alemar. He was staring at the void.

"Ready?"

He drew off the coverlet from his fully clothed body.

They rose. The wives and children slept soundly. Hastily they re-created their bedrolls such that it appeared they still occupied them. Darting from tent to tent, they filtered their way to the edge of the camp. A sentry had just passed by.

They glided into open desert, the night consuming them. They went east, the least likely direction. Ahead lay a slope gnawed by nature, where the land climbed into a series of rugged hills, full of cover, with plenty of rock to hide spoor.

In between remained two leagues of flat ground, where they could easily be overtaken. At first they moved slowly, hugging the earth, stopping behind brush or mounds of grass. Once they had traveled beyond the range of even sharp-eared sentries, they paused.

They reached inside their collars and withdrew identical gold necklaces, each adorned with a single large emerald. Standing close to one another, they touched the jewels together and concentrated. First one amulet, then the other, flashed with a jubilant green light, alternating more and more rapidly until the glow became constant. Alemar and Elenya stepped away, satisfied.

Now let the Zyraii dare to give chase.

Moonlight gave them a clear view of the terrain. Sure-footed, swift, and well rested from the ten days with the tribe, they no longer had to pace themselves or hide what they could do. Elenya set the speed, her lean legs thrusting the sand and soil behind with each step.

Alemar smelled the clean desert wind, felt it caress his hair. Although there were no trees to dodge nor logs to leap, he was at home. No distance or change of nations had taken away his legs, nor the jewel at his throat.

Dawn would soon pale the silhouettes that slipped past them every few strides. Elenya, her initial, exuberant burst of energy spent, had let Alemar lead for the long-term jog. As the flush of excitement leaked away, they no longer dreamed so freely of avoiding pursuers who knew the land and outnumbered them by many dozens, but no sounds of pursuit had reached them.

Still, there was a peculiar sense of unease in the air. It had become increasingly distinct within the past hour. Finally Elenya commented on it, and Alemar pulled out his amulet to check it.

It glowed now not simply with the pleasant forest green of their own spell, but with the deep tones that warned of foreign magic being cast upon them.

They turned worried faces toward their trail, but still could detect nothing.

"They have a sorcerer," Elenya said grimly.

"They must," Alemar agreed. They heightened their speed.

The amulets were now hot with warning, yet the twins could hear no one behind them. A new shadow grew on the path. It emerged low and square, only the regularity of its shape distinguishing it from the increasing number of rocky knolls that pimpled the region. Alemar and Elenya slowed, but retained their route, straight toward the feature. They were quite near before the light of the moons finally allowed them to identify it.

They stopped.

Alemar could now feel the heat radiate from his skin, bereft of the cooling wind of his passage. The meditation born of steady exertion broke.

They faced a mound of stone set, without mortar, slightly higher than they could reach, a cube some fifteen feet along each base. They could see no openings. Marks of weather indicated considerable age; its surface was free of vestiges of recent habitation.

They realized their error. The source of the magic was not the Zyraii behind them, but the object in front of them.

"Let's go," Elenya said in anxious tones.

Only then did they see that they had entered a vaguely defined circle, its borders indicated by crumbling marker stones. They could guess its meaning, but nevertheless they tried to step back.

They could not. Each attempted, unsuccessfully, to get heels or toes to lift from the earth. Elenya's obscenities blistered the air, voice tinged with panic. Alemar struggled harder, finally dragging his foot painfully across the ground—a few inches, no more. The effort made him pant. Worse, the heaviness in his soles spread to his calves, then his thighs. He heard an impact behind him. Elenya had fallen. She lay in an unnatural posture, unfolding slowly, as if incapable of controlling her muscles. Numb now from the waist down, he swayed like a coastal sapling.

They heard the sound of stone sliding against stone. A section rose from the top of the sepulcher, emitting the stench of air long confined, accompanied by the rustle of dry cloth.

Alemar sank to his knees, fighting for consciousness. Dread kept his eyes open, watching as a bluish, glowing specter flowed out of the opening. Manlike arms reached out toward them as the wight issued its siren call.

Each thought took far too long to circuit through his brain. He was crawling toward the cairn before he could, at last, put away his shock and conceive of a means to fight. Elenya writhed, snakelike, spittle on her lips, though managing for the moment to retain her distance from the wight and its sorcery.

"Ec lu tinacht. Jin drenne o lieul . . ." The words creaked out of Alemar's throat, each syllable more painful than the last. The wight hesitated.

Tingles coursed over Alemar's neck and face, returning remnants of human sensation. *"Monacht abba Poseth!"* he yelled.

The specter wavered. Its cry thrust agony into Alemar's temples.

"Poseth!" Elenya cried.

"Poseth, lama ti Poseth!" the twins shouted in unison.

The wight exploded, splintering into shards of blue radiance. The psychic impact pounded the twins into the dirt. Each flicker of blue flame sped up as it went, circling the others, somersaulting, broadcasting the ecstasy of release. A hundred souls grown small from centuries of captivity and domination expanded to their full glory. For a moment, it was daylight.

But the dread did not leave.

Weak with exhaustion beyond the physical, Alemar and Elenya raised onto their elbows, but their relief was smothered. Another wight floated out of the vault's interior, its azure fire dwarfing that of its predecessor, the malevolence of its spell mocking the earlier failure.

But it held back, unable to prematurely calm the psychic chaos caused by the twins' counterattack, shrinking from the odor of exorcism. It laid the heaviness on the bones of its prey, draining all but the strength to remain awake, and waited.

Alemar heard hoofbeats.

The phantom acted abruptly. It roused, flowing foglike down the surface of the cairn to reassemble at the base, not ten feet from where the twins lay. There it hesitated a moment, reluctant to leave the source of its power. It proceeded forward gradually, opening its noncorporeal lips and uttering a strident, potent call of invitation.

The hands and knees of the twins responded, grudgingly, closing the gap.

A single rider and his oeikani galloped forward into the faint, early dawn illumination. The wight reared, facing the newcomer.

"Haiii-yahhh!" the rider shouted, drawing his scimitar. The wight opened its arms and grew until it was as tall and as wide as the mount, the glitter of its eyes betokening its hunger.

The man flung himself from the oeikani at the last moment, landing so suddenly and with such poor preparation that he knocked himself out. The oeikani passed through the wight and collapsed, its momentum tumbling it over three times. The creature laughed with joy, the blue of its shape momentarily deepening.

As it turned back toward its human victims, ten more Zyraii rode into the site, beasts flecked with foam. Fear immediately contorted their faces. They shrank back. Lonal thundered between them on an exhausted stallion.

"Dismount! Surround them!" he yelled.

They obeyed instantly, two men automatically rounding up the animals, which warbled their nervousness and would have scattered if not prevented. The wight screamed at them, but although knees shook, the tribesmen remained upright, keeping just outside the markers of the circle. They drew scimitars.

"Forget the steel! Get torches!" Lonal cried.

The wight held its ground, evaluating its opponents, while the men holding the oeikani retrieved resin-soaked shafts of bound sage from the saddlebags and threw them to the others. Alemar and Elenya stirred. Another ghostly scream shook the initiative out of their attempt. The specter advanced.

Lonal lit his torch. Rapidly the others followed suit.

The wight bellowed. As the light grew, it became faint, little more than a blue tinge on the walls of the mound. The Zyraii held the torches above their heads, the pallor of their faces revealed.

The creature began to whirl its arms in circles, spinning until it lost all human configuration. Currents of air rose, a whirlwind with a blue, stationary core. The siren call increased. The twins moaned. The tribesmen fought back the urge to step into the circle and had difficulty keeping their eyes open. One of them fell down.

A gust doused the torches.

Angrily the wight flowed outward in order to envelop Alemar and Elenya. Lonal lit his torch again with one stroke of the flint and flung it straight at the thing. The flame snuffed out, but the advance was halted. The wight screeched and spat blue tendrils at Lonal.

Lonal shuddered as if arrows of ice pierced him. By now, most of his men had relit their brands. They waved them again, causing the wight to retreat toward its mound. It coalesced once again into human outlines. For a moment it almost possessed a true visage, that of an ancient, weary man, but other countenances coruscated within and upon the first, reflections of the souls held inside.

It glared at the men, hatred fervent. It hissed at their torches, and at the increasing light in the east. The men were grim, but they waited resolutely.

Ten interminable moments later, the wight retreated, slimelike, up the surface of the vault, and disappeared inside, drawing the stone cover back over the opening.

When they were sure it wouldn't return, the men sank to their knees. Three times they touched their foreheads to the ground toward the point where the sun would soon rise. The oeikani ceased to struggle against the grip on their reins. Murmured prayers came from many lips.

Alemar lay still, awake but unwilling to move. He ached. It humbled him to think how little his physical resistance had accomplished. Elenya groaned, not completely aware of her surroundings even now, struggling to stay conscious only out of terror of falling asleep while still in that place.

Lonal and his Po-no-pha did not attempt to enter the circle until after the orb of Achird had risen above the line of the hills, and direct light hit the mound at last. The piled stones lost a little of their sinister aspect, though the sensation of dread continued to permeate the vicinity. By that time, Alemar had risen to a sitting position, and Elenya lay comfortably. The man who had leaped from his oeikani woke up.

At Lonal's terse command, only two of his men and he himself entered the unholy ground. They gripped each of the Cilendri and their bruised comrade by the armpits and dragged them past the marker stones as quickly as feasible.

"You do us honor, Kulam," Lonal told the recovering Zyraii. Kulam stared about uncertainly.

"Is it gone?" he whispered.

Lonal nodded. "The power of God proved more than it could defy. But it was a close thing." He filled in the man quickly, but did not elaborate. None of them cared to stay in the area any longer than necessary. The twins stood, shaky but on their own power. He ordered them onto the backs of two oeikani. They hung on to the Zyraii riders as if frightened of the height. Kulam glanced once at his dead animal and pursed his lips. Then he climbed behind one of his fellows.

"You will be compensated," Lonal told Kulam, and glared at the twins. "I know some people who will be glad to see that you receive two oeikani for your one."

IX

Two naked breasts.

They were petite, but firm and well proportioned, light pink nipples untouched by motherhood.

Keron blinked, not really sure that he had opened his eyes. The sensation of relief had awakened him. Lerina was leaning over him. One of her hands held an abalone shell between his legs, the other directed his penis toward the shell while his bladder emptied.

He tried to rise, but his body was a statue. Even the most insignificant muscle failed him.

"Relax," Lerina said.

He did. Vague memories told him this was not the first time she had tended him so. In fact, by now it seemed natural.

"You're really awake," she said, shaking him perfunctorily. She lifted the shell away.

"I think so," he murmured.

"Your fever broke a few hours ago."

"How long has it been?"

"Three days."

She rose and left momentarily to dump the urine. He glanced around. The cave had lost its uninhabited aspect. His mattress was a large blanket stretched across the smooth sand at the rear of the chamber, a gentle bed created by the ocean of ages past. Along the tunnel to the outside, niches and natural stone shelves had been filled with small items such as blankets, flasks, and in one instance, a book. A basket of considerable size stood against a wall next to his clothing, his weapons and belt in a neat pile on top of them. There was a depression in the sand next to him.

Lerina returned, a soothing, nude presence.

"Have you stayed with me the entire time?" he asked.

"I had to. It seems that some barbarian murdered people in

Eruth, and my uncle forbade me to leave the house. I had to slip out in the night, and had I returned, I would have been closely watched. I managed to bring enough supplies for the time being."

"Your pardon. I've made trouble for you."

"It's nothing. Drink some water," she said, and handed him a flask.

He sipped. Some of his dizziness went away.

Lerina pointed to the wound on his side. "I almost gave up on you. But once the infection was defeated, you began healing so quickly I could see the changes over the course of hours."

He sensed the unspoken query. Poor Obo. The old man was probably half-dead. He was a greater mage than the king suspected.

"Come on," she said. "You stink. If you can walk, it's time to give you a bath."

Again he tried to rise, but barely sat up. Lerina had to wrestle him to his feet. Securing herself under his uninjured shoulder, she walked him toward the cave mouth. Here the sand floor gave way to water-sculpted, convoluted folds of rock. Keron navigated the irregular surface cautiously, his feet relearning their function. Although Lerina grunted under the burden of his weight, Keron thought he would float away. The fever had purged him of all tension. He had never felt so insubstantial.

They labored to a tidepool, under the blinding light of day. Clouds splattered the sky, decorations without promise of rain. They couldn't see the mainland from their location, but could feel its bulk. Keron stopped, calf-deep in the ocean, and stared to the south. He remained there for some time.

"What is it?" Lerina asked eventually. He had forgotten she was there.

"The sea."

Perhaps she understood. In any case, she left him alone until he returned to the here and now.

She had to help him to sit down. He bellowed as the salt water struck his thigh, but she shoved him down and proceeded to wet and scrub vigorously at his undamaged areas. The stinging gave way to the luxury of being cleaned. His thick scabs softened and tugged less vindictively.

He lived.

He knew Obo was only part of the reason. He let Lerina work for a few moments, gathering his thoughts.

"I owe you my life."

The cake of soap was a coarse concoction common to the region, and she handled it enthusiastically. She paused only a moment. "No, you don't," she said.

"Seriously. The spell could only—"

"I know what I did. But it wasn't a job, so you don't owe me anything."

She lifted one of his legs as he balanced on a submerged rock, and began meticulously washing his toes. "As a matter of fact, I would have been less likely to help you if I'd felt I had to. I don't like having to do what people tell me to."

Keron had to smile. "Still, if you hadn't helped me, I would have ended up like my companions in Eruth. I won't forget."

The memory troubled him, but she didn't allow him to dwell on it. Her hands worked with the skill of a masseuse, seducing his body to relax. It hardly startled him when she became intimate with the soap, or that she did it with the platonic disregard of a nurse.

"I take it that your sympathies lie with the royalists," he added, "or I'd be in a cell manacled to my sickbed, if not dead."

"My sympathies are with Cilendrodel. I don't care to be on either side of your war."

He coughed up a small amount of phlegm. "Still, if it becomes known that you aided me, that will serve as a declaration in itself."

"Then best it not become known," she said demurely.

She gingerly rubbed at the edges of the stitches on his thigh, more of an examination than a cleansing. "It's amazing. This was obviously infected yesterday." As she rinsed the soap off his waist, she added, "Do you always wear a belt under your pants?"

He clutched his hips suddenly, then reddened as he recalled seeing the belt in the cave. "I'm sorry. It feels odd to be without it."

"It seemed valuable."

"It is. A family heirloom. I try to keep it out of common sight. When did you take it off?"

"Yesterday. It seemed so cold, and you were shivering."

"Thank you."

She hurried through the rest of the cleaning, and helped him back to the beach. Then she soaped herself down in the shallows and waded out to dunk. She vanished, leaving swirls of foam, which she obliterated as she burst back up through them, spouting like a dolphin. She joined a swell as it gathered and died against the beach, and walked the last short distance to him with rivulets dripping from her breasts, chin, elbows, and fingers.

It made him hungry to watch her.

"Let's eat," she said, as if reading his mind, and headed for the cave. She brought out the entire food basket.

Food, Keron thought. Yes, he remembered what that was.

She cut up a mosh, a staple of the Cilendri forest. Full of fluid and soft enough to chew with gums alone, it struck Keron's strained system lightly, a satisfactory choice for the transition between water and solid food. Lerina sliced each piece only the width of her small finger, almost so thin that the flesh folded over itself, and fed them to him one by one. It took a considerable amount of time to consume the single fruit.

"Enjoy it. It's the last of the fresh stuff," she warned.

"Am I complaining?" He smiled.

Twice she left her finger near his lips even after he had taken the slices.

Cold porridge followed the mosh, which they ate silently, enjoying the sun. As it grew warmer, they moved into the cave again, Keron preferring to crawl on his own power for the exercise. Walking made his head resent being up so high.

The cave still smelled of human perspiration, tempered by salt drafts. He noted bits of mica in the walls. Though humble, it seemed to him more secure than any number of luxurious accommodations in which he had found himself.

"Rest," Lerina commanded as he refused to lay back on his blanket.

"I have rested," he said. But to humor her, he put his head down and closed his eyes.

A moment later, he opened them, and felt the fog-breath of late afternoon.

He heard soft snores beside him. Lerina was curled in a little-girl bundle, oblivious to the world.

"My company's that boring, eh?" he murmured. She didn't respond.

Before long, he noticed his belt just beyond the end of their feet. He dragged himself stiffly in its direction, took it, and caressed it in his grip. It was an impressive piece—a strap of dragon hide decorated with gold embroidery, the symbol of a dragon in flight set with rubies on the buckle. It still showed no wear, though he had worn it for years now, not to mention all the others who must have owned it.

Without attempting to wake up Lerina, he crawled toward the opening, clutching the belt. In places, he could almost walk, bracing against a cave wall with his free hand to compensate for his thigh. The act provided a small bit of self-sufficiency he needed at that moment.

The sea rumbled a few steps away, beckoning, but he deliberately ignored it. Finally, he unbuckled the belt and wrapped it around his waist.

The power came on him like fire, a fierce jolt unlike the sensation he had always known. He sweated and shook as if his fever had returned. But the strength was there. He stood up straight, the wound in his thigh only a nagging itch. He took a few firm steps, stooped, and tore a section of stone from the outcropping at his feet. He threw it as hard and strong as he could, watching it arc and land at sea many hundred yards away, so distant the splash was hidden in the swells.

Satisfied, he unbuckled, falling instantly onto his good knee as his other leg gave way. It took him several moments to control the shuddering of his muscles and the agitated state of his lungs.

So she'd saved his life again. Ah, what a fool he was. Of course Obo wouldn't have been able to work his spell when other magic sapped the energy for its own use. Keron stuck the belt between his teeth and crawled, somewhat meekly, back toward his sickbed.

He replaced the belt and began to climb onto the blanket, only then noticing the marks in the sand in front of the spot where Lerina liked to sit. Curious, he leaned over and was able, after some guessing, to see that she had sketched the figure of a sleeping man with her finger.

He spent some time just looking at his small, naked, slightly overwhelming nurse. His thoughts tried to wander leagues away, but they kept coming back to the present moment, location, and companion.

"I'm in trouble now," he muttered to himself.

"Follow me," Lonal said.

The sun was kind, though it was midafternoon. The twins did as they were told, abandoning the erection of their tent. Around them, the tribe prepared to settle in for a day or more. Good forage had been found.

The war-leader followed the track of the sheep out of the camp, occasionally glancing ahead where the preemptive whistles of the shepherds originated, as the latter endeavored to keep their animals orderly. Soon he diverged, leading them into open desert, which in this region abounded in short shrubs and cacti, crossed often by snake tracks or the spoor of small mammals. When they approached a stand of spiny plants that stood like trees, columns often as high as a man, he stopped and faced them.

"I trust you are both feeling miserable?"

Alemar and Elenya looked worse than they had when they had first arrived. Crimson webs filled the whites of their eyes, dark lines beneath, and their hair was matted and disarrayed. Elenya had to endure the sting of her sunburn, as well as the exhaustion of her battle with the wights. She now wore her full complement of clothing. They had not been permitted to rest all day, as the tribe had been setting out as they returned that morning. Lonal was only a little better off.

"You don't like life among the T'lil?" the war-leader asked.

"Would you?" Elenya replied coldly. "In my position?"

"It is not often that God sees fit to change someone's gender," he answered. "But if I guess correctly, you would not have been happy in our land as a woman. The solution of the ken saved us both."

"Thanks."

"But the solution is only a first step. The tribe can't continue to coddle the two of you."

"Why bother?" Elenya asked, and threw up her arms. "Why not let us go our way?"

"I have my responsibilities," Lonal said firmly. "In this instance, I must act to protect the holy relic, to which you will go should I set you free, and there is the matter of Am and Roel's family. Do not forget the duties you have assumed. For the moment, they give you your only worth among the T'lil."

"I am honored," Elenya said sarcastically.

"It is time you realized the seriousness of your position. You, Yetem, have mocked the lessons our Ah-no-ken have tried to teach you."

"Oh, really?"

He gestured at the landscape. *"Ho koso quell ka kem?"*

She pursed her lips. Lonal sighed. "Well? What's the answer?"

She didn't speak.

"Tebec?" Lonal asked. "Can you answer the question?"

Alemar glanced at his sister. Abruptly, irritably, he said, *"Quell ka rhyme koso."*

"Your brother at least learns out of politeness. Yes. This is flat country. Not a difficult question, Yetem. But no—we're barbarians, and our tongue is beneath you. I see it in your upturned nose."

She pointed her face toward one of the mesas in the west. "Will I lose my soul if I don't learn to speak God's language?"

"Perhaps. You will certainly lose your life. It is not normally my duty, but I'm going to give you three lessons before we walk back to the camp. For your sake, pay attention." He stepped over to the stand of cacti and drew his dagger, with which he tapped the thick mesh of bristles covering the closest specimen.

"This is the *boro*. It is very common to this region. Its name means succor."

The *boro* in front of Lonal stood as high as his waist. The war-leader plunged the dagger into the crown and efficiently carved out a circular piece. Using the blade as a skewer, he lifted the section out, exposing a rind similar to the melons of the twins' homeland, but much thicker. Alemar and Elenya peered in. The core of the plant was filled with liquid.

Lonal produced a stiff, hollow reed from his scabbard, inserted it into the *boro,* and sucked. He swallowed and handed the reed to Elenya. She and Alemar each sipped some of the juice.

"It's very good," Alemar said.

"Given the choice between water and *boro-ra,* I would drink *boro-ra,*" Lonal said. "But one must not abuse God's small charities." He pointed to the wound he had created. "This plant is endangered." He replaced the plug in the exact position it had formerly occupied.

"The *boro*'s skin is virtually impregnable to its native enemies. But once breached, parasites may attack it, or the sun evaporate its cache, and kill it from dehydration. This individual, hopefully, will seal its damage and survive."

He then removed a small cloth pouch from the goatskin satchel he carried and poured the chalkish meal it contained in a continuous circle around the base of the *boro*. "This meal poisons *picteor* beetles, the worst parasite."

He cinched the drawstrings of the sack. "This is the first lesson, which you have perhaps guessed already: Water is never to be taken for granted. Learn its sources, and do all within your power to see that they are preserved against future need."

For once, Elenya was not irreverent.

They continued deeper into the wasteland. Lonal wandered in no specific direction, or so it seemed to them. Eventually they realized he was following a peculiar type of mark in the sand.

He stopped next to a mound of earth pocked with holes, each about the diameter of a human wrist. He motioned them to stay and tiptoed up to the site. Leaning close to several of the holes, he examined the traces left in the loose soil surrounding each opening. He nodded to himself and reached within his satchel once more. He withdrew a mouse.

The creature tried to scurry between Lonal's fingers, but the war-leader thwarted it. He produced a coil of twine, a metal barb resembling a fish hook at one end. He plunged the point into the mouse's abdomen, made sure it had anchored firmly, and let the rodent free at the lip of the hole he had selected.

The mouse hobbled painfully, but swiftly, out of sight, trailing the twine. Lonal allowed the coil to unravel without resistance; soon it went slack.

They waited. Gradually, Lonal nurtured the strand back into a coil, finger by finger. It grew taut. Lonal jerked.

The twine shuddered, thrashed. The man pulled as fast as he could.

When it emerged, the end of the twine seemed to have grown thicker. Lonal stood, holding up a snake half as long as he, a narrow, delicate specimen with a swollen gullet, the point of the barb protruding entirely through its skin in the middle of the bulge.

He held the snake in front of Alemar. "Cut it in two," he ordered.

Alemar drew his saber and halved Lonal's catch. The hind section flopped to the ground, where it writhed.

Lonal cut off the end of his twine and flung the head of the snake, mouse and all, past the mound. The blood pouring from the severed end splattered the burrows. They could hear the muffled thrashing of its death throes through the sage for several seconds.

Lonal picked up the tail and held its markings up to the sunlight. "This is an *iltrekal-hasha-sor,* the moonsnake, the most venomous thing in all Zyraii. If one should bite you, you will die in less than an hour. Only once in our history has a man survived it—Umar, the greatest Hab-no-ken ever to have lived, who healed himself. Fortunately, they prefer to remain in animal burrows such as this *hussa* mound or other underground tunnels. They only come out at night, and they do not bother creatures as large as men, unless you bother them. Never pitch your tent in open desert without checking for their traces."

He shoved his supply of twine into the satchel. "This is the second lesson—the desert has a thousand ways to kill you, large and small. God did not place us here as a reward, but as a test. If you would challenge this land, know the magnitude of what you do."

As he spoke, Lonal's hands had drifted to his sides, to rest on his waist, just above the sword belt. Before either Alemar or Elenya could move, he had drawn demonblades from duplicate scabbards and flung them simultaneously at their chests. Both landed hard at midtorso level, butt first, and flopped to the ground even as the targets dodged.

Elenya drew her rapier. Lonal folded his arms and smiled. Alemar, winded from the impact to his solar plexus, merely dropped his jaw, literally breathless at the thought that anyone could control two throwing knives with either hand at the same time.

"What was that for?" Elenya demanded.

"May I?" Lonal asked, gesturing toward his knives. Two wary observers allowed him to retrieve them, wipe off the dirt, and slide them into their scabbards. Elenya sheathed her rapier only after he had looped the flaps shut over the handles.

"Lesson three," the war-leader observed calmly, "is that people must help each other. God gave us challenges, and he gave us the social qualities that bring us together to meet those hurdles. When one is offered help, one should take it. Don't tempt good fortune. I could have killed you just now, but I have hopes that you will be valuable to me, given time. Out there"—he swept his arms across the arid tracts of chaparral and ruptured stone—"are nigh twenty thousand other sons of Cadra, thirsty for foreign blood. We are not a tolerant people. If you are welcomed by us, consider it an advantage not to be wasted. I am the son of Joren, but even my father's fame and my own reputation will not protect you should you stray from the embrace of the T'lil."

Elenya seemed ready to retort, so he held up a hand. "You aren't reconciled to stay. Otherwise you would listen to your teachers, Yetem, and cooperate with them. Be like your brother, with his natural desire to study regardless of the conditions. Perhaps you will succeed in your escape next time, and it could be your ruin. The wights should serve as a warning. Those crypts are old, and they litter our landscape in odd places, away from the common routes. Lost children have been attracted to them from miles away. You were drawn to that particular site because you couldn't recognize the taint in the air. Any adult born in this land would have been in no danger."

"We didn't thank you for our rescue," Alemar said.

"No, you didn't. I am, in a sense, offering you the chance to show your gratitude. I won't ask how you ran so fast—your bedrolls still held warmth when we discovered you missing. Nor will I ask how you possessed the sorcery to destroy a wight and set its captive souls free. It is enough that we riders saw the aura of your magic and could locate you in time. You are more than you seem. So be it. Remember that you are in my debt."

The first bat of evening whisked overhead, though the sun hung clear of the horizon. Lonal turned and headed back toward camp. He let the twins follow as they might. The war-leader's confidence was overwhelming, Alemar thought. Soon he and his sister were trailing close behind, reflecting on the war-leader's advice.

Only once did Lonal stop and speak to them again, just before they entered the camp. He seemed deeply intrigued.

"Do you believe in auguries?" he asked.

XI

The Snakeback Hills had earned their name. They twisted with serpentine abruptness, jagged S-curves as rugged as the Ahrahikte Mountains hanging over them in the west. The T'lil seldom ranged so far, but Joren and his clan needed the pasturage to be found on their slopes. Furthermore, Setan was nearby, and Joren reasoned that it was an auspicious place to be with the child due.

No doubt she's in labor now, he calculated. Alone, he climbed over a precarious section of scree toward firmer ground near the ridgeline. He had already crossed the back of the snake three times, though it was early in the day, and would probably continue his destinationless trek until the light failed. Here, it was said, an ordinary man could be closer to God than any spot in all Zyraii. From any high point, God's Peak could be seen challenging the sky, so near that the glow of the moons could be seen on her snowfields in winter.

Would God consider his prayers? Was he worthy?

As he stopped at the crest to view the mountain again, his foot dislodged a large stone, sending it crashing down the grade he had just vanquished, into the scree. It created a small but noisy avalanche.

"Help! Help!"

Joren could just hear the voice once the din of the slide had diminished. "Where are you?" he yelled.

"This way! In the hole!"

Joren searched the hilltop. Guided by continuing cries, he finally located an opening in the ground a short way down the other side of the hill.

"Don't get near! It crumbles!"

The warning came just in time. Though the earth appeared to be granite, near the hole it had cracked, and some pieces at the lip were loose. Two chunks fell. Dust billowed up out of the pit.

"Thanks."

"Sorry. How did you get in there?"

"The hole wasn't here until I walked by. The mountain must like to eat holy men."

Joren climbed what appeared to be a secure boulder to one side of the opening, from which he could manage to peer within. The sun's angle favored him. He could see a grime-covered Zyraii in the gray robes of a *hada* Zee-no-ken, standing in the center of a near perfect spherical chamber within the ground. It was hard to imagine what had made the hole. Joren could only guess that the upheaval that had built the hills themselves had left a giant bubble within the rock, trapped until the Zee-no-ken's misfortune exposed it to the light of day. It was just a little too deep to allow the man to jump out. Moreover, the geometry of the chamber made climbing impossible.

"I don't suppose you have a rope with you?" the Zee-no-ken asked.

Naturally Joren had a rope; he wouldn't have gone wandering in the Snakeback Hills without one, and before long he had anchored it to the boulder and thrown the free end to the trapped man. Soon wiry, middle-aged hands emerged, followed by the gaunt, but obviously strong, figure of the priest.

"Thank you," the Zee-no-ken said. His robes were torn, exposing a pair of scrapes, but the vigor of his climb out and the ease with which he handed the rope back to Joren belied any serious injury.

"How long were you in there?"

"As of dawn, two days."

"Would you like some water?" Joren asked, noting that the other had none.

The man accepted the goatskin without hesitation, and drank one long, fulfilling swallow. He seemed entirely satisfied with that. As Joren knew, Zee-no-ken had control over their bodies in ways that mystified other human beings. Two days without water in this land often killed.

"I am Esidio. I am in your debt, Po-no-pha."

"I am Joren, war-leader of the T'lil. And you're welcome."

Esidio seemed surprised. "I assumed you to be searching for a lost goat, but a man of your station would not do so. God must have designs on me to send such a rescuer."

"I would have no idea about that," Joren said. They prudently put a little more distance between themselves and the pit.

"Surely you're here for some reason?" Esidio smiled gently.

Joren paused long enough to coil his rope. Could it be that God had heard him? "I came seeking counsel with myself. My wife will soon give birth."

The priest had probably not seen a baby in decades, but he nodded understandingly. "Your first?"

"Yes, if all goes well. The other three times I have been given girls."

"Ah. Have you considered another wife?"

"She is my other wife."

"I see."

Joren nodded, and they sat down together to view God's Peak. Near midday the currents of the heat in the air made the mountain's contours shimmer, as if it were melting into the heavens.

"You don't seem at all disturbed that you might have starved to death in that hole," Joren wondered out loud.

"I was disturbed while I was in there. Now that I'm saved, it doesn't make any sense to fray my nerves worrying about what would have happened if you hadn't come along. I don't mean to seem indifferent. In fact, I would feel much better if there were a way I could express my gratitude."

"Well," Joren began. "I see you wear the gray. . . ."

Esidio smiled paternally. "I know your mind, but your question would no doubt be answered simply by walking back to your camp. My talents can be of better use to you. Ask me a question whose answer means as much to you as my life did to me, then accounts will be squared. But have caution. If the Sight were straightforward, one such as I would not fall into holes in the ground."

"You're right. Give me a little time."

"No hurry. I hadn't planned on going anywhere today."

Joren struggled with opposing moods. On the one hand, he could hardly contain his eagerness. On the other, he worried that he might choose a frivolous query, or one whose reply would be indecipherable. To pass the time, he offered Esidio food from his pack. The Zee-no-ken readily accepted, selecting a modest quantity of dates, which he ate promptly, taking care to collect the seeds and return them to the pack. Rummaging further, he uttered a cry of delight.

"Locusts!" He held the open sack up and poured several of the salt-roasted insects out. "I had forgotten it was the swarm year. They haven't reached the hills yet."

Joren pressed the sack toward his companion. "Enjoy. Not quite the same as getting them hot from the fire, but good nonetheless."

"And coffee!" Esidio cried. Joren had to grin. Zee-no-ken were so different from the phlegmatic Ah-no-ken and Bo-no-ken. Though they were considered highest ranked among the priesthood, he had never yet encountered a Zee-no-ken who sought to conceal his emotions. "Let us take it to my camp. It's not far. I'll heat some water, and we will share a drink while you ponder."

"You seem poorly supplied. How is it that you survive up here?"

Esidio shrugged. "I have lived alone in these hills for twenty years, and it's never seemed hard to me. But I miss the things the land can't provide. I visit Setan so seldom."

They descended, Esidio instinctively selecting a path that taxed their endurance the least. Joren could see no trail. Though unhurried, the pace swallowed the distance. Before long they entered a gorge, steep slopes of rock rising on either side. Joren automatically checked the sky above the Ahrahikte to be sure no clouds hung there. They followed the stream bed deeper into the hills.

Finally Joren heard the trickle of water, a sound he found impossible to ignore. They rounded a bend, and in the shade on the south side in front of them, he saw a rivulet working its way down from far above, filling a tiny pool and diffusing into the cobbles downstream, where all sign of dampness quickly disappeared.

"Fill your waterskin," Esidio suggested.

Joren did so, cupping a handful and tasting it. He sighed. Unlike that of the oases in the steppes, this water didn't have to be made into coffees, teas, or wines to be palatable. Perhaps the priest was not so deprived after all.

They left the pool and immediately mounted the opposite bank. There, sheltered by steep slabs of granite, and high enough to be safe from flash floods, Esidio had created a living space.

Kindling was neatly piled to one side. A grass mat covered a flat spot beneath an overhang, and deeper within the cleft, Joren spotted casks of wine and urns of wheat and other dry goods, with a lattice of sturdy limbs to protect them from foraging animals. The firepit was in the center of the area, under the open sky.

"My home," Esidio said, "though I am more often out among the hills."

Joren grunted his approval and began to gather wood to start the fire. Esidio got out the coffee beans and dropped a handful into a stone mortar. While the war-leader coaxed the tinder, the Zee-no-ken ground the beans with the pestle. The flame caught, and Joren nursed it into a true fire.

"How long has it been since you spoke to anyone?" Joren asked.

Esidio chuckled. "I visited Setan only three months ago. But in my younger days, I once spent eight years without seeing another living soul."

"Didn't you miss company?"

"Of course. But the solitude suited my purpose."

"But so long without a woman . . ."

"I have yet to believe that a man can keep God and a woman in his heart at the same time."

In due time, the water boiled. The priest stretched his coffee cloth over the hoop and poured the grounds onto it. Joren helped pour water through into a clay pot. Esidio filled two mugs and placed the pot on the hearthstones.

"To rope," Esidio toasted, and they sucked in noisy, sudden swallows in the manner of the Zyraii.

"This is an excellent brew," the priest continued. "I can't recall that I've ever had a coffee so fine."

"There are some advantages to being a war-leader. This is *olom.*"

"Ah. The traders' best. My uncles used to speak of it. It used to be more plentiful, before the tributes became so small." Esidio inhaled another sip. "How is it these days?"

"There is talk again that Azurajen will try to build a fort in Zyraii lands."

"More work for you."

"More than I care for. But at the moment, the tribes still hold the trade routes. I worry most what will occur in the next generation." His face suddenly became pensive.

"You have found your question," Esidio said presently.

"Yes," Joren said firmly. "I have. Are you ready?"

"At your convenience."

Joren chose his words carefully. "What may I do to help this new child of mine deal with the threat of the traders, that I would not ordinarily think to do?"

"Even if it's a girl?"

Joren paused. "Yes. Even then."

Esidio set down his mug. "It is a worthy question. The T'lil's taste in war-leaders is improving. What was the name of that last fellow?"

"Storith."

"Yes. Rash sort. Made me glad to have been of the Alyr." Standing and dusting himself off, he pointed to Joren's just emptied mug. "You can use that to masturbate into if you'd like."

"I beg your pardon?!"

Esidio chuckled. "This is no casual procedure. If the topic had concerned yourself, I would have asked for your blood. If about your enemies, your spit. Since it deals with your offspring . . ."

"I see." Joren passed the mug from hand to hand. "I don't have to do this in front of you, do I?"

"Of course not. I'll start my preparations here. Come back when you're done. My only requirement is that it be fresh."

"All right." Joren picked himself up and left before he could doubt the situation too much.

When he returned, a bitter taint filled the air. Esidio was leaning over a tiny brazier from which thick, viscous smoke coiled. Tendrils vanished up the priest's nostrils, never seeming to be inhaled. His eyes were half-closed, showing only the whites. Over the fire another pot warmed, a small one filled with green liquid.

Esidio's back straightened as he heard Joren's feet scuffle on the granite. His hand reached for the mug.

"Quickly, before it cools."

Joren gave him the mug. Esidio inverted it over the pot, letting the semen drip out. It dissolved immediately, leaving no trace, though the consistencies of the fluids had seemed so disparate. Soon after, the mixture became as transparent as water.

"Good. The question can be answered," Esidio announced. "This will only take a moment. Please don't speak."

Joren chose a spot a dozen paces away, where his back could rest against stone, and waited. Esidio already acted as if nothing existed but the clear liquid into which he stared, lids half-closed again, but this time more naturally. The brazier continued to smoke, surrounding the vicinity with more of its noxious fumes. Esidio was unperturbed, but Joren blew away traces that wandered his way. Soon the coals consumed whatever substance had been placed upon them, and the air began to clear. The priest was still except for the subtle signs of his lung action, and the more obvious, rhythmic tremor each time his heart beat.

Then, abruptly, he picked up the pot and dumped it on the ground.

Joren nearly bit his tongue to keep from asking what was wrong.

Esidio sighed very deeply, and Joren noticed beads of sweat on his forehead. The priest didn't answer, only crawled deep into his storage niche. Joren heard a heavy lid opened and set down again. Soon Esidio crawled out again carrying a scroll, its finely wrought container incongruous among the Zee-noken's other, humble possessions. He opened the roll and searched, all the while ignoring Joren. Finally he stopped at a specific passage, and recited from it.

"They, of dragonkiller's blood,
Will the Eastern Deserts wander
In search of ancient weapons
Against an ancient enemy."

"Esidio?" Joren asked softly.

He seemed calmer. He closed the scroll and said solemnly, "I must end my hermitage and return to Setan." Then, more confidently, he looked at Joren and said, "And you must prepare yourself for a lifetime of challenges. This," he said as he held up the parchment, "is my copy of the prophecies of Shahera, the greatest master of the Sight ever to have lived. She foretold the waning of the Calinin Empire, for which she was executed."

"What does this have to do with my question?"

"Everything. Yours was that question which I, like all my kind, wait for—in dread or longing, depending on the circumstances. One never knows when it will arrive. Today the Sight reached out and showed me strands of time and chance that may affect the life and history of half the continent. I saw the Zyraii that may be; I saw the Zyraii that would have been had you not asked me to make this augury."

"All in a few moments?"

"Yes. And I will live with it for the rest of my days. I can't reveal more to you. You are too near the crux of events, and the cloth is still in the loom. We both have our parts to play—you will be the one who acts, without knowing the outcome; I will know the outcome, but do nothing. Each with one exception."

"What is my exception?"

"The answer to your question: See that your son is taught the High Speech of the Calinin. He must be ready when the prophecy of Shahera is fulfilled." His voice lowered. "As must I be."

"The High Speech?" Joren repeated, mystified.

Esidio stood, holding the scroll and gazing in the direction of Setan, turning his back to Joren. "Go, my friend. We will hear of each other again, though we shall not meet. Remember what I have said, but tell no man save your child."

Joren was already far away, the priest's instructions etched absently like an ancient childhood lesson. *Your son*. Like Esidio, he had been answered more completely than he had anticipated. The journey out of the hills was short.

XII

As Lonal and his companion watched, the riders wheeled and charged toward the target again. The westerner, as usual, seized the lead, her cowl flapping wildly, spilling some of her dark tresses. She let go of the reins, guiding the oeikani with her knees, and reached toward her quiver. In one motion she pulled an arrow free, cocked it back, and fired. The bundle of hide jerked on its pole as the arrow struck. The other archers were only a moment behind. The bundle spun and flopped, bristling like a pin cushion from this and previous passes. The ground nearby was littered with spent shafts, both those that had missed and those that had been flung free by subsequent impacts. The target nearly shredded, the riders pulled up, dismounted, and began to sort out their arrows from the rest.

"Impressive," Lonal's companion said, nodding toward the stranger. They watched as she tucked her hair back into her cowl. The clan of T'krt had been joined by the T'lan and the Ena during the past day, and formal wear was necessary. In fact, Lonal and Ulnam, war-leader of the Ena, had never seen each other's faces, though Lonal was betrothed to marry Ulnam's daughter when she came of age. "Is the other one that good?"

"Possibly, but Tebec doesn't show off like that."

"Four hits out of ten," Ulnam added. "He must have started young."

"No," Lonal said. "Actually, Yetem tells me that in his country, they only use the long bow. It is forest country. They hunt large animals, which they approach in stealth, and need the extra power to bring them down. Not like us, who have to hit the small creatures that scurry from rock to rock, from oeikani-back. He neglected to learn the bow until he arrived here; those in his land required too much upper-body strength."

"He does have narrow shoulders for a warrior," Ulnam admitted.

"Where they come from, it is the men who have teats and nurse the babies after the women give birth," Lonal said gravely.

Ulnam held his composure for almost the count of five, then the façade cracked. They shared a hearty guffaw. It did Lonal good to joke. Too many others within the recently arrived clans had not been pleased to hear the story of Tebec and Yetem. Outside of the T'krt clan, loyalty to Lonal was not as entrenched, and a few voices dared to speak of heresy. None, of course, would dare to dispute Toltac's word, for he was opsib over them all, but people muttered all the same. Ulnam and Lonal had always been on good terms; it was gratifying to see that this had not changed.

In some ways, it was easier for Lonal than for the westerners themselves, who were once more the center of attention. All the T'lan and the Ena wanted to view firsthand this man-who-didn't-look-like-a-man.

The contest was over, and the participants left to join their families. The reunion celebrations that had taken up the past day would have to yield to the necessity of movement. The most desolate and most dangerous portion of the migration lay just ahead of them—the journey through the pass of Hattyre. Lonal and Ulnam surveyed the low, blistered hills to the east.

"When do you expect it? As we enter, or at the fork?"

"I never know what to expect where the Buyul are concerned."

"True."

They became grim, and parted, each off to their responsibilities as war-leader, Ulnam looking after his clan, Lonal the authority over all three. Lonal rode back to the rear of the clan. His war-seconds could handle the front well enough; his greatest worry was the stragglers. A dragging end could put the caravan in danger, should the raid happen at the wrong time. They had to make speed over Hattyre.

Things were proceeding well. Soon virtually every member of the clan was under way. The only exceptions were two women, one elderly, the other in late youth, who stood several hundred paces behind the departing end of the caravan. The old one was removing her clothes and handing them to the other. When she was naked, she sat her frail body down in the dirt beside the trail. The younger woman bundled the clothing in her arms and headed back toward the caravan. The old woman bowed her head and did not look up again.

Lonal watched respectfully, as he had done many times. The old woman left behind was Mada's grandmother. He had foreseen this. She had barely kept up in the flat; she couldn't be expected to maintain the pace needed through the pass. He nodded to Mada's wife, the woman carrying the clothes, as she reached his position.

Lonal turned back to his duties, inevitably thinking of the time when he might be in the old woman's place. Of course, as a Po-no-pha, he would keep his garments—his weapons, too, if he were selfish—and would hear the high Ah-no-ken recite the hour-long rite of death, but he would wait in the desert all the same. The fact that he would return one day to the world, and the woman would not, was only occasionally comforting. He couldn't decide which was better—a sudden death in battle or, like Mada's grandmother, to be able to choose the time and place.

He worked his way gradually through the procession. The broad, amorphous columns of the earlier part of the journey were consolidating toward the gap in the hills ahead. Soon they would be able to travel only two or three abreast. Then they would be vulnerable.

Shigmur joined him.

"The first night's watch has been assigned," the war-second reported. "What about them?"

He pointed not far ahead. There, Tebec and Yetem walked beside Fumlok, their wives and children following. Having lost their oeikani to Kulam, the twins had to travel on foot. They owned two other animals, but they were of the drelb breed and suitable only as pack animals. Yetem had already returned the mount she had borrowed for the contest.

"I want them to participate. They need the experience. But I want eyes on them. Put Tebec on guard at the pens for the first watch, the same for Yetem, late watch. I'll think of something else tomorrow."

"Yes, war-leader."

Tonight's camp should be secure, Lonal calculated, but there was no certainty. He prepared himself for the first of several sleepless nights. When would they strike?

There was no incident. They reached the first campsite and, unlike previous stopovers, staked out the tents before nightfall. Lonal was pleased. The location was large enough for everyone, and all approaches were plainly visible. He stood beside the firepit, where the ritual flame had yet to be built, and stared farther up into the hills, wondering what threats they held. His first wife brought him some broth.

Tebec soon strolled up.

"Nannon abat se," Lonal said.

The other replied smoothly in Zyraii, then reverted to the High Speech. "Fumlok has explained that we are in danger of attack by another Zyraii tribe."

"Yes. The Buyul."

"Each time he tries to explain why they would want to attack us, I don't understand."

"It's simple. The Buyul don't like us."

"Why not?"

Lonal shrugged. "Before I became war-leader, this pass was Buyul territory."

Tebec nodded slowly. "Then wouldn't another way be safer?"

"This is the best route. I wouldn't have taken it if I didn't intend to keep it."

Lonal began to stir the coals of the long dead campfire. He frightened a small scorpion from its lair in the shade of one of the hearthstones. Its brood clung to its back. He flipped the creature over with a charred faggot, dumping off the little ones, and swiftly picked it up by the tail, holding it just short of the stinger.

He waved the arthropod in front of Tebec, swaying it so that it would not crawl up his fingers. His free hand indicated the orange markings spotting an otherwise dull yellow body.

"Not poisonous," he explained, and threw it back onto the charcoal. The offspring, gray as the sand and rock of the area, swiftly crawled back aboard. "It is called dukham, after the greatest sinner of all Zyraii. As punishment for his godless life, Dukham was reincarnated into the first of this particular species of scorpion, a creature so lowly it is denied even the luxury of a powerful venom."

Tebec, however, was not going to let the earlier topic be dropped.

"Why did you take the pass from the Buyul?"

Lonal considered telling him, but that would take far too long, and there were more important tasks for the moment. He settled for the simplest reply.

"Because I don't like them."

The apprehension thickened throughout the next day, as the three clans of the T'lil made their slow progress up the hills. The way was not difficult; it was simply impossible to hurry. Each stray noise brought palms to the hilts of demonblades. They stopped only when the heat was fiercest, and continued on in spite of the sweat and the taxing climb. They saw a pair of the rare wild sheep of the region, several hawks, many snakes—but no hostile Po-no-pha.

"Do you suppose they've lost their balls?" Ulnam asked Lonal, after one of many patrols had returned with the same news: the Buyul were not to be found, nor were there any fresh traces.

"They haven't forgiven me yet," Lonal answered, and sent out more scouts.

The war-leader was near the westerners as they traveled through the pass. As they topped the crest, their view of the land suddenly expanded eastward. Ahead, the relatively easy road they had followed up the western slopes transformed into a twisting, double-backed aisle, cutting through a gradually receding series of parched ridges. Somewhere in that desolation the road forked, one way heading south, toward Buyul lands, the other east, to T'lil ground. That was the point of greatest danger. Lonal stared at the peaks that concealed it.

But the twins looked farther, past the hills to the incongruous sight near the horizon.

"Norym," Yetem gasped.

It took Lonal a moment to translate from the High Speech. "Trees," he corrected. Small wonder that the Ah-no-ken had not yet taught them the Zyraii word. In this land, the term only had true meaning in the valley beyond the hills. They were so far away that any hint of green was distorted by the atmosphere into a kind of blue gray, but the westerners obviously knew they were viewing a forest. The foliage meandered from north to south, a languorously winding track a league or more wide, occasionally thickening or narrowing, with several islands. Had Lonal not been preoccupied with his duties, he might have shared their awe. They were witnessing the lifeline of Zyraii.

"Ahloorm," Lonal said.

"How long until we get there?" Tebec asked.

"Five days."

They continued to gaze at the river, transfixed, until their family had left them well behind and they had to hurry to catch up. Lonal remained at the crest, where he could reconnoiter. Soon Shigmur came to report.

"We have been up and down the hills well past the border, and the odor of the Buyul is exceptionally faint. I don't understand it."

"Neither do I," Lonal answered, checking the low sun in the west. "As soon as camp is made, I will go to Toltac. It is time to undertake the Trance of the Searcher."

Toltac's words were a measured drone. Lonal was no longer consciously aware of their content. He breathed deeply, and then more deeply still, the oxygen stimulating the *rashemi* in his lungs. He relaxed each muscle group, one by one, unsure whether this was at the Bo-no-ken's command or his own idea, and not caring which. His body felt heavy; it was too much effort to move it. He went numb.

And he was out.

Below him, he saw his own body, with Toltac hovering dutifully over it, still uttering his monologue. The haze of smoke from the brazier made the tent hazy and ill defined. He lifted farther up, and found he was outside. The camp lay below him, on a shelf of land a mile east of the pass, dotted with cooking fires and filled with the bustle of early evening activity. Though it was night, he could see the people, tents, and hills as if the sun were still up.

He began to float. Suddenly, the camp was no longer below. In rapid succession, his ethereal eyes sought out and found the places of his concern. He scanned the ridgetops that overlooked the road, checked the woodless dells and nullahs where groups of men might hide. Time meant nothing; it seemed to him as if he arrived at each new spot the instant he left the previous one. He recrossed the ground his scouts had patrolled the past two days, and cast deeply into Buyul land. He followed the route the caravan would take out of the hills all the way to its end. And finally, he felt the tug in the small of his back. He had to return. In what seemed to be the next moment, he opened his eyes.

Toltac leaned over him, looking concerned.

"How long?" Lonal asked.

"Four hours," the high priest stated. "Most of the camp is asleep. You should get some rest. Any luck?"

"None," Lonal said in answer to Ulnam the next morning.

"Where are they? Why are they invisible?"

"I don't know."

"Perhaps they are waiting simply to make us nervous."

Lonal took out his demonblade and applied the whetstone. "The longer they wait, the less advantage they have. We will reach the fork before noon."

"What I wouldn't give to be riding through this pass with nothing but my best Po-no-pha." Ulnam sighed, glancing at the ranks of women, children, animals, and goods. "We could clear the hills in one forced gallop."

"Under those circumstances, the Buyul wouldn't be interested in attacking."

"That's the trouble with enemies. They never cooperate."

The war-leader of the T'lan joined them, and had nothing more to report. *Where are they?* Lonal thought. He mistrusted the evidence of the trance, though it merely corroborated the physical reconnaissance of his scouts. He knew the unpredictability of travel in the astral form. He might have been viewing some strange parallel world, or perhaps it was the actual pass of Hattyre he had seen, but in some other time. Perhaps the Buyul had clouded his vision, in the unlikely event that they had found a sorcerer so powerful. He wished they had the services of the Zee-no-ken. Though Toltac was well schooled, the Zee-no-ken were the only true magicians of Zyraii. But the Zee-no-ken rarely devoted themselves to such mundane matters as military spying.

The Buyul *had* to be out there.

For the most part, they made good speed. Much of the way was downhill, and at each high place they were spurred to new hope by the tantalizing sight of the Ahloorm. Soon they reached the fork. The road split, passing to either side of an eroded mountain. Massive piles of rocks and three shallow box canyons provided plenty of places for ambush. The caravan took the left fork, continuing east. Each step along that route took them farther from Buyul territory.

Lonal hovered near a T'krt family as they transferred gear from a pack animal that had caught its leg between two rocks and broken it. One of the owners was already honing his butcher knife. Though infrequent, each such small delay rasped on Lonal's nerves. Each time, the war-leader expected to hear the cry of Buyul raiders. This time, as before, he worried for nothing. The animal was cut into large sections, most of the meat bartered to other families, and the caravan crawled onward. They made camp that night well down the fork. Lonal slept poorly for the third night.

They poured out onto the valley floor in the afternoon of the next day, having forsaken the midday rest in order to gain speed. They could no longer see the river on the horizon—their elevation was too low—but they were now well within traditional T'lil holdings. To either side, promontories thrust out into the flatland; once beyond these, they could see an enemy coming for miles. Lonal waited at the rear of the column, alert for any pursuit from the pass behind, but the last of his people had reached the plain and the anxiety was lifting off his shoulders. They were safe.

Then, directly ahead, where no scouts had thought to patrol, a horde of white-robed men rose from behind shrubs or out of the trenches they had dug, brought their oeikani out of concealment, mounted, and charged the front of the caravan at full gallop.

"Torovet!" Lonal cried. He cursed. Almost all of his Po-no-pha, like himself, were toward the rear or along the sides, guarding from attack from the promontories. The front was exposed. They hadn't expected attack from their own land. T'lil demonblades whisked into palms and the warriors sped to meet the assault.

They were too little too late. The Buyul line splayed out into singles, each rider plunging between the retreating ranks of women, children, and elderly, toward the locations where livestock were gathered. Flails struck, shouts rang out, and soon sheep, goats, and oeikani panicked and began to bolt. Then just as quickly, the Buyul disengaged and, though driving the animals farther from the caravan whenever the opportunity arose, drew weapons and prepared to meet the warriors.

The invaders separated as widely as possible, likewise the defenders. The raid fractured into dozens of individual contests. Demonblades flew. Some went wild. Some were blocked by shields. Blood splattered the field, part of a Buyul ear falling with it. Then a T'lil went down. As the demonblades were exhausted, scimitars replaced them.

Lonal hurried forward in vain. He was too far to the rear to make a difference. He reined up. He could spend his time more effectively being a war-leader and organizing his people's disrupted defense.

But now, the Buyul were in full retreat. If forced, they traded slashes, but in the main, they sought to escape. The raid evolved: now the objective of the Buyul was to drive livestock farther afield, and that of the T'lil to prevent it.

Lonal got the women and old men into tight formation, keeping the animals that remained securely in tow to thwart a possible second wave. Those of his Po-no-pha who, like himself, had been caught at the far rear, he ordered back to position, suspecting that a contingent of raiders might appear there yet. Then he scanned the conflict once more.

He saw it immediately. Six choice purebred oeikani, unsaddled and fleet as the wind, had been driven by their fear far from the caravan. Riders of both tribes pursued them, the Buyul in the lead. However, well ahead of either group of riders, actually gaining on the oeikani, were two lithe figures *on foot*.

Elenya narrowed her eyes to keep out the grit kicked up by the oeikani. She and Alemar were only a few body lengths behind the panicked animals. Her lungs were on fire, her legs throbbing, and her amulet fiercely radiant, but they had the momentum. She sidestepped a shrub that appeared abruptly out of the dust. Alemar split away, approaching the oeikani from the right side. She took the left.

She was even now with the rearmost animal, but she ignored it, as did Alemar. One by one, they caught up with the others. As the lead beast veered to the left, she leaped onto its back and seized it by the mane.

For several moments, all she could do was hold on. The run had winded her; she had no strength left to deal with a terror-stricken mount. She let it run freely, allowing it to become accustomed to her presence. When she dared, she glanced back and saw that Alemar had successfully landed on the second oeikani.

Finally she gripped the mane and tugged. All six animals veered. She pointed them back toward the caravan.

Immediately, the party of Buyul pursuing them began to close the gap. Elenya tried to circle, to buy time. The Buyul were themselves being chased by T'lil warriors.

Inevitably, the Buyul bore down. But the raiders' mounts were not as fresh as those they chased. Elenya and Alemar were starting to pull away. The lead Buyul flung his demon-blade, forcing Alemar to duck. In a few more moments, however, the Buyul were too far behind, and were forced to break off in order to avoid their own pursuit.

Elenya and Alemar raced for the caravan, only to be blocked by two more Buyul who had left the main battle. The latter waited. Elenya knew there was no point in trying to circle them. Instead, the twins charged straight ahead. The Buyul spurred their oeikani and met them at full run, scimitars extended.

Elenya drew her rapier. As the warrior thrust out his weapon, she jabbed him in the forearm. He dropped his weapon. She quickly glanced back. Alemar simply blocked his opponent's slash. The Buyul did not attempt to engage again. Like the rest of their tribe, they retreated southward. The twins reached the lines before other enemies could bother them, the six oeikani rescued.

Only when they were safe did Elenya feel the pain in her shoulder. She had been too slow. The Buyul's scimitar had bitten her. She clapped her hand over the cut and forgot about it. There was still a fight going on.

Lonal had watched most of the twins' adventure, but was occupied with his responsibilities. The raid was nearly over. A Buyul leaned far down from his saddle and scooped up a lamb. Another had lassoed a oeikani and was pulling it in tow. The others either had their prizes or were in full flight. Lonal shouted orders, sending the warriors whose animals were the fleetest out to the pursuit, keeping the others in reserve to protect the women and goods. Then he saw Yetem riding out, the cloth against her shoulder stained a dark crimson, with a quiver on her back and a bow already strung.

"Na tet!" he yelled at her, but she was oblivious, already racing to catch up with the Buyul.

Lonal heard Tebec shout also. The westerner started after her, but stopped almost immediately and reached within his collar. Lonal saw him withdraw something attached to a gold chain, the actual object hidden in his fist. He pressed it to his forehead. Green light flickered through his fingers.

Yetem suddenly relaxed her arm, even as it had been drawing back an arrow, and reined up. She stared back at Tebec. He held his fist to his forehead for a moment more. Strangely subdued, she started back toward the tribe.

Lonal, eyes riveted to Tebec, waited until the latter had restored the chain inside his garments. He hurried to check the status of his tribe.

All told, three of his Po-no-pha were dead, several more wounded, one mortally. The Buyul had left five on the field, and as many more had hung limply from their beasts as they fled. More dead than there should have been, had he not been taken unaware by Buyul guile. His mood was black as he rode over to the twins. Tebec was bandaging the wound near his sister's collarbone.

"Do you want to start a vendetta?" he asked sternly.

"Is this a war or not?" she demanded, equally sharp. "We could have quadrupled our effectiveness with arrows!"

"So could the Buyul. This is *torovet*. We must conduct ourselves with honor."

"They attacked us! How honorable is that?"

"If the Buyul had let us pass unmolested, they would have had to concede that the pass belonged to the T'lil."

"I don't believe it. This whole fight happened just so you could all prove your manhood."

Lonal was so angry he could barely continue to use the High Speech. "I should have realized one such as you would not understand."

She started to retort.

"No," he said. "If you are without honor, you aren't free

to judge us. Until you learn the laws of battle, keep out of it. Stay with the women."

He didn't permit her to respond. Tebec prevented her from following, pressing her down firmly in order to finish tending her wound. Lonal wanted the tribe moving. They would make a forced march into the valley, deeper into T'lil territory, where they could lick their wounds and he endure his shame in peace.

XIII

The bottom of the fishing boat passed over, three fathoms up, barnacles plainly visible on her hull through the crystal water. Lerina giggled, creating bubbles. She and Ethmurl were safely camouflaged among the coral and kelp of the ocean floor. If Lerina guessed correctly, the men in the boat were searching for her and/or the murderer of Luo of Eruth, never dreaming they were so close to their goal.

She was breathing normally, though she still occasionally felt the urge to reach up to her face and feel the membrane of the airmaker. It was strange to think that she could actually breathe more easily underwater than could a fish. Fish, after all, had to keep swimming at least in order to keep water—and oxygen—flowing through their gills. She watched the bubbles of her exhalation race one another upward.

Ethmurl nudged her. The boat was out of sight. They set out, keeping just above the profuse life of the bottom, she a few strokes behind to his right. So much to see. Anemones, crustaceans, coral, fish, silt rich with flickers of color. She had caught glimpses of all of these on her many dives over the years, but had never been able to float next to the thing she was looking at and examine it at her leisure. Air had always been the limitation, driving her inevitably back to the surface. Now, with the magic of the artificial lung, she was free.

But old habits died hard. She realized that she was holding her breath. She quickly exhaled. It caused her to sink a few inches, until her vest absorbed more air from the surrounding water and returned her to weightlessness. The vest, too, was a joy: no more energy wasted simply trying to maintain a specific depth. Moreover, at the surface she could keep her head above water without being forced to tread.

She tickled an anemone with a pebble and watched it close.

A tiny squid rewarded her with a squirt of ink and an arrow-quick dash into a crevice. She delighted to watch crabs dragging their stolen shells across the sediment. She was getting used to everything seeming larger than it actually was.

And the noise! She had never realized how pervasive it was. In the kelp, the shrimp rattled their single claws endlessly, calling to her with their aquatic voices. Though it was difficult to determine which direction sounds came from, the variety never diminished.

All too soon it was time to stop.

She didn't want to, but neither did she want to tax Ethmurl. He was much better, but he still had a great deal of recuperating to do. No sense in endangering his progress by tiring him out swimming. Whatever advantages the healing spell had provided now seemed entirely gone; he mended like a normal man. In a way, that was reassuring.

As he had instructed her, they rose slowly, never exceeding the pace of the smallest of the bubbles they exhaled. She had never heard of the strange pain and death experienced when divers who used the airmaker surfaced too quickly, but she doubted Ethmurl would invent such a story. He had admitted they were not going to be deep enough to worry about it today; it was simply a good habit to maintain. Before very long they were topside.

"That was wonderful!" she exclaimed as soon as she had removed her mask.

Ethmurl was subdued. He scanned in the direction that the boat had gone. It was not in sight. He rechecked their beach. They had been careful to cover their signs, and the cave entrance was small, seeming to be only a shadow in the rock. Apparently the men in the boat had ignored the islet.

"Oh, you worry too much," she said.

He shrugged and helped her unbuckle the straps of her vest. "I don't think I can change at this age."

As she held her equipment, Lerina marvelled again at the workmanship. The headgear seemed so delicate, only a framework of goldlike metal across which stretched the transparent membranes, one for breathing, one for vision. The vests were more substantial, heavy out of the water, shaped so as to collect air in front of the chest and upper abdomen, with a hole for the head and a buckle behind the small of the back. Hers was blue; Ethmurl's was black.

"Should we give these back to the faernak now?" Lerina asked.

"Yes," he replied. "No one knows how to make these anymore, except the straps, so it's best not to take chances." At the back of the headgear, two shark-hide straps could be adjusted to provide a perfect fit.

While she held everything, he waded deeper and removed an engraved ring from his finger, lifted it to his mouth, and whistled through it. He had not waited long before a man-size tentacled shape brushed against his leg. Lerina handed him the airmakers and vests, which he gave to the creature. They watched it put everything into a pouch at the base of one of its many-suckered arms, after which it returned quickly to deeper waters.

"I still can't believe it found you," Lerina said, not nearly as startled as she had been when she had first glimpsed the faernak earlier that day.

"It knows where the ring is, and never wanders far."

"Aren't you afraid it will damage the airmakers?"

He smiled. "They're far safer there than any place I can think of. The thing is well trained, and long-lived, and I wouldn't care to try and forcibly take anything from a faernak under any circumstances. In fact, they were specifically bred for this function."

"Who bred them?"

"Alemar."

"Alemar Dragonslayer, the great wizard?"

He nodded. "The founder of Elandris. In order to build and maintain the cities beneath the sea, he made hundreds of thousands of airmakers. Or, to be truthful, his sister Miranda did. However, neither of them cared to share the secret of their manufacture, so it became vital to protect each one. They bred the faernaks to caretake the devices whenever the owners had to make journeys away from Elandris. In our own dwellings, of course, we have special troughs to keep them secure. It's surprising how few have been lost over the centuries since the great wizard vanished."

"You mean no one has learned how to make them since?"

"Alemar and Miranda were the greatest sorcerers in history. There's a great deal they could do that no one else has been able to. Killing dragons, for example."

The sun had virtually dried them already. They sought refuge from its heat in the cave. Ethmurl lay down immediately. This had been the first day he had tried anything strenuous; it had clearly taken a great deal out of him. Lerina leaned back against the cave wall.

"Do you suppose it's true, that the Dragon of our day is the child of the pair that Alemar killed?"

Ethmurl brushed away an insect. "It's possible. Dragons live thousands of years. Gloroc could have been an infant of several centuries at the time that Faroc and Triss were defeated. It would explain why he wants to conquer Elandris. He can't have revenge on Alemar himself, so the next best thing is to steal the empire away from his descendants."

"He seems to be succeeding."

Ethmurl made a wry face. "Not entirely. We royalists have kept nearly half the kingdom free for almost a hundred years. It's as if the Frog were waiting to make his move. In any case, he seems nowhere near as formidable as his parents."

"And where do you fit in, Ethmurl?"

He met her glance. "I serve my liege."

She didn't press the matter. Soon she flipped up the lid of their food basket. It settled back down with a hollow *pud*. "We have to leave tonight. You seemed to be all right in the water today. Do you think you can make the trip?"

"We might as well try."

"Good," she said. "Get some rest."

Night had closed in by the time she woke him up, darkness muted by Urthey, the smallest moon. Lerina felt odd to think of wearing clothes again, and it would be stranger still to see Ethmurl covered. It seemed a shame.

"We can leave almost everything," she said, taking only her garments and the water flasks. "I'll get it another time."

"My belt," Ethmurl said, and picked it up.

"Why not just wear it?" she asked.

"No," he said, sounding strangely determined.

It made her wistful to think of leaving. The cave had always been a favorite place, but with Ethmurl present, it had become very special indeed. She felt safe here.

She led. The water put vigor back in her body. They dripped dry in the shadow of the bluff and put on their clothes, she the tunic she had come in, he his trousers and a quarn shirt she had taken from her father's wardrobe. Actually, he wore clothes well, she thought. She suggested that he proceed ahead of her up the bluff. She knew the terrain and could support him should he slip. He agreed.

The forest welcomed her as they merged into the underbrush. Its fecund odor had never seemed quite so precious. She had always had plenty of forest and less than she wanted of the beach; now finally the situation was reversed. He rested. The bluff had been almost too much for his wounded thigh. Several times she had been forced to brace him to keep him from losing his balance. She found a broken branch and gave it to him to use as a walking stick. She walked on his other side, holding his hand.

The leafy canopy above reduced the night to velvet blackness. She guided them by instinct. "Watch out," she murmured as they found and stepped over a huge root.

His grip was strong and reassuring. He was not the invalid she had discovered many days before. In a way she was disappointed that he was no longer utterly dependent on her, but it also excited her. She squeezed tighter.

Progress was slow. Though Ethmurl didn't complain, she heard his sucked-in breath whenever he stumbled, and periodically she felt twinges of pressure in her hand. She deliberately paced herself as slowly as she dared, and made him stop frequently. He would wait, sip some water, and stoically trudge on. He assured her his discomfort was only the stiffness of his muscles, but she worried nevertheless.

Hours of this finally brought them to the rear of Garthmorron Hold, well after midnight. They heard an owl chitter as it flew overhead, and oeikani shuffle in the stables, but no human noise. All the lights were out in the buildings. They decided to walk openly through the vegetable gardens. Not only could they move more quickly, but if their silhouettes were seen, they would look like they had every reason to be there.

A dog barked.

Lerina stopped, heart thundering. Ethmurl was still.

The windows of the hold remained black. The barking came from the far side of the grounds, and soon tapered off. Eventually Lerina remembered to exhale.

She was so nervous that she nearly tripped on a squash. They continued on at a measured pace, and before long they had reached the copse in which her father's cottage nestled, tucked in a private spot not far from the central courtyard. She lifted the latch and pushed. The door creaked, as it always did, but an instant later they were both inside.

She felt little prickles of perspiration over her neck and throat. She made sure all the curtains were drawn and lit a candle. The room opened out. The chamber they had entered was the only large room. It contained a cooking hearth, a dining table, stools, an armchair, and some crates and chests. To one side was a small bedroom, to the rear the door to the outhouse. A loft was above, the only access to it a steep ladder in a corner.

Home. Safe. Many times she had told herself otherwise, but now it was a palace—at least until the end of the month, when her father would return. She savored the sight of it, then, for one of the few times in her life, barred the doors.

"You did it!" she told Ethmurl.

He swayed, set his belt down on the table, and sagged onto one of the stools. "I wasn't sure I'd make it."

She giggled. "Now we won't have to worry about food or water or being discovered. They'll never look under their own noses."

"If it's all right, could I not worry about it tomorrow?" he asked wearily.

It was hard to suppress her enthusiasm, but she knew Ethmurl well enough by now to know that he wouldn't complain unless his need was genuine. "Here," she said, pushing the door of the ground-floor bedroom wider. "This is my father's room. The loft's mine."

He stood once more, with effort, and headed toward the door. Lerina helped him onto the tick and removed his boots for him. He didn't bother to undress or get under the blankets. Seeing his exhaustion, she left as soon as he was settled, bidding him a good night.

She practically shook with adrenaline, and used some of it checking the cottage. Nothing seemed disturbed, though it smelled of being closed up for a length of time. She hid Ethmurl's belt in a chest and paced. But there really was nothing to do, and she knew that the morning would bring an early confrontation with a disapproving great-uncle. She automatically started up the ladder to the loft.

And paused.

"No." She smiled, and turned around and headed for her father's bed.

XIV

It *was* a forest.

As they approached, parrots glided from tree to tree, their bright colors almost shocking to behold after the drab country the tribe had just covered. Jungle was more accurate a description than forest. Life abounded. The trees were high, broad hardwoods, their shade the parent of climbing vines, elephant grass, shrubs, giant ferns—all without exception vibrant with the green born of plentiful water. The racket of birds, insects, and small animals never ceased.

Most of all, it smelled like life, Alemar decided. Strange that his senses were so attuned to the scent after only a month in the desert.

The caravan did not enter the jungle. The road from the pass of Hattyre to the Ahloorm had run almost due east across the valley, but now that the river had been reached, the long line of men and livestock turned north, travelling parallel to the heavy growth, along a deeply cut track that ran to either horizon. Occasional stone markers, a novel sight, demarcated the road boundaries and measured the distance. Periodically trails merged with the main highway, but always from the west. The only ways heading into the jungle were no more than footpaths.

The shepherds let their flocks range freely in the wide grasslands extending toward the left, which they had first reached the previous day. However, the animals were prevented from feeding on the eastern side, beyond what they could nibble from the fringe of the road as they passed.

"The forest of Ahloorm is sacred," Fumlok explained. "Do not let sheep and goats inside. Do not cut living wood."

Po-no-pha of the three clans disappeared periodically into the foliage to hunt, observed with envy by the twins. The hunters brought back all manner of game, particularly birds, though the most heralded prize was wild boar. Women, including Peyri and Omi, were allowed to enter and pick berries and melons. The first evening, Shigmur invited the twins and their family to share the pork his women had roasted.

On the second day, the T'lan split from the group, heading back toward the west. The twins could see an oasis on the horizon, one of many fed by the Ahloorm's subterranean branches. The parting provided an excuse for celebration—the dangers of the migration were behind them, and now they had reached the richest of their many pasturage regions, in a year of good rains. The festivities lasted an entire night and day, the T'lan families leaving one by one for different sections of the range, with a large assembly accompanying the ken directly to the oasis.

Two days later, the Ena copied the pattern, leaving the T'krt to continue north.

Elenya sat on the ground with her back to one of the magnificent *hoeanaou* trees around which the clan had camped. She stared at the forest. The sun filtered through small open patches in the canopy, but had yet to climb above the tops of the trees and shine directly on the tents. Alemar still slept, and the women were ignoring their odd husband.

"Good morning."

She recognized his boots out of the corner of her eye, but continued to meditate on the distant leaves. "So—the war-leader deigns to converse with someone who doesn't know the laws of battle."

"I even converse with children and infidels," he said. "How is your wound?"

She smiled impishly. "What wound?"

"In your shoulder," he said. She enjoyed his puzzled expression. "You were hurt in the Buyul raid."

"Was I?"

"Yes. I saw the cut myself. Your robe is still stained." He pointed to the brown section of cloth. But in silent dispute, Elenya pulled open the top of her garment. Where the cut should have been, Lonal could see only a scar, and though it was fresh, it was completely healed.

Lonal's face clouded. "Have there been Hab-no-ken in the camp without my knowledge?"

"No. As a matter of fact, my brother and I have never seen one since coming to this country."

"Then how did you heal so fast?"

Again the smile. "It pleases me not to tell you," she said. "Now, do you have business here? I was enjoying the view alone."

"Do you want to see the forest?" he asked.

She looked at him. He carried a quiver and bow, which he gestured toward. "Bring your own and follow me." He turned and headed straight for the river.

His abruptness caught her off guard, but by the time he vanished from view of the tribe, she was one step behind him.

Almost from the first, the soil was spongy. As it became even less firm, Elenya realized they were not walking on ground at all, but on a network of plant growth. She had wondered where the river was. At no point in their journey had they seen an open flow. Now she knew that the forest *was* the river. The plants were the banks; if not for their roots, the water would spread over the plain and evaporate, never even coming close to the sea. They had to travel single file most of the time, sometimes cutting their way through vines and brambles. Lonal didn't speak, and Elenya was far too distracted by the scenery to initiate conversation herself.

They penetrated deep into the area, until the land grew so swamplike it threatened to swallow them unless they placed every foot with extreme care. The surroundings opened up, the ubiquitous shrubs unable to find permanent foundations from which to grow, leaving a swath of territory to the water grasses and trees. The whole place hummed with insect life.

"I propose a contest," Lonal said. He strung his bow and indicated that Elenya should do the same. They had found a comfortable spot to rest on a small island of solid ground.

"I will shoot a bird. See if you can hit the same bird with your own arrow, before I can hit it a second time."

He hardly had the words out of his mouth before he grabbed an arrow and let fly. A parrot above screamed and began to flutter earthward. An instant later, it jerked with the impact of another arrow. Before it landed, two more shafts had knocked it this way and that in the air.

Lonal got his legs wet up to the shins in order to retrieve the bird. It bristled with all four arrows, every one firmly lodged in its plump torso. There probably wouldn't have been room for another.

"Not bad," he said. Two of the arrows were his own, marked

with a red line down the side of the shaft; two were Elenya's, with a double yellow band just short of the nock. "Now it's your turn."

She smiled. Unlike him, she nocked her arrow serenely and waited, with bow relaxed, for a suitable target. She ignored three likely choices. Then a queeble launched from a low branch. She waited until just before it passed behind a tree, then let loose. The trunk obscured the result.

A moment later, Lonal fired. The arrow caught the queeble just as it reappeared, only a moment before it nose-dived into the grass.

Elenya found it. Her own point had struck the hindquarters. Lonal's shot had gone through one eye and out the other.

"You like to cheat, don't you?" Lonal said.

"Always." Elenya smiled, graciously acknowledging that this time it hadn't worked. "That was a superb shot."

"I have had a lot of practice. You were introduced to this weapon only a month ago."

"I learn quickly."

"Let us hope so," he said.

They sat on a log. Lonal held up the first bird and pulled out a bloody arrow tip. "Imagine that this was a man."

"I don't follow you," she said.

Lonal removed all the arrows, gave Elenya her own to wipe off, and dropped the carcass between them. It was little more than a mass of blood, feathers, and ruptured meat. "We did this from a distance, in a matter of moments. Suppose we had been shooting at a man. Better yet, at four different men. It's not hard to imagine four corpses in as many seconds."

"Maybe not. What if they had bows, too?"

"Then make it six corpses," he said sadly.

Elenya decided not to be flippant.

Lonal continued, forcefully. "Picture a field of men. They are Po-no-pha. There is no greater glory for them than to meet an enemy, one to one, and prove themselves the greater warrior—the best shot with a dagger, the best rider, the most daring. They have distinguished themselves in raid after raid. They go forth with courage and ability.

"And they are mowed down by men who wait within stone bunkers, from afar. Often they never see the men who kill them. They fall and rot on the rocks, their many kinswomen abandoned to fate. Their land is stolen."

He stood up, braced his bow against the log, and unstrung it. "I condemned you last week more strongly than I should have. But I was reminded of matters which do little to help my temper. And I was angry at myself. I let the tribe's vigilance go slack just when the Buyul could take advantage of it. I brought you here to try to amend my lack of judgment."

"I don't need an apology."

"This isn't one. I was right to chastise you. My error was in not being prepared. It is my responsibility as war-leader to see that, when my expertise is next called upon, I will better meet the test. I've thought of one thing I might do."

He held up a red-striped arrow. "The Zyraii are all sons of Cadra. We understand each other. Our warriors wage *torovet*. We fight, we steal from our enemies, we risk our lives, and, if need be, we take lives. But taking life is not our objective. Raids are a way to win honor and material gain, not to murder. We have a saying: 'The desert kills enough.'

"But now, more and more often we face the armies of the traders. They have no conception of *torovet*. They wage *war*." Lonal plunged the arrow symbolically back into the body of the ruined bird. "They do not care if the blood of Cadra is completely wiped from the surface of all Tanagaran."

Lonal sighed. "My father was killed by traders. And I have been unable to fulfill my vendetta. Over the past few years I have realized the root of the problem—we Zyraii do not *think* like our invaders. We don't understand their rules, if they have any, and therefore we do not anticipate their actions. I have been waiting for someone like you.

"I will be frank. I need you. I have seen your skill and your nature. You and your brother have clearly received long and hard training in the military arts. You understand the type of fighting which my people must now learn. Am I wrong?"

"No," Elenya said.

"I have yet to win your loyalty, but I can hope. I offer you an opportunity, at least. I don't know what goal you came to Zyraii with, but I can provide another of depth and honor. Help our nation remain free."

"Do I have a choice?" she asked.

"God gives us our roles to play. You lost your life your first day in our country by stealing water. I gave it back to you. Now you owe me, and you owe the family of Am and Roel. Until that debt is discharged, you are not free. If you decide to leave, I must order my Po-no-pha to hunt you down and kill you. But whether you cooperate with me or not is another matter."

His tone became almost confessional. "My father was once given an augury concerning my life and the threat of the traders. Because of it, I had to learn the High Speech. He would never tell me why. I never needed to use the language until you and your brother arrived. I suspect you are somehow part of the answer to this challenge. Why else would God have put me through all the trouble you've caused?"

She watched a squirrel race from branch to branch, automatically calculating the lead and force needed to shoot it down. "If I agree, when do we start?"

"Everything has to wait until you are an adult. It is more than three months until the next rite of the *pulstrall*. If you have advanced in your studies to the satisfaction of the Ah-no-ken, you will be permitted to participate. Po-no-pha do not listen to the advice of children."

"Or women."

"In your case, that has been taken care of."

"So you say."

"There will be problems. But God has performed a miracle, and my people believe in God."

Elenya plucked at the queeble. She had tasted one earlier that week and enjoyed it. It had pleased her to be able to choose one during the contest. Maybe she wasn't always able to make the rules, but sooner or later, she'd get what she wanted.

"I'll think about it," she said. "Let's get back to camp. It's time for breakfast."

XV

Lerina slid back and forth on the film of sweat between their bodies. Her hair cascaded over Keron's face, smooth and ticklish. He didn't brush it away. She straightened up, the filtered light through the drapes catching the glisten of her breasts and collarbones. She rocked gently back and forth, the bed creaking pleasantly. Keron inhaled deeply. She had the skill of a veteran and the enthusiasm of a novice.

She coaxed it out of him with full, firm plunges and lifts. He clamped hands on her buttocks and strengthened the rhythm. It was more than an orgasm. To a man who thought he was dead only a month before, it was resurrection. Long after it was over, all he did was lie there and hope for more.

Lerina collapsed against him, tears in her eyes. "Good, huh?"

"No."

"No?"

He laughed. "No. It was too intense. I wouldn't survive another one like that."

She kissed his nipple. "You'll survive."

She rolled off and nestled against his side. Soon she giggled. "To think I have Uncle Ossatch to thank for all of this."

"Beg pardon?"

"If he hadn't virtually confined me to the cottage until my father comes back, everyone would have started to wonder by now why I'm spending so much time here. It's not like me."

Keron smiled and put an arm around her shoulders. "What will you tell your father about us? Will he punish you, too?"

"I doubt it. I'll tell him what I told Uncle Ossatch—that I ran off for a week with a fisherman's son. He'll probably laugh. He did last time."

"Last time?"

"I did it before, when I was fifteen."

"You were a brazen young thing."

"I had wood for a brain. He was eighteen, and seemed so heroic. That was the period in my life when I thought all fishermen brave adventurers. By the end of it, I preferred the smell of the fish to that of my lover. And a fish would have been more interesting company."

"So now you've graduated to smugglers."

"Why not? They make better lovers." She began to throw on clothes. "I'm late. I'm supposed to help Brienna with the evening meal. Best not have her come looking for me."

She bent down and kissed him here and there. "See you after dinner? I'll save you some roast."

"Where else do I have to go?"

She pranced down the loft steps, sprite as a fawn.

The islet stood nearly a mile off the coast, a forlorn piece of rock only a few feet wide, barely above the surface, the perfect design to poke holes in the hulls of unsuspecting vessels. A huge lantern had therefore been mounted on it, at the top of an eight-foot pole. The spot was visited only occasionally by Cilendri coast watchers, in order to fill the lantern's reservoir or relight the flame when doused by storms. The night was still and clear. One moment the beacon was deserted, kept company only by the waves. In the next a man was there, pulling off his airmaker and buoyancy vest, dripping salt water.

Keron sniffed the ocean breeze, welcoming the air to his chest like a lost friend. He wore a pair of seal-hide breeches, weapons at his waist, his belt hidden underneath the garment. Goose pimples rose, but he faced the wind, standing firm. He was strong again. Three days before, he had felt the touch of sorcery that told him that *King's Ransom* had returned and Obo was near enough to work his spell. Within hours he had completed the remainder of his convalescence. His relief was acute. He had first won the protection of a healing spell over a decade before; to him, recovery from injuries, however great, should not have involved so much time. At last he was whole.

And alone.

Back in Garthmorron, supper would be over. Lerina would be back in the cottage. She would have found his note, and the one paltry gift he could leave. Keron felt a lump rising in his throat.

He could still turn back. But they would come for him,

sooner or later, and find Lerina. Perhaps he could leave behind old duties and loyalties, but he couldn't risk her safety. Moreover, he had a specific job to do.

"Forgive me," he whispered.

He sat down to wait in the dark and wet.

Admiral Warnyre paced the poop deck, staring out at the foggy night. His plans had gone awry, and he didn't like it. Furthermore, he was rapidly running out of time to do anything about it.

A man climbed the steps and approached. Warnyre turned.

"Yes, Ensign?" It was Enret, one of the last people he had cared to see. The junior officer had always been one of Keron's number-one aides.

"It's time to send the boat to the rendezvous, sir. Bhaukom and I request permission to man it."

Warnyre frowned. "I had planned to send Robbern and Nals."

"I know, sir. But the captain and me—we go back a ways. I'd like to do this for him."

Still another wrinkle, Warnyre thought. But he made his mind up quickly. "Very well, Ensign. Proceed."

Warnyre watched the dinghy being lowered. As he expected, Nals soon joined him on the poop.

"Change of plan, sir?" the midshipman asked meaningfully.

"Yes," the admiral replied. "Lay low for a while. Don't do anything unless I tell you."

Nals left. Soon the dinghy was lost in the fog. Warnyre went to his cabin to get out of the weather. In a way, he was glad Enret had volunteered to take the boat. It was known that Warnyre favored Robbern and Nals. If anything happened to Keron while in the company of those two, suspicion would fall on him. Additionally, Robbern and Nals might have failed, just as the Claw had done. The passive route was safest. There was no reason to think that Keron would connect him with the ambush. He would play the innocent, until another opportunity arrived.

It was long after those aboard *King's Ransom* could hear the plop of the oars that they could make out the dinghy. Many of the crew leaned over the railing, straining to see. Yes, there were three men aboard. A cheer went up—quietly, for they were still in Dragon's waters. A rope ladder went over the side. Warnyre saw Keron seize it.

He climbed alone, Enret and Bhaukom staying with the boat to help secure the winches to raise it to its berth. The large party waiting on the main deck surged forward to greet their returning captain. Warnyre remained at his vantage point near the stern. He lost sight of Keron in the press of bodies.

Then the crowd parted. Keron stood in the center, staring at the entrance to the staterooms. Nanth had just emerged, and waited for him there. Keron seemed reluctant to approach, Warnyre thought, but then the captain was striding forward. He gave his wife a long embrace, enduring much good-hearted teasing from the crew in the process. Warnyre stifled his jealousy and started to climb down from the poop.

"Oh, my love," the admiral heard Nanth say, "thank blue sky and sea that you've come back safe and living."

Keron touched her cheek gently and turned to the man who had just appeared from the doorway. "We have Obo's talents to thank for that."

The wizard bowed slightly. "I slept for a week after the crisis passed. I should *hope* you're grateful."

Warnyre cleared his throat.

Keron faced him, no longer smiling.

"At your service, Admiral Warnyre," Keron said, and saluted, palm to chest.

The admiral nodded stiffly. "You're a hard man to kill, Captain. The news from Eruth was not optimistic. It seems a miracle you made it back."

"It was. A case of luck, really."

"You must tell me more."

"Not just yet," Keron said amiably. He waved an arm toward the crew. "Well? Where's the rum?"

The liquor appeared instantly. Keron and Nanth were led back into the throng. Soon someone thrust a stein in Warnyre's hand. To his annoyance, he was called on to make the toast.

The admiral had not forgotten how to be charming when the occasion demanded it. "To Captain Keron Olendim, of the House of Alemar," the admiral stated heartily. "Welcome home."

The crew applauded, and the celebration began. Warnyre, however, retreated to a spot on the poop deck, where he could sip his rum in peace. The men ignored him. They had surrounded Keron and were plying him with questions. Warnyre was patient. He'd find out sooner or later how the man had slipped the trap.

Obo retreated below, disdaining the rowdiness. The crew didn't forget that they were in enemy territory. The lookout and night watch remained sober, and as before, the running lights were left unlit. Nevertheless, the party was boisterous. Keron was a popular officer, Warnyre had to admit. It was one of the reasons he hated him.

Robbern briefly joined the admiral. "Stay close at hand tonight," Warnyre told him. The man nodded and disappeared below.

It was some time later that he noticed the captain and his wife begging their leave and heading for their quarters. Warnyre did not share the knowing smiles of the crew. What would she tell him? he wondered. Nothing. He had not touched her. Warnyre had learned early to be a cautious man. He had wanted to be sure Keron was out of the way before he actively pursued Nanth. He would find a way soon.

The drinking was still going strong when Warnyre made his way back to his stateroom. He opened the door, stepped in, and tapped the striker of his lamp. The wick caught.

"Good evening, Admiral."

Warnyre jumped. Keron was leaning back lazily on his bed. The admiral recovered quickly. "To what do I owe the honor, Captain?"

"I thought you might want a report on my mission," Keron said matter-of-factly.

Warnyre closed the door. "I had thought tomorrow morning would be more appropriate."

Keron reached in a pocket, withdrew something, and threw it to the admiral. "I found something in Eruth. I thought you might be interested in it."

Warnyre caught it, held it in his open palm. It was an amath pearl.

"Have you ever seen that before?" Keron asked.

"I've seen many amath pearls."

"Notice the flaw. It's quite distinctive. The last time I saw that pearl, it was in the sea chest of this very ship."

Suddenly Warnyre whistled sharply.

"We seem to be upset, Admiral."

"You won't live to bear witness against me," Warnyre swore, and drew his rapier.

The door opened. Enret stuck his head in. "Did someone whistle?"

"What?!" Warnyre yelled.

Enret lifted the head of an unconscious man into view. "If you wanted Nals here, he seems to have fallen suddenly asleep. Poor Robbern isn't doing much better." Behind Enret, Bhaukom waved cheerfully.

Warnyre spun toward Keron, who simply raised a blowgun to his lips and fired. Warnyre clutched at the pin in his chest. His rapier fell, then his body, battering the floor with an ignominious thud. He wiggled there, awake and struggling, but unable to stand.

Keron came forward, picked Warnyre up by the front of his clothing, and hoisted him above his head. "I used Mother's Breath. You can try moving your muscles all you want, but they won't work in coordination. Unfortunately it won't kill you."

Warnyre goggled at the single arm holding him toward the ceiling. Suddenly everything made sense. "You—you have the belt of Alemar!" The words were garbled by the effect of the poison, but understandable.

"Yes. Had you known that earlier, your ambush would no doubt have been successful. The belt doesn't do much, you know; just makes me strong. I see now that I need something to make me stab-proof."

Enret, with Bhaukom immediately behind, dragged in the limp bodies of Warnyre's henchmen. "What do we do with these, Cap'n?"

"Put them in the brig. I want them alive."

He dropped Warnyre, leaning the man's back against one of his sea chests. "I want all of you alive. There are others like you out there, and you can tell about them."

"Never," Warnyre mumbled, but he failed even to convince himself.

"Think again. Send Obo to me," Keron called after his departing mates.

"No need," the old wizard said, and stepped into the room. He stooped over the admiral. Warnyre looked into the frightening depth of the sorcerer's eyes and choked.

"We will find the truth," Keron reiterated. "It's no trivial thing, a navy man defying the authority of his superior officer. For my sake I have to make sure my case is thorough. We will set sail for Firsthold before the night is out. The king himself will be the judge of your guilt."

Warnyre groaned.

"Lady Nanth has been pining for the children. She will be pleased to return to the capital," Obo said.

"I imagine she would be," Keron said in a reserved tone. Obo shot him a puzzled look. As Warnyre drifted off into a drugged haze, he felt Keron lift his head by the hair. The expression on the captain's face seemed more melancholy than victorious, and his voice was vengeful.

"You owe me more than you will ever know," he said.

XVI

An old priest named Gerat led Alemar and Elenya more than a league from the T'krt camp in the central reach of the Ahloorm Basin, alone and in silence, and stopped in the middle of open desert. The place was a curious mixture of terrain. Several outcroppings of brittle, volcanic rock pockmarked the landscape, the sands varying from miniature, fine-grained dunes to patches of coarse material. Silt from prehistoric flows of the Ahloorm could be found in the areas where the sage was thickest. Gerat reached down and broke off a chunk of ancient lava, his grip stronger than one would expect of a priest.

"What is this called?" he asked.

Alemar sighed. *"Seti'i."*

The old man made no overt acknowledgment of the correct answer, merely stepped over to a ridge of sand and picked up a handful of its grains. "This?" he asked Elenya.

"Mah," she replied.

Gerat was an aged, gaunt Ah-no-ken rarely possessed of either enthusiasm or impatience. His expressions and manner were etched into him as deeply as the lines on his face. Dour and owning a monotone voice, something in his speech nevertheless caused his words to remain in the memories of those he instructed.

Gerat pointed to the coarsest sand. *"Choo,"* Alemar answered.

Gerat nodded slightly. Soon he picked up another handful from a dark section of earth where a pool had been not long before, a remnant of the sudden, thunderous rain earlier in the week. He stared at Elenya.

"Mud," she snapped.

The Ah-no-ken waited with his infuriating calm. He never criticized, never complimented. He also never allowed his pupils surcease from his lessons. Alemar opened his mouth to word the answer, but Gerat said, "No. I asked *him.*"

She sighed. *"Leism,"* she said curtly.

Gerat looked at the mud in his palm. "What is the significance of *leism?*" he asked.

She could think of several uses for that particular handful, but held her tongue. The past four months had taught her that spite washed completely past Gerat. She cited the passage: "After God created the world, He took the mud of its shores and made from it the first men, that there should be physical containers for the souls that He took from His being. Man's original substance is recalled each time he spits, or bleeds, or urinates, creating mud again from earth and the fluid of his body."

"And the lesson that *leism* gives us?"

"That man should guard his fluids—drink water only to the extent of his actual requirement, spill his seed only into a female, and let blood only as ritual and war demand. There is power within the liquid of the body, which devils and sorcerers may twist to their own ends."

Gerat nodded. "Good," he said. "You are ready."

"Ready for what?" Alemar asked presently.

"Next week, the youth of the T'krt journey to the oasis of Shom, to perform the rite of *pulstrall,* as do all boys in their thirteenth year, if, as have you, they have absorbed the teachings required of them. The other Ah-no-ken have decreed that you will go. My vote is the last."

Gerat began walking back toward camp, drawing the twins with him as he spoke. "You have been trained very hard. You have been with us four months—hardly long enough to learn what a man must know. But the *pulstrall* comes only once a year, and it is not appropriate that you, who are grown, should be as children. We had no concern for you in the physical tests, but a man who knows nothing of language and law is not a man. You have done well."

It seemed odd to finally hear his judgment. Gerat had early been given the responsibility for the twins' education. He had drowned them in Zyraii. During the first few weeks, Fumlok had been allowed to explain the difficult concepts and points of grammar, but as the twins' fluency in the desert language reached a proficiency equivalent with Fumlok's weak command of the High Speech, the lame man appeared less and less often, and finally, not at all.

"This ceremony—we've heard it mentioned often. What's involved?" Alemar asked.

"It lasts eight days. A small party of Ah-no-ken and Po-no-pha will take you to Shom, a place used only for the *pulstrall*, and you will be put through tests to prove that you are ready to become men. You'll find out the rest when you get there."

"What happens if we fail to pass the tests?" Elenya said.

Gerat shook his head. "How can a boy not become a man? That is God's design. The *pulstrall* does not create manhood; it celebrates it."

"Stranger things have happened," she said to herself.

Sometime later, Gerat asked, "Is it true that you do not have circumcision in your homeland?"

A false dusk fell as they returned to camp. Motherworld, full and swollen on the eastern horizon, held off darkness. Elenya paced off her restlessness, waiting for dinner. The tents and people beamed back the ocher and beige of the great planet, the illumination so altering appearances that she scarcely recognized Lonal as she passed by him. She started at the sound of his voice.

"Good evening," he said.

"What's good about it?" She used the High Speech, knowing that however comfortable Lonal might seem speaking it, it required effort on his part.

Unruffled, he replied in the same language. "I have heard that you will go to Shom. Congratulations."

"So I'll have my adulthood back. That's half a recovery," she said sarcastically.

Lonal pursed his lips. "I suppose I could persuade the Ah-no-ken to reconsider. You could always go through the *pulstrall* next year."

She decided to drop the banter. She knew Lonal could keep it up as long as she. Instead, she asked, "Am I really to participate?"

"Of course. Why shouldn't you?"

She glared and turned away. "May you be reincarnated as a sand tick," she said as she walked away. It was a powerful slur.

"Don't be angry," he said, and caught up with her.

"I thought you might be the one person here who would give me an honest answer."

"I gave the appropriate answer."

She stopped. "Is it that hard to think of me as a woman?"

"It has been decreed that you are a man. Even I am not above the law. Otherwise the matter of your gender would never have become as complicated as it is."

"So—you admit it's complicated. I had begun to think the whole tribe considered it nonexistent."

Some of Elenya's neighbors were watching. Here, deep within T'lil territory, the tents were spaced widely by Zyraii standards, but still closer than Elenya liked. She led them around her own tent, managing at least to cut off the view of Omi and Peyri.

Lonal sighed. "I can't understand someone who fails to acknowledge good fortune. Be glad that you're participating. Never mind the talking I had to do with the elders to beat down resistance to the idea. Women are not allowed at Shom—ever. But according to the decision, *you* must be. Some of the tribe want to use your 'manhood' as an issue to displace Toltac and myself."

"I'm sorry for any inconvenience," she cooed.

He found a date pit on the ground and picked it up. "It mystifies me. I would have thought that having your adulthood denied for four months must have been the worst insult, but you act as if you'd prefer not to have a soul."

"I happen to like being female. And I don't believe in souls. Do you?"

He squeezed the date pit. "Of course."

She smiled. "No, you don't. I can tell. You believe whatever furthers your goals."

"I believe I see why you became a warrior. No man would put up with such a wife."

She paused. It was strange how she and Lonal always ended up baiting each other. For a moment, she almost admitted that she was intrigued by a Zyraii who didn't swallow his people's gospel whole. Despite his attempts to make her obey, he himself seemed the most understanding of her urge to sway tradition.

"You're not like the others, Lonal. Why is that?"

He avoided her eyes. Had she embarrassed him? It occurred to her that a nonconformist here would be a lonely individual.

It surprised her when he answered seriously, "It's my father's doing. In order that I learn the High Speech, he sent me to the cities. I used to feel it was unfair that I could not be taught the same lessons as any Zyraii boy. Now I am glad. I can see God's plan. It was done to help me fulfill my destiny."

"You have a destiny, too," she said pensively. "What is it?"

"To become opsha."

"What's that?"

"The military ruler of all the Zyraii people."

The thought captured her interest. She pictured one man ruling all of the steppes, an authority over all its bickering factions. "Why haven't I heard this title before?"

"There has never been an opsha. The tribes have not been united since the sons of Cadra left their father's tent more than a thousand years ago. Many have tried. I will be the first to succeed."

His tone said he believed it. Elenya did, too, though she knew that the people had split into twenty tribes and over a hundred clans since the patriarch of Zyraii begat his fifteen boys. "That's a bold claim."

"Had I been raised as my brothers were, the thought might never have occurred to me. I could have lived exclusively among my own clan for all of my life, and have been content to be war-leader of the T'lil. But my journeys have shown me that there are possibilities beyond what has always been true before. Does that seem strange to you?"

"No. Not anymore."

He stood up straighter, facing her. "I have watched you in the drills. If you were larger, a bit older, you would be a nearly invincible fencer."

"Thank you," she said, puzzled by the shift in the conversation.

"I would like you to know that, had it been possible to defy custom, I would never have insisted on these months of lessons for you."

"I'm used to training," she said. "I've been training from the moment I left my cradle."

"It will be different, once you return from Shom. You can ride as a warrior—then you will feel what it is like to be Zyraii. A child is nothing. You will have rank. Maybe you will find that the desert is not such a terrible place. God made it hard, but that's part of the beauty of it."

His fervor attracted her, but he had missed the point again. She wasn't a Zyraii boy.

"Tell me," she said, her voice regaining some of its curtness, "when the *pulstrall* is over, will Tebec and I ever be allowed to go to Setan?"

"No," he said, glancing toward the east.

"That's very good," she said. "Most of your countrymen look northwest when I mention the place."

He flicked away the date pit. "What you want has been strictly denied by Toltac, and no one, myself included, will defy that edict." Elenya regretted the withdrawal of their brief camaraderie. "We can help each other, westerner, but only if you give up your fantasies. There is nothing for you in Setan."

"How are you so sure of that?"

"There is a good well, a school for the ken, and some ruins. Despite the stories they love to tell in Surudain and Nyriya, there is no hint of treasure."

"We've tried to tell you it's not treasure we're after."

"Then what is it you want?"

Elenya closed her mouth.

"You see? If your reasons for seeking it were innocent, you would tell me," Lonal said calmly. "Setan is reserved for the ken. I myself have only been there once. Unless you were *hai-Zyraii,* you would never be allowed near. It is not a place for warriors. In fact, all men must strip off their weapons within the boundaries of the school. I suppose you could have legitimate purposes there—if you wanted to become a priest. Is that what you're after?"

She sighed. "No."

"Then forget Setan. Only those who prove themselves to Zyraii deserve to see it."

As Elenya entered the tent, she startled Peyri. The woman almost spilled the pot of millet that she carried. She set it and its steaming contents in front of Alemar and hurried back behind the purdah, face averted. Elenya was used to it. She was neither man nor woman; to Peyri's mind that left only demons and rythni.

Alemar stared morosely at his bowl as she sat across from him. They began to eat. She still disliked the desert cuisine, but it kept them going. In fact, the aridity preserved meat, her favorite staple, over periods of time that would have rotted it in Cilendrodel.

"What's wrong?"

"Rol has a fever."

Elenya shrugged. "Why should you care?"

"We are responsible for this family," Alemar said.

She winced at his tone. For his sake, she lied and said, "I only meant that he's a strong boy. He'll be well in a few days, probably sooner."

"I hope so. Peyri has lost three sons now. She has never seen one live past puberty."

Elenya briefly pictured Rol's wisps of facial hair, grown since their arrival. To her, it indicated the accelerated life of the Zyraii—Alemar's beard had only recently filled in at the thin places. Most of the tribe married within a year after the *pulstrall,* and had half-grown offspring by the age of the twins. By forty, their teeth were worn away from the sand that inevitably migrated into their food, and their grandchildren far outnumbered the years they had left to live.

"Well, if it's serious, what can you do?"

"I don't know."

He was angry about his impotence. She herself had known the emotion all too often these past months.

"Alemar, how long are we going to stay here?"

He slowly ate a bit of millet. She hadn't asked that question since shortly after they had arrived in the Ahloorm Basin.

"Nothing's changed," he said. "We've nothing to gain by leaving except a long run or death."

"Do you care?"

He lifted one of the unlit lamps to fill it with oil, its chains tinkling as he lowered it. Its reservoir wasn't particularly empty. "How do you mean?"

"You get enough to eat. You keep your mind occupied. And those women wait on you as if that's all they were ever meant to do. They'd probably lick you clean if you asked them. I think you're getting to like it here, just the way it is."

He replaced the lamp. His hands inevitably came away oily. He scrubbed them in the cleansing sand. "I wish you'd be kinder to them."

"Why?"

"They're victims, too. They didn't choose us."

"They help keep us prisoner," she argued.

"They've done us no harm."

"Alemar! We came to this country with a purpose!"

"We came here in search of a myth," he murmured.

She sank down to her haunches. Soon she picked up her bowl and jabbed halfheartedly at her food. Alemar remained in the corner by the cleansing sand, doing something out of Elenya's sight. When he returned to his place, he handed her a flower.

She blinked. "What's this?"

"For your hair. I picked it today, when we were in the desert with Gerat. They only bloom one or two weeks a year."

Tears. "Thank you," she said hoarsely.

He arranged the petals over one of her ears. "I know it's been harder here for you than for me. The legend may be true. Maybe not. But we're here now, and have to live as best we can."

"I'm so tired," she said.

They said nothing for a while. The noises of the camp quieted. Alemar blew out all the lamps but one. The rest of the household went to sleep. Soon they heard the distinctive boom of sand shifting out in the dunes, a sound that had shocked them their first nights in Zyraii.

"What is that called?" Alemar whispered.

"Ohoom," Elenya said. They managed wan smiles. They scooted nearer and nestled against each other, two tiny tidepools in the midst of a beach with no ocean.

XVII

"I am Wilan,"

The Zyraii who spoke seemed to loom above the gathering of boys, voice frighteningly deep. He was a figure meant to be obeyed. Alemar and Elenya recognized the title; it meant man-maker.

"You will do as I say in all things," Wilan announced. "When I tell you to speak, you will speak. When I tell you to be quiet, you will be silent. I have the power to send you back to your mothers; the *pulstrall* can wait for you for another year. Do you understand?"

"Yes," some of the boys whispered.

"Do you understand?"

"Yes!" they replied.

"Good," Wilan stated crisply. He paced the line of boys, all of them in a neat line facing the oasis of Shom, several hundred yards distant. To either side, three other priests waited, imposing in their light blue robes, veils, and cowls, though not as intimidating as Wilan. Alemar and Elenya had been required to dispense with their veils, and they felt exposed in front of Wilan's authority. The men were all strangers.

"You have come here as children. You will leave as men. You will walk the path that your fathers walked, endure what they endured. You have been trained in the things a man must know. Now we will see if you have taken the lessons to heart. Can you hunt? Can you recite the laws? Do you understand the arts of war? Do you know your duty?"

The twins had never seen an Ah-no-ken who so resembled a warrior. For a moment, Wilan met each of their glances. They both had to look away.

"If you are slow-minded, I will find that out. If you are frightened, I will know. If you cheat, lie, whine, or seek to curry favor, I will expose you. You are not safe behind your mother's purdah. Every deficiency, every scrap of false pride, the leadenness of your feet, the awkwardness of your tongues, and the pallor of your young asses will be there for all to see. I am here to find your weaknesses.

"Becoming a man may not be all you think. You see it as your chance to ride with the warriors, take women to bed, win honor in *torovet*. But being a man is to play the Bu. If you shame yourself, your next life you may be born a goat. If you fail to provide for your family, you may be born to a mother with sour milk. God is watching, and judging. So, too, you must be able to judge yourself. This is the primary lesson of the *pulstrall:* Know yourself. Don't expect to leave here with the illusions you arrived with. Soon you will crave them back."

Wilan paused, his attitude becoming almost wistful. "You cannot be a boy again. This is perhaps the hardest lesson. There are no second chances."

By the end of his speech, Wilan had arrived at a pile of equipment. In the center stood a stack of small tents, scarcely more than windbreaks, with accompanying guy ropes and stakes, one for each boy. Near them were goat-hide flasks, uniform in size, filled with water. A few other accessories, such as small butchering knives, flint and steel, and coils of thin rope, had already been picked up by the three assistant Ah-no-ken, who proceeded to distribute them to the group. There were no real weapons, nor any food.

"God placed us on Tanagaran with only our hands and our wits," Wilan continued. "It is good to remember that, should all our material gains be lost, we still will have God's gifts." He nudged the tents. "Unlike our ancestors, you will have a few tokens of civilization. For this is the gift of your fathers, and should you be struck with poverty, at least you will have your heritage. Take these, in honor of him who begat you."

After each boy had been given his gear, he went to the stacks and took the tent off the top and whichever flask was nearest. No choices were allowed. Wilan waited until they had formed their line again.

"The first thing you must learn is that, to be a man, there are times to put family and commerce and amusement aside. A time when there is only you and the world. No one can help you, even if they stand at your side. Go." Wilan pointed to every direction. In every direction was open desert. "There is your fate. Go out and meet it. For the next three days, you will roam the land. Keep solitude. If you encounter one another by chance, take opposite paths. Survive, and return before dusk on the final day. You will have no company. You must see for yourselves that there is no one as lonely as a man."

The four adults abruptly turned and headed back toward the oasis. No opportunity for questions or protests was offered. The boys looked at one another, but were afraid to speak. Finally Elenya kissed her brother, balanced her tent pack more comfortably on her shoulders, and set out for the west. Alemar shrugged and started eastward.

A few boys hesitantly followed suit, each in a somewhat different direction, until a little over half the group remained. Then suddenly all of them acted, walking quickly as if to atone for their lack of initiative. By the time Wilan and the other priests had reached the palms, the meeting place was barren.

At first, Elenya was pleased to be by herself. It was the first time she had been allowed to since she and Alemar had crossed the Ahrahikte range. It felt like freedom. Not quite, for she was deep within T'lil territory and escape was still not worth the risks, but the lack of observation was a genuine luxury.

The furnace in the sky had not yet stolen the morning's pleasantness. She put as much distance as she could between herself and the starting point, without taxing her body, and spent the heat of the day in a niche among some rocks, her tent fabric serving as an awning.

By the time Achird had burned its trail across the western sky, Elenya no longer felt quite so enthused. She was hungry. Soon she would be thirsty, too. The skins held about two gallons—enough to seem heavy during the morning walk, but in this climate, to drink less than that in one day would sap her vitality, particularly for one not born in the country. By strictest conservation, she could ration it and still not be totally enervated by the end of the three days, but realistically, she would have to find water. That was, of course, part of the point of this section of the *pulstrall*. Thanks to the oasis, the region possessed several springs, and enough underground moisture to support plants like the boro, but first she had to find one or the other. In the meantime, her stomach was empty. She had actually hoped she would find a snake occupying the niche she had chosen to rest in. Snakes were not nearly as fast as some other sources of food, accustomed as they were to being the predator, and they provided a substantial amount of meat. She rolled up her awning and set out.

Dunes, outcroppings, and sandstone flats surrounded her, devoid of any obvious source of sustenance. As dusk settled in, she occasionally heard or saw small creatures scuttling over rocks, but trying to chase down any of them would be an exercise in futility, and even if she did catch one, the amount of edible meat would scarcely be enough to stave off her hunger pangs. She passed a patch of *elbraksh* brush, its thin leaves curled almost into thorns until the next rain opened them again. She would probably be able to find a *pommyt* nest somewhere within it, but the bird's eggs were so small they weren't worth tearing her skin or clothing for.

The sun was down, but the light still good, when she spotted a shrike wheeling in the sky. A few moments later, it dove out of sight into the distant sage. Seconds later, it fluttered off toward another stand of *elbraksh,* a thrashing creature in its grip. Elenya smiled and headed toward the site.

She paused several hundred yards away, until she had seen the shrike fly off, then hurried to the *elbraksh* before it could return.

Just as she'd expected, the shrike had left its catch, a small but plump sand-runner, impaled on the thorns of the brush. The lizard still shuddered spasmodically. For a moment Elenya felt sorry for it. Its gruesome end might have been avoided if the shrike had possessed talons with which to slay quickly. But why regret a situation from which she benefited? If the shrike had been so well fed that it had decided to hunt more while the light was good, that was its misfortune. Elenya removed the sand-runner and absconded with it.

The bulbs Alemar had found were tucked into a cranny between two boulders, in the pocket of loose soil that had collected there. He returned three to the spot and carefully tamped the dirt down again, put eight in his sack, and bit down on the last. Sweet juice gushed over his tongue. Alemar had seen the variety in bloom near the river. It sported a cornucopia of flowers on a knee-high, thick stalk, multiple blooms and multiple colors on each stem. Ironically, the pollen would induce nausea if swallowed, but the bulbs were considered a delicacy. They seemed far too small to produce such a spectacular plant. All that remained above ground here had been one withered shred, just enough to alert Alemar to the presence of the bulbs. Those he had left would wait, if necessary, several years for enough rain to flower, though lesser rains would prompt underground growth.

He sat on one of the boulders and watched the sky shift to deep oranges, pinks, purples, and reds. Flamboyant sunsets were the rule in Zyraii. He virtually ignored them now. But when he did stop to notice, he never failed to be overwhelmed. The desert did have its advantages.

The air was cooling rapidly. Before the light failed altogether, Alemar rose and searched for a campsite. The rocks were not only hard, they attracted creatures. The dunes not far away promised better.

Elenya spread out her tent and reached for the stakes. The hides were well sewn, she noticed. She wondered whether any of the girls of the T'krt had been the seamstress. It brought to mind one of the last nights before she had left for Shom:

"What is that?" Elenya asked. Meyr had just come out of the tent, carrying a small bundle.

The girl paused, eyes wide, mute. Meyr always did her best to avoid any sort of contact with her strange "parent." Finally, still without comment, she held out the object.

Elenya let it unfold, and recognized it. At the same time, Peyri stepped out, noticed the pair, and hurried forward. It was she who answered the question.

"It is a tent for the *pulstrall*. A boy will use it during part of the time he is at the oasis."

"What boy?"

"Any boy. It doesn't matter. She is required to make one."

"Why?"

Peyri hesitated. Suddenly she turned to Meyr and said, "Take it to Clan Mother. She is waiting."

Meyr nodded submissively, gingerly lifted the tent out of Elenya's hands, and scurried away.

Peyri sighed. "This is not a matter that men need be interested in."

"Is it forbidden?" Elenya said testily.

"No," Peyri admitted.

"Then tell me. I'm just curious. It's not as if I'm plotting something."

Peyri hesitated. Always, the internal debate. The women never were sure how to act with Elenya. A true Zyraii, no doubt, would not have asked his wife such a question. Finally, Peyri said, "Last year, Meyr began her bleeding."

Elenya raised her eyebrows. "So?"

"You don't understand? It is time for her to be a woman."

"Of course it is," Elenya said. "Is there something unusual about that?"

"I don't think being a woman in your land is the same as being a woman here."

"That's true."

Peyri continued, "To become a woman of the Zyraii, she is taught all she will need to be a wife. In the year after she starts to bleed, she must show that she can do all of these things alone. She must be able to cook both the common foods and the ritual ones. She must make a garment for every member of her family. She must cure hides. She must understand how to please her husband when she goes to his bed, and how to prevent the children from happening at the wrong time. The last thing is to make the tents for the boys to use in the *pulstrall*. Now she can be married. When the new men come back from Shom, she will be ready."

"Meyr is going to be married?" Elenya said, surprised.

"No. She *can* be married. A man must want her. Sesheer has been of age for two years now. But no one has asked to wed her."

Now, out in the desert, Elenya debated with herself as to which was the easier ritual: the abrupt but respected one demanded of the males or the drawn-out, unpublicized female one.

With her luck, she was glad not to have to endure both.

Task done, she squirmed feet first into the cloth cocoon she had created. She wondered who had ended up with Meyr's tent.

Alemar awoke to the sensation of something creeping down his neck. He sat up so fast he lifted the hide off one of its poles and collapsed the tent.

Sand trickled down his spine.

The moons told him it was a few hours before dawn. Nothing stirred, except the air flowing over the dune, bearing with it the fine spray of granules picked up from the earth. Small drifts had piled up against Alemar's sleeping body, until it had entered his collar. Irritated, he stood up and shook out his clothing.

He realized immediately what he had done. In this particular region, the prevailing winds always changed direction shortly after midnight. He had left the open end of his tent exposed to them. Wearily, disgusted with himself, he proceeded to uproot his shelter and reconstruct it facing the other way.

Dawn smelled imminent, but the sky offered only diamonds on black velvet. Elenya couldn't make herself sleep any longer. She began to tremble, though she was perfectly warm inside her blankets. She shifted until her head lay outside the tent, where she could stare upward and feel the faint kiss of dew landing on her face.

A billion stars, a billion grains of sand. And her. One woman, man, man/woman. Who was she? A bastard child on a quest, sent by a father she had scarcely ever seen. One half of a set of twins.

She couldn't understand why she wasn't happy to be away from the Zyraii. She didn't belong with them. They all treated her like an aberration. The strange man with tits. An embarrassment. Did Lonal really think that the other tribes would play along with the farce? How could the T'lil themselves have accepted it so blithely? She wished she were God; it was handy to have people obey you to the point of denying their own sight and touch.

The jumping rat could derive enough moisture from the dew and the seeds it consumed to never need a true drink. That was the sort of creature that belonged here. Not a woman.

She reached into her collar and pulled out her necklace. The jewel was agonizingly faint, a small green flicker now and then. Alemar was miles away. But at least he was there.

Alemar felt the tiny pulse of heat on his chest and knew at once it was the amulet. It said nothing articulate, only that there was someone else thinking of him. He hung on to the knowledge, the faint chitters and rustles of dawn desert life failing to bring him out of his soliloquy.

A new day. Soon it would be a new month, a new year. Would he still be here, in the desert? Or would there be a path suddenly open in front of him, making his course of decision clear? He knew what had been expected of him when he departed for this country. He could guess at Lonal's plans for him. He hadn't resisted either influence on his life. That struck him as strange. He should have some idea what *he* wanted to do with himself. But no, it had always been his way to be passive and wait. He was over twenty years of age now; still he had no idea what he was waiting for. He had always let others lead him their way.

What were the choices? To plow ahead with his and Elenya's original quest, and ignore the lessons in prudence they had gained from the Zyraii? To return home empty-handed? He hadn't felt such lack of direction since his mother had died.

It startled him to think of her. She wasn't so long dead that he forgot her often. No, what surprised him was that he had not recently felt the disconnectedness her passing had created. No one could replace her as an individual, but the sense of a home, a place he belonged, had not been fretting him. Foreign though it was, he now had a family and, transient though it was, a home. He didn't know whether to be grateful or to grieve. He realized he had been touched irrevocably by Zyraii.

He got up. The next year would come soon enough. Best to take this day all by itself first.

XVIII

In the first weeks after Ethmurl had gone, Lerina liked to spend middays meandering along the high bluffs. The fog would usually be well off the coast, providing her with a broad view of the ocean while she herself was camouflaged by the forest. She would watch as the ships of the Dragon's blockade maintained their patrols, catch glimpses of the fishing boats of her own people, and imagine that she saw other craft, always at the horizon or on the edges of incoming fog banks. Those who knew her might have thought her behavior odd, but ever since puberty she had habitually spent long periods alone away from the hold, and none were the wiser that she was now haunting the woods more than the beaches.

This day she broke her ritual, cutting short the time spent watching the Dragon Sea, and drifted deeper into the woods. Inland, Garthmorron was a treasury of virgin lumber, little exploited since the Elandri war had disrupted trade between Cilendrodel and the civilized world. The roads were infrequent and seldom traveled. The forest devoured her, the subdued light beneath the canopy guiding her toward her objective. Before long she found it, growing at the base of one of the mammoth trunks.

The shrub was in flower—tiny white blossoms to accent the earth tones surrounding them—but the abundant, delicate leaves were what she wanted. She stripped off a few handfuls, sniffed them, and wrinkled her nose. She folded the leaves into a piece of cloth and stood up.

A fluttering in the underbrush caught her attention, giving her heart a surge. A patch of ferns swayed and parted briefly, clearly revealing minute, nearly human outlines. Pinpoint eyes glinted up at her, then were gone. She stepped forward, alert, but the movement of the plants had stilled entirely, leaving no trace of her small visitor.

"Rythni," she whispered.

She might have searched, but knew from experience and legend that she wouldn't find anything. She gathered her composure and walked back to her father's cottage, holding the cloth of collected herbs in cupped hands.

The water had boiled, and she was pouring it into the teapot to steep when her father opened the door. She jumped, recovered herself, and greeted him as he entered.

"A fine day," he answered, obviously in a good mood.

"I thought you went hunting."

"Did. I came across a fine hart almost inside the grounds. He's hanging from the tree near the smokehouse, already gutted."

She winced at the image.

"Now, now, you know you like venison as much as I do." He arranged himself in the room's only real chair. Cosufier Elb-Aratule was ruggedly handsome, a small man just beginning to display the waning of youth. He sniffed the air.

"What's that you have there?"

"Amethery."

His face fell. Lerina felt the blood rush to her cheeks. "You have a problem?" he asked.

"Not if I drink the tea." Her attempt to sound flippant fell short.

Cosufier straightened up slowly. "Apparently you had an interesting holiday with that fisherman's son." He kept judgment out of his voice. He hadn't pressed her over her somewhat dubious excuse for her absence, nor would he now.

"I'm afraid so."

"Are you sure this is what you want?"

"As a matter of fact, I haven't decided." All at once, Lerina felt her reticence vanish. This was her father, not the gossips of the village or the unsophisticated sons of woodcutters and silk farmers.

"Oh?"

The scent of the amethery was thick, approaching the strength necessary for its purpose. "I was thinking what would have happened if my mother had chosen to drink."

Her father said nothing.

"Don't try to reassure me. You were both very young, and

Mother wasn't the kind of person to let something happen that she didn't want. She must have considered it."

Cosufier cleared his throat. "Actually, *we* considered it." Lerina wondered if it were guilt she detected in his tone, but realized she preferred not to know the particulars. "And so might the father of this baby, whoever he may be."

She paused. "He is someone committed to distant lands and responsibilities—and I think to another woman and her children."

For the first time, her father seemed worried. "Who?"

She shrugged, inwardly laughing at herself. "I don't know. He never told me his true name, I'm sure of that."

"What have you gotten yourself into, daughter?"

"He wasn't like anyone I'd ever seen before. He impressed me—the way you impress me, Papa. And he needed me, at least for a little while. I knew he wouldn't stay, but that didn't matter. I took what I could, and he loved me back as best he could. I didn't worry about getting pregnant. Why should I? I've used amethery before."

"But now you're not sure," Cosufier deduced.

"I don't want to raise a child alone, but I also don't want just any offspring. I don't know who Ethmurl really is, but he had something inside him that no boy of Garthmorron has to offer. This baby could be someone very special. That's my difficulty. If I conceived another dozen times, I might never produce a child to match the one in my womb now."

"Will the child exhibit the qualities of the father if he isn't present to raise it?"

"That's a long question, Papa. My short answer is: At least it will have a chance."

"Wait until Uncle Ossatch hears about this."

Her smile was involuntary. "I'm sure Uncle Ossatch will deny it came from his side of the family, but it does seem to run among the Elb-Aratules."

"At least I was able to do the honorable thing." Cosufier sighed. "This child of yours won't have that sort of buffer."

"I survived. So did you." However dull Garthmorron might have been, it had nurtured her.

"You want the child, then."

"I don't know, Papa. I really don't."

It took a few moments for it to sink in, then Cosufier suddenly stood up, adjusting his belt in a feigned attempt to seem casual. "Well, I have some chores I should be doing. . . ." But he only made it halfway to the door. "You know," he said finally, "your mother and I planned brothers and sisters for you, though we never had the chance to have them. I'm still young enough to enjoy being a surrogate father."

"Thank you, Papa."

"I'll see you in a few hours."

She kissed him and he was gone, leaving her stroking her abdomen and wondering if it would ever again be as firm as it was now.

A short while later, she poured a full cup of the tea—more than enough, she thought. She emptied the remainder of the pot onto the ground outside the back window, and set the cup on the windowsill to cool. It would be ready in a few minutes. By that time, she would have decided.

She climbed into the loft. She lay in her bed, which had never seemed too large until Ethmurl had left, and pulled out the scrap of doeskin she had hidden under her pillow, spreading it out on the bed to read the hastily scrawled ideograms of High Speech. She could have simply taken it from memory.

> Lerina:
>
> I leave like a thief in the night--because I could not face the hurt and judgment of your eyes. I cannot share with you the reasons why I leave, but believe me when I say that they have nothing to do with you. I said it once lightly, but now I repeat in sincerity: "Thou art the queen of all women." I love you.
>
> —Ethmurl

With the note, he had left four jewels. She picked up the largest one. It glittered magnificently. She had never seen anything comparable, not even among the late Lady Dran's finery. If and when she ever needed to convert it into cash, she would receive enough to live on for several years, at a better standard than she was used to.

But at that moment, it had no allure. They were four rocks. Pretty, and precious to some, but nevertheless hard and giving no love nor warmth. What kind of legacy was that? She slipped her hand under her blouse and felt the area around her navel. It was warm, living, containing a potential for beauty unmatched by jewels.

She had made her decision. She wanted a better reminder of him than rocks.

She virtually sailed down the stairs from the loft. She would have to tell her father immediately; it wasn't fair to make him wait all day. She almost giggled at the expression she knew she'd soon see on Uncle Ossatch's face. But first, she turned to the windowsill to dump out the amethery.

The cup lay on its side, its contents dripping off the outer edge. Brows furrowed, she picked it up. It had a wide, flat bottom, and even a stiff breeze wouldn't have knocked it over, had there been one, which there wasn't. Her father? Not like him.

Then she saw it. A tiny set of footprints led across the sill, etched with spilled tea, evaporating to nonexistence as she watched. She searched, but the rythni had gone, and had left no other traces.

As any Cilendri knew, a mother couldn't have asked for a better omen.

XIX

It was Dark Night, the night on which neither the sun, nor its sister, nor Motherworld, nor any of the moons were in the sky. It was a time when the gods withdrew their surveillance, when the forces of the supernatural were unbound, and when men conducted those rites that needed power to sanctify. Across the face of Tanagaran, every culture maintained its superstitions and observances concerning Dark Night, and Alemar and Elenya were prey to old beliefs and childhood myths. This was the moment when the face of the world they knew turned its back on its mother planet and Achird, the sun, away from its origin and its foundation, and looked out at the immensity. Here in the desert, the magnificent clarity of the dry, high altitude cast jewels in the ebony ceiling above. The air lived. Existence never seemed so limitless, and man so small.

A knot of Zyraii surrounded them, but despite the presence of humanity, Alemar and Elenya felt the loneliness and desolation of the land, a sensation that had not truly left them since they had separated to observe the first section of the *pulstrall*. The beauty and the terror of the wasteland once again stole their equilibrium.

They had reached the end. They had spent their time alone, and had all returned, some worse for wear, but alive, to endure the other tests. They had proved their knowledge of the blade and rope; they had broken oeikani; they had recited the laws of the So-de'es from memory. Now on the eighth night, one ritual remained.

At a word, the youths were formed into a long line. Ahead of them stood the Menhir of T'lil, flanked by three large fires. Wood fires. The stone was something of an enigma, a chunk of rugged, convoluted rock possessing glints of metal ores. It reached shoulder height, half as wide as it was tall, nestled in the midst of the fine sand that bordered the palms and grasses of the oasis of Shom. No rock of this type existed elsewhere in Zyraii. It was the most valuable of all T'lil relics. The oasis was the center of their territory; no member of another tribe would be permitted here while a T'lil lived to defend it. Alemar knew this was no boast. The Menhir, in a sense, gave this Zyraii tribe their everlasting souls, and there was no physical object more precious to them.

Wilan took to his position directly in front of the stone, facing the line of boys.

"Ai Nannon!" Wilan cried.

"Ai Nannon!" the boys echoed.

Behold God! A phrase spoken only on Dark Night.

"Nannon welcomes you to the Bu," Wilan said. His voice carried such impact that it rode over the detachment Elenya and Alemar normally felt listening to the Zyraii language. Even words that they scarcely understood moved them. "You have all done well. It is time for the final acknowledgment of your new status."

The old man looked down the line—about twenty boys, all afraid. The adults took up stations at either end of the line. The youths eyed them nervously.

One of the priests stepped to center stage. He reached to a tiny scabbard on his belt and withdrew a shiny, very wicked looking instrument. The blade was shorter than the handle and was shaped like a fork. The outer edges were dull; only the insides of the prongs were meant to cut. The man raised it above his head and waved it once, slowly, across the boys' range of vision.

A boy next to Alemar hiccupped.

"Take off your clothes," Wilan ordered.

The boys hesitated. Although it was not considered immoral for males to bare themselves before other males, once past toddler age Zyraii usually disrobed only within the confines of the home tent, among immediate family. It was a practical custom—in the desert, one did not expose one's skin unnecessarily to the sun. The men merely waited, and one by one the boys began to obey.

They threw their bundles of clothing a few paces behind them. Alemar felt the isolation of his light complexion, but the sensation vanished as he noticed the many furtive, and some open, glances at Elenya. One or two of the boys stifled smiles, more of them displayed fear. They had known she was there, but suddenly it mattered. They looked to their elders for guidance. The older Zyraii merely avoided looking, but some of them, for the first time since the *pulstrall* had begun, stirred nervously.

Elenya held her chin high, chest out. But a trickle of sweat worked down each side of her torso.

Wilan alone looked her in the eyes. "Nannon forgive us," he breathed. Then, full-voiced, he demanded of the line: "Hold out your *sheys*."

The blood flushed Alemar's cheeks as he complied. Down the line, knees weakened. Elenya stared at her pubic hair for several moments, shrugged, and kept her hands at her sides.

The Ah-no-ken with the surgical knife waited where he was. Two other men walked over to one end of the line. The first carried a small earthenware pot, suspended from a hemp net, which had recently been heating over one of the fires. The other held the severed tail of a oeikani, the hind end smooth and whiplike, the tip heavy with its knot of hair.

The pair stepped in front of the first boy. The priest with the oeikani tail dipped it into the pot. The brush of hair emerged dripping a thin, greasy liquid, which the man rubbed over the boy's penis. This procedure was repeated down the line.

At first, the fluid felt like it would burn away Alemar's skin. Soon it cooled, then numbed. Within a few moments, he could scarcely feel the area where the ointment had been applied. He felt bereft. He glanced at Elenya. She raised her eyebrows and looked repeatedly at her companions, much to their dismay. The anointers had skipped her.

Alemar doubted that she minded being left out, just this once.

They heard a cry at the end of the row, and turned. The man with the knife stepped away from the first boy, blade dripping. The boy was shaking, but it was apparent that his outburst had been one of shock, not pain. Directly behind the surgeon, another priest collected the foreskin on a stone plate, and a third removed something from a basket he carried and helped the boy to wrap it around his wound. The boy was pale.

The second boy obviously would have liked to run, or at least twist away, but he did neither. One look at the knife, and the man who wielded it, made it clear that he should stand absolutely still during the procedure. This time, everyone watched closely, though they held their places.

The surgeon wasted no time. While a fourth man held a lamp near, he grasped the foreskin, pulled it taut beyond the end of the glans, and cut swiftly downward. The newly circumcised man jumped after all, but by then the affair was cleanly and efficiently accomplished. The surgeon did not smile or otherwise react; he maintained a calm, detached concentration on the task at hand. His job was one that required no mistakes.

Alemar wondered if his heart could really beat so quickly. He watched the boy ahead of him, seeing clearly for the first time that the basket contained leaves of the husura—broad, soft fronds found at the very edges of the water of the oasis. They had been soaked in a milky, pasty concoction.

Then it was his turn.

It ended before he could consider the various ways to retain his composure. Like most of the others, he jerked away after the knife descended, but it had not hurt. It felt like a glove being removed. He watched dumbfounded as the last man helped him wrap the leaves around. The odor of the bandage curled his nostrils, but its touch soothed his fingers.

The surgeon stepped in front of Elenya, knelt down, and for the first time his meticulous, methodical routine faltered. He stared between her thighs as if he had forgotten momentarily that she was in the group. She faced him squarely, although perhaps more nervous than any of the young men, and read in his expression the conflict within. He had, quite possibly, been performing this duty for more than ten years; by now, his opinions regarding the ritual were chipped in rock.

She surprised herself. She felt no anger, nor even defiance. The emotion was embarrassment. She wished she could do something to ease the man's difficulty.

In another moment, the knife descended, severing a tuft of pubic hair. The second man, nonplussed, took the hair and added it to the plate, now almost covered with foreskins. The sight made Elenya a little nauseated, glad for the darkness. The third man didn't bother to reach inside his basket.

In what seemed like both seconds and hours after it had started, the surgeon reached the last boy. He cut.

"Oops," he said, pulling back his knife.

The boy fainted.

The surgeon burst into intense laughter, so hearty that he almost dropped the foreskin as the Ah-no-ken with the plate reached for it. All the grown men immediatly joined in, some with tears springing from their eyes. One by one, the initiates understood, and began to chuckle and guffaw. The priest who held the lamp pulled smelling salts out of a pocket and woke up the stricken one. When he came to and saw that he was whole, his laughter swamped them all. They were all whole.

The man with the plate carried his burden to the central fire.

"Nannon gives you manhood," Wilan intoned. "What do you give in return?"

"Our childhood!" they cried.

The man dumped the plate over the fire. The blood and fluids sizzled on the coals, the odor of burning flesh powerful. As the scent permeated his nostrils, Alemar acknowledged what he had felt the first dawn after the *pulstrall* began. He had been marked by Zyraii. The scars would remain, for better or worse, physical and emotional.

The youths were led one by one to the Menhir of T'lil. There, each spilled a drop of blood from their wound onto the stone, which was encrusted with the remains of many such offerings. When Elenya's turn came, the surgeon pricked her finger with the ceremonial knife.

"This is the blood of T'lil, joined with the blood of T'lil. Let the sons be one with their fathers, and their fathers' fathers. Blood is the force of Nannon within the living body."

"Emat ha temi," they all replied. "The truth is known."

Wilan raised his arms slowly toward the stars. "God is watching you," he said.

Alemar saw merely points of light and filigin blackness, but only a small part of him doubted that Nannon was out there.

"Now your souls are awake. Now you play the game for full stakes. A sobering thought." Behind Wilan, two pair of men brought forward near bursting goatskins sloshing with liquid contents. The men/boys began to smile.

Wilan at last smiled, too. "Let's not let it be too sobering."

XX

"Admiral," the lookout called.

Keron climbed onto the poop deck for a better view. "What is it, Shel?"

"A sail, sir. I see the colors now. It's Lieutenant Enret's skiff."

Keron stared in the direction indicated, and before long was able to make out the flash of color just above the swells. Enret had made good time.

Keron paced the deck. Sniffing the air, he caught the aroma wafting from the galley. Lobscouse again. At times it seemed the stew was the cook's only recipe. He picked up a belaying pin from its holder and spun it in his grip. Its hardness soothed him. He had always favored the kevel as a weapon. Coupled with the strength of Alemar's belt, its impact was devastating, and it could be used in extremely tight quarters. He slapped it against his palm. He hated waiting. He never liked working through intermediaries.

One more short wait should have been easy to bear, after the months he had already endured, but it was not. It had been almost a year since he had left Cilendrodel. The trial of Warnyre was history; the spy network within the navy's upper ranks had, so the loyal hoped, been uprooted. Keron had been promoted to Warnyre's old position as admiral of the northern fleet, and was highly favored by the king. The time had not seemed to drag then, but, he reminded himself, there had been plenty to do at the capital. Now, back in northern waters, he could think of only one thing.

Would she still be there? Had she forgotten him in the way of impressionable young women?

Did she forgive him?

He lost himself in reverie until he heard the bump of the skiff against the hull of *King's Ransom*. The ladder was flung over the side. Others began hoisting the small craft aboard. Enret's young but balding head appeared above the railing.

Keron himself extended an arm and helped his junior officer aboard. Their greeting was warm. "You look weary from your expedition, Lieutenant," Keron stated. "Share a glass of apricot brandy with me in my quarters while you give me your report."

The light bouquet of fermented fruit filled the stateroom, vaguely reminiscent of the perfume used by Lady Nanth, who had not accompanied her husband this trip. The glass snifter clinked against Enret's teeth.

"I'm not sure how to tell you this," Enret said.

"Spit it out, man!"

"I'm sorry. You . . . might want to take a healthy swallow first."

"What is it? Is Lerina well?"

"Oh, quite. I saw her myself, from a distance. I admire your taste, m'lord."

"Well then?"

"She was almost flushed with health, you might say. A trim and spry young mother."

Keron tilted his brandy snifter back and took three large gulps.

Enret tried not to, but smiled anyway. "She had twins, a boy and a girl, about two and a half months ago."

Keron did some calculations. He had been gone for eleven months. "What do the locals say about the birth?"

"Well, that was a difficult subject to broach. Apparently it's one of the choice bits of gossip in Garthmorron at the moment. No one seems to know who the father is. The little lady isn't telling. It seems she disappeared for a week last year. Everyone seems to agree that timing is somewhat significant."

"I'm afraid it is. Anything more?"

"I didn't think a stranger asking questions about it would be a good move. Someone did comment that the babies were just as black-haired and beautiful as their mother." He glanced involuntarily at Keron's midnight locks.

Keron left his seat and opened the door to his chamber, making sure no one was outside. He told Enret, "You and Obo are the only two people besides myself who know of my connection to this maid of Garthmorron. If it were critical to keep it secret before, it is now triply so."

"Of course, m'lord. Your reputation at court means as much to me as it does to you."

"It's more than that. Half the nobles in Elandris have bastard children; I wouldn't lose much, except, of course, in my relationship with Lady Nanth. No, this is more grave than that. These are children of the Blood. The Dragon will want them dead. The fewer who know the truth, the fewer who can endanger my offspring."

"I understand."

"This news changes my plans. I will have to go to Garthmorron."

"Is that wise? As you implied, many eyes are upon you."

"I will be gone less than a night. In the meantime, we set course for the Thank River delta."

"Why?"

"I have some pearl diving to do."

The Thank River drained most of Cilendrodel, as well as the wilderness to the north, spewing out into the northwest corner of the Dragon Sea. Its muddy effluent stretched far out to sea—a ship could be completely out of view from the coast and still know that the river was near. Creatures unknown elsewhere in the world inhabited the microenvironment where fresh and salt water met. And farther offshore, where the silt plateau suddenly dropped into deep ocean, lived the creature most famous to every jeweler of ten nations—the amath oyster. It fed on the nutrients dumped by the river and grew the largest and finest pearls known to civilization.

The amath did not surrender their treasures easily, however.

Keron handled the tiller of the skiff while Enret sat toward the prow. *King's Ransom* wallowed at the horizon, near the crag that had identified the spot where Keron wished to go. Rowboats and a small sloop lingered at various places throughout the area—other crew members trying their luck.

Keron was certain his real motives for coming here were hidden. The Thank River delta was part of the normal patrolling area of the northern fleet, and to stop and hunt for pearls was common. No member of the present crew had been with him when he had visited the location ten years earlier.

"Furl the sail and drop the anchor," Keron announced. "This looks like the right spot."

"Deep water here, Admiral. Are you certain?"

"Yes."

They put on their vests, weights, and airmakers and leaned backward into the ocean. Once under the surface, they fastened a rope to one another. At Keron's signal, they began to descend. He could see the submerged cliff already. He was right. This was the place.

Ten years fell away. He had been an ensign. His royal blood was thin enough that it had won him only two things—an officer's commission and the belt of Alemar, and his mind was full of ways to make his fortune and fame. He had spent two years with the northern fleet, smuggling and living a sailor's life, before he had thought about the amath. He and another ensign named Brenck had laid a plan.

Keron glanced at Enret. Poor Brenck. It should have been he who accompanied Keron into the depths. But the ensign had been killed long ago in a battle with a Dragon's ship. Soon Keron would know if their hopes had borne fruit.

They went deep. In fact, they would go as deep as Keron had ever gone, and that was fundamental to the plan. These waters were often exploited. Though amath pearls were rarely found, and pursuit of them was hard work, their worth nevertheless enticed many fortune hunters. So a given oyster could seldom remain for ten years without being molested—unless it was below a certain depth.

Down. Keron and Enret watched the jumbled sea growth of the cliff pass by. Now all they could see were shades of blue and deep green. Soon they would enter a gray limbo where light was a stranger and life wore shapes that men imagined only in dreams. At that level, an amath need not fear the intrusions of humankind.

The pressure squeezed uncomfortably by now. Keron signaled a halt. Dim as the world around them was, it took him several moments to spot the projection in the cliff. It seemed to be only silt-covered rock, but Keron knew differently.

He tapped Enret three times on the elbow. The lieutenant nodded. Keron continued down alone, the line connecting them gradually unravelling. Enret's presence served one purpose: to watch Keron. At this depth, such a precaution was essential.

Keron felt light-headed. He didn't notice any other symptoms, but he knew his body was undergoing physiological changes. He had to be alert for their effects. He breathed very deliberately, never holding his breath, never allowing his inhalations to become shallow. Finally he reached his goal.

Camouflaged by silt and barnacles, the amath was as long as Keron, its horny body covered by jagged points and ridges. Its mouth zigzagged like a giant clam, wide enough to swallow large fish, though, like its smaller cousins, the oyster fed only on plankton. It was twice as large as when Keron had last seen it.

Its mouth, which had been open a fraction of an inch as Keron approached, shut forcefully, pummelling the man with a strong jet of water. To reopen it would take the strength of several men, normally more than could find handholds with which to try. The only practical way to open an amath was to chisel it free of the rock to which it had adhered itself, and carry it bodily to the surface. Aboard ship, it could be pried open.

The uncooperativeness of the amath was the reason they were never harvested below a particular depth. Regardless of the riches that might be won, few divers would risk rapture of the deep or other pressure maladies. Nor was it advisable to attempt strenuous labor deep down, and the amount of time required to chisel loose an amath meant a long return ascent in order to avoid the bends. Taking into account the fact that only one amath in hundreds contained a pearl, it was not surprising most divers went after the easier ones.

But most divers did not wear a belt that increased their strength many times.

Keron anchored his feet, found a firm grip on the upper shell, and pulled. It felt like trying to rend stone. Perhaps he had miscalculated. Perhaps he had let the creature grow too large. Then he heard a groan. The mouth opened a crack. Keron yanked. The oyster's great muscle released. Keron kept pushing until he had bent the shell completely back and broken the joint. The delicate inner body was exposed.

The blood in his temples pounded fiercely. He fought to return his breathing to normal, doing nothing more strenuous than staring at his accomplishment. When he had recovered, he withdrew his knife and carefully slashed at the ugly mass of flesh. He peeled away the layers at a specific point.

And there it was. A perfect, tremendous pearl.

Keron had made sure it would be there. He had learned how to culture normal oysters as a boy. The trick was duplicating the feat with an amath. The king of pearls had never been cultured, except by sorcerers, simply because opening an amath was so difficult. If men did succeed in spreading the huge jaws, they usually inadvertently killed the bivalve in the process.

But Keron had his belt. A decade before, while he had held the oyster open, Brenck had quickly inserted the seed pearl—itself a quality amath—into the proper spot. They had returned a few months later to be sure the oyster had lived.

Keron held up his prize and began to laugh. And kept laughing.

It wasn't until he felt a strong tug on the line that he became aware of his peril. He rapidly secured the pearl in his game pouch, and pressed the right-hand stud on his vest. It inflated just a bit, taking him gradually up five feet, then levelling off. He repeated the action. Everything seemed to be going in slow motion. His brain gave the command to his finger to press, and only many seconds later did it obey.

There was Enret—up toward the right. No, to the left. He blinked. He saw two distinct images of his lieutenant. He blinked again, and there was one.

He stopped. He had just enough composure to know that he had very little. He waited. Eventually, Enret tugged on the line. Keron knew better than to trust his own thinking. Enret's tugs would tell him when it was safe to ascend. It would be stupid to win so great a prize and cripple his body forever by rising too swiftly. He abandoned all power of decision to the rope, moving a single increment whenever he felt the signal. He clung to consciousness.

In this manner he reached Enret's position. Keron was feeling better by then. They continued up together, a lazy ascent that gave Keron plenty of time to exult. If he did nothing else in this life, he would always be known as the creator of this mighty pearl.

In the boat, Enret's eyes went wide to see the amath dropped out of the pouch. "By the gods! That is the largest I have ever seen."

"There is a larger one among the crown jewels, and others lost to Gloroc," Keron said modestly. Inside, he was laughing constantly, and this time it was not the effect of nitrogen narcosis.

"What now?" Enret asked.

"Back to Garthmorron—to the only lady fit for this jewel."

XXI

Long before they reached the oasis where the main camp of the T'krt was situated, Alemar and Elenya could smell the rich odor of cooking meat. Pork, and lots of it. Though they were many leagues from the Ahloorm, someone must have done some travelling and staged a massive hunt, for it was only there that the boars could be found. It was not until they rode into sight that the twins could guess the reason.

A party of Po-no-pha chanting the T'lil song of life were marching toward them, veils undulating with their singing. The parade surrounded the initiates and lifted them from their saddles onto their own shoulders, and carried them in that fashion the remaining distance to the camp. The entire community had gathered. Jathmir and Toltac, impressive in their red robes, waited at the forefront of the throng. After the new men had been lowered to their feet and lined up, the two Bo-no-ken bowed deeply.

Hands reached forward and removed the veils from the initiates' faces. Jathmir turned to the crowd.

"Behold, the future of our tribe!"

Then the formality vanished. Relatives rushed forward, friends cried congratulations, and the pits containing the roasting meat were opened. The feast began.

Shigmur found the twins. "Well done. I see you made it through the recitations?"

"I never knew God could have so many laws." Alemar sighed. "But we remembered them all." His Zyraii was fluid. Elenya was almost as proficient. However, there was no question that remembering and repeating the laws of the So-de'es had been the most difficult trial of the rite of passage.

"Good. Now just a march of Urthey, and you can really enjoy being a family man," Shigmur said.

"I can?"

Shigmur cleared his throat. "You mean no one has told you?"

"Told us what?"

He pointed at Urthey. The tiny moon was scarcely visible in the daylight. It had been new on Dark night, and would be new again in ten days. Then he paused. "Never mind," he said mischievously.

They couldn't coax anything more out of him. He invited them to the party that his family, in cooperation with Omi, Peyri, and their children, had prepared.

Elenya was stuffed. She lay on the ground behind her tent, staring at the blood of the darkening western sky. Alemar and other nearby revellers were out of sight. She was feeling good. The food and wine had been superb. Many of the tribe had complimented her on her completion of the *pulstrall,* and she could tell the coments had been sincere. Even the weather had been blessed. She felt warm and secure. One hand wandered to her crotch and smoothed the wrinkles in the cloth. She murmured, and continued to stroke lightly with the two middle fingers.

"Good evening."

She sat up abruptly. The shadow standing nearby held out a skin of wine.

"What do you want?" she asked sharply.

"I've been throughout the camp to congratulate each of the new men," Lonal said cordially. "I saved you for last."

"Thank you, war-leader."

"I would have thought you'd be too drunk now to have much frost in your mouth," he said, the white of his smile brightening the dusk.

"I'm sorry," she said. "I was enjoying being alone."

"It looked that way."

"Blasphemer." Her cheeks were burning.

"Your grasp of our language has certainly improved." Lonal laughed. "How does one swear in yours? My tutor never taught me."

She pursed her lips, bound not to speak. He waited patiently. Eventually she relented.

"You can't swear in the High Speech. It was the formal language used in the schools and at the royal courts of the

Calinin Empire. You'd have to use one of the vulgar forms, and those are unique to each region."

He nodded and sat down beside her, offering her the wineskin. She took a deep draft. "What would the greatest insult be in your country?"

"To call someone a northerner."

"Why?" He was sitting so close she could catch his scent, even over the feast odors on her lips.

"Cilendrodel is at the far north of civilization. Only savages live in the forests and wastelands beyond. I suppose we're sensitive about our provinciality. Barbarian is a big slur as well—anything that implies one is not part of cultured society."

"I see. Well, northerner, it is good to be able to profane one another."

"Yes, it's very manly," Elenya said.

He sighed. "I am trying to be friendly."

"I'm not," she answered.

He frowned. "I wonder how good you would be at a manly sport."

"Oh? Which one?"

"I might challenge you to a wrist-wrestling contest."

Wine exaggerated her guffaw.

"Are you a coward?" Lonal suggested.

She lay down on her stomach and put out her left arm, her strongest. He scuttled into position and locked his palm around hers.

"On the count of three," he said, and began counting.

She pulled immediately. She almost had him down before he tensed. Suddenly his arm felt like iron. He held it there for several moments, while she continued to try to force him down the last few inches. At his leisure, he applied more force and simply laid her arm down.

"I hope a scorpion crawls into your bedroll tonight," she said.

He didn't let her up. The grip was so tight she had to scoot forward in order to relieve the pain. They were now so close their breaths mingled. "You're goading me like a child. What is it you want?"

She angled herself so that the front of her robe hung open, granting Lonal an enticing view of her cleavage. When his glance shifted, she leaned quickly forward . . .

. . . and kissed him.

Lonal's eyes went wide. He sat back, widening the distance between them and watching her carefully. "Why did you do that?" he demanded.

"I wanted to."

"Are you trying to seduce me? I thought you didn't like me."

"I don't."

"Then why?"

"I wanted to see what your reaction would be." She helped herself to the wineskin. "I wondered if you'd still be able to think of me as a man with my legs wrapped around you."

He took the wine away from her. "Perhaps you've had too much of this."

"Perhaps not enough."

He shook his head. "You're too good a fighter to waste as a breeding ewe."

She leaned toward him. He shifted away.

"I think you're tempted," she said. "Am I right?"

He hesitated.

"You're too honest." She smiled. "You want to say no, but you know it wouldn't be true. Why not do what you feel?"

"Men don't love other men," he said firmly.

"I don't believe that."

"There may be those who do, but they are brought to punishment if their habits are made public. A war-leader cannot be so daring. He must be a paragon, or lose the loyalty of his people."

"I am an invented man, and everyone knows it."

"But they obey the edict."

"Especially you," she said hotly.

"The law is a powerful force among my people. I would be stupid not to use it as best I can."

She grabbed the wineskin back from him and turned away. "Leave me alone," she murmured.

He waited several moments, then climbed to his feet and did as she asked.

The celebration lasted for two days, then life resumed its normal routine in the T'lil camp. The new men strutted about enough to get used to their new status, then their seniors began to reteach them humility. Families who had gathered from far ranges for the occasion returned to their herds, leaving a few of their young men. Fumlok told the twins that the latter were preparing to patrol the trade routes. There had been trouble with some of the caravans this season, though he would not specify what kind. They were told to make themselves ready as well.

Urthey waxed, showed its red-and-orange face, withered to a crescent, and disappeared once more. That night, Elenya preceded Alemar to bed. He lingered in the common section, caught up in contemplation. On the whole, life among the T'lil had improved. Their newly instated adulthood had eliminated much of the distrust they had been subject to. They were officially T'lil. Their skills could now be looked on as community assets, and therefore the tribe was more prepared to accept and compliment them. And the ceaseless lessons were behind them.

He could hear activity on the other side of the purdah. The wives had been carrying themselves more proudly in the past few days. The improvement in the status of the twins evidently reflected upon the women.

Eventually Alemar retired to his niche, though he was not sleepy. He could hear soft snores through the cloth that separated his and Elenya's sections. He had only just lain down when the curtain to the common area parted.

Omi stood in the opening, holding a lamp in front of her naked body.

His heart skipped a beat. She knelt down just inside the entrance and waited. The flickering light danced across her body. She was not beautiful. The stretch marks on her abdomen told the story of the children she had borne. Yet Alemar was not repulsed. He saw something alluring in her shyness. She smelled female.

"What is it?" he murmured.

Her breathing contained a hint of panic. "It is the Night of the Wife. Urthey has come and gone one time since the *pulstrall* ended."

"I don't know what that means."

"You are a man now. A wife must serve her husband."

"Oh."

When he failed to say more, Omi bit her lip. "You do not desire me? I am ugly?"

"No, no. It's just unexpected." Alemar almost didn't get the words out. His mouth had turned to cotton.

"I can go away," she said. "It is not demanded of you."

"Do you want to go away?"

"I . . . I want to serve my husband."

Alemar took a deep breath. He stared at the matting, mind in turmoil, trying to ignore Omi's presence. He stayed that way for a long time.

When he glanced up, Omi was trembling. Tears welled on her eyelashes as she turned to go.

Tears did not come easily to Zyraii faces, not even those of the women. As she reached for the curtain, his paralysis vanished. *"Na,"* he said.

Omi stopped, automatically obedient. Timorously, she placed the lamp to the side and crawled closer to Alemar. He frowned when she paused.

"What's wrong?"

"We didn't know what to do," Omi said slowly. "We needed to ask you. Your brother—Peyri will go to him later if he wishes. What is correct?"

Alemar smiled. "Tell Peyri to stay where she is. My 'brother' will not be offended. I will explain things in the morning."

Omi suddenly beamed. She almost pranced out of the niche, disappeared behind the purdah, and popped back into sight happier than Alemar had ever seen her.

"We try always to be good wives, but some things are easier than others," Omi explained, snuggling into Alemar's bedroll as he lifted the blankets.

The sensation of a warm body against his seemed foreign. Omi scooted against him and lay on her back, eyes shyly downcast. Alemar was on his side. At first, he only stared at her—at the crinkles of her nipples, the pattern of her body hair. Finally he reached out and cupped one of her breasts.

It was soft, a membrane of fluid, mobile and yielding to the touch, not firm and definite of shape as he had expected. It seemed odd to find such a pliant spot floating on such hard, prominent ribs. And it was cool, unlike the rest of her torso. He held it until it warmed under his palm.

She stroked his side, callused hands surprisingly gentle. She was looking at him now, searching his face. It was his turn to avert his glance. He felt terribly young. He was as exposed as he had been on Dark Night. The scab was gone now, but he was still *changed,* and it had stolen his confidence.

Omi realized what was happening. She uttered a short laugh, the first compassionate laugh he had heard in this land, sweet enough to assauge his nervousness. She made him lie back, and gently proved to him that some things were the same as before.

XXII

Her father had left for the main house only a minute before Lerina heard a knock on the door. He must have forgotten something. Then why the knock? She glanced out one of the windows and saw the silhouette of a man. She couldn't make out his features, but she didn't need to. She rushed to fling open the door.

He was dressed in black seal hide, the uniform of an Elandri diver, his hair still tousled from his swim. He was more handsome than she had remembered. She stared. He did likewise, a long time straight at her, then at the baby at her breast.

"I waited to name them," she said. "I wanted you to be here to help me choose."

He took the baby from her and cradled it. It protested. "Ssssh," he told it. "You may never see your father again. Have some respect." To their delight, the infant obeyed, burbling contentedly and falling asleep in his arms the way newborns will.

"So small," he murmured.

"They didn't feel small coming out." She smiled. "And they're twice as big now as they were then."

"Is this the boy?"

"No, the girl. I was considering calling her Elenya, after my mother."

"A good name. How about Alemar for the son, both for my own father and my famous ancestor, the Dragonslayer? At least he will bear some mark of his heritage."

Lerina's eyes went wide. "You weren't joking—you *are* the king of Elandris!"

He chuckled. "No." He suddenly realized where they were and entered the cottage. Lerina closed the door. "I am a very distant cousin of King Pranter, so far that were I not royalty, no one would have bothered to calculate the relationship."

She raised the baby boy out of its cradle and brought him forward. "But you were worth a healing spell."

"Not for that reason, exactly. Any of the Blood who can make the talismans of Alemar work—the belt in my case—is looked after by the king."

"The talismans?"

"We have a great deal to discuss," he said. "How long until your father returns?"

She knew then that he was here only for the night at most. But by heaven, she would make the most of the hours they had.

Lord Dran had apparently been contentedly asleep. He shuffled into the great hall of Garthmorron Hold, Lerina in the lead. Dran was a stout man. The gray in his voluminous beard made him appear almost elderly, though Keron knew him to be just over forty.

Outside an owl screeched. Mice rustled under the floor. It was that hour when one's own breathing sounds like a gale. The light came from a few candles, supplemented by the nearly dead embers in the fireplace, just enough to define the carvings, brasswork, tapestries, and paintings that decorated the walls.

"I'm sorry to disturb your rest, my lord," Keron said. "It was important to talk to you when no others could hear."

Dran looked askance at Lerina, then to the quiet figure of Cosufier Elb-Aratule, who waited in the background near the hearth, then back to Keron. "Just who are you, sir?"

"I am Keron Olendim, admiral of the northern fleet of royal Elandris. I am the father of Lerina's twins."

The sleepiness vanished from the lord of Garthmorron's eyes. "You are a bold man to come here. What is to stop me from rousing my household?"

"Nothing," Keron answered seriously. "Though capturing or killing me might take more than you imagine. I believe you will be well satisfied to have heard me out, however."

Dran turned to his gamekeeper. "Cosufier?"

"Hear him," Lerina's father said simply.

Dran sank into one of his sumptuous sofas. "Very well, then. I'm listening."

Keron produced a pouch and inverted it. He caught the amath pearl as it rolled out, and lifted it up for Dran to see.

"Take it. Examine it."

Dran's hands trembled as he reached for it. Cradling it carefully, he placed it next to the candle and peered at the iridescent surface for a full minute.

"This is real," he whispered.

"And it is yours," Keron said. "Assuming, of course, you agree to my plan."

Dran sat up straight. "You'll not bribe me into your war, sir. We've suffered enough disruption of trade. Garthmorron is neutral."

"The war may force you into a decision of one sort or another before too many years," Keron said. "But I respect your position. I am not suggesting a political alliance. This is a personal matter."

"Go on," Dran said, suspicion evident, though he kept a paternal grip on the pearl.

"You lost your wife and son a number of years ago, and have not been inclined to remarry. Garthmorron is at present without an heir."

"That is correct."

Lerina had taken a seat next to Keron, who put his arm around her. "I cannot stay here to care for my children. I am married, with sons and daughters, and an important station in Elandris. Soon, I suspect, my duties will not even allow me to return to Cilendri waters at all. I have two choices. I can be separated from Lerina and our offspring, or take them with me."

"And I would go," Lerina interjected.

Keron's expression was bittersweet. "It hinges on you, Lord Dran. You see, these children are of the Blood. They are the descendants of Alemar Dragonslayer. As such, they have potentials and a heritage which must not be wasted. I would gladly take them to Elandris, and endure the mutters behind my back, and will if necessary to ensure that, should they be the ones to remanifest the great wizard's full power, they will be properly trained to apply those talents to our efforts against Gloroc. But I prefer not to do so. In Elandris, they would be targets. In the last decade, Gloroc has begun to systematically assassinate any who carry Alemar's blood. He has already succeeded in killing two of my children—one of them a girl child of four years." His voice became husky.

"You want to hide them here," Dran said.

"Yes. If the Dragon doesn't know about little Alemar and

Elenya, he can't hurt them. At the moment, only we in this room, and two of my most trusted men, know of their origins. I will not even tell the king unless it seems necessary. It is my wish that no one else learn of them. Even the children themselves must not be told until they are of such an age that their discretion may be trusted."

"What do you want from me?"

"To adopt the twins as your heirs. They will grow up with the amenities of landed gentry, and it will not seem unusual when they are provided with special education and training. I will send one of the men I spoke of earlier to look after them, and teach them what they will need to know. Raise them well, and our pact will be fulfilled. You need not actually leave the estate to them, if that is disagreeable to you, nor do you need to cater to us royalists in commerce or military dealings. For this you will receive the pearl, which as you can see is worth as much as your entire hold, and a generous yearly stipend."

Dran stroked the pearl. "Surely you realize that I could never convert this into cash?"

"It is a token, Lord Dran. If I thought you could be bought, I would never have made this offer. You would be just as likely to sell me out to Gloroc."

"That is true. At the same time, by helping you I am opening myself up to the Dragon's retribution."

"Yes. You are."

Suddenly Dran smiled. "The Frog is getting too bold. I would enjoy putting a thorn in his side."

"Then we are agreed?"

"I have spent too much time without an heir. Why not have two?"

"Tongues may wag," Lerina said. "Even though you were nowhere near when the children were conceived."

"Scandal doesn't seem to have disturbed you," Dran said good-naturedly. "If anything, I would consider such gossip a compliment to my virility. Though my chamberlain will be aghast."

"Poor Uncle Ossatch," Lerina murmured.

"Oh, he'll be glad to see his great-nephew and niece looked after," Dran declared, and turned to Keron. "When will you send your man?"

"As soon as I return to the capital."

• • •

Musicians lifted conch shells to their lips and began the dirge. The pallbearers climbed the steps of the dais, the first of them closing the casket lid. They waited for the signal from Keron, then lifted their burden and followed the admiral from the great, royal Hall of Final Respects. No burial at sea for this man. That ritual was respectable enough for commoners, but Obo of Mirien had been one of the greatest servants of King Pranter, a fine and capable wizard, and deserved interment within the walls of the Lesser Mausoleum.

Keron strode impassively between the ranks of grievers, many of them from the royal houses of Firsthold, capital of Elandris. Obo's reputation had reached many ears, though the man himself had forever hidden in the background of court life—his face would not have been recognized by most of those present. In fact, Keron mused cynically, the turnout would never have been this large had not the king himself briefly come to pay his respects. To those seeking to curry favor, the funeral had become the place to be.

They passed the Greater Mausoleum, its marble columns stretching almost to the city dome. Perhaps one day Keron would himself be brought to that place, attired in finery as magnificent as that he wore today, to join the ranks of the Blood who had lived and died since Alemar Dragonslayer had built this, the first of his cities beneath the sea. At the Lesser Mausoleum, the Keeper of the Tomb was waiting.

Keron saluted the old man. "I give to you this servant of the king," he said ritually.

"What name shall be entered in the Record of the Dead?"

"Obo Iremshan, son of Ibo and Phelopeen."

"Let him pass, and find his place among the generations who have labored for the House of Olendim."

The pallbearers approached the threshold, which they did not cross. An equal number of the Keeper's assistants received the coffin as it came forward. They carried it inside, to the niche within which it would be deposited and sealed, marked by a plate of brass containing Obo's name, age, rank, and the nature of the tasks he had accomplished for the rulers of Elandris.

It was done. Keron turned, thanked the pallbearers, and ambled down the steps, a dark expression tainting his features. The crowd had already largely dispersed. Lady Nanth joined him as he reached street level. He held her hand and walked with her toward the vast palace.

"My condolences, Admiral," stated Lord D'rul, a former naval commander who had served with Keron's father. "And congratulations on your promotion."

Keron thanked the man tersely and quickly excused himself. He could read D'rul's motives. Upon his return to the capital, Keron had found himself raised not simply to rear admiral in charge of the northern fleet, but admiral of the entire navy, following the recent assassination of one of his cousins. It was obvious that Keron was very much in the king's favor. Furthermore, incautious tongues had been wagging, and most at court suspected—correctly so—that Keron possessed one of the talismans of Alemar Dragonslayer. So he was now the object of courtiers and hangers-on. All the bilge of the empire wanted to be his friend.

"He was a good man," Nanth said of the deceased. "It was so sudden. He seemed in good health only last week."

"Obo was old. I am relieved he got to die of natural causes."

"He healed so many. He couldn't save himself, though."

"He only worked with wounds. The Lesser Art, he called it. Nor do I think he wanted to thwart nature."

"I will miss him."

"So will I," Keron stated emphatically.

Nanth and he seldom talked about important matters. She would obviously have liked to continue, but they had reached the palace door that would take Keron to his offices. "I have business to attend to, my lady. Obo left some final wishes. I will see you at home soon."

She opened her mouth, but he had turned the corner before she could protest. He cringed a little at his gruffness, but in truth he couldn't enjoy Nanth's company until the matter on his conscience was cleared.

He greeted his secretaries and locked himself within his sanctum. He found a cup of hot tea waiting for him. He raised it up to toast the bald figure on the other side of the room.

"Now you are dead, and are free to serve me," Keron said.

Obo smiled and raised his own cup. "And a fine retirement it will be, I hope. The tension in this city could be cut with a kitchen knife. Too much for this tired old frame. If I had stayed much longer, I would have died in truth."

"Your need and mine have come to terms," Keron said. "It gives me hope, master wizard. Teach my children well."

"I will," Obo said seriously. "You will be proud of them."

"If I ever see them again," Keron murmured. As full admiral, no doubt he would be unable to leave the capital for a decade or more. "Give my love . . ." He choked on the phrase.

"I will," Obo said kindly. "She will understand, if she's half the woman you've described. She'll realize that all men have their duty."

"I forgot mine, for a month," Keron said, in a haunted tone of voice. "Now I'll have to pay for that lapse the rest of my life."

In a voice more fatherly than he had ever heard Obo use, the wizard said, "Do not blame yourself. If not for the Dragon, you could have chosen another path. Blame Gloroc. It is he who warps the lives of every man in the kingdom."

Blame the Dragon he would. But it wouldn't be enough. Keron had known of his lack of choice before he had met Lerina, and had still loved her. If the fates willed it, he might have his vengeance on Gloroc one day, but he could never erase the fact that he had cruelly toyed with the life of an innocent young woman.

XXIII

Ret a Jheheph was a rich man. Half the wagons in the caravan belonged to him; the other half to the traders who had paid his stiff fees. If he were so inclined, he could ride within his own personal coach, cushioned in velvet and canopied in fine Cilendri silk. Furthermore, where other merchants endured the journey from Azurajen to Surudain without the comfort of their wives' company, Jheheph always brought at least five of his favorite concubines, and provided each with accommodations nearly as luxurious as his own. The oeikani beneath his saddle was of the most exclusive, thoroughbred stock. Ret a Jheheph was used to having his way.

A man was blocking the path of his caravan.

The stranger was alone, waiting atop a hardy desert oeikani, in the center of the wide, shallow rut through which the wagons were travelling. Ret a Jheheph recognized the white garb. He smiled. He had been expecting this.

The Zyraii rider maintained his position, though the caravan's pace did not slacken. As the gap between him and the lead wagon shrank, the assistant caravan master looked questioningly at Jheheph.

"Continue on," he commanded.

Finally, when the caravan was only a few dozen yards away, the Zyraii began walking his animal backward. Jheheph shrugged. They were close enough. He signalled a halt.

Jheheph himself rode to the head of the line, a slave beside him with a broad feather fan to ease the effects of the sun. He waited casually on his thoroughbred. Soon another slave brought a platter of dates. Jheheph ate one very slowly, and spat the pit out in the direction of the Zyraii.

"You are in the way, Po-no-pha."

"I am Shigmur of the T'lil," the rider replied. "You are entering my tribe's land."

"So?"

"Tribute is required."

Jheheph smiled. "Surely you are mistaken. The Alyr and the Olot took no tribute."

"We are not Alyr or Olot. Pay the tithe, or you may not cross our land."

Jheheph raised his hand. Abruptly, two archers hidden in the lead wagon stood up and fired arrows.

The Zyraii ducked to the side. One of the shafts missed entirely, the other caught him in the veil. He was moving instantly. The archers fired again, but the rider weaved out of the way. By the third set of shots, he had gained speed and was soon out of range.

"Too bad," Jheheph muttered.

"Do we chase him?" the assistant master asked.

"No. We'll be seeing him again."

R'lar broke the arrow and pulled it out of Shigmur's cheek. It was a clean wound, in through the mouth and out the side of his face. All things considered, it was as minor an injury as he could have hoped for. Granyet brought a bandage.

"That was a true feat of *haiya!*" R'lar exclaimed.

Others added their congratulations. Alemar and Elenya hid their own incredulousness. Even Lonal, up at the crest of the hill with the lookouts, was gazing at Shigmur with envy.

No wonder the Zyraii people had a reputation for being fierce.

The twins climbed up to the vantage point. The caravan was emerging from a series of low, weather-pocked hills and was now threading its way west, to the rugged terrain in which the Zyraii were hidden, across the small flatland that marked the border of T'lil territory, where Shigmur had issued his challenge. This was the main trade route between Azurajen and Surudain.

"Where is the end of it?" Elenya asked, trying to determine where the line of wagons stopped. "Are they all this big?"

"No," Lonal answered. "This is the largest I have seen."

They waited. Finally the tail end reached the valley floor. In the meantime, the lead wagons reined up. Their passengers climbed out and began setting up camp, though it was still early in the afternoon.

"They won't dare the hills at night," Lonal deduced.

"It was as the Olot and the Alyr told us," one of the seconds said. "They have no intention of paying us our rightful tithe."

"They smell the fort two days behind them, and it gives them confidence," Lonal said.

"What can you do about it?" Alemar asked.

"We will fight."

"What?" Elenya exclaimed. "Where are you going to get the warriors? Can't you see how many men-at-arms are riding next to those wagons?"

"It is a matter of honor. They have ignored our rights. We can't let the precedent be set. The T'lil is the last tribe on this route with the might to challenge them. We'll attack tonight."

Ret a Jheheph sent away his concubine. He would have no women tonight. He was waiting for a different kind of excitement. He sucked his pipe and waited, in a soft chair, staring out at the moonlit terrain.

He could almost hear the minds of the barbarians. He sniggered. They would not have any ideas that he had not already anticipated.

Not far away, three men waited next to a dim lantern. At first glance, one would not say that they resembled each other. The first was obese, with a heavy black beard and clothing similar to a guard. The second was gaunt and balding, wearing gauzy, effeminate robes. The third was small, wrinkled, and very brown, dressed in only a loin clout and headband. Nevertheless, they were the same in one respect.

They all waited, Jheheph with the calm of the man whose money has always bought him what he wanted, the three others with the vigilant attitude of craftsmen called upon to perform their very best work.

Suddenly the sentries began to shout.

In the muted light of the moons, Jheheph could see a line of shadowy, four-legged shapes bearing toward the caravan from all directions. Within a few moments, he could hear the beat of oeikani hooves.

The small brown man cried out and pointed at the sky.

For a moment, it seemed as if stars were falling. Then the streaks became fire arrows, which landed between and upon the wagons and coaches. The sentries ducked behind cover and wielded their own bows, sighting their targets whenever riders lit fresh arrows.

Just as he had predicted; Jheheph smiled.

Women began pouring out of the wagons and tents, collecting in the center of the encampment, out in the open. They knew the Zyraii code would save them from harm—as long as they stayed out of the battle and out of the way. Jheheph's concubines lorded it over the slave girls.

Most of the fire arrows did no damage. Some struck the dust, some bounced off the starched hides placed on the wagons specifically to fend off such attacks, others changed direction at the last instant and fell wide. The three men by the lantern concentrated, keeping their eyes on the sky, focused on each new volley.

A few wagons were not so lucky. Their owners rushed to try and smother the flames with blankets or sand. But their efforts were often futile; the Zyraii had treated their missiles with oil. Soon several wagons became bonfires.

None of Jheheph's own were touched, however. He sucked another lungful from his pipe, enjoying the narcotic buzz, amused by the frantic activity around him. After all, the less merchandise that arrived in Surudain, the more valuable the remaining goods would be. And those would be his.

The three men were sweating now, though they had never risen from their positions. They were stretching their skills to the limit. A pity, thought Jheheph. Good sorcerers were scarce in the Eastern Deserts. Moreover, those with real talent were seldom for hire; they seemed to have their own methods of making themselves rich. But these would do. If he could make it through the Zyraii web just once without being forced to pay the tithe, all the merchants of the Sea of Azu would flock to be part of his caravans.

The twins answered Lonal's summons and joined him on the hilltop from which he had chosen to observe the battle. They could see fires burning below them, but not nearly as many as there should have been.

"They are using sorcery," Lonal stated.

Alemar nodded. "They are creating wards around the wagons. Certain magicians have the talent."

"Whatever it is, it's effective. I need your help."

Alemar exchanged glances with Elenya. They had been expecting this, ever since they had first detected the spells. They had agreed upon an answer.

"No."

Lonal scowled. "You mean you don't have the skill?"

"No, we could probably do something. We simply don't wish to."

"I see," the war-leader said flatly. "You were willing to fight the Buyul."

"We had no choice. They attacked us."

"You're trying my patience. If you won't be warriors, you might as well stay in camp and be shepherds."

"If necessary," Alemar said.

Lonal turned toward Elenya and met the same determined refusal in her expression.

"To hell with you, then," Lonal told them. "We will fight without your help."

As Shigmur's oeikani deftly avoided a shrub, the war-second realized how much easier it was to see his surroundings. He glanced to the horizon. Motherworld had risen. He lit one more arrow and let it fly, then retreated out of bowshot. The rest of the Zyraii riders did the same.

The caravan had suffered, but not greatly. Shigmur had seen some of his own shots swing wide, and knew that his tribe's markmanship was not to blame. He saw several Zyraii bodies on the ground nearer the wagons, and even more dead oeikani. The archers were good. Furthermore, the night had never become properly dark. Serpent Moon and Urthey had not set, and now Motherworld was up, bright and more than half-full, with the Sister soon to follow. Not only would they be easier targets now, but he could see some of the caravan guards mounting their oeikani in order to chase them. It was at this point Lonal had planned the retreat.

Shigmur waited for the horn notes from the hills. Soon they came. Carry on, they said.

So be it. Shigmur lifted out another arrow, making sure he got none of the oil on his hands, and reached for his striker. The T'lil began to close in again.

Why didn't they stop? Jheheph was no longer amused. The barbarians had lost the advantage of the dark. His own mercenaries were out among them now, breaking their formation. Yet the fire arrows kept falling. Suddenly, Jheheph jumped to his feet.

"That's one of *my* wagons!" he yelled. His slaves tried to snuff the blaze, but it got away from them. A cargo of rare birds and their cages began to go up in smoke.

The caravan master ran over to the sorcerers. "Do something!" he cried.

The thin, effeminate man was startled. The arrow he was warding struck the coach of one of Jheheph's concubines. Jheheph was incensed.

"My lord," the small brown man said firmly, "do not interrupt us."

Jheheph nearly struck the man for his temerity, before he saw that his threats would only worsen the sorcerers' performance. Jheheph left them alone, turning his anger once more toward the Zyraii riders.

He saw one of the barbarians fall off his animal. Elsewhere, two of his guards were hit by demonblades. His side was suffering casualties, but Jheheph was confident that the odds were in his favor. The Zyraii could not harm the wagons without coming within range of the well-protected archers. Now the Sister was beginning to rise, and it would soon be almost as light as daytime.

He did not see the single Zyraii bearing down on him until almost the last moment. The white-robed warrior burst through the outer line of wagons, whipping his wounded oeikani to a frenzy of speed. Jheheph felt his heart quail, but in another instant his personal guards had collected between him and the Zyraii, pulling out swords and nocking arrows. The rider changed direction. Only then did Jheheph see the torch in the man's hand.

"Stop that man!" he shouted.

Many tried, but the wagons and other guards were often in the way, and the Zyraii was a phenomenal rider. Though both man and oeikani had been struck more than once, their agility had spared them fatal blows. Horror-stricken, Jheheph saw the torch flung into the very wagon he wanted most to save.

"My carpets!" he screamed, as a fortune in fine weaving caught fire.

He was so aghast that he barely noted the rider's escape. The man was not so lucky on the way out. Once clear of the caravan, he presented an open target. They failed to stop him, but his back fairly bristled with wood and feathers by the time he won clear.

Something in the way the rider weaved away from the arrows, as well as his size, jogged Jheheph's memory.

Two young Po-no-pha found Shigmur beside his dead oeikani and brought him back to camp. He was unconscious, but momentarily still alive.

Lonal and the twins arrived simultaneously. The war-leader leaned over Shigmur. The war-second's clothing was drenched in blood, his skin white. He still had seven arrows in him; it was hard to say how many others might have struck him.

Lonal looked up angrily. "This might have been avoided had you chosen to help."

Alemar squatted down and touched Shigmur's back. His fingers came away bloody. "Get me water," he told Elenya calmly. She ran to comply.

"I won't accept responsibility for his death," Alemar said, "but I will for his life."

"He hasn't much of that left," Lonal said.

"I can save him."

Shigmur opened his eyes. He was lying on a blanket under a tarp. It was daylight. Lonal was leaning over him with concern. Yetem was standing behind him. Not far away, Tebec was soundly asleep, looking strangely pale. Many other Po-no-pha were near.

"How are you?" the war-leader asked.

Shigmur wasn't sure. He had fallen unconscious with the certain knowledge that he would not awaken again until the next life. He couldn't tell if this were a dream or if he had simply been reincarnated with extraordinary quickness. He could still feel the places where the arrows had struck. They felt like bruises. He sat up.

"How long has it been?"

"It is early afternoon after the battle," Lonal said.

That did nothing to relieve Shigmur's confusion. "Has there been a Hab-no-ken here?" he asked.

"In a sense," Lonal said, gesturing toward Tebec.

Yetem stepped forward. "Hold out your hands," she said.

He did so. She dropped seven arrowheads into his palms. "I thought you might want those to keep as souvenirs."

"Thank you," he said, wiping the bloodstain off one of them.

"I will do that . . . though I am tempted to send them back where they came from."

"You'll have your chance," Lonal said. "Go back to sleep."

Elenya walked with Lonal a short way from Shigmur's resting place, out of the hearing of the others nearby.

"I, too, would like to thank you," Lonal said. "And I will be sure to tell your brother."

"You're welcome," she said. "I'm curious, though. If you knew there might be a battle, why didn't you bring healers with you?"

"Hab-no-ken do not come at a war-leader's order." He glanced back at the shelter. "Tebec doesn't look good. . . ."

"They'll both be on their feet by morning. My brother will feel weak for a few days, Shigmur for about a month."

"Can they travel?"

"On a litter, yes. Why?"

"Then they can join us at the ambush point. I think Shigmur would want to be there when we confront the caravan."

Ret a Jheheph was in a foul mood. The sorcerers stayed out of his sight, his slaves' bodies smarted from his lash, and the concubine who had presumed to complain about her burned coach had been forced to walk the entire previous day, until the soles of her feet, unused to even the slightest effort, had begun to bleed.

They had not seen the Zyraii. A few of the slaves, seeing the bodies of the slain riders, dared to hope that the barbarians had decided to cut their losses and had permanently retreated, but Jheheph knew this was a fantasy. The desert men were too stubborn for that. Jheheph would have his chance for revenge.

It was near dawn. Motherworld was high, as was the Sister, and the east was pale. The caravan had been travelling for two hours, penetrating the thickest part of the hills through a narrow defile. The guards kept their glances on the boulders and ridges to either side of the road. The pace was brisk; everyone wanted to reach the plain as soon as possible.

Suddenly the lead wagon and team disappeared in a cloud of dust.

Jheheph rode forward, and soon he could make out the trouble. A pit had been dug across the road and concealed.

The wagon and oeikani had fallen within. It was too deep for them to pull out by themselves, forcing the caravan to halt.

Jheheph looked to the slopes even before the shouts rang out. Hundreds of white-robed Zyraii revealed themselves. They were armed with bows. Some of the arrows were already burning. The caravan guards rushed for cover.

The Zyraii did not shoot. The mercenaries, after a sporadic initial volley, realized that the barbarians were deliberately giving away the advantage of surprise, and they stopped short. If this were an ambush, it was a strange one.

Jheheph could not fathom it, either. Either the Zyraii were going to fight, or they weren't. Both sides waited several tense moments, then a single man stood up from a hiding place and walked down to the roadway immediately in front of the trench.

"Don't shoot," Jheheph ordered his men. His curiosity was aroused.

The man in the road stared straight at Jheheph. "I've come to give you another chance," he said.

Jheheph's jaw dropped. He recognized the voice. It was the same Zyraii who had first confronted them two days before, who—so Jheheph had believed—had also set fire to his precious carpets. But surely it was a trick; that man must have died of his wounds.

As if reading the caravan master's mind, the Po-no-pha untied his upper robes and removed them. When he turned his back, several of the watchers in the caravan gasped. Jheheph stared at the scars and began to shake.

The man turned back. "I ask again—pay the tribute. If not, we will fight again. As you can see, the sons of T'lil are not easy to kill." He put his garment back on and stood there, waiting.

Jheheph licked his lips nervously. He called the small brown wizard to him. "What is this sorcery?" he demanded.

The sorcerer shrugged. "How should I know? I make wards, that's all."

Jheheph stared at the Zyraii, and at the others up the slopes, and at the spot in line where his carpet wagon should have been. He could fight. He could have his slaves fill in the pit, he could send his mercenaries up into the rocks. They still outnumbered the barbarians. They could win. If he hadn't felt confident of that fact, he would not have challenged the T'lil in their own territory.

But—was it worth the loss of cargo like his carpets or his birds? The wealth he had with him now, though only a small part of his fortune, was still staggering. It would serve no one if turned to ash. He had depended too much upon minor magicians. And what good were the best mercenaries against warriors who could rise from the dead?

He called his quartermaster to him. The words nearly choked him; he uttered them only through clenched teeth:

"Pay them."

XXIV

As the Po-na-pha returned to the main T'lil camp in the pastures of the Ahloorm Basin, Omi ran frantically out to meet the twins at the corrals.

"Come quickly," she said.

"What's wrong?" Alemar asked.

"It's Rol."

They left their oeikani with another Po-na-pha and hurried back to their tent. Omi ran to the partition and lifted the cloth, beckoning them into the women's section. The twins knew it was serious. This was the first time the wives had ignored the sanctity of the purdah. Peyri was stooped over Rol, who lay stiffly on his mat, a feverish sudor on his brow. He grimaced and held his lower belly.

Meyr and Sesheer got out of the way, and immediately Alemar was kneeling next to the boy, face grim.

"What is it?" he asked.

"I don't know," Peyri said. Her tone surprised Alemar. There was no fear in it, only the resigned attitude of someone who has lost all hope. "It was the same with his older brother."

Alemar drew back the thin sheet and examined Rol. The boy, who in times past had shrunk away from any contact with his foster father, seemed too deep in pain to care. Alemar noticed the tautness of Rol's abdominal muscles and pressed, once, lightly, on the right side above the pelvic bone. Rol cried out.

"Pus gut," he said, in Cilendri. The words were an echo from the past. Behind his heart, he felt a sore, kicked feeling, like that he had felt as a child when ridiculed by his companions or cheated of a special treat. But this was an adult hurt, not capable of being put from his mind like those of younger days.

Elenya put a hand on his shoulder. He took it within his own. "Are you certain?" she asked gently.

"Just like *her,"* he said hoarsely.

The twins felt the women watching, understanding neither the reasons for their reaction nor the foreign language. Alemar felt an old, useless anger grow, and was determined that—this time—he would do something to stop it.

"Where can I find a healer?" he demanded abruptly. "A Hab-no-ken?"

Peyri only seemed more despondent. Finally Omi replied, "Rol is only a boy. Hab-no-ken are not summoned to heal a boy."

This made him more angry. "What is the use of healers if they won't heal?"

Omi shrugged—a Zyraii woman's shrug. "Rol is not important enough. Lonal would have to send Po-na-pha many leagues."

"I will go."

"Lonal will not let you," Peyri said with certainty.

"We'll see," Alemar said tartly.

"I thought *you* were a healer," Lonal said.

"Of wounds and injuries," Alemar answered. "I can do nothing for Rol. A Hab-no-ken must be brought."

"No," Lonal said.

"Why not?"

"He is only a child. Should I waste the time of warriors on his behalf? The nearest Hab-no-ken is in the hills." He indicated the rugged terrain to the west. "It is a day's ride there, and another back."

"No one would 'waste time' but me."

"Do you think I would let you go alone?" Lonal sighed as a parent would when a child is being petulant. "Have you no pride? A man should not be frightened that God has chosen to test his son."

"Next year, Rol will be one of your warriors. Would you abandon him then?"

"That is not the issue. What use is sickness, if not to weed out the weak? What better way for a warrior to play the Bu, than with nothing between himself and fate?"

Alemar showed teeth. "Should I unheal Shigmur, then?"

Lonal shook his head. "I am not arguing that the healers' work is not good. But if we depend on them, we will lose the cutting edge that the desert demands. Rol will have to wait until a healer visits the camp of his own accord."

"That may be too late."

"It is all I will offer."

"I'll duel you," Alemar said.

Lonal stopped. None of the others present spoke.

"If I win, you'll let me go. If you win, I'll do as you say," Alemar continued.

Lonal pursed his lips, scanning the surroundings. R'lar and Shigmur stood near him. Elenya was near her brother, with their wives cowering in the background. Several children played not far away. "The boy is not even your blood kin," he told Alemar.

"Choose your weapon." Alemar's hand wavered near the pommel of his saber.

But Lonal did not move. The two men stared at one another. Soon even the children became silent and began to pay attention to the confrontation. A locust hopped noisily between the two men.

Abruptly, Shigmur stepped forward. "I will go with him, war-leader."

Both Alemar and Lonal looked at the war-second in surprise. Alemar noticed the shift in Lonal's mood and tried to control the sweating of his palms and the slight quiver of his fingers. The pommel was hard and warm.

Finally Lonal shrugged. "According to reports, Hab-no-ken has been spending his Retreat near the spring of Triple Spires." The war-leader pointed again to the western horizon. "Maybe you will find him there."

Alemar blinked. "I can go?"

"It seems to matter to you, far more than a duel matters to me." Lonal turned to Shigmur. "Take Zhanee and go with him. Be back within three days."

"Thank you," Alemar said.

"Don't. You have no guarantee that the healer has finished his meditations. He may choose not to come. The Hab-no-ken are not bound to cure all the ills of the world. But I'll allow you the chance. Remember it."

"I am surprised," Shigmur said, the bounce of the saddle warbling his words.

"Why?" Alemar asked, eyes riveted forward, though the

hills that defined the western boundary of the Ahloorm Basin were still hazy and purple in the distance, and the configuration called Triple Spires would not be visible for many hours.

"Since he came of age, Lonal has not lost a duel. It has been two years since anyone in the camp challenged him to the *ju-moh-kai*. I thought he would fight you, just for the fun of it."

A small chill flowed down Alemar's spine, though if it had been necessary, he would not have hesitated to fight. The son of Keron Olendim was no petty swordplayer.

They veered away from a stand of *elbraksh*. Zhanee skirted the far side of the brush, his short bow strung, alert for game, leaving them alone for a moment. "I want to thank you for stepping in when you did," Alemar said.

"I owed you that," Shigmur said. "But I don't believe it had anything to do with Lonal's decision."

"No?" Alemar listened more carefully. Though he had come to know Shigmur better than any of the T'lil warriors, the war-second had always been tight-lipped about his own opinions.

"Lonal needs your cooperation. I think he understands now that he can't force it out of you. This trip is his way of showing you that he can be flexible."

"That would be nice." A sand-runner burst out of hiding nearby, snapped up an insect, and was gone again. "Why is it that he is so driven?"

Shigmur wiped the sweat off of his brow and readjusted his cowl. "Lonal is weighed down by his destiny." He sighed. "He bears the legacy of his father. I do not envy him the burden."

"Who was his father?"

"Joren," Shigmur said reverently.

"A great man?"

"He was a war-leader such as the T'lil have not produced in three centuries, though on the surface he seemed a simple man. He had faith in God's goodwill, a ready laugh at the antics of children. You'd never catch him lost in somber thought like you do Lonal. But when it comes to battle, he could pluck a hair off the balls of a rival war-leader's oeikani before the other was aware that his camp was being raided. He made the name of the T'lil one to be respected. None would attack our caravan when he was present. The T'lil nation could have doubled in size if he had wished it, but he believed in peace with our brothers born of Cadra. He saved his enmity for the traders. When the men of Azurajen came to build a fort at the pass of Zyraii-ni-Zyraii, Joren was there to stop them. He held them at bay for two weeks, and would have won the battle altogether had he not been betrayed by the Buyul and the Fanke. All Zyraii sings of that last stand, and therefore expectations are laid on the son of Joren."

"Then the fort was built. Is it still there?"

"Stronger each year. They call it Xurosh. Many Zyraii warriors have died trying to raze it—not only the T'lil, but the Alyr, the Fanke, the Buyul. Most especially the Olot, in whose territory it was built. They stood by Joren and fell next to the cream of the T'lil. Also, there is another trade route, from Palura to Nyriya, through the lands of the Olot, Hapt, Aikal, and Zainee tribes. The traders of Palura want to build another fort along there. If they succeed, Zyraii control of the desert may be lost. It is critical that we destroy Xurosh."

Alemar recalled the maps he had studied in his youth. The cause of strife was plain. The fertile Azu region had only one outlet to the wealth of the old kingdoms—through Zyraii.

"I wonder what I would do in Lonal's place," Alemar said sometime later. "I know what it means to live in a father's shadow."

Alemar dumped out the scorpion before he put on his boot. He stood, his shadow a long, thin patch of darkness extending toward the desiccated hills ahead. Shigmur and Zhanee were breaking down the simple camp they had made the evening before.

"See?" Shigmur said of the badlands. "Much better to hunt this terrain in the light. As it is we'll have to pray the oeikani don't twist their ankles."

Alemar agreed, though he regretted the delay. He had, however, been thankful for the rest. He had only recently recovered from the healing. Shigmur no doubt was worse off. He urged them to move quickly, and soon they were riding toward the three thin rock spires that dominated the nearby landscape.

Shigmur led them to the spring in a shady nullah on the south side of the spires. It was a permanent water hole, blessed with two full-grown whitedown trees, seldom seen away from the river. The trees had just begun to shed. Alemar watched the puffs settle on the surface of the pool, each tiny black seed carried windward on dozens of white, hairlike filaments. The seeds might travel a hundred leagues before finding a rooting place with enough water to sustain an adult tree.

"The spoor of a man," Shigmur announced as he stooped over a patch of mud. "Many traces, all made by the same pair of feet, over many days."

The three men checked for other signs while the oeikani filled their seemingly bottomless reservoirs with the spring water. They found remnants of old meals, charcoal, more footprints.

"Where is he?" Alemar demanded.

Shigmur shrugged. "Obviously his permanent camp is not here. We can wait. He may need to come for water soon."

"Let Zhanee stay. We can split up and search the area."

Shigmur bowed his head. "No. It's better we stay together."

Alemar paused. "You still don't trust me, do you?"

"Lonal would have my manhood if I lost you."

"I'm hardly going to run away with Yetem still back in the camp."

"I know. That's why Lonal let you come, with only two Po-no-pha to accompany you."

"What if I said I would duel you?" Alemar asked.

"I would laugh," Shigmur said.

Alemar popped his knuckles one by one. "All right, then—we stay together. But I can't just sit and wait. You know something of this area—where else would a man be likely to be found?"

Shigmur mulled it over while he filled his waterbag. "Well, I might look for an ordinary man along the game trails or at a salt flat. Since we are seeking a Hab-no-ken, perhaps we should climb the spires."

"Why?"

"Some of them . . . like to fly."

"They like to what?" Alemar was certain his Zyraii was deficient.

"They fly through the air—gliding like a vulture."

Alemar decided that the Po-no-pha was not joking. "Just how do they manage this?"

"I have only seen it once. They jump from a high place, like the spires, inside a cage of light wood. The cage hangs from a great cloth canopy. The winds carry them many miles."

Alemar looked at the imposing height of the nearest spire. "I hope I live to see this miracle," he announced.

• • •

He got his wish. Two hours later, as they negotiated the convoluted trail up the spire, Shigmur suddenly reined in and pointed skyward.

"Look!"

A brilliant triangle of green had separated from the upper reaches of the rock, passing far overhead without sound. From that distance, the man and the apparatus that supported him looked like dark specks on the cloth. It flew well.

"That must be him," Shigmur said.

Alemar's hope sank. The glider sped in moments over badland terrain that would take men on oeikani-back hours to cover. Yet he saw little choice but to follow.

"Come on," he said sourly, "let's try to find him when he lands."

They had lost him. Alemar was sure of it. They had only been able to track the glider for a few minutes, and it had taken half the day to reach the point where, as best they could determine, it had landed. Now the sun was descending, and despite searching through the heat of noon, they had found no trace of the contraption or the man who allegedly flew inside it.

They meandered down a shallow gorge, the clop of their oeikani hooves echoing repeatedly from one side to the other. While Shigmur and Zhanee continued on, Alemar stopped, overcome by the sensation that he was being watched.

He jerked his head suddenly toward a glut of boulders to his left. There, a man stood so still that, though he was in plain sight, he was difficult to see, in spite of the bright green robes he wore and the wide straw hat on his head. Even as Alemar stared, the figure seemed to fade in and out. Finally the young Cilendri noticed the pulse coming from his amulet.

Of course. The man was exerting a simple spell of concealment.

The man in green realized the ineffectiveness of his magic. It abruptly ceased. The stranger called out to the two Zyraii, who had not yet noticed that their companion was no longer with them.

"May I help you?" he shouted.

Shigmur and Zhanee spun in their saddles. The war-second

was the first to regain his composure. "Our apologies for disturbing you, holy one. We seek a boon."

"I am on Retreat," he said. The words weighed like stones on Alemar's hope. "What do you need of me?"

Shigmur nodded toward Alemar. "It is best for him to explain."

The Hab-no-ken shifted his glance. Alemar had not seen eyes with such . . . *extra* depth since the last time he had seen Obo. The man was about fifty, though that was hard to tell for certain. The desert wore out bodies early. If his green robes—the first of that color Alemar had seen in Zyraii—seemed incongruous, so did the kindness of his face. Alemar had never thought to see that emotion so firmly set in any Zyraii countenance. He was reminded of Rictane, Lord Dran's old stablemaster, who had worn that look at his own wake.

"My . . . son needs a healer. I don't know what to do for him. I need your help."

"You have a strange accent," the Hab-no-ken said. "Where are you from?"

"Cilendrodel."

"Yet you wear the robes of a Po-no-pha. What tribe?"

"The T'lil. T'krt clan."

"Our war-leader adopted him by rite of *niutap,*" Shigmur explained.

"Indeed?" The healer seemed increasingly intrigued. Alemar had the unnerving sensation that the man was looking not so much at him as through him. "This son—did you bring him from Cilendrodel?"

"He is also mine by virtue of *niutap.*"

"Yet when you speak of him, I see a woman in your mind, and a forest."

Alemar jumped.

"Be at peace, Po-no-pha," the healer said reassuringly. "We will have plenty of time to talk." He jumped nimbly down the boulders and lit on a spot between the mounted men. "My name is Gast. As I said, I am on Retreat, and ordinarily I would refuse your summons. But it is not every day I find a man who can see a Hab-no-ken when a Hab-no-ken does not wish to be seen. My rituals can be broken. Let us see what is wrong with this boy of yours."

XXV

Obo found Alemar by the graveside. The boy was kneeling in the forest mulch, gaze locked on the recently turned earth. If he had heard the old wizard approach, he did not show it. Obo remained back among the foliage of the trees, too caught in his own sorrow to offer any words of consolation.

The heavy, bitter shroud of failure settled on his shoulders. Intellectually, Obo knew he was not the cause of Lerina's death, but it was not easy to believe that in his heart. Though Alemar would never say it aloud, Obo could hear the question *Why, if you could save my father, couldn't you save my mother?* It would do no good to remind his young ward that sorcery was not a chosen skill, but the development of talents one might, or might not, be born with, and that Obo, like all wizards, was limited in what types of magic he could perform. That excuse would not change what had happened.

Alemar was virtually a man now, at his full height, strong and black-haired like his father. He had the short but lithe physique so prevalent among the House of Olendim. A fine boy—a fine man. To see him so bereaved dried out Obo's throat, made his arms shudder with pent-up anger at the fates. Of all the trials Alemar could have faced, the death of his mother was the worst. Obo had seldom seen a parent and child more emotionally close. It would be a long time before he recovered.

Elenya had already accepted the tragedy. She was hard, that one, full of her mother's spice and her father's stubbornness. Though she had loved Lerina as deeply as her brother, Obo knew Elenya would find a vent for her outrage—she would blame the world. Alemar would keep it inside, find a way to blame himself. He would have to be watched.

Obo found his own hope in that fact. If he could help the boy through this, that would partially make up for his unsuccessful attempt to help Lerina. Alemar, along with his twin, had shown the marks of the Dragonslayer's power more than any of the dynasty. More than that, he was a good person, of the kind Obo had seen far too seldom within the royal family in Elandris. Obo would not let so much human and sorcerous potential be warped by grief.

The wizard heard a subtle rustling in the dead leaves at the base of the tree next to the grave. At first, Obo could barely make out the tiny, manlike shapes, then they walked into the light. He stayed very still, watching the rythni as they came to Alemar and touched him lightly on the knee. The young man's trance broke. He lifted one of the fairy creatures in his palm.

Obo heard the rythni speak in a shrill, singsong voice. Alemar answered briefly, in the same language.

Obo smiled, and stopped worrying so deeply. The boy had his sister, his grandfather, Lord Dran and his household—too many who cared for his well-being to let him slide into permanent melancholy. And if these were not enough, the rythni would be there, with their laughter and music, special allies that few other humans in Cilendrodel could claim.

Obo watched for a few more moments, then slipped quietly away. The wizard had one pressing task yet to perform, a duty that he would have given a great deal to avoid. He felt very old. He wanted to put it off. But there was no way around it. *He* would have to know.

Obo found parchment and pen, and prepared the letter that would take the news to Elandris.

XXVI

"How is he?" Alemar asked as he dismounted. He and his companions looked as if they had spent the entire day on a forced gallop. Elenya couldn't help but gawk at the outlandish stranger in green, from the weathered hat to the scraggly beard. Her brother had to repeat the question before she answered.

"He's in pain, but alive."

Gast stared equally hard at Elenya as he handed his reins to her. "Yetem, my brother," Alemar said, then introduced the healer.

Gast shook his head in amazement. "You must have played the Bu very strangely in your last life to have been reincarnated in a body like this."

Alemar was already hurrying toward the tent. Gast followed.

Elenya stood, flabbergasted, then turned to Shigmur and Zhanee. The war-second chuckled and said, "He is Hab-no-ken," as if that explained everything.

Elenya hurried to deal with the animals, wishing she could unload the chore on a wife, but grooming and husbandry were male tasks. She corralled them, threw out feed, and jogged back to the tent.

When she ducked under the flap, complete silence greeted her. Omi, Peyri, Meyr, and Sesheer stood in a huddle near the purdah; Alemar waited alone on the opposite side. The priest knelt in the center, cradling Rol's head in his palms. Gast's eyes had glazed over. Rol, lying supine and naked, glanced drowsily at Elenya. After a few twitches and moans, he fell asleep.

Elenya's amulet gave out a dull warning. She and Alemar exchanged glances. She hardly needed the hints. She could smell sorcery at work.

Where was his talisman? How was he focusing his power?

The healer returned quietly to alertness. He stood up, laying Rol's head carefully back on its pillow. "I'll need your assistance," he told the twins.

"Certainly," Alemar said. "How may we help?"

"The technique I must use will create some pain. Even in his sleep, he may thrash. It could endanger his life. Station yourselves at his shoulders and knees, and be ready to hold him down should it be necessary."

They took up their positions, Alemar at his foster son's head. Gast began breathing in an exact, slow-paced rhythm, his hands limp against the skin of the boy's lower right abdomen.

Elenya stared. It seemed as though Gast had not moved at all, but something was odd. Eventually, she realized what it was. The tips of the healer's fingers had disappeared into Rols' body. The boy stirred, and the twins held him firm. By this time Gast's fingers had sunk in to their entire length.

She saw the Hab-no-ken begin to manipulate Rol's abdomen, searching by touch for the root of the illness. Then his limbs began to shake. His breathing lost its rhythm. Her amulet began to flicker.

He's losing it, she thought. *His spell is breaking up.* She saw Gast lick his lips. He had gone pale, and looked much older than a few moments before.

Then, suddenly, she felt a vibration through Rol's body. The Hab-no-ken looked startled, but he bent his efforts back to the task. Soon Elenya deduced from the shifting of his hand muscles that the healer was pinching something. He remained there for a full minute, then carefully lifted away his hands. Rol's flesh was unmarked.

Gast held a bloated, angry-looking, oblong section of tissue over the boy's unmarked belly. "Bring your chamber pot," the priest ordered the women.

Omi rushed into the back of the tent and returned with the urn. Gast dropped the appendix inside. Immediately a horrendous pus stench filled the room. Omi held her nose and left immediately to dump the pot.

"If I had not come when I did, it would have burst internally, and then no power of mine would have saved him," Gast declared. "I almost failed. I shouldn't have interrupted my Retreat." He turned to Alemar. "How did you do that?" he demanded.

Alemar was shaking. "I felt your need, and . . . the energy came."

"That sort of power must be properly channeled in childhood, or you'd never be able to use it as an adult. Why didn't you tell me you'd been trained in the art?"

"I didn't want to waste any time getting back here."

"Do you know how rare you are?" Gast whispered.

"The man who taught me gave me some idea."

"Why couldn't you save the boy yourself?"

"My master only knew how to heal wounds and injuries. That's all he taught me."

"The Lesser Art," Gast said. "It's all some healers can manage. Disease has a different taste. Yet I sensed in you the ability to use the Greater. You mustn't let that go to waste. It will fade if not developed."

"What do you mean?"

"I can teach you. Become my apprentice; come with me into the hills."

Alemar began to tremble. Elenya understood every bit of his turmoil.

"I am a prisoner here," he said desperately.

Gast frowned. "I'm not sure what you mean, but rest assured—no one in this land interferes with the prerogatives of a Hab-no-ken. If I decide to take you with me, only the word of the High Scholar could stop me."

That had done it, Elenya realized. Alemar choked short his reply, almost to tears. She grabbed him by the elbow and dragged him toward the exit. "Excuse us," she told Gast. "My brother and I have to talk."

They walked away from the tent, ignoring the glances from nearby tents, and of the children in the area who had collected in hopes of seeing the Hab-no-ken. They spoke in Cilendri, Alemar unable to keep the quaver out of his voice.

"You have to go," she insisted.

"How can I?" he croaked. "I couldn't leave you here."

In truth, the thought of living alone among the tribe terrified her, but she stifled her own desires. "You know what this would mean to you. When will you get an opportunity like this again?"

He sighed. "Mother is dead. I can't save her after the fact."

Elenya knew Alemar was not as reconciled as he was pretending to be. He wanted to go, but he was afraid. What if he succeeded in learning the Greater Art? Lerina would still be dead. It had been a comfort of sorts to believe that nothing could have saved her. He would lose that buffer if he went. If Elenya didn't do something to jolt him, he would rationalize himself into staying. The fact was that she could survive without him. She had to think.

Then it came to her.

She pressed close to him, activating the amulets. She bespoke him with all the force she could muster. *"Hab-no-ken complete their training in Setan."*

He hesitated, shocked. She was reaching him.

"I can continue with our plan by myself," she said. "That way, we will double our chances of getting there."

He nodded, the light of excitement growing in his pupils. She had eliminated his dilemma in the most straightforward way she knew—she had made it his duty to go with the healer. By his expression she knew she had done the right thing.

Now all she had to do was reconcile herself to the consequences.

"No," Lonal said.

"You have no choice," Gast said. He held up Alemar's wrist, around which was tied a piece of green cloth. "I exercise the right of *Hab-shah*. He is no longer T'lil. He belongs to all Zyraii."

A small crowd had gathered. There were murmurs. It had been decades since any of the clan had been selected to become a Hab-no-ken. It had never happened to an adult.

"Silence!" Lonal shouted.

He was obeyed. He continued to the healer, "This man has designs on reaching Setan."

Gast shrugged. "Then he shall succeed, should he complete his apprenticeship. I will not permit him near the sacred grounds unless it is clear to me that he will do them no harm. In any event, it is my responsibility now, not yours."

Lonal was adamant. "He is Po-no-pha. You propose to take a warrior and transform him into the very opposite of what he has been?"

"God makes those choices," Gast said. "Tebec has the gift. Whatever else he has done with his life, it would be a crime to let that talent be squandered."

"He can serve the tribe well just as he is."

Gast smiled, unintimidated. "Do you challenge the *law,* war-leader?"

Lonal was silent. Some of the observers held their breath. No one within the tribe, short of the Bo-no-ken, would have dared challenge the war-leader in such a manner.

"No, I didn't think so," Gast said presently.

Lonal turned to Alemar. "You will abandon your brother?"

"I don't wish to. But I will."

Elenya swallowed hard.

Lonal muttered under his breath, "I underestimated your resourcefulness. Very well, then, you will go."

"Thank you, war-leader," Gast said pleasantly.

Lonal stared at Alemar. "I should have dueled you," he said.

Elenya waited while her brother and the Hab-no-ken returned to the tent to prepare for the journey. Omi followed behind Alemar, a stricken, plaintive look on her face. Lonal watched them as well, and it was only after they were out of sight that he noticed Elenya.

"I could be gone, too," she said, using the High Speech. "If Tebec could find a way out of your web, so can I. Then where would you be?"

"I don't follow you," Lonal said.

"You want something from us, but you've never offered anything in return."

"What you want is impossible for me to give."

"Setan?" she asked. She was confident now. She would get him on the defensive. Someone had to bear the brunt of the loss she felt. "Ah, but look at what just happened. My brother has found a way there. Surely you're not so uninspired that you can't think of another. Be creative. How could *I* be allowed in Setan, and still obey your precious laws?"

"You were born an infidel. It would be a crime merely to let you near the holy grounds. Unless . . ."

"Yes?"

Lonal scratched his beard thoughtfully. "Some dispensation might be made . . . if you were *hai-Zyraii.*"

"Go on."

"In that event, it would be permissible to take you to the site. Once there, you could petition the ken to let you enter the boundary. I cannot promise that they would do so."

"If I agree to help you, will you do this?" she demanded.

He paused. "Yes," he said finally, with conviction. It satisfied her. Lonal was a man of his word, if nothing else. "But becoming *hai-Zyraii* may not be as simple as you think."

"I'll find a way," she replied.

XXVII

Keron felt footfalls behind him. He turned. The elderly figure in embroidered robes smiled.

"My lord King," Keron said, bowing his head.

Pranter, rightful king of Elandris, joined his cousin. His Majesty was now one hundred five years of age, an occurrence remarkable not so much because of the sheer number of years he had lived, but because of the war and attempted assassinations he had had to live through to get there. He still stood straight, pupils bright, voice authoritative, a living tribute to the skill of the best healer/sorcerers in the known lands. He had been the pillar of resistance that had held Gloroc at bay for decades. He might die soon, but no doubted that he would face death as stubbornly as he had Elandris' great enemy.

"Come to watch your boy?" the king said cheerfully.

"Yes," he replied. "However, I have been standing too long. Why don't we find seats in the gallery?"

Keron and Pranter ambled slowly up the shallow steps of the amphitheater, to one of the seats reserved for the king. Below, on the polished marble floor, the chief wizards of Elandris conducted their tests. Once each year, members of the royal family collected in this hall—never too many at the same time, for that would tempt assassins of the Dragon—to bring forth the talismans left by their revered ancestor, Alemar Dragonslayer. Even as he walked, Keron kept his eyes on the activities. The talismans included his belt, and at the moment, one of his younger cousins was wearing it, trying to lift weights. Keron still vividly remembered his sixteenth year, when suddenly the massive iron barbells had risen in his arms like a basket of cotton. He was the first in three generations to be able to activate its magic.

"Val's a capable young man," Pranter said, nodding toward the lean, dark-haired youth waiting his turn at the weights. The king had difficulty getting into his seat, which Keron tactfully ignored. Pranter was proud and never enjoyed having to be helped. "Though the four winds know if he will have the gift."

Their banter was informal, this being one of those rare times when they could speak freely. Only the wizards and the sons of Alemar entered this place. It was the family's sanctum, and only they would know the results of the tests undertaken this day.

Pranter lightly stroked his scepter. Perhaps the most famous of the devices the great wizard had left behind, it could, with a thought from its owner, create a ward that would defy both physical and sorcerous threat. It was Pranter's badge of office, his proof above all else that he was a true son of the Dragon-slayer. Only those of the wizard's lineage were closely enough attuned to stimulate the talismans. No once since the wizard's time had been able to use all of them.

"My heart is troubled," the king told Keron. "Gloroc has become more aggressive lately."

"There have always been lulls and swells," Keron suggested.

"True, but the Dragon has usually been cautious. Old age will not claim him for five thousand years. He can afford to wait until a fool comes to the throne, or until we make a military mistake. His strategy is shifting."

"My lord knows best," Keron said. He knew by then that this meeting had not been by accident.

"How long have you been admiral of my navy?"

"Over fifteen years, Your Highness."

"About twenty, then, since you ferreted out the Eel, Warnyre."

"Yes."

"There are more like him now within the court. Some, I'm sure, quite close to the throne. Who knows whom Gloroc has swayed to his ends? He corrupted my own grandfather with his powers."

Keron did not dispute his liege. The fact was that, since those times, the Dragon had remained sequestered within his palace, seen only by his high commanders, and none of the royal family of the present generation had been physically close enough to him to have come under his mental spell. Still, the lesson of Pranter's grandfather, King Othwind, was hard to ignore. That incident had caused half the kingdom to fall to Gloroc.

"I jump at my own shadow," Pranter continued. "If it were not so draining, I would use the scepter and sleep inside a ward every night." He held up the device, which he would soon hand to the chief wizard to be used in the tests. "But as a matter of fact, I haven't been able to use it for years."

"My lord?"

"Oh, I know. I shouldn't tell anyone, not even you. You might be an agent of the Dragon." Pranter cleared his throat. "But I would like to trust someone."

"I'll try to be worthy of it," Keron said firmly, though the king's gesture made him uneasy. Pranter had not lived so long by being naive. Was the king baiting him? Was the scepter genuinely useless?

"Look at them," Pranter said sourly. A pair of his grand-nephews were testing the amulets, a pair of gold necklaces adorned by single emeralds. Reportedly, they had been used by Alemar Dragonslayer to communicate telepathically with his sister, Miranda. They would also warn the wearers if spells were being cast nearby, and it was rumored that the wearers could transfer their speed and agility back and forth between themselves, squaring it in the process. "No one's been able to use those for a thousand years. I wonder why we bother to test them. How many talismans are active today? We can't count the scepter. That leaves your belt and the globe. A few toys against the strength of Gloroc."

"We are still a mighty kingdom," Keron said.

The King shook his head sadly. "Gloroc will find the chink in our armor. I fear he may have his chance, come the succession."

Keron pursed his lips. The king had uttered a treason that, coming from the lips of any other citizen of Elandris, could have earned execution.

"What do you think of my son, Admiral?"

Keron felt sweat pop out of his pores. The truth? If he were suspect, his life could depend on how he responded.

"No," Pranter said presently. "I won't force your answer. I'll say it myself: My son is a good man, cultured and obedient, but he is not made to rule an empire. He would crumble under the burden."

"The people are loyal to him," Keron said without emotion.

"That is the problem. Imagine the unpopularity of a decision to deny him the throne, in place of, say, a member of a lesser house who has distinguished himself militarily, and who, unlike the prince, can control one of the talismans?"

"Are you serious?" Keron whispered. "It would be cause for civil war!"

"That is true . . . unless the crown prince were already dead. Let us say that an assassin of the Dragon managed to reach him."

Keron felt a cold snake crawl up his spine. He couldn't believe the king was serious. "Could you bring yourself to do such a thing?" Keron asked.

"The answer, I'm afraid, is no. I love my son, Admiral, does that surprise you? But curse me for a sentimental fool. As long as I retained my vigor, I had hoped that time would solve the problem. Now it is too late. I am on my last legs. Even if the prince should die, and I should name you my heir, all would say that it was the act of a senile, grief-stricken man. No, the only safe succession is the expected one.

"But I carry a heavy conscience. My son is safe, but is the kingdom? Will my weakness open the breach through which the Dragon inserts his power? Ah, if only some of my younger sons were of the right mettle. Why did you have to be such a distant relative?"

A shout rang through the hall. Down on the floor, Keron's son had put on his father's belt, and was holding the barbells far above his head, with one hand. The wizards converged around him.

"You see," Pranter said. "The Blood of Alemar is strong in your line. My loins have betrayed me."

It was late. Keron had paid his respects to the king and departed with his son to celebrate activation of the belt. The talisman had always been the easiest of the devices to use, but to have two living individuals able to make it function had not happened for generations. Unable to publicly proclaim the event, Keron and Nanth staged a hearty supper which their other children and representatives of royal houses attended. Val was so taken with himself he didn't even notice his father leave the feast early.

The Chamber of the Oracle echoed the breathing of the

ocean. The room, a windowless hemisphere accessed only by a single corridor, lay deep within the palace of Firsthold, many fathoms under the surface. Keron squatted on the polished floor and set down his small burden. It fluttered in its deep bowl, expanding its jellylike parachute membrane. Keron hesitated a moment, then thrust his hand into the bowl.

The ospris wrapped its tendrils around his fingers. He withdrew his hand instantly. Streaks of fire penetrated his skin wherever the ctenophore's appendages had touched him. Drops of salt water fell from the tips of his spasmed fingers, dribbling onto the slick marble.

He sat down, cross-legged, facing the dais, and allowed the poison to take effect. His body quickly became leaden. He heard the blood of his carotid arteries flowing behind his ears, listened to the humming of his brain, and noticed the slight swaying of his torso with each pulse. His head felt like it was floating away.

He waited.

The stinging of the ospris faded. His meditation deepened. Somewhere within, a nagging voice reminded him that the oracle had not replied to a question in four years.

He waited twelve hours. His legs slept, but he did not. And then the Oracle of Miranda stood before him, her complexion preternaturally vivid, her figure firm and young. She was dressed in plain white, a contrast to her night-black hair. Her expression, as if she had living eyes with which to observe him, contained compassion he had never associated with her.

"I have come, nephew," she said. The voice, clear, feminine, and youthful, originated at no specific point. "What is your question?"

He could see her, he could hear her, he could even smell the traces of perfume, but he knew that if he were to stride forward to touch her, she wouldn't be there.

"What may I do to defeat the Dragon?"

She chuckled. "Do you know how many have asked that question of me in the last century?"

"Yes."

"And yet you ask it?"

"Yes."

Miranda's robes shuffled as she paced slowly about the dais, her movement creating sound but no wind. "Do you think you are worthy to hear the answer?"

Keron thought for several seconds, then shrugged. "How am I to judge?"

She came to the very edge of the dais and extended her hands. "Come forward," she said.

He struggled to his feet, almost unable to make his numb legs work. When he had approached, Miranda took his head between her hands. Keron felt a disorienting buzz. Something pressed against his temples. The contours felt like fingers and palms, but the sense of energy was beyond the limits of any fleshy touch. It seemed to reach inside his head.

He watched Miranda's expression change from calm concentration to surprise to bright-eyed interest. "At last," she murmured.

She disengaged and returned to the center of the dais, the excitement evident in her every step. She spun, facing Keron again, and said, "Listen carefully."

"I will."

"Know that there are talismans of Alemar not accounted for. Seek those that were left in Setan. Only one of the Blood may fetch them. This is vital. Send no one after them except children of the Dragonslayer. After the talismans are in your hands, one will appear who can make use of them. Then, perhaps, Gloroc will be defeated. That is all."

She blew him a kiss and was gone, like a dandelion in a sudden gust.

There were only three men in the private study of the king: Pranter himself, Keron, and Gelle, chief royal historian. The latter spoke.

"There came a time, after Alemar had built the empire and brought it to glory, that he grew tired of rule. He left the day-to-day administration to his great-grandson, Imt, and retired from public life. Thereafter, he dwelt in his chambers deep within the palace, engaged in sorcery, and appeared only at special occasions. By the time of Harath the Third, he had vanished altogether, except to rumor. At Harath's coronation, it was Miranda who placed the crown on the king's head. She herself was rarely seen.

"Then, two centuries later, Alemar suddenly came into the light and requisitioned a group of architects and construction personnel, as well as quarry workers and sailors. He took command of one of the fleet's best cargo ships, and sailed to Carajen in the Gulf of Anrahou. From there, his caravan went into the Eastern Deserts, at that time an empty land. For some years, shipments of food goods for his work crew followed, along with various materials and additional artisans.

"Then, as suddenly as he had gone, Alemar returned, along with his helpers who, though they were asked to speak of what they had labored upon, said nothing. Occasionally one of them would attempt to do so, and be stricken dead on the spot. In due time, all these individuals lived out their natural spans, and not long after Alemar and Miranda disappeared from the kingdom without announcement. Of the place in the Eastern Deserts, the only trace we possess is the name: Setan."

"Then we don't know where this place is?" the king said.

"No, sire. There is a Setan within the land of Zyraii, a nomad nation. It is some sort of holy relic. No one is sure how it obtained the name. It could be the same place."

"Do we have maps?"

"None that we could trust, my lord. The Eastern Deserts have never been part of the empire."

"The facts fit," Keron said. "It is very conceivable that Alemar could have left talismans—perhaps his most powerful—in this place."

"Why?"

"Perhaps to keep foolish men from trying to use them inappropriately. Perhaps to hide them from the Dragon."

"The Dragon did not appear until my great-grandfather's reign," Pranter argued.

"But the Dragonslayer knew the child of Faroc and Triss was out there, waiting for its time. He may have prepared for the eventuality."

The king sighed, but nodded. "Very well. We are beggars. We can't afford not to investigate the possibility. But tell me this—which of my kin will I burden with this duty? The Dragon watches us all. He knows the wizard's brood. The moment one of us removes himself from the protection of royal Elandris, the risk is very great that the Claw will find him. And even if he should slip away successfully, the absence of any of the Blood will be noticed. The wrong questions will be asked."

Keron had already considered this, and had an answer. He asked first that the historian retire. The king and the scholar both scowled, but eventually yielded to Keron's insistence.

"Well, Admiral? What is your inspiration?"

It tumbled out. For the first time in twenty years, Keron told someone the story of his bastard children in Cilendrodel, whom he had seen only twice in their lives. "I have often thought, now that they are fully grown, to bring them to Elandris," he concluded. "Their mother has recently died. But I have seen no reason to endanger their safety. But the risk is now justified. They could make their way from Cilendrodel to the Eastern Deserts and back without Gloroc ever suspecting that any of the Blood were abroad."

"Your resources always delight me," Pranter stated. "It is good. If the Dragon were aware of their existence, they would have been killed before now. See to it, then."

"Yes, my liege. But may I ask a boon?"

"Of course! You have given an old whale his first bit of hope in two decades."

"Let me send the amulets of Alemar to them. I have a feeling that they might be able to make use of them. Obo says that they show a considerable talent with sorcery."

"Obo!"

"He has served me in Cilendrodel these past two decades, my lord."

Pranter grinned. "I wonder how many other surprises you have hidden? I agree with your thinking. Alemar and Miranda were twins, after all. If the guess is wrong, what have we lost? Go, then—and plan every move with caution."

Keron left, trying to move with decorum, but inside he felt the oppression of many years dissolve away. At last the road was open to involve his life with the children so often in his thoughts, and through them, to touch again the spirit of their mother.

"Lerina," he whispered softly.

Now, whatever the result of the quest, their offspring would leave a mark for all Elandris to note. He could offer that much to her legacy.

XXVIII

The blistered landscape stretched from horizon to horizon, bereft of movement, greenery, or human construction. They saw eroded hills, deep gorges, cliff walls of yellow, brown, and orange rock. The sky was clear, the air hot and dry as it flowed past their faces. Alemar was awed. How could so much land be so empty?

He hung hundreds of feet above the world, dangling, with nothing between himself and the uncompromising badlands below. All his instincts told him he should be falling, but he wasn't. In fact, he and Gast were rising, carried by a thermal that seemed to grow stronger as they sailed higher. Gast laughed, his peals only half bridging the broad gap between his glider and that of Alemar. The rest of his mirth was stolen by the sky.

They didn't talk. Even on earlier flights, the only words spoken in the air had been Gast's instructions or Alemar's questions, but now the younger man had mastered the art of the glider well enough that they had no need to converse. They paid silent obeisance to the wind.

Now I'm a dragon, Alemar thought, not missing the irony.

Alemar stared wistfully at their campfire, watching scarlet cinders rise into the night sky. Their gliders lay many steps away. They themselves had to maintain a substantial distance from the flame; the dry brush burned fiercely and quickly. Strangely, they had had no trouble finding the fuel. Desolate as the land seemed, it supported a wide variety of life. They knew where to obtain what they needed.

"What do you see in the sparks?" Gast asked.

Alemar shrugged. Gast had a blunt way of asking questions, though he rarely asked. Alemar wasn't sure he was prepared to analyze his state of mind.

"She's been in your thoughts a great deal."

"I miss her. Is there something wrong with that?"

Gast didn't say it, but Alemar could tell that the answer was partly yes. It made him angry.

"Master—we've been out here for months, and all we've done is wander about, or fly, or eat and sleep. I came with you to learn to heal."

"The first step is to heal yourself."

The answer puzzled Alemar. "I'm healthy now," he protested.

"Are you?" the Hab-no-ken answered, a twinkle in his eye.

"Yes, of course."

"Is there nothing that troubles you?"

Their campfire popped. Alemar stared back at Gast, unable to read the healer's expression. The latter wore his straw hat, though it was night, and the shadow concealed his face.

"Naturally, I'm troubled, now and then. Does that mean I'm not healthy?"

"Exactly."

Alemar frowned. "Then how is any man healthy? Name someone who is perfectly content."

The glitter of teeth from Gast's smile was visible within the shadow. "I am not talking about any man. I am talking about Hab-no-ken. You may be a vigorous individual with no sign of infirmity. That is fine if you are to be a warrior, a shepherd, a merchant. To be a healer you must rethink your concept of health. You cannot give to another what you do not have yourself."

Gast threw a chip of dung on the fire. "The power to heal is like fire. When it is blazing, it is awesome. But when nothing is left but embers, it must be banked and nurtured, or it will expire. Think of the wounded you have healed—could you have helped them if you had been injured at the same time?

"Do you imagine that magic falls out of the sky for us to toy with? That is a myth. The only magic is the sorcery within. For example, consider this trinket." Gast lifted the chain of Alemar's amulet. "You think it gives you strange abilities. That is not accurate. The wizard who made it created it as a means of focusing powers he had within himself. Around another man's throat, it is only a necklace. It works for you because you have the same abilities as the maker, and because the pattern of your energies matches his closely enough to trigger the device. I might suspect he was your ancestor."

Alemar said nothing.

"Men like to wrap their magic in talismans. It saves them from searching within themselves each time they weave a spell. But the sorcery itself does not come from the object. Once the creator has died, the device loses its power. Ultimately, an adept needs only inspiration and practice to allow him to focus his gift. Dragons are said to know this—they use no talismans. Neither do Hab-no-ken.

"Your talent can be affected by what would otherwise be minor factors. Right now, one of the things standing in your way is your guilt at having abandoned your sibling."

"Isn't a certain amount of that natural?" Alemar asked defensively.

"Of course. But nevertheless, your ability is going to be affected by it, and by anything else that causes you stress. You have to be able to measure the degree to which you are hindered and take that into account. You've seen for yourself what may happen if a Hab-no-ken tries to stretch himself too far. I let my curiosity get the better of me when you arrived. I nearly killed your son because I ignored the fatigue that sent me into Retreat.

"Your talent has been allowed to stagnate. The sorcery within you has been directed in other ways for most of your life. In time there would have been no chance to awaken the Greater Art. The energies would have been sapped to other purposes. You must realize how fragile your internal magic is, and give it succor.

"There are good reasons why Hab-no-ken observe the ritual of Retreat. It may seem that I am teaching you in reverse, but you need to understand how vital this time of recuperation is. Before you come into your power, you must know how to preserve it. If you can't cope with the concerns you have now, then you will be lost, because they are nothing compared to those you'll have after you become Hab-no-ken. What will happen when you face a situation when you have three people badly in need of healing, and you have only the strength to save one of them? You can try to help them all, and fail—perhaps at the cost of your own life. Or you can help the one you can and leave the others to fate, and be grateful that you made a difference. In the end, you must still be able to live with yourself.

"This is why Hab-no-ken have the authority to refuse to heal. If they exhaust themselves, they may never aid anyone again. The power needs a clear, unworried mind. If need be, we go on Retreat every year, sometimes for two months, sometimes as much as five, and during that time we forget the world and its tensions.

"This is your first step. We will stay here in the badlands for as long as necessary. We will fly, we will sleep, we will stare at rocks. There is plenty of time. Once you realize that, you will be ready to start learning."

It bothered Alemar to realize how hard a labor it would be, simply to do nothing at all.

XXIX

The fort at Zyraii-ni-Zyraii, which the traders called Xurosh, straddled the gorge through which the trade route flowed. The main structure had been erected on the northern cliff, accessible only via a small side road that branched off from the highway a mile to the west, where the grade was not as vertical. The smaller building, across the chasm to the south, could be reached only by the bridge that connected it to the main fort. The small keep commanded a site where arrows could easily be fired through archery slits at the highway, or great stones, already prepared, dropped. Boiling oil could be poured through machicolations in the bridge battlements. The barracks could hold a small battalion.

"Give me your opinion, war-second," Lonal requested.

"Formidable," Elenya answered.

They had come, alone, to a hilltop where they could get a clear view of the fort without being themselves noticeable. She scanned farther. There were no alternate courses through the pass other than the road and the riverbed next to it, and these were equally vulnerable to attack from above. Cargo could only travel via the road. Even unburdened, oeikani would have difficulty negotiating the ridges. To get to their present vantage point, Lonal and Elenya had climbed like goats. The next good pass was a hundred leagues away.

"It's a perfect ambush point," she said.

"This was true even before the fort was built," Lonal said, "and the traders have made sure to secure their advantage. The only way to gain control of this spot now is never to have lost it."

He pointed to the small keep. "That was where my father died. The merchant's army trapped him there with about two dozen men of the T'lil and the Olot. They wanted the spot because that's where the spring is, the only permanent source of water in this region. They starved him for a fortnight, and when they feared to wait any longer, they stormed the summit. They must have lost hundreds of men in the attempt, but they took it. They built the keep on his bones."

He sighed bitterly. Elenya had heard much of the story before. Joren had led Po-no-pha of the T'lil to the aid of warriors of the Olot, who had been taken unaware by the mercenaries the Azuraji merchants had hired. When it was clear that the trader intended to seize the pass, Joren sent messengers begging reinforcements from other Zyraii tribes. But the Buyul and the Fanke refused to do so unless their own war-leaders commanded the defense. There was no time to resolve the issue. Surrounded, Joren held the cliff tops for as long as he could. Men of the Alyr came, but they arrived too late.

"We should have taken the mountain back immediately, no matter how many men it would have cost," Lonal declared. "But the tribes would not band together. My father was perhaps the one man they might all have followed, given time enough to swallow their obstinacy. They argued with one another until the fortress was completed. Now we are left to face this monstrosity."

That was a good description, Elenya thought. Xurosh didn't belong in a land whose people built no permanent structures. The great stone battlements broke the natural lines of the gorge. It was a blot of civilization against the otherwise pristine scenery. The land was no longer as God had made it.

As she watched Lonal stare at the outpost, she understood things about him for the first time. There was more than grief at work. Joren's last stand had determined the focus of his son's ambitions. On the one side, Lonal had to vindicate his father's failure. On the other hand, the defense of the mountaintop had become legendary. Thanks to its fame, and Joren's impressive early career, Lonal might actually win the loyalty of all the tribes. The myth-loving Zyraii wanted the vendetta fulfilled.

Xurosh was the key. It was the root of the war-leader's single-mindedness. It didn't really matter to him what else he did with his life, as long as he dealt with this place.

"I will take it down," he said. "Have you thought of a way to help me?"

"Yes."

• • •

"We poison the well," Elenya said.

The tent was filled with the war-leaders and war-seconds of the T'lil, Alyr, and Olot. Toltac, opsib of the T'lil, sat to one side with Gham, opsib of the Olot. Many were disgruntled by Elenya's presence. She was not only a woman—though none would voice this objection aloud—but was also only recently promoted to war-second. It did not seem appropriate that she should be spokesman, but Lonal clearly deferred to her, and made it obvious that he expected everyone else to do so as well.

"We all agree that we don't have the lives to waste taking Xurosh by storm," she continued, "so we have to use their weak point against them. There is only one well. If it is tainted, everyone in the fort will be affected."

"There are women inside. They would be killed, too," pointed out the war-leader of the Olot.

"We've thought of that. The poison we will use won't kill anyone. It will only paralyze. We'll make sure that the women recover, but the men don't."

"What poison are you speaking of?"

"Mother's Breath."

"Only sorcerers can make Mother's Breath. Where do you plan to get it?"

"I can make it."

Murmurs echoed off the goat-hide walls. A few pairs of eyes gazed at her with alarm. Sorcery not of the ken was just short of demons' work.

"It will require a large amount of human blood," Elenya said. "But if we take a little from all of the men in the camp, it should be enough."

The war-leader of the Olot stood up, facing Lonal. "You're going to let a witch bleed us?"

Lonal's tone was offhand. "Are you afraid, Quasham? Would you rather spill your blood on the walls of Xurosh, until you have none left?"

"Who is to say if the blood will be used only to make poison? Should we endanger our souls?"

Lonal shrugged. "I will be the first. Thereafter, if you don't wish to donate, I will be glad to take it from you. We could get all we need from a single corpse."

Elenya smiled. Lonal was stretching the facts in order to enforce the bluff. In fact, Mother's Breath required that the blood be utterly fresh, dripped hot from the wound directly into the mixture at an exact point in time. The blood of a corpse would only be effective for moments after death.

"We aren't as worried about tainting the well as what happens afterward," Elenya said. "We may take the fort, but we have to keep it. The T'lil are not sufficient alone. We can hold Xurosh, yes, but the supply lines must be kept open. We need enough Po-no-pha to harass the traders, should they try to lay siege. They must be convinced that it will be too dear a cost to them to retake the outpost."

"If we can keep Xurosh for one season, we will have won," Lonal stated. "The merchants of Azurajen cannot afford to lose business for long. They will soon be willing to negotiate. Paying us tribute will rest easier on their minds than having the trade route completely blocked."

"How are you going to reach the well?" asked the war-leader of the Alyr. "It is guarded."

"That's true," Elenya said. "But it is guarded from men, not women."

"For good reason," the man continued. "We would not permit a woman to become involved in acts of war. Are you suggesting heresy?"

"It's not necessary to use women," Elenya said. "It will be enough if the traders merely *believe* that only women are near their well. The reality will be different. We happen to have at least one Po-no-pha who can disguise himself as a woman very well."

During a break in the discussions, Lonal was relaxing by the edge of the oasis. Toltac joined him.

"How do you think it will go?"

"As soon as they're done with their cavilling, they'll accept the plan," Lonal said confidently. "They have nothing to lose. They don't have to commit their forces until after they know if the poisoning of the well has succeeded. Once that occurs, they will hurry to be on the winning side."

"Yes. That was my perspective, also."

The Bo-no-ken seemed pleased with himself, in the mood to talk. Lonal didn't mind. As war-leader and opsib, they had no peers within the clan. Their political relationship kept them from becoming confidants, but they had often conversed at great depth and, quite unknown to themselves, would have regretted losing the chance to continue.

The high priest chuckled. "Do you remember that night when you brought back Yetem and Tebec?"

"Of course. Why?"

"That was the longest night of my life, save the night I spent in the caves of Setan. A time of hard decision. I have never told anyone this before, but I am convinced God spoke to me that night." He lowered his voice to a whisper.

"What did He say?"

"He said, 'The problem is faith. When you believed she was a man all things were correct. What is simpler than to believe once again she is a man? With sufficient faith, all things are possible.' I then knew God's mind. The whole matter was a test of our belief. But I knew He wouldn't leave it there. There had to be a reason why He would test us in this particular way. Now it is obvious."

"It is?"

"Yes. How else would we have this needle to thrust in Xurosh's eye? As was said, it would be heresy to endanger a female. So God has provided for us a man who looks like a woman. I see now why He had to speak to me."

"He indeed works in fascinating ways," Lonal said.

"What I also never understood before tonight," Toltac added, "was why *you* wanted the westerners. It could not have been only what you told us that night in council, though that was no doubt true. Now I perceive your plans. How far ahead you think! I am impressed."

Lonal demurred. "I had hardly thought of the plan of the well back then. I didn't know Yetem could make Mother's Breath until very recently."

Toltac chuckled. "No, not that. I was watching carefully today." Indeed, observing was all Toltac could do. Though his authority was deep, the Bo-no-ken had no voice in military matters. "The idea of poison was not popular. It is not manly."

"But it is our only hope."

"I agree. But still, it was wise of you to divert the dissension to another target. You place Yetem, with all his 'oddness,' to the forefront. It is then easy for all concerned to direct their dissatisfactions at him. You, though you are the policymaker, are safe in the background."

"I suppose you could see it that way," Lonal said, but his face clouded.

"It is a good scheme. In the event of failure, the blame can fall on Yetem, yet you can claim most of the credit for success. If your father had possessed that sort of subtlety, he could have become opsha."

"Perhaps I am like you," Lonal said presently. "Perhaps God speaks to me, and tells me what to do. I only see the significance of the acts later. Perhaps He sent Yetem to me for this very purpose—to be my foil." He faced Toltac. "It is comforting, to have His presence, guiding my destiny. But is that all there is to it? Are we all merely players in God's game? Are we the dice, once thrown, that have no choice in how the roll is thrown? Sometimes it seems that God is on my side. But what should happen if I choose not to do what He asks of me?"

"Do not speak of apostasy," Toltac said firmly. "You have always been a devoted servant of God. Even the noblest have doubts. What is better than to fulfill your destiny? Especially one as glorious as yours seems it will be."

"Yetem is good company," Lonal interjected suddenly.

"You have been spending a great deal of time with him," Toltac noted. "In fact, there—"

"There is talk about it, I know. Be comforted—it has no basis in fact. Still, I enjoy the time I spend with him. It never fails to be . . . educational. I think this would be true in spite of his usefulness to me."

"Be careful of the urges of youth," Toltac said.

"I am not a boy. I can feel what I want."

Toltac pursed his lips. "Perhaps it is time you took another wife. A distraction would do you good."

"I don't need another wife."

Toltac frowned. "I wonder if you know yourself as well as you think," he said.

"What do you mean?"

"Suppose the plan against Xurosh fails. Suppose that, in order to continue to pursue your ambition, you need a scapegoat, and Yetem is the only one available. Would you still want his company?"

"Are you saying I would betray him?"

Toltac shrugged. "You tell me."

"I would prefer to consider it when and if the situation arises," Lonal said sharply.

"That may be a luxury. God may test you. He chooses His own time."

Lonal stared at the oasis.

Toltac tried to sound sympathetic. He was not Ah-no-ken, who swallowed the word of God whole and regurgitated it, believing it inviolate; his sect of the ken knew that God's work took place though the hands and tongues of men, and believed it their task to shape that creation. He could note and accept that Lonal lusted for the westerner. It would be heresy to consummate it, and if Lonal were caught, Toltac would not hesitate to pass judgment upon him, but the opsib was not shocked. It was merely new evidence of the inscrutability of God.

"The Lonal that I have known would have only one choice," the opsib finished.

XXX

"Steady now," Gast warned.

Alemar held the head of the viper still, the upper fangs draped over the rim of the urn, while Gast delicately milked the venom out. The snake slapped its tail angrily against the sand. Alemar never loosened his grip.

"How poisonous did you say these were?" Alemar asked.

"Compared to what?" the healer responded, calmly stroking the snake's gums with his wooden implement.

"The moonsnake."

"Oh, not nearly so potent," Gast assured him. "It would take you several hours to die, if a big one got you."

"Wonderful."

"The problem with manhunters is that they are not so retiring as the *iltrekal-hasha-sor*. They bite many people every year. If they'd behave themselves, we wouldn't have so much work."

Gast and Alemar had spent the previous week boiling and distilling mixtures of various herbs and minerals. The apprentice had not precisely been pleased to learn that they had to acquire some of the poison in order to finish making the antivenin.

"There, that one's done," Gast announced, sitting back.

Alemar held the head of the manhunter so tightly the snake probably couldn't breathe, and walked several dozen yards from their work area to the cleft in the rocks where they had captured it and its companions. He let it go with a firm toss. The snake wriggled instantly into the hole. Alemar returned, gingerly avoiding any shady spots that might hide more of its kind.

Gast cautiously opened the netting where they kept the other manhunters, taken earlier in the day. He inserted the capture stick, with its tiny lasso at the end, and looped the cord around the neck of one of the occupants. He withdrew it, closed and reweighted the netting, and held out his prize so that Alemar could grab it just behind the head.

"Such a fine, fat one." The healer smiled.

Alemar could feel the snake's firm, defiant muscles struggle against his palm and fingers. "How many of these do we have to do?" Alemar asked.

"Why, all of them," Gast said, pointing at the dozen remaining in the netting.

"Good morning," Gast told the plant as he gently dug away the soil at its base, exposing a tuber of imposing size. Alemar watched in disbelief as the healer continued to murmur to it, an endless monologue of encouraging remarks, compliments, and good wishes, such as one might babble to an infant. Gast didn't stop until he had completely removed it from the earth and held it up proudly for Alemar to examine.

The tuber was gnarled and ugly, but the healer had assured his apprentice that, when dried and pulverized, it would form the most important ingredient of several medicines.

"Fine baby, healthy baby," Gast told it, and gestured at the upper plant, which was still attached. "We will let it dry on its own. The tuber will absorb the juices of the stalk and leaves and become more potent. It will be ready to use next month."

The Hab-no-ken kept his prize cradled carefully in his hands as they walked back to their camp. Ahead of them lizards scurried in fright from one long patch of shade to another. The day promised to be hot. "Always reassure the *whakeesh* when you harvest it," Gast cautioned. "The feelings it absorbs as it dies are those that will be stored in its flesh. If you insult it, or treat it with indifference, healing effects will be ruined. And always take it on a summer morning, when it is both refreshed from the cool of the night and ready for the challenge of the new day. By sunset it is tired."

They were in a bunker in the earth, a few minutes' walk from the oasis of Nher, in the northern regions of the territory of the Alyr, the only spot that Gast might be able to call home. Down in the cool underground air, Alemar and his teacher worked by the light of oil lamps. The shelves around them were filled with Gast's pharmacopoeia, both the drugs themselves and the scrolls that outlined their preparation. Alemar's head buzzed with information about the potions, powders, and ointments that he had helped prepare. Gast required that he memorize the major ingredients and their applications, although, thankfully, he was permitted to consult the scrolls for the exact procedures and proportions.

The Hab-no-ken held up a vial. It contained a thick, viscous oil, taken from the frogs who lived in and near the oasis. "A sip of this once a day for a few weeks, and a child with bent limbs will grow firm and straight." Gast shook his head in amazement. "People think we are magicians, but most of our art is recognizing the sorcery within these bits of nature. For every person I heal with my powers, there are thirty I cure with little more than a bit of knowledge." He waved at his library. "Most of the men who discovered these medicines had no trace of the power."

Alemar nodded patiently.

Gast looked at him understandingly. "I know you've been waiting a long time. But these are the real tools," he said, waving his hands around the room. "They are the basics. You have to know them first. Sooner or later, you'll be grateful." He tapped his chest seriously. "In the times when the feeling in here fails to stir, you will always have your lore."

The healer and his apprentice were leaving the oasis, on foot, leading pack animals. They had stayed seven weeks. Alemar was reciting formulas, oblivious to the moment. As they were crossing a sand dune, Gast stopped short. He seemed to be listening. Alemar heard nothing out of the ordinary—only the wind, the scree of a distant bird of prey, the scurrying of lizards in the brush. Eventually the healer said, "Sit here. There is something you must do."

Alemar shrugged and sat cross-legged on the top of the dune. Gast said, "When I reach the outcropping ahead, put yourself into the Trance of the Listener, and wait for my instructions."

Gast trotted off quickly, taking the animals with him. Alemar watched him descend the slope, cross another dune, and finally settle on top of the jumble of rocks. Then the apprentice did as he was bid. Eyes closed, breathing deeply, he easily slipped into the first-level trance.

"Good," Gast bespoke. The healer had entered the Trance of the Speaker. *"Now—listen. Seek no farther than the mound upon which you sit. A voice is crying out to you."*

Gast withdrew. Alemar could sense him observing, but nothing more. What could he mean? Alemar began to listen, this time not just with his ears.

He heard grains of sand tumbling endlessly down the lee side of the dune, propelled by the breeze. He heard a lizard sigh. There were roots deep under the dune—he could smell the water they brought up from below, feel the surge of the sap.

And he heard pain.

There was no cry or moan, not even strained breathing. But it was pain nonetheless. Someone was hurt. No, some*thing*. There was no human intellect involved. Alemar concentrated, but he could not recognize the pattern of the creature's thoughts. Its agony drowned out any other impressions.

Location, then. Alemar sent his awareness in widening arcs. He made contact again. The thing was behind him, to the right, about twenty paces distant.

"Good." Gast said. *"Awaken. Tend the injured."*

Alemar opened his eyes. He walked slowly in the direction he had sensed. Only when he was quite near did he see it.

It was a tortoise.

He knelt down beside it. He had seldom seen the tortoises of the desert. They hibernated ten months out of the year, buried deep in the sand. Even during the few weeks when they were active, they were hard to find, for they likewise burrowed in order to escape the heat of the day. This specimen, a mottled gray individual only as long as Alemar's outstretched hand, was out much later than he should have been.

The reason was apparent. A small, thorny twig was caught in its collar. It could not dislodge the item, nor even withdraw its head into its shell. The barbs had dug into its flesh, and movement only caused it to be skewered more deeply. Drops of ichor had stained the sand beneath its neck.

The tortoise was aware of Alemar. It tried to retreat into its shell. The thorn prevented it. It glared at the man defiantly, opening its formidable beak. Small as it was, Alemar took no chances. He walked over to the nearest stand of brush, broke off a piece, and when he had returned to the tortoise, inserted the stick between its jaws.

It clamped down and wouldn't let go. Alemar tugged and, while the creature's neck was stretched, pulled out the thorn. The wound was superficial and would heal unattended. He left his patient to its own resources, its mouth still full of wood.

He was halfway over to Gast before he realized that this had been the first healing of his apprenticeship.

"Don't belittle it," Gast warned. "You have to start small and work up. To stop pain, you must be able to find it."

"I hope my next patient is more cooperative."

"Possibly. Now that you've healed a tortoise, you can move on to vipers."

XXXI

"Twelve silver crowns," the caravan master insisted.

"Very well," Shigmur grumbled. It had been a long bargain, full of melodrama. The price was now at the current market value, however, and both parties knew it. They had only argued for the sake of form. Shigmur reached for his purse and counted out the coins before the arrangement could be altered.

"A wise investment," assured the master, watching the money drop into his palm. "A man isn't safe out in that desert, travelling with just a wife and slave girl. The barbarians might've had you for lunch."

Shigmur nodded. "I heard they burned a whole caravan not six months ago."

"Nearly. But don't worry. They won't bother us. We're too large, and we pay their tithe, anyway." The man tucked away the payment. "Be ready at dawn. We don't tarry for stragglers."

Shigmur assured him they would be prompt, and the man reentered his gate, disappearing behind the whitewashed adobe walls of his estate. The master of the caravan was also the mayor of Thiebef, the last village on the road out of the city-state of Surudain. This was the departure point for caravans heading to the Sea of Azu region—chiefly to Azurajen, but also to Shol, Palura, and the minor communities adjacent to the inland sea. East of the village lay the beginnings of Zyraii land.

He began walking back to one of the village's many inns. He was nervous, but none would have guessed it. His walk seemed smooth and unconcerned. Passers-by would see him as a moderately well-to-do Shol leather-maker, identifiable by the style, workmanship, and predominant material of his clothing. The only weapon visible was a scimitar, a common article for any head of household in these lands.

He resisted the impulse to draw up his nonexistent veil each time a stranger passed.

He entered the inn and knocked on a door on the second floor. "Who is it?" demanded a female voice in badly fractured Azuraji, the trade language.

He answered then heard the bar lifted inside. "You'll have to learn to speak it better than that,' he chided as he stepped in.

And then he burst into laughter.

Yetem controlled her grin by the barest margin, and quickly shut the door.

"It isn't funny," Lonal said.

The war-leader stood at the far side of the room, adorned in the traditional garb of a pregnant Shol wife: floor-length skirts, loose blouse, full sleeves, shawl draped over the shoulders, complete with an extremely prominent abdomen. Shigmur couldn't help but think of his wife when she had been eight months along. He examined the effect from several angles.

"The shoulders are still a bit wide for a woman," he decided. "But we can't do much about that. The padding looks good."

Yetem stroked Lonal's bare chin. "He looks young, no?"

Lonal slapped her hand away. His face was white where the beard had been. He did indeed look years younger.

"I've heard all grown men shave in Ijitia," Shigmur said diplomatically.

"I should move there," Lonal said flatly.

"Here," Shigmur said, picking up the final portion of the disguise. "No woman of Shol would be without her veils—some stranger might see her shame." He draped the multiple layers of gauze over Lonal's head and secured them with a braid around the temples.

Lonal now was utterly covered, save the hands, which he had shaved as well. Yetem had painted the nails. Few would guess that the person in the gown were anything other than a rather large, expectant Shol mother. One had to be very close to make out the outline of the face at all. This, of course, didn't improve Lonal's vision.

"How I wish I could bring myself to ask another man to do this," the war-leader said passionately.

"It will only be for a few weeks," Yetem said cheerfully.

"I know," Lonal said.

Yetem's disguise was much simpler—nothing more than a

calf-length skirt split up the sides all the way to the belt. She was naked above the waist. Although an upright woman of Shol was expected to sequester herself from the eyes of unknown men, it would be presumptuous for a slave girl to even think of doing the same.

"I'm ready," she told Shigmur.

The war-second glanced inquisitively at Lonal. "Go," the latter urged. "I will stay here like a good wife."

They filed out the door, and didn't speak until they were well out of Lonal's hearing.

"He'll go crazy, having to just sit and do nothing until we get to Xurosh," Yetem said.

"His hate for the traders will sustain him. Lonal always chooses the hardest roles . . . though this time I think you may have him beaten."

"It won't be any worse than others I've had to play," she replied.

The wineshop brimmed with activity. Merchants and travellers had been gathering for days; this was the last night before the caravan left, and they meant to make the most of it. Shigmur and Yetem took a table near the front, near the circular platform where entertainers tried to entice tips from the clientele. At the moment, a musician was plucking at a stringed instrument unlike any Yetem had ever seen before.

They had not been there long when a lanky man-at-arms from Ireon joined them at the table.

"The name's Jiustog," the soldier said. "You're journeying with the caravan?"

Shigmur gave him a name and replied affirmatively.

The man smiled beguilingly. "My uncle was in the leather trade. Tried to bring me into it when my sire died. Is it your only source of income?" he asked, staring fixedly at Yetem's breasts.

"I supplement it," Shigmur answered. "One silver crown," he added, saving Jiustog the effort of asking.

The man nodded, eyes still on Yetem. "A mite high, but worth it." He laid the coin on the table. Shigmur covered it with his palm.

Yetem stood. Jiustog took her arm. "I have a room right upstairs," he said.

Shigmur observed them as long as he could. The soldier

had his arm about Yetem's shoulders, and she was laughing at his comments and caressing his side. "What will God have me do next?" Shigmur muttered under his breath. The musician had finished his song and a pair of companions were carrying tip boxes through the crowd. One of them paused in front of Shigmur.

"Sholi?" the man asked, using the language common to Shol and Zyraii.

Shigmur hesitated. "Yes."

"What part?"

Shigmur quickly put more money in the tip box. "Rejen," This was the capital, the only large population center.

"That was my birthplace," the man said cordially. He seemed to want to talk more, but a pair of jugglers from Tunaets had taken the stage. The man hurried to finish collecting.

Shigmur sighed. The last thing he needed was to run into a man from Shol. It would have taken only a little more conversation for the man to have realized that Shigmur's accent was Zyraii, not Sholi. It was for just that reason that he had selected a caravan that had few travellers from Shol. He relaxed only when he saw the musician and his cohorts leaving the wineshop in search of another establishment in which to perform.

He settled back to watch the jugglers, and suddenly realized that Yetem was beside him.

"Is everything all right?" he asked.

"Of course." She poured herself more wine.

"You're back very soon."

She shrugged. "Some men are faster than others. By the way, you didn't charge enough."

"Oh?"

"Yes. He didn't even bargain. Next time start with three silver crowns."

The jugglers were very good. Shigmur learned that they were going to be among the caravan. A man at a nearby table waved at their antics and called out, "It's going to be an interesting trip, don't you think?"

"Yes," Shigmur replied.

"Faha ebruzh hephanemeni," Yetem said.

"Faha ebruzh haphenemeni," Shigmur repeated patiently. She tried again, and once more pronounced it incorrectly.

Shigmur laughed. She couldn't manage the accent, and butchered Azuraji grammer. Nevertheless, during ten days with the caravan, she had picked up a pidgin version of the trade language that was enough to make herself understood.

"Let me try with them," she said, and nudged her oeikani forward. Soon she had caught up with a pair of Surudainese merchant's sons, and struck up a conversation.

Shigmur listened to them laugh. Yetem was a favorite within the caravan. If only a few had purchased her services, it was only because of the prices she commanded. Shigmur had been astonished to discover how much he could get. The others had been won over by her cheerful manner and ribaldry. She had by now ingratiated herself with nearly everyone and gathered a great deal of information.

Shigmur waved away a cloud of dust. The hardpan and mesa terrain was familiar to him. The caravan was within the T'lil borders. He had, in fact, known the Po-no-pha who had come to collect the tithe. They were over halfway to Xurosh. Most of the expedition consisted of Surudainese and Azuraji traders, but nearby rode the jugglers from Tunaets. The other foreigners included a pair of young drelbs on a rare foray into the Far East, a jeweler from Tamisan, a blacksmith from Numaron, and the soldier from Ireon. The latter frequently dropped by their wagon at night, still hoping that he might be able to rent Yetem's favors for the same price as he had at the wineshop in Thiebef.

Gradually his glance returned to his side. The canvas sides of their wagon were up, allowing the breeze through. Lonal was perched matronly on thick cushions, visible but silent to the world. Even with the veils, it was obvious what he was looking at.

Finally Shigmur said, "If you were to have her, none but I would know."

"I would know," Lonal answered wistfully.

Shigmur nodded. It would be a long road.

XXXII

The palace of Gloroc trembled. Throughout the structure, even down in the kitchens at the lowest level, the Dragon's servitors felt the vibration and tried to quiet their fears. But their master's distress infected them all, as he reached out aimlessly with the powers that had subdued half a kingdom. Soon many crawled into the corners and tried to hide, others became incontinent, and two commited suicide. Even those with strong wills, who were able to detach themselves and understood that their paranoia came from Gloroc and not from the recesses of their own minds, quailed. They had never before known anything that could make the Dragon afraid.

Only Gloroc's high commanders knew the cause of the turmoil, because they alone had been trusted with the knowledge. Of them, only Beherrig, commander in chief, could bring himself to approach the great portals and enter the Dragon's Hall.

Inside, the psychic turmoil was much greater. It made him momentarily nauseated but he succeeded in closing the doors, and crossed the antechamber to the edge of the royal pool. There he took off his robes of office and laid them on the tiles. He would go to Gloroc naked, as all men were when they met the Dragon face to face, whether their bodies were clothed or not. Beherrig took one of the airmakers that waited in the trough by the edge of the pool and fitted the gear over his face, then dived into the water.

He swam the length of the entry corridor carefully, breath regular and controlled, wary of his master's irrational state. Gloroc was at the far side of the tremendous chamber.

The Dragon no longer resembled the gigantic worm of Beherrig's youth. The serpentine torso was longer—now eight times the length of man—and covered with an iridescent mesh of scales. The sight of his teeth could render a man impotent. Two pairs of legs, rudimentary though they seemed compared to the rest of his form, were large enough that he could wrap his talons completely around a human waist. The huge wings fanned out to either side like leather sails—Beherrig had to struggle to maintain his position against the current created by their frantic strokes. Only the eyes were the same—deep jewels of indigo that consumed the self-determinatiion of all who looked within them.

"Master," Beherrig called when Gloroc failed to acknowledge him.

No result. The Dragon spasmed, sweeping continuously toward the shut doors that dominated the ceiling of the hall. His body slammed against the vartham, shaking the entire building once again. But the dome had been built to defend Gloroc from attack, and even his formidable physical strength had no effect. Beherrig concentrated and bespoke his master again.

The answer nearly blacked him out. *"Beherrig! Aid me! It is time!"* This was the rational part of the message; beneath were garbled images and hallucinations that would have been deadly if focused. The crisis had rendered Gloroc helpless. It was all the Dragon could do to coherently communicate his need. But Beherrig had been forewarned, and knew what to do. It was simply a matter of summoning the courage.

The man no longer hesitated. He swam with all the speed and stamina that his well-trained, middle-aged body could manage. His route took him directly past Gloroc. Once, a thrashing limb nearly disembowelled him, while twice the turbulence caused by the wings forced him to the side. But he won past, to the thick gold wheel that controlled the roof portal.

Beherrig braced his heels against the floor and gripped the ring, which stood as high as his chest. The spindle wouldn't turn. It was designed for the Dragon himself, and when others were occasionally called upon to use it, the duty fell to two strong men. Gloroc thrashed, and the whirlpool caught Beherrig and flung his feet out. He held on to the metal and set at it again, hoping Gloroc would regain enough composure to manage it himself, but knowing that they couldn't afford to take the chance. The change was imminent; already the Dragon's gills fluttered wildly.

"I am dying," Gloroc bespoke, and the fear he transmitted desiccated Beherrig's strength. The man despaired, barely keeping a grip on the ring.

Yes. The Dragon would die. Beherrig would die. Dreams of empire would shatter. Nothing had ever been more certain. He hung slack, arms outstretched, while Gloroc's violence stilled. For the first time in his life, Beherrig heard the whimper of a dragon.

Perspective suddenly returned. The Dragon had withdrawn into himself, freeing his servant of his psychic influence. Before he could be drawn in again, Beherrig ground his feet into the stone and strained.

The tumblers moved, picking up momentum, their engineering so perfect that, once started, they pulled their operator with them. Beherrig held on instinctively, legs trailing behind as he was pulled in faster and faster circles. He let go just in time to see the sight of his life.

The great dome split down the middle, each side vanishing into its niche. Gloroc, mentally trumpeting his elation, thrust with all limbs through the widening crack, swimming upward and leaving behind a cometlike stream of bubbles. From vantage points all across the underwater city, citizens looked up in awe at the plume racing surfaceward.

As they patrolled the tower tops of the city, sentries saw a geyser rise high above them and sprout wings. When the Dragon's exultation reached them, it knocked them to their bellies or off the air funnels they guarded into the ocean below. Gloroc glided over his throne city and felt the membrane burst inside, flooding his virgin lungs with air, shutting his gills forever. The waves heard dragon laughter for the first time in fifteen centuries.

Gloroc was an adult now, no longer restricted to the seas. Nature had removed the single greatest impediment to his ambitions. Let the sons of Alemar beware.

XXXIII

The woman knelt at the edge of the oasis. She was naked except for a leather loincloth. Like most Zyraii, her skin was slightly copperish, but Gast could tell she was not a native. Zyraii women never went naked in public. She was dipping waterskins into the pool to fill them. Alemar stared at her breasts as they swayed back and forth over the water.

"Been a long time since you've seen that much woman?" The healer smiled. Alemar did not react. He remained in the shade of the palms that surrounded the pool, rigidly holding the baskets which they had come to fill.

Then Gast felt it, tickling the edges of his senses. It was unmistakable. No Hab-no-ken could have ignored it. At once, the older man was in a nostalgic reverie, recalling his own apprenticeship and that potent, irresistible moment when the power manifested.

"Who is she?" Alemar asked, not bothering to take his eyes away.

"A slave."

"She is . . . is . . ."

"Yes."

They regarded the girl for a few moments. She was about Alemar's age, healthy, youthfully lean, and blessed with long, luxuriant hair. She filled the waterskins listlessly. When she turned toward them, her glance was vacant.

"What do I do?" Alemar asked plaintively.

"You will heal," Gast stated. "Come. Let's go back to the tent. You'll have to prepare for this."

The slave finished her task and lifted as many of the skins as she could carry, taking them back toward the tent of the patriarch of the oasis. Gast guided Alemar in another direction.

• • •

"Now?"

"Yes," the Hab-no-ken's apprentice replied. "Is there a problem with that?"

"No, no," the patriarch answered. He glanced over at Ilyrra. His slave was churning butter. "I would be honored to do all I can. You are welcome to her." It was good luck to favor a Hab-no-ken, as any Zyraii knew. Yet he was puzzled. The last time he had noticed, the healer and his student had been engrossed in their work, boiling their concoction. This sudden interest in his slave girl had taken him by surprise. The young man did not seem, even now, particularly urgent with lust.

The patriarch shrugged. He pointed to the screened grove, his own retreat for times such as this. "Wait there. I will send her to you."

The slave girl appeared out of the fronds surrounding the tiny clearing. She stopped at the edge of the blanket on which Alemar waited, perfunctorily removed her loincloth, and sat down near him. The mottled sunlight created patterns on her shoulders; a faint breeze toyed with the ends of her hair. If not for the perpetual aloofness reflected in her face, she would have been beautiful.

"How may I serve my lord?"

"What is your name?" Alemar asked.

"Ilyrra," she said, expressionless.

"Lie here, on your stomach," he said, pointing to the center of the blanket and reaching for the small ceramic jar at his side.

She obeyed. He dipped his fingers in the jar and began rubbing the cream it contained onto her sunburned shoulders and back. She seemed surprised, the first active emotion she had shown.

"You'd waste that on a slave?"

"Why not? There's plenty of it." At the moment, this was particularly true. Alemar and Gast had spent the past three days making it, taking advantage of the local plants. They had been obtaining more water for the process when they had encountered Ilyrra at the pool.

"Your master should be more careful of you. Too much exposure to the sun will ruin your skin," he added.

She shrugged.

"Talk to me," he said.

"If it would please you."

"Yes. It would."

"You are one of the strange priests they talk about—the Hab-no-ken."

"An apprentice, only. I've only been studying with my master for eight months." He finished applying the salve and sat back. She rolled on her side, facing him.

"Is that why you're not . . ." She gestured at her own body.

"None of the Hab-no-ken are required to refrain from sex, as far as I know."

"You asked for me. I . . . my master thought . . ."

"Don't bother about that right now. Tell me about yourself. Talk to me about your past."

She frowned. "No."

"Where do you come from?" Alemar insisted. "It's important that you tell me."

She hesitated. "Shol."

That would explain why she knew the language. Cadra, founder of Zyraii, had also come from the plains north of the sea of Azu. The dialects were still very similar.

"You were not a slave there," Alemar said firmly. "True?"

She was staring at his chest. There the green of his robes had become greener still. He reached inside his collar and removed the amulet. He wouldn't need it. The sorcery welling up inside him needed no focus. A power was awakening that he had never suspected existed within him. The amulet was simply acknowledging the presence of the magic.

She stared at the brilliance of the amulet as he put it down, but he turned her eyes to his own. "Speak," he commanded. "Don't stop. Tell me of your life, from Shol until you came to this place."

She quailed, but could not turn away from him. Gradually, almost without her conscious volition, her mouth began to form words.

"My uncle was a tax collector for the khan . . ." she began.

Ilyrra heard the commotion and hurried to the balcony. Down in the inner courtyard, four large men in the uniform of the khan's guard were dragging her uncle across the flagstones. There was blood on his face.

She heard a crash in the servants' quarters downstairs; porcelain shattering on the floor.

A hand appeared on her shoulder. She jumped. But it was only her older cousin Hameela.

"What is happening?" Ilyrra asked. "Why are they doing this?"

Hameela, as usual, was handling the crisis with far greater composure than Ilyrra. "The khan must have discovered how much money Father has been keeping for his own purse. We are ruined. We must flee for our lives."

They heard heavy boots on the stairs.

"They are coming into the women's quarters!" Ilyrra cried, disbelieving.

"We are too late," Hameela said. Her eyes darted around the room. "Here," she said, shoving Ilyrra bodily toward a trunk in the corner. She opened the lid, removed the top layer of silks it contained, and urged her cousin inside. The fit was tight, but Ilyrra managed it. Hameela replaced the silks and closed the lid.

Ilyrra heard Hameela move away from the trunk. Then came the sound of men's voices. There was a scuffle and rude laughter. Ilyrra put a knot of silk in her mouth and bit down on it. She could tell—from the tearing of cloth, from the heavy grunts, from the vibrations of the floor beneath her—what was being done to Hameela. The noises never seemed to stop. At no time, however, did she hear her cousin give them the benefit of a single whimper. Finally, when Ilyrra could hardly bear it anymore, it was over.

But the silence was worse. Long before the footsteps had faded, before the wailing of the other women of the house had stilled, Ilyrra wanted to leave her hiding place and run. Where she would go she did not know. She was a daughter of respectable birth; she had never seen much beyond the confines of the women's quarters of her father's and her uncle's houses. But at least she would be away from them. It took all her small store of discipline to force herself to stay where she was.

It became quiet. Now and then, she detected a muffled thud in some far chamber, nothing more. Her own heartbeat began to overwhelm her ears. At last, tentatively, she began to push on the trunk lid.

When she had lifted it a few inches, it was suddenly yanked out of her grip. A huge, heavily scarred guardsman smiled down at her.

"*No!*" she screamed.

She opened her eyes, barely recognizing the foliage above her. A pair of hands gently held her head. She struggled to free herself.

"Not yet," Alemar murmured. "You must see this through."

"No! I don't want to!" she cried, but her will was not the equal of his. The memory continued.

He was hairy. He stank. Her strength was nothing against his. He threw her to the floor, his claws made ribbons of her delicate gown. When she tried to bite him, he lost patience, stunned her with a backhand across her cheek, and rolled her on her belly to enter her from behind.

She squeezed her legs together, preventing his penetration. This only increased his anger. He held her pinned with one hand around both her wrists and grabbed a lamp from a vanity table. He spilled the lamp oil between her legs and mounted her once again. Either the slickness or the violence of his effort prevented her from keeping him out.

She felt it pierce her, deep and bruising, where no man had been before. She nearly fainted. He ignored her pain, thrusting stronger and stronger with each stroke. She could feel the heat of the blood as it trickled out of her. She put her face to the floor and cried until her tongue lay in the dust and her hair was matted from her tears.

The patriarch heard an almost inhuman scream from the grove and jumped to his feet. "What was that?" he demanded.

Gast pulled gently at the patriarch's sleeve, beckoning him back to the mat where they were sharing tea outside the latter's tent. "Sometimes healing is a painful process."

"What is happening in there?" the patriarch insisted.

Gast smiled warmly. "A Hab-no-ken is being born. Be at peace, Abisha. Not many are privileged to witness this."

She had, mercifully, fainted at last. She woke as he withdrew, but lay limp, unable to rise. The man rolled her over on her back.

Two more guards were standing beyond the one who had just violated her. He stepped away to let them have their turn.

She managed to get to her feet. She opened her eyes, saw the glowing amulet next to the blanket, the shrubbery to every side, her own perspiring body. She tried to fight off the arms surrounding her. Despite the clothing on his body and the care with which he held her, she could not distinguish between the man with her now and the rapists of her past. She twisted away, tearing a sleeve of his green robe. He stopped her, made her turn, and she looked into his eyes.

The spell comforted her, reassured its firm, loving, unstoppable nature. Finally, of her own accord, she lay back on the blanket and let him proceed.

The guards took her to the slave pens of Rejen, where she was auctioned to repay the khan for her uncle's embezzlement. Her jailors raped her as well. She was sold to an Azuraji merchant, who amused himself with her for a few weeks, then brought her with him on a caravan to Surudain, intending to sell her in that city.

Because of her beauty, her master had high hopes for a good bid. But Ilyrra had died in her uncle's house, along with her virginity, her honor, her faith in the world. She would speak only if ordered to; she would lie passively when men had her; she had to be coerced into eating. Even on the block, the bidders could see she had no spirit and would not give the merchant his minimum price. In disgust, rather than sell her below what he asked, he removed her from the auction. On the road home, when the Alyr demanded their tribute, Ilyrra became the merchant's contribution.

The patriarch's sons had won the lottery to decide who would own Ilyrra, and brought her to live at the oasis. Here people were kind to her. As long as she did her share, she was left alone. But it didn't help. She was ruined. She could not go back to what she was before.

One of the patriarch's grandsons, near her age, became infatuated with her and began to hint that he might take her as a concubine, give her children. His attentions were not unpleasant, but she could only think of the day when, at last, her body would fail her, and she could be at peace. Spurned by her lack of response, the boy gave up on her. She didn't care. So it had been until the moment the Hab-no-ken's apprentice had called her to the grove.

Ilyrra felt as if she were waking after a long sleep, though when she opened her eyes, she could tell from the deep shade of the clearing that it was only sunset. The young healer was beside her, asleep. She sat up.

She wasn't quite sure what had been done to her, though she remembered every bit of it. She knew that she had fought the process. She had been through a part of her life with a vividness easily as powerful as the actual occurrence. Yet now, she could look at those same events at a distance, as if they were part of another person's life. She could see the crippling effect of her own withdrawal. She knew now that it was not just events and evil men who had ruined her, but her own refusal to cope, to strive for a better life. For the first time, her misery was where it belonged—in the past. And, unless she let it, the past couldn't touch her anymore.

She got to her feet, drained but also aware of a new, quiet strength inside herself. The old healer met her as she came out of the grove. He looked at her carefully, burst into a broad smile.

And, to her astonishment, so did she.

It was so quiet he could hear a drill beetle gnawing at the dead cork of one of the nearby palms. It was only after Alemar had stirred that he realized Gast was seated next to him. They were in their tent.

"Good morning," the Hab-no-ken said.

Alemar was exhausted, but he had never felt more peaceful. "Is it always like this?"

"What you did was ambitious for a beginner. Soon you will be able to judge your own limits."

"And Ilyrra?"

"See for yourself."

They went outside. Alemar kept a hand on Gast's shoulder to steady himself.

They spotted Ilyrra in the grainfield to the east of the oasis.

She was taking bread and tea to the grandson of the patriarch. Her straight posture and the vigor of her step told Alemar all he needed to know.

"I am proud of you," Gast said.

Alemar smiled, and they began walking back the way they had come.

XXXIV

Xurosh loomed ahead of them, rocky and impregnable. The caravan master rode up to the tollhouse, identified himself, and paid the fee. Soon the main gates opened like iron jaws and the conglomeration of humans, beasts, vehicles, and goods flowed in.

The jugglers were already at it, whirling and tossing knives to dazzle their new audience. Just behind them came the leather-maker from Shol, his pregnant wife sequestered in the coach, his slave boldly displayed on a oiekani at his side.

The guards hooted merrily, jesting boisterously concerning the best uses for the supple thighs that peeked through the slit skirt. Elenya flashed a smile back at them and flicked the cloth to show more leg. The sentries laughed, a pair of them promising to investigate the matter further when their round of duty was over.

The leather-maker arranged for quarters on the ground floor of the inn, so that his spouse would not have to climb stairs in her condition. He came back to the coach and, with the help of the slave girl, assisted the soon-to-be mother into the building. A few of the fort's residents spared them a disinterested glance before they vanished into their room.

"At last!" Lonal sighed, pulling off his veils. He began to loosen the shawl.

"Don't be so eager," Elenya cautioned. "You have to be female a bit longer."

"Yesterday would be too soon," Lonal stated flatly. "Remind me never to get pregnant."

"I don't think it's possible," Elenya said.

"I have seen too many strange things happen. I can believe anything now."

Elenya knew Lonal was actually well pleased. They had maintained their masquerade all the way from Surudain. They were where they wanted to be—inside Xurosh, with no one suspecting that they were Zyraii. Now, finally, he could do more than sit on a wagon.

Lonal began to smear animal fat on his chin and sharpen his knife to shave. One last time. It wouldn't do at this point to have someone accidentally come near enough to his veils to see the dark smudge of a beard through them. Shigmur and Elenya refreshed themselves as well.

"Have a look around," Lonal said presently. "See if anything is different than what our spies have reported."

It was not uncommon for visitors to Xurosh to tour the sights. The fortress was a spectacular edifice. Though roughly made and unornamented, its sheer massiveness was daunting. The favorite vista was from the bridge. None thought it strange to see the Shol leather-maker casually negotiating its length, his slave girl holding a broad parasol to shield him from the sun.

"They must have used thousands of men to build this in so short a time," Elenya said. The main fortress was large enough to house a brothel, two wineshops, stables, an open-air bazaar, exercise yards, and two inns, including the one in which they had left Lonal. The small keep on the other side of the gorge contained the barracks and mess hall of the permanent garrison.

"The merchants can accomplish a great deal when their profits are in jeopardy," Shigmur said.

On closer examination, the construction bore evidence of the haste of its construction. The walls were native stone, chunks of irregular rock held more by their own weight than by the mortar. Only the bridge had been hewn—some of the major corbels obviously quarried elsewhere—and set with precision. Given time and lack of interference, a group of men could literally pull Xurosh down.

But it was much better, Elenya decided, to leave the great work in place. If it could defend Azuraji and Surudainese, it could defend Zyraii.

She peered down through one of the machicolations at the

road below. The height was dizzying. She saw a child dribbling water from a cup over the edge. Long before it reached the earth, it separated into hundreds of small, perfect spheres. Elenya selected one and watched its descent. It shrank out of visibility, though she saw the splatter as the impact obliterated it and its fellows.

The child's mother slapped him for wasting water.

Shigmur and Elenya ambled on, toward the courtyard of the south keep. If the north fortress were not formidable enough, the smaller structure dissolved any fantasies of direct assault. The keep could only be reached by the bridge. It stood on a solitary promontory, cliffs on every side. An iron gate lay ready to drop and seal off the entrance. Even if the outer fortress were conquered, the keep would stand. Even if the occupants were trapped within, they could still drop missiles on the trade road. The barracks contained a huge stock of foodstuffs.

Then, too, there was the well.

Elenya spotted it as she and Shigmur crossed the threshold. Here was the reason why Joren had held the peak, and why the traders could hold it now. The natural spring had been capped, and a small gazebo built on top of it. It stood in the center of the keep. A pair of guards relaxed under the gazebo roof, watching the day's traffic, making idle conversation with those who came to draw the water—usually slave women of the fortress, occasionally another of the keep's soldiers. The two T'lil warriors knew without testing it that the guards would not permit a man they did not know to come close to the well. It was not that the men of Xurosh particularly feared that the water would be violated; they simply knew that this was one of their weak spots and took measures to insure their security. They had stores of wine and other liquids, including barrels of water, to fall back on. Lonal and Elenya were depending on the fact that, in the daytime desert heat, nothing was as popular as cold, pure drafts freshly drawn from the well.

This afternoon was no different. Women were drawing urns-full and carrying them on their shoulders back to the northern fortress, which had no source of fresh water. All had to come from this one spring.

Elenya and Shigmur completed their tour. At their query, they were told that the gate was lowered at midnight. She smiled to herself. The plan was by no means faultless, but it had a decent chance. She made sure to smile coquettishly to the well guards as she followed her "master" across the yard.

The caravan took advantage of the safe haven, the first in many leagues, and decided to remain at Xurosh for three nights. Two hours after sunset on the last evening, two figures crossed to the south keep, walking slowly down the center of the causeway. Both appeared to be women, one slender and half-nude, the other entirely clothed and obviously heavy with child.

Lonal waddled expertly, as he had practiced endlessly in their room. Elenya matched his pace, walking gingerly herself. He noticed.

"What's wrong?" he whispered.

"I'm sore," she replied.

He chuckled. "Well, you should be."

In only two nights—and days, for that matter—Elenya had established a reputation among the garrison. Shigmur had made it apparent as early as possible that his slave was not simply a servant. The price for her went up several times, but the garrison didn't seem to mind. Most were posted to Xurosh for two-year indentures, and their opportunity to spend their wages was restricted. In any event, they received no complaints.

"Make it obvious," Lonal added. "It will amuse the guards."

"It amuses *you*, you blasphemer," she accused.

They fell silent as they neared a small party of people walking the other way. The humor couldn't take the bite off of their nervousness. The hope of the Zyraii nation revolved on the success of their actions within the next few minutes. All the rest had been preliminaries. They had to concentrate, he on his awkward gait, she on her tart's swagger. They were already in the shadow of the keep's broad portal.

Elenya realized she was squeezing the handle of the bucket in her hand so tightly that her knuckles were white. She relaxed her fist, swinging the container indolently at her side.

The eyes of the sentries by the well, not to mention others patrolling the tops of the battlements, were drawn to her body like flies to dung. She smiled broadly. Soon they had reached their destination.

"Quite a walk for the lady," one of the guards said cordially. Elenya recognized him. She had entertained neither him nor his companion, but she had seen them in the company of one of her earliest customers, laughing in a wineshop and glancing in her direction. They knew who she was—and did not suspect she was a threat to them.

For an instant she forgot every word of Azuraji she knew. When she did reply, she couldn't keep the tremor out of her voice. "My mistress is a plainswoman. They can give birth and be riding a oeikani an hour later."

As she spoke, Lonal reached the rim of the well, which stood about three feet higher than the paving stones, and peered down, as if trying to discern the water in spite of the darkness, aloof from the conversation. The guards ignored him. They knew that Shol women did not speak directly to men outside their family. They much preferred to watch Elenya. They perhaps took note of how the pregnant woman had settled her distended belly on the well's rim, but only assumed she was seeking relief from the constant weight.

Elenya noisily dropped the catch bucket into the well. The rope unwound, the spindle twirling in its metal sockets with a clatter. A splash reverberated from below. As she operated the crank, she kept up a ceaseless banter.

"My mistress thought the fresh well water would do her good," she said. "You would not believe what we have had to drink on the journey. There isn't a drop of decent water between Surudain and Xurosh, and coffees and wines are hard on a woman with child. Are either of you fathers?"

They hesitated. Both said no. She could tell at least one of them was lying. She caught them staring downward, and fingered her necklace. The jewel rested precisely halfway between her nipples. "Do you see what my master gave me? He said his beauty should have something beautiful to show off. Do you like it?"

She held up the green stone, exerting a mild command to make it sparkle. The guards watched it—or the area near where it swayed—with unabashed scrutiny. They hardly paid attention to the words she uttered, not particularly caring how badly she mangled their language or how trivial her subject matter seemed to be.

Nor did they notice the faint hiss of powder dropping into the well from an open seam in the front of the pregnant woman's clothing.

In due course, the bucket reached the top of the well. Elenya transferred the water into her own container, which she set on her shoulder, a statuesque pose. Her mistress stepped away from the rim. As they walked off, the guards were treated to a broad whore-smile, and hungrily watched as the night and distance obscured her figure. If there was any sign that the veiled wife's burden was less heavy, the men failed to notice.

They heard a merry laugh from the center of the bridge.

"A cheerful strumpet, isn't she?" said one of them.

XXXV

Shortly after dawn, the bugles sounded at Xurosh.

Elenya watched the sentries suddenly burst into activity. No one took the time to wonder what the Shol slave girl was doing on the battlements. They were preoccupied by the sight beyond the walls.

A band of Zyraii had rounded the last bend and were waiting in the roadway, calmly regarding the fortress.

As the echoes of the horn faded, bodies came pouring out of the barracks, both in the southern keep and the northern fortress. The commander of the garrison appeared from the brothel doorway. And a strange thing happened.

The commander was walking very slowly, barely able to get each foot in front of the other in time to stay upright. His arms, busy putting on a leather armor vest, stiffened and would not complete their chore. Eight paces from the building, he stopped altogether. A pair of prostitutes watched from the doorway, terror on their faces.

"Sorcery!" screamed voices from the bridge. In the barracks, over a dozen men could not rise from their beds, though they breathed and some had opened their eyes. Many of those who did rouse were afflicted like the commander, moving strictly in slow motion—able to speak, fully awake, but without control over their own bodies.

Elenya sighed in relief. It had been an uncertain thing, determining how much the well would dilute the poison. If too strong, the men would have been instantly stricken, and blame would have fallen on the water they had just consumed. Too weak, and the Mother's Breath would have made the soldiers sluggish, but far from incapacitated. The proper range had been achieved—the tainted water had its effect hours after the drinking, and, though it hadn't frozen all of the victims, it had rendered a large number useless. Given time, the heat of the day, and freedom from suspicion of the well water, most of the fortress would succumb.

"What are you doing up here?"

Elenya jumped. The vice-commander of the garrison was standing behind her, obviously displeased. She almost slipped into a martial stance before she controlled her surprise and remembered to look frightened, as a slave girl would. The question had been rhetorical. The man rushed past her with hardly a second glance, joining his lookouts farther down the battlements.

She sighed in relief, and decided to return to the inn. There was no sense in directing any more attention to herself.

The vice-commander's name was Falol, she had learned. He was a great, hulking mercenary from Calinin South, a career soldier with a sharp mind. He had always maintained a clear head in the taverns, with several ales in him. Elenya didn't like it that he was still unaffected. Falol seemed more, not less, capable than the commander. She stalled at the top of the stone steps that led to the courtyard. She was just able to hear Falol talking with his subordinates.

"What are they doing, just sitting there like that?" one of the sentries said. "What are they trying to prove?"

"It's a small party. We could easily take them," said another.

"We will stay in the fortress," Falol said emphatically. "As far as I'm concerned, they can sit there until their scrotums wilt."

"But why are they showing themselves?"

Falol turned back toward the inner community. "Where the devil is Yllam? I sent for—"

Elenya sensed someone coming up the stairs at her back. It was an elderly man in a full-length azure cape, long white hair to his waist behind, long gray beard to the same level in front. As he brushed past her, she momentarily caught the lunatic-like brightness of his pupils.

A sorcerer! God's unholy names! None of her espionage had uncovered him. Xurosh had a mage. Curse the five spheres of heaven!

The sorcerer looked out at the T'lil and grunted.

"Well?" Falol demanded. "What's their scheme? What is this affliction that has taken the commander and the others?"

Yllam seemed unperturbed, unintimidated. "I cannot read minds, Vice-Commander. For all I know the desert men are out getting some sun. I can detect no spells."

"What is the cause, if not magic?"

"I did not say that sorcery was not involved, merely that none is being cast now. I will have to examine the stricken. Perhaps it will become clear."

Elenya scampered down the stairs, cursing the Zyraii God and the deities of a dozen other nations.

Yllam leaned over the prostrate form of the commander, which had been taken to the officer's private suite at the main inn. The paralyzed man lay where the two soldiers had deposited him, barely shifting his limbs at all.

The commander uttered something. It came out so slow and distorted that Yllam could only guess the meaning.

"Be at peace, sir," the wizard said. "I will do all I can." He turned to the pair of men who had carried in the burden. "Wait outside. I don't wish to be disturbed."

They obeyed immediately. They had never seen Yllam angry, and were sure they never wanted to.

Yllam looked into the commander's pupils, waving a candle flame toward and away in order to examine the speed and degree of dilation. He smelled the man's breath. He felt for temperature and a faint warning bell sounded in his memory. He rummaged through one of many pockets on the inside of his cape and produced a small mirror. He took sweat from the officer's forehead and wiped it on the glass.

He set the mirror on the small vanity table, and dusted it with orange powder. The powder sizzled on the glass. When it was done, the ash left a distinctive pattern. Yllam grunted, both in triumph and outrage.

"Mother's Breath!" he hissed.

At that moment, he heard a man's muffled cry of pain from outside the room, and the sound of at least one body striking the wall. The door burst inward. A burly man in Shol leather charged inside, a bloody dagger in hand. Behind him came a slender, dark-haired woman.

"Hass-tah!" the wizard shouted. The man's lunge was aborted. He fell as if tripped. Yllam began to wave his hands in a brief pattern.

"Elique naddath!" the female cried. The jewel between her breasts blazed with green splendor. Yllam felt the potency vanish from his lethal spell.

But the wizard's disadvantage was short-lived. He began twirling in a circle, his cape flaring wide. His attackers reeled back as if struck by a tornado-force gust of wind, their hair and clothing flapping wildly, though nothing else in the room was affected. They were forced to shut their eyes and hold up their arms against the pressure.

Yllam stopped. That would do it. Now that the initial surprise was over, he could sense that the woman was not his match in the arts. She would not be able to stop him a second time. He raised his arms.

A demonblade rammed into his throat. He staggered back, slamming his skull against the wall behind him, and sank to a sitting position.

A pregnant desert woman strode forward from the doorway and yanked the knife out of Yllam's throat. "Quickly!" she called to her companions in a male voice. "We've made a hell of a racket!" Through the open portal, Yllam saw the upper body of one of the guards, blood pooling underneath the head.

Yllam saw them pause just long enough to slit the commander's throat, and as they left, the great darkness claimed him.

A knock came loudly at the door of the Shol leather-maker. Inside, Shigmur, Elenya, and Lonal all felt their hearts jump, but the war-leader signalled calm, settled his veils once more over his head, and lay down on the bed.

"What is it?" Shigmur called in Azuraji.

"The garrison," came the reply. "Open the door."

Shigmur did so. A pair of enlisted men were waiting outside. "What is the problem?" Shigmur asked.

Their eyes darted about the room. They did not seem hostile, merely worried, young, and unhappy. They kept their tone respectful, but unequivocal.

"There has been treachery inside the inn. Four deaths. The vice-commander has ordered every guest to be confined to the cellars. You are to come with us."

"But my wife—"

"I am sorry, lord. There are to be no exceptions. The barbarians are outside the walls, and we do not have time to sort the innocent from the assassins. It is for your own protection."

"I must talk to the caravan master," Shigmur said.

"Talk to him in the cellar. He'll be there."

Shigmur frowned, feigning annoyance, and grumbled his assent. "May we take our possessions?"

"Only what you wear, m'lord. You'll have to leave your weapons here, and let us search you."

Shigmur pretended to be outraged, but did not resist. They were quick and respectful, but thorough. They found no weapons other than the unconcealed scimitar in his belt and seemed reassured. Elenya voluntarily lifted her skirt. The guards looked hard at Lonal and made a decision concerning the bounds of military propriety, not suspecting that their choice had saved them from instant murder.

The dungeons of Xurosh were small, intended only to house the occasional miscreant or belligerent drunk. When the fortress had been built, no one had wanted to chip jail cells out of solid rock. Therefore, faced with the problem of incarcerating a sizable number of people, the cellars were the only convenient choice.

Lonal, Shigmur, and Elenya had laid claim to a corner near the door. A few dozen others shared whatever niche or cranny presented itself. A few, victims of the poison, remained eerily in the positions in which they had been placed. The cellars were full of barrels, casks, crates, and boxes. Hams, sausages, and strings of garlic hung from the rafters. The odor was full and appetizing. The air was genuinely cool. Aside from lack of mobility, in many ways the room was more comfortable than those in thc hostel above.

This was a fine mess, Elenya thought. That Falol was too sharp. She cursed the need to have exposed their presence inside Xurosh by killing the sorcerer. Given much more time, the vice-commander might ferret out the truth. She supposed they were fortunate to have accomplished the murder without being caught in the act, but it was only half luck. Falol had managed to thwart them even without knowing their exact identities.

Above, all of Xurosh might be stiffening to the effects of Mother's Breath. The army of T'lil that waited in the hills outside the walls would be able to swarm in and meet no resistance. They could take the fortress even if she, Lonal, or Shigmur failed to open the gate. But they would not move without the signal. With the gate closed, even a small contingent of alert guards might slaughter hundreds.

Of course, no signal could be sent when the three of them were locked in a cellar.

They didn't have much time. One way or another, the water would become suspect. Also, the poison lasted little more than a day and a night. Assuming the worst, by dusk of the following day, the entire garrison could be fully recovered. She had to do something.

She licked her dry lips. . . .

Of course!

She leaned close to Shigmur and whispered in his ear. The big war-second grunted and strode to the doorway.

"Hey, out there!" he called.

"What do you want?" answered one of the sentries.

"How about some fresh water? The stuff in the barrels smells like oeikani dribble."

Some of the prisoners murmured agreement. They had been content with the wines and ales, but good water was more than welcome. The guards, told to remember that their charges were technically still guests of the fort, found the request reasonable.

The water arrived a half hour later. The sentries made everyone stand back from the door. They briefly unlocked it, placed a large bucket within, and secured it once more. Elenya noted with satisfaction that both guards had droplets of the liquid on the edges of their mustaches.

The dutiful slave, she filled a dipper and toted it to her master and mistress. Both tipped it to their lips, as did she. Then, at Shigmur's order, she served the entire assemblage. Some might not have bothered to drink had she not made it so easy for them, but as it was, only one declined, a Surudainese mason, who seemed to be completely satisfied to continue to get fantastically drunk on the keg of brandy he had discovered.

The hours dragged on.

The first hint of panic came from the loud wife of an Azuraji merchant, when she discovered that her husband was not simply ignoring her, but was as immobilized as those afflicted earlier in the day. She screamed and ran to the door to rouse the watch.

The guards did not respond.

A man near the door knelt down and peered through the crack at the bottom of the door. He saw the boots of their jailers. They did not move.

"It's got them, too," he moaned.

Fear spread. They had discovered that others in the room were as rigid as the merchant. They shouted and pounded the walls and the door. The merchant's wife wailed.

"Control yourselves!" Shigmur boomed. "They can't hear us all the way down here. They'll send someone soon."

"What if they don't?" someone asked.

"Then we break the door down. Let's wait and see."

In their condition, the group was ready for any assertion of authority. They squabbled, but eventually saw no harm in the idea. They returned to their places, some whispering nervously among themselves.

The lull lasted perhaps a quarter of an hour.

Someone noticed then that the merchant's wife had grown silent. She wasn't the only one. In fact, less than a third of the prisoners were active, and some of these found upon rising that they could no longer move with their normal speed. The man who had discovered that the guards were paralyzed checked Shigmur, who failed to respond. His wife and slave girl were also unnaturally quiescent. He and two other men decided that they had waited long enough. They began to kick the door.

Their blows were less powerful than they should have been. They tried prying the door with barrel staves. Eventually it began to weaken. Though well constructed, it hadn't been intended for abuse. It began to slope on its hinges. In the meantime, one of the three slowly sank to his knees. He was unable to rise. But others, encouraged by the success, had come forward to replace him.

"That will be enough," announced a commanding male voice.

They stopped. The Shol leather-maker, his wife, and his slave had suddenly come to life. The wife threw off the veils covering his head, and they saw that he was not a woman at all. Among the things he had hidden under his skirts was a scimitar. He handed his companion knives.

"Who are you?" asked one of the merchants.

"Our people own this land," Lonal answered.

"Zyraii!" The man blinked. "It was you! You've poisoned us!"

The mood of the group became ugly, but none were courageous enough to charge just yet. Lonal continued forcefully.

"Sit down and be silent! You will recover. You're not the ones we're interested in. We just want you out of the way. Resist us now and you'll be killed."

They looked at the sharp weapon in his hand. There had been no quaver in his voice. One by one, they complied. Elenya soon came forward, filled the dipper with water, and went to the Surudainese mason. Drunk as he was, he recognized the meaning of the dagger tip she put to his throat.

"Drink this," she said.

He drank. When he was done, she tied him securely to a crate.

Lonal noted with satisfaction that even those who had tried to break down the door were moving appreciably slower. "Now we wait," he told them.

Vice-Commander Falol was once again on the battlements, gazing at the intimidating cluster of Zyraii. The sun beat down mercilessly. Ordinarily at this hour, only those on posted patrols would be out under the open sky. Falol wiped off the sweat and drank another deep draft from his flask. The Zyraii, in their audacity, had erected awnings over the patch of road they occupied.

The Zyraii had every reason to seem confident. The vice-commander had only a quarter of his garrison left. Falol was worried. He could smell the treachery, and suspected the speed and accuracy of his mind were all that would allow him to exist another day.

The party of Zyraii outside the walls was not sufficient to threaten Xurosh's military strength, much less her structural invulnerability. The true enemy was inside the walls, had murdered their wizard and was slowly stealing their ability to fight.

Then the group outside the walls . . . were waiting.

"Lieutenant," Falol told the junior officer at his side. "Raise the main gate."

"Sir?"

"Raise the gate. But be sure the men who operate it are alert enough to drop it again at a moment's notice."

"Yes, sir," the lieutenant said, still mystified.

The gate was raised. Falol noted that activity in the Zyraii encampment instantly increased. Figures converged. Discussion was taking place.The vice-commander was patient.

Finally a single Zyraii on an oeikani cantered toward the fortress. "Hold your fire," Falol commanded. The rider slowed as he reached the halfway point. He craned his neck toward the open entrance. He reined up and called out a word, probably a name.

Falol decided that the man was coming no closer. "Archers!" he shouted.

Only a dozen shafts flew out, far fewer than normal. The Zyraii, his caution high, spurred his animal out of the path of the volley, then turned and flew back toward his countrymen. Once his back was turned, the reserve volley was released.

Fatally struck, the oeikani stumbled and rolled, flinging its rider to a battering impact on the dry clay of the roadway. The man—stunned, unconscious, or dead—did not get to his feet.

"Keep firing," Falol called. He also ordered the gate dropped. Arrows thudded to a halt in the unresisting body of the Zyraii. The archers didn't stop until they could se the blood seeping out of the man's white robes.

Falol smiled grimly. That had shown the barbarians some bite.

So—the Zyraii were waiting for a signal. They expected an ally to open the gate and allow them to enter. He sipped more water, concentrating hard as the cool fluid flowed down his gullet. He would have to make sure the signal never came.

Who were the traitors? He had confined every civilian in the fortress. Naturally, those most suspect were the visitors staying at the inn. They would have been most able to approach and depart from Yllam's room without being caught. There was the Surudainese mason, several Azuraji merchants, the Shol leather-maker and his nubile slave . . .

A slave who had been on the battlements when the bugle sounded, where she had no reason to be.

"Lieutenant!" he yelled.

His officer was crossing the courtyard below. "Sir?"

"Put the Shol leather-maker and his whores in the dungeon. I want to *speak* to them."

The man, propelled by the savagery of his superior's voice, hurried to comply.

XXXVI

Shigmur gave the door one last kick. The latch shattered. Lonal shoved it open, knocking over the inert forms of the guards on the other side. Elenya noticed that one of the people in the cellar had jumped at the noise. She walked over to him and shook him. He seemed to be completely under the influence of the Mother's Breath, but to be sure, she inserted her little finger up one of his nostrils. He snorted and tried to attack her, but the poison had slowed him down, and she easily subdued him. She trussed him up like the Surudainese mason for safety before checking the cellar's other occupants.

"All clear. They won't be following us," Elenya said.

Shigmur and Lonal had dragged in the guards. Lonal was procuring the clothing off one of them. He tossed the other's sword to Elenya.

She caught it, unsheathed it, checked its balance. "Not the best," she murmured.

"I'm sure you'll use it to its potential," Lonal said confidently.

When they had taken what they needed, Lonal and Shigmur dispatched the sentries. Being compelled to kill helpless opponents soured their mood. They didn't tarry over the bodies.

They mounted the wide stairs in slow, mouse-quiet strides. They keened their ears, but any activity in the world above was muffled by the stone walls and massive flooring over their heads. Only when they reached the door at the top could they hear the clunk of boots in the kitchen beyond. In the next moment, the door opened.

Lonal struck, mortally wounding two of the four soldiers in the kitchen almost before they knew they were under attack. The bodies obstructed Lonal's efforts to reach the rear pair. One of these hurriedly tried to draw his sword; the other turned to run. Elenya took out the first, Shigmur the second, both with demonblades.

Their dying gurgles were loud.

Elenya and Shigmur had just had time to retrieve their knives when two more of the garrison rounded a corner. They flung again. The lead soldier ducked behind the butchering table. The other sidestepped less successfully—the demonblade glanced off his ribs.

The wounded man ran out, shouting loudly. The other stood, kicked the demonblades behind him, and chose a position just beyond the narrow entryway to the inn's dining hall.

Lonal didn't hesitate. He plunged across the room. The soldier parried stoutly. The man was good. He had not tried to delay the three of them out of a suicidal impulse; he assumed he would be able to hold them the few moments needed for reinforcements to arrive. He would have stood a chance, Elenya decided, watching him. His Tiandra Block was classical, worthy of an academy instructor. An excellent, temporary defensive strategy. But he faced the war-leader of the T'lil.

Lonal thrust repeatedly, pulling his jabs short to gain speed. The soldier blocked the first two; but from then on he was always a fraction of a second too late. Lonal opened superficial cuts all over his opponent's torso, limbs, and face. In a few moments, the man was too disoriented to stop the killing blow to his heart.

Shigmur and Lonal pushed past the dying man as fast as they could, racing for the main entrance to the inn. Elenya stayed in the kitchen, succeeding in barring the exit there, as well as the one small window. The inn was meant to be defensible; they would turn that to their advantage if possible.

Lonal reached the doorway. A large party of men was bearing down on the entrance. He had no choice but to stand his ground and try to hold the portal, leaving Shigmur to try to secure the two windows.

Metal clashed. The foremost soldier was halted by the war-leader's weapon. The garrison ignored the windows for a bit too long. Shigmur managed to close off one and reach the other in time to harry the man stepping through.

The battle was furious. The Zyraii knew that they stood little chance if the inn were breached. For the moment, the enemy could only attack one at a time, but it would take only one suicidal charge to force them away from their position of strength. Shigmur's first antagonist had fallen dead across the sill, eliminating the possibility of easily closing the shutters.

It was a temporary stalemate. The garrison men were not the equal of either Lonal or Shigmur. Furthermore, many of them were sluggish with Mother's Breath. Intent on their jobs, Shigmur and Lonal didn't notice Elenya join them.

"The horn!" she cried.

Lonal ducked a slash and chopped off the man's sword hand. Elenya repeated her entreaty. This time it registered. During the lull while the crippled man got out of the way of his comrades, Elenya and Lonal traded places.

Once free, Lonal lifted to his lips the ram's horn that hung on a chain around his neck and blew a series of six notes.

Falol was on the battlements when he heard the horn blast, and he knew immediately what it meant. The call was repeated several times. It echoed off the mountainsides.

The vice-commander looked to the road. The Zyraii had stood and were mounting their animals. Another horn call rose from their center. Moments later, a far larger party of Zyraii appeared around the bend in the road.

"Archers!" Falol shouted. The bugle blared. Men running to the fight at the inn turned and rushed to the walls. The guards at the gate house doubled their alertness.

Falol cursed. Only a handful of his soldiers were moving normally. Several others were trudging slowly to their positions, but most had simply not stirred at all. There should have been nearly one archer for each embrasure; instead, there was one for every ten.

The Zyraii were charging en masse, riders in the lead. In their wake ran foot warriors carrying ladders.

"Fire at will!" Falol growled, picking up his bow. Almost at the same moment, an arrow whizzed past his nose.

The soldier next to him crumpled and fell, shot through the ear.

Falol ducked behind the merlon. Arrows were pouring over the battlements. He could see at least three of his men down. Most of the others, like him, had sought refuge. He peered out through the embrasure to his left. Zyraii warriors had risen from hiding places behind the rocks near the fortress, and were applying covering fire.

Falol took aim, fired, and hid behind the merlon again.

When he looked, the warrior he had shot at was limp across a boulder, a shaft protruding from his chest.

The Zyraii archers were more exposed than the men of Xurosh, but the nuisance they created was critical. The fortress bowmen now had to guard themselves and divide their offense between two sets of enemies. The riders were well within range now, but were suffering minimal casualties. Within moments they would be at the walls.

Falol shot three more arrows, and received one through the sleeve for his trouble. The scratch on his arm swelled his anger. There were Zyraii everywhere! The fortress was fighting back like a child.

The first ladder slammed into place nearby. He helped push it over before the climbers could start. The man next to him took a demonblade in the throat.

Screams rang out as a cauldron was tipped, drenching the Zyraii trying to ram the gate. Two of them went to their knees, clutching their scalded flesh. The others picked up the ram, stood in the sizzling puddles of oil, and resumed the effort.

The gate would hold, Falol knew. But the garrison, crippled as it was, would not be sufficient to keep the ladders away forever. Soon it would be time for swords, he thought, laying a sweaty palm on the pommel of his weapon.

He saw flickers in the sky. The barbarians were sending fire arrows over his head, into the wooden market stalls and awnings in the courtyard below.

Lonal, Shigmur, and Elenya knew as soon as the shuttered window of the inn burst that they couldn't hold the room. They back-pedalled into the kitchen, their enemies close behind, and reestablished themselves at its entrance. Lonal, the most rested, held the passage.

Shigmur and Elenya had only a brief respite. The door to the kitchen's side exit smashed inward, and solid blows were landing on the window. They moved to intercept the intruders. These three openings were the only inlets. If they all survived, they could hold the kitchen. Their next retreat would be the cellar door. That would put them in a disadvantageous position on the stairs.

Elenya felt blood trickling down her ribs, and knew she had been wounded, but she couldn't feel it. There was only the heat in her muscles, the steady pull in her lungs, and the burden of making a decision each second on which her life depended. She held the side door. A huge, burly man, seeing her slight form, tried to overrun her and only met his end much faster. His body tripped the next man, who became fodder for her swordplay. The one behind him was sluggish, no doubt from the poison, and lasted only a few seconds.

Caught in battle fever, she lost all sense of the happenings around her. It was only when her opponents hesitated that she smelled the smoke.

The pause was momentary, but suddenly Elenya could hear the desperate sounds of war from the battlements. Behind her attackers, she saw figures scurrying to put out fires. Many of the stalls had been disassembled during the morning, the awnings rolled up, but lack of fully functional workers had prevented completion of the task. Most of the arrows landed on stone or packed dirt, but several had found fuel. She saw an Azuraji civilian from her caravan beating out a burning wagon, only to be struck himself.

The garrison soldiers redoubled their attack. With each fresh opponent, Elenya wondered how long she could keep up the pace. The wound in her side—a shallow slice—bothered her now. The loss of blood would weaken her.

Another man down. She could almost count the number left. Was it five, six? If she could last, they would soon run out. The rest of the garrison was too busy now with the attack beneath the battlements or the fires to reinforce the group attacking the inn.

Something grabbed her ankles. She tumbled backward, landing hard on her rump.

One of the men she had defeated was still alive and had managed to tackle her. His grip was weak, however. She pulled free as she fell, rolling backward and regaining her feet in time to meet the charge through the door. She parried, halting the progress of the lead man.

A jab from the side clipped her elbow.

She spun, instinctively lashing out. Her sword thudded into the leather armor of a garrison soldier.

The side! He should not have been there. She retreated, blocking two enemies at once, and her heart caught in her throat.

Shigmur lay on the floor by the window, an arrow through his throat. Three men had climbed in over the sill, and the archer was standing just outside. The first man had come for her, the other two were closing in on Lonal.

Falol swung his blade like an axe, hewing a gash in the head of the Zyraii at the top of the ladder. The warrior fell, knocking off the next two climbers. Falol allowed one of his men to take his place, so that he could reconnoiter the battle.

At three places down the battlements, Zyraii had achieved the top and had established footholds. For the moment, these parties were being held at bay, thanks to the armor worn by the garrison, but the ladders continued to appear, and there were not enough men left to fend them off.

Down in the fortress, two buildings were burning. The firefighters had all given up in order to defend the walls.

They were losing. Slain desert men were piled in layers at the foot of the walls, but the demons would not be stopped. Falol lifted his horn and sounded the retreat. They would fall back to the southern keep.

The soldiers in the rear ranks responded with obvious eagerness, hurrying in an orderly fashion toward the bridge. But Falol and others in the front rank remained. They would hold the walls and the gate until their comrades were safe.

Falol hefted his sword once more; and discovered that his arm moved more slowly than it should have. He was stiff all over.

It had him. The Zyraii sorcery was affecting him, making him useless. He would be mown down the next time he tried to engage in battle. Falol felt his gorge rise at the prospect.

No. He refused to be helpless. While he retained control over his body, he would at least determine how he was to die. He wouldn't give a barbarian the satisfaction of slaying him.

A ladder slammed into place at a nearby embrasure. Falol stepped forward, waited for the Zyraii to scale most of the way, and plunged downward to his death, taking the lead climber with him.

Elenya screamed, but it was unnecessary. Even as Shigmur had silently died and Elenya had been driven from her position of strength, Lonal had finished off his foe. He turned in plenty of time to meet the new attack coming through the window.

His attackers stopped short. Realizing they had failed to

surprise their victim from the rear, they sidestepped. The archer at the window recognized his cue and fired at the war-leader.

Lonal had noted how Shigmur had died, and was ready. He leaped out of the arrow's path. Before the bowstring had stopped vibrating, the archer received a demonblade in his chest.

Elenya and Lonal hurriedly joined each other, trying for the cellar door. They were blocked off by the rush of men. Instead, they backed into a corner, and were instantly surrounded.

There were eight of the garrison left. They, fresh and well armored, regarded Elenya and Lonal for a moment. The latter were both wounded. Sweat poured down their faces. Their breath came in wheezes and rasps.

"Who's first?" Lonal grinned.

They heard the horn blaring. A shadow of doubt filled the soldiers' eyes.

Lonal and Elenya seized the initiative. They worked in unison, one attacking while the other covered. The eight, daunted, yielded a pace, then another. One man went down. Lonal and Elenya remained in their corner.

"Get the bow!" one of the soldiers cried.

The rearmost man scurried to the window and plucked the bow out of the dead archer's grip. Lonal and Elenya pressed again, but decisive moves eluded all parties. The skirmish was aborted. The crowd departed. The man with the bow took aim and released.

Lonal caught the arrow in his fist.

The garrison soldiers stared at the war-leader, who took the arrow and broke it in two. Suddenly they made up their minds. The horn of retreat, the shouts and the clatter of running boots outside, and the smoke streaming in from the common room all had its effect. First the man with the bow threw the weapon down and bolted. The others were only a few steps behind him. They made for the bridge and the southern keep.

Elenya, when she had caught her breath, said, "That's a good trick. Will you teach it to me?"

"I just learned it myself," Lonal answered.

For a few moments, all they could do was stand in place and feel exhausted. Then, slowly, they found their demonblades and picked them up. Elenya also took Shigmur's and returned it to its sheath. As she kneeled over the body, she thought how serene the war-second looked. He had died the warrior's way, as he would have wished.

"He will play the Bu again," Lonal stated passionately.

She nodded sadly. "There's a fight out there," she said. "We'd better go."

They emerged from the small service alley beside the inn into a cloud of smoke. It took them a moment to see that the men swarming on the top of the battlements wore white robes. The last of the garrison were vanishing over the bridge. The gate of the southern keep was closing, threatening to abandon a pair of mercenaries who, slowed by poison, were not able to run fast enough.

The only remaining active resistance to the invasion was by the gate house. The guards had held the great portal of the main fortress until their companions were safe. Now completely surrounded by Zyraii warriors, hope cut off, they fought all the more desperately.

Elenya and Lonal rushed to the fray. They were almost too late to be of any use, but Lonal killled a soldier just in time to prevent him from stabbing a Zyraii in the back. When the rescued Po-no-pha turned to them, they saw it was R'lar.

"Well met, nephew," the war-second said.

"My pleasure."

R'lar hugged his sister's son, then noticing that only Elenya accompanied him, said, "Shigmur?"

Lonal bowed his head.

Their grief was cut short by the sound of the iron gates rising. Zyraii riders flowed into the courtyard. The bloodshed was momentarily over. The Zyraii had taken the northern fortress. The only battles still being fought were against the fires.

The victors, when they realized Lonal was among them, raised a shout and gathered around him. Quasham, war-leader of the Olot, though he had lost an eye in the attack, shrugged off the man who was bandaging him and, handing Lonal his demonblade, kneeled down before him.

"I will follow you, opsha!" he declared.

Lonal reverently spotted the weapon with blood from one of his superficial wounds, and handed it back to Quasham. But he postponed other congratulations, turning instead toward the southern keep, which reared its formidable mass on the other side of the bridge.

"Secure the fortress. When night falls, we must take the keep, before they discover the source of their affliction."

The fight was not quite over. There would be more lives

lost, and possibly more snags like those caused by Falol and the wizard, but God was with them. Lonal doubted the garrison would hold the spot as long as his father had. Joren's spirit would rest easy tomorrow.

XXXVII

"There is a dragon in the sky!"

The messenger stopped in the center of the briefing room of the Royal Elandri Naval Headquarters, out of breath. Many of those in the room knew the man; he was not the kind to joke. Keron was the first to rise from his stately chair of office. The other high officers were right behind him. They ran, full-speed, to the building's tower.

They climbed up the inner walls of the great ventilation shaft, frustrated at the slow, lazy spiral of the stairs. Finally they emerged on the watch platform at the top, their elderly and middle-aged bodies complaining of the exertion, and stared in horror over the battlements.

It was true.

The Dragon wheeled joyously in the air above Firsthold, sunlight resplendent on his body, awesome in speed and size.

"He has wings," one of the vice-admirals whispered. "He flies."

Many of the men could not take their eyes off Gloroc, but soon Keron and a few of the others turned toward the northern horizon, where they spotted a large warship. It was not one of theirs. Not far from it a ship of the harbor patrol was burning.

The high officers had met because they had not received word from their northeastern patrols for almost a week. Now they understood why. Even the fleetest scout ship could not outrun a dragon. As if in confirmation, Gloroc opened his great jaws and spouted a purple, narrow bolt of flame. It was so bright the observers had to turn away.

"Gods! How can we fight that!" asked one of the tower guards.

"His supply of flame is limited," Keron said.

The Dragon glided over them, its great, dark eyes directed at the royal palace. Soon Keron and all those on the platform felt the insides of their heads violated by triumphant, malevolent dragonspeech.

"Spawn of the wizard! I have come for you! I will have back what was stolen from my parents! See if you can stop me!"

One of the catapults on the top of a nearby tower flung a load of rock shards at the Dragon. He ignored the attempt. Gloroc stayed high, out of range of the city's seige engines and far above any attack the ships of the harbor patrol could mount. The shards fell harmlessly into the ocean, sinking and ultimately settling on the city's dome.

He still respects our strength, Keron realized. He did not, however, understand why the Dragon had come. Gloroc had always been cautious. What did he hope to prove here, at the stronghold of the royalists? Like most of the cities built by Alemar Dragonslayer, it was completely underwater, save for the tall ventilation towers and the Tower of Trade, and the only access was through the towers or the airlocks far under the surface. The airlocks, if kept sealed, were impregnable, and the towers had the advantages of height and the catapults permanently mounted at their tops. The Tower of Trade, where merchant ships loaded and delivered their wares, was even now being barricaded. In addition, the home fleet was huge. Furthermore, Firsthold had been built on beds of thrijish coral. The proximity of the coral negated the Dragon's sorcery, reducing him to dependence on his physical powers alone. How could Gloroc, with one ship to back him, pose any significant threat? To come close enough to use his flame or physical strength would make him vulnerable to counterattack.

The Dragon flew back to his ship, dipping so low that the men in the towers momentarily thought he had collided with it. When he rose again, he had something clutched in his foreclaws. He flew straight to the center of the harbor; and hovered over a particular vessel.

"That's the *White Lady!*" one of the admirals cried.

Then Gloroc dropped his burden. An instant later, the flagship of the Elandri fleet was surrounded by brilliant orange flame.

Oil! Gloroc was carrying receptacles of burning oil. There was no need to endanger himself trying to use dragonflame. He could stay at a safe height and simply bomb his target.

The flame around the *White Lady* fell away. The vessel was untouched.

A cheer went up from the tower top. Like most of the important ships of the fleet, the *White Lady* had a wizard aboard. Hers was Hecren, one of the best. He had set up a ward to protect her.

The Dragon seemed unperturbed to see that he had failed. He streaked back to the horizon, rendezvoused with his ship, and returned to the Elandri flagship with another fire bomb. His shot missed, or perhaps was deflected off the edge of the ward, and fell into the ocean, briefly setting the waves alight.

Again, Gloroc paid little attention; he simply flew back to his supply ship. Keron saw his strategy and began to issue commands.

"Send more wizards to the *White Lady!*" he roared at a pair of the aides standing by. They gawked in surprise.

"How—how many?" one asked.

"Ten, if you can find them! Just hurry!" To others he yelled, "Send twenty ships after that Dragon's boat!"

They soon heard trumpets playing the song of attack. Sails began to rise, and men could be seen scurrying across the wharf and docks. Anchors rose. By that time, the Dragon had bombed the flagship three more times. Seeing the activity below, he increased his speed.

Nothing that big should move that fast, Keron thought. The only times when the Dragon slowed was to pluck pots of oil from his ship and to rain his deadly gifts on the *White Lady.* He took careful aim now, and never missed.

Hecren's ward was holding, but the ship was staggering in the water with each impact.

"Why don't they move?" asked one of the tower guards. "A moving target would be harder to hit."

One of the rear admirals explained. It was hard enough maintaining a ward over an immobile object. At this point, the wizard didn't need any more challenges.

Another fire bomb. Two. Three. Four.

"Hang on, Hecren," Keron whispered to himself. He saw two separate dinghies speeding toward the beleagured ship as fast as their oarsmen could row, a sorcerer riding in each. Another was nearly ready to leave the quay. The *White Lady* was now afloat atop a film of burning oil. Stray bursts of fire licked at her hull. The first dinghy paused at the edge of the area, daunted by the obstacle.

The Dragon arrived with another bomb. He dropped it. Both

the container of oil and the ward exploded at the same time, engulfing the ship in a fireball. The men in the dinghies covered their faces against the heat. When the burst settled, the officers in the tower could see that their proud flagship was burning from prow to stern. Men, clothes and hair on fire, were leaping from her decks into the ocean.

None of them could keep the Dragon's laughter from their minds.

Keron gritted his teeth, but would not take his eyes away from the carnage. Gloroc had made his point. The royalists could stay in their impregnable cities. Their ships, however, would have to ply the seas, where they could be destroyed one by one at the Dragon's leisure. Without the navy, free Elandris would have no supply lines.

The Dragon sailed gracefully to the northeast, his mirth audible until he was only a speck over the horizon. His ship had turned to run. Keron could see its lines; she was built for speed. Almost a dozen royalist ships were closing on her. They might catch her. The Dragon might protect her. It didn't really matter.

"Admiral Olendim!" a page called from the top of the stairs. "The king sends for you!"

The king was in the royal observation dome, a structure at the top of the palace from which one could view the harbor, towers, and nearby ocean in all directions. It was made of the same vartham as the city's great roof and would resist even dragonflame. Pranter stood just inside the transparent walls, morosely watching the *White Lady* burn. Keron approached and waited quietly by his monarch's side.

Pranter was painfully thin. He no longer seemed part of the solid, real world, but rather a wraith somehow visible in the daylight. He couldn't walk without assistance, and even standing still, he wobbled. In one hand he clutched the scepter of Alemar Dragonslayer.

"We see it all now so clearly," Pranter said weakly. "The Dragon sequestered himself these past decades because he was maturing. We knew it would happen one day. Now the skies are his. Our doom is upon us."

"I'm not ready to give up yet," Keron said.

Pranter smiled humorlessly. "We don't have much time on our side, boy."

"There is one chance."

The king raised one eyebrow high. "Oh?"

"We have to kill the Dragon."

Pranter chuckled. "I wish I was young enough to share your optimism. I have dreamed of that impossibility, praying that any moment your children would return from the desert, or some inspiration would be sent by the gods. But it has been two years. Your twins have died, Keron. All our hopes have died. It is time to cut our losses."

Keron swallowed. The taste of his own bile was bitter. He could not deny that he, too, had decided that Alemar and Elenya had perished on their quest.

Pranter tapped his scepter pensively. "The talismans must be taken to safety—away from Elandris. We may lose the country, but our heritage from Alemar the Great must be preserved. You are the man I trust most to execute the task."

At first, Keron was not sure he had heard right. "You're asking me to run?"

"In a way. Would you rather remain as head of the navy, and have to watch your ships turned to charcoal? I need you to continue the fight, and to do that, you have to find higher ground. It doesn't exist here."

"What of you, my king?"

"My place is here. I am on death's doorstep. What point to make me a refugee? My body would not survive the journey. I will stay, where the loyal can rally to me, and keep the kingdom free as long as heart and body will bear it. That's how my life can best serve a purpose."

"I don't like abandoning you," Keron said.

"Forget me. There is more than one dynasty or kingdom at stake here. I do not believe Gloroc will stop when Elandris is defeated. He is not like the dragons of old; he has lived among humans too long. He has learned ambition. In time he will want the world."

Pranter extended his arm, offering the royal scepter to Keron. The admiral hesitated.

"Take it."

He did so reluctantly. It felt alive; he could almost feel a pulse running down its handle.

"This is the one thing he fears—this and all the artifacts our ancestor left behind." The speech made the old man's body shake. "We must keep the threat alive, or he will come to rule us all. Do this for me. Choose your own men and your own destination, and be gone. Be invisible. Be a threat."

"I'll prepare at once," Keron replied.

Nanth was in the parlor showing their youngest daughter how to embroider. Keron watched from the doorway for several moments before revealing his presence. Nanth was no longer the carefully crafted beauty of two or three decades earlier, and their marriage, a prearranged affair that had never been perfect even before Keron had encountered Lerina, had endured some unpleasant moments. But as she turned and smiled at him, it was hard to bring the lie to his lips.

"Val and I are going to the palace," he said as he kissed her head and that of his daughter. "We should be back in a few hours."

He didn't return her smile, but Nanth wouldn't think that strange. There had been little to be happy about in the two weeks since the Dragon had appeared above Firsthold.

Keron met his son just outside their home. The boy was doing his best to hide his red eyes. Both of them had decided he should not try to bid his mother farewell; Val wasn't mature enough to put up a convincing façade.

They set out for the palace. Keron's bodyguards automatically dropped into place behind them. The streets were lightly travelled, although it was barely dusk, normally a social hour. There was a strange pall about the city, a grimness. They felt unhappy eyes peering at them from the upper-story windows. The ocean above, normally crystalline, was tainted by sediment.

Two blocks down they came upon the site of a looting. Someone had broken into the storeroom of one of Firsthold's best inns. The city militia was restoring order. A pair of men in uniform started toward Keron's group, recognized him, and turned away again.

It's beginning already. Keron had heard reports of fighting the previous night. Rationing had been put into effect the day after the Dragon's attack. The mood of the city was growing thicker. Keron's final project as admiral of the navy had been to send a huge fleet of ships to T'jet with the sole purpose of bringing back as many provisions as could be stuffed into the holds. There were more ships, with more skilled wizards aboard, than the Dragon could intimidate alone. He would have to rouse his navy. The ships, unlike Gloroc, would be vulnerable. The royalists could, at least, cause the enemy pain.

In the meantime, those left behind in this city, or of the other communities of free Elandris, felt the noose tighten about their necks.

Keron and Val left behind the bodyguards at the entrance to the palace, walking in stony silence through side corridors to the king's chambers. The sentries admitted them, and they soon stood in a parlor rarely visited by any save the king, his family, and inner household servants. The king and a bald man in a captain's tunic waited at the rear of the room, near an alabaster statue of Miranda.

"Enret," Keron said, clasping hands with the captain. His longtime friend nodded back.

To one side were almost twenty carefully assembled packs. Each contained a talisman of Alemar Dragonslayer. Most of them would be leaving Firsthold for the first time in more than a millennium.

One by one, the others joined them. Keron examined their faces as they assembled in front of him. Good men. The best that he and Enret could pick. He met their glances with compassion. Every one of them was leaving behind a wife, mother, sister, or child—loved ones who would have to guess at their man's fate. Only the king and the men themselves would know how they left the city.

Soon they were all assembled, but one. Enret noted the hourglass and coughed. "Should we leave anyway?"

"He has to go," the king said. They waited a short while, and the last man appeared.

Keron rarely saw his cousin, Treynaf. The latter was an effeminate, dour man nearly as old as the admiral. He wore his hair close-cropped, like the ancient wizard-kings of Acalon, and was not popular at court, but he was able to activate the globe of Alemar, which he even now nestled in his hands. Pranter insisted that any who could use the talismans should accompany the party. That was why Val was present.

"What news, cousin?" asked Keron.

Treynaf rubbed the crystal reverently. His eyes briefly glazed over. "I see a long swim," he answered tonelessly.

That was hardly news. They couldn't risk travel by ship, nor would they stop at cities along the way, for fear that the

Dragon would somehow pick up their trail. They would literally swim to the coast.

It was unfortunate that Treynaf was not more worthy of the globe's potential, Keron though. He could have foreseen useful things, such as the Dragon's recent attack.

The king stood. The others bowed to him.

"Follow this man," the king said, pointing his scepter at Keron. "He will be your monarch now." With a trembling, unsteady hand, he placed the head of the scepter against the wall behind him. Double doors suddenly became visible and opened inward, revealing a narrow, unlighted tunnel that smelled of stagnant air.

"May you all outlive the Dragon," Pranter declared.

Enret took the lead, letting the others follow single file. At last only Keron was left with the aged, rightful ruler of Elandris. Pranter suddenly swayed, maintaining his balance only by placing his hand on Keron's shoulder. When he was steady, he handed the scepter to the younger man.

Keron took it reluctantly. As two weeks before in the observation dome, he thought he felt a throb of power within the device. He found it hard to look at; it was a thing he had never dared to hope to own.

"Take it!" the king insisted. "Stick it in Gloroc's eye!"

Keron nodded. The king turned and sat down. There was nothing more to say. Keron entered the tunnel, touched the doors as Pranter had instructed earlier, and watched them close. The light vanished.

They walked wordlessly down the passage, guiding themselves by touch. The tunnel was featureless—simply a flat floor, an arching roof, and smooth walls. The sound of their own breathing was fantastically loud.

Finally Enret called, "Wall here, Admiral."

Keron slipped past the others. The end of the passage was blocked. He touched the partition with the scepter. A massive door slid to the side, revealing an airlock on the other side, its contours made visible by dim phosphorescence.

The party filed in. There was nothing to indicate the chamber had ever been used. It seemed to be chiselled out of native coral and sealed by extreme heat, though there was no char. The only highlight was the broad, circular hatch in the center of the floor.

Keron sealed the opening through which they had come,

and they put on their airmakers and vests. Two men opened the flood ports. The chamber began to fill with seawater. Keron sighed at the scent of free, honest ocean. As soon as the room had filled, they opened the hatch.

They came out on the underside of a huge coral formation. Keron, the last man out, closed the hatch behind him. At a touch from the scepter, the spindle spun from the inside, restoring the lock. From this side, the hatch was a barnacle-encrusted circle of coral, perfectly concealed in the shadows.

The city was to the east, most of a league away. The magnificent vartham dome shone in the night waters. Their gazes lingered on her lights.

Keron signaled, and they set out, hugging the ocean floor against the remote chance that the Dragon had stationed observers near the city. They soon vanished into the murk.

XXXVIII

As Alemar and Gast made their way down the road at the western edge of the Ahloorm River, they unexpectedly ran into a large encampment of Zyraii. The group had settled under the canopy of a grove of *hoeanaou* trees, where they were feasting and drinking wine. They proved to be the Hysic, the smallest clan of the T'lil, in the midst of their migration from the river basin to the far parts of their range. Children ran out to meet the Hab-no-ken, followed not long after by the Hysic's solitary Bo-no-ken and a party of elders.

"What is the occasion?" Gast inquired, after he had accepted an invitation to join the festivities.

"The siege of Xurosh has ended," the Bo-no-ken replied. "The traders have sent their soldiers home."

Alemar took the wineskin that had been thrust into his hands and listened keenly, eager for news of Elenya. He had not seen her since he had originally left with Gast. They had visited the T'krt twice in recent months, but she had not been there. She was among the warriors who continued to defend the fort after the Zyraii had taken it.

"Yetem has become *hai-Zyraii,*" a very young Po-no-pha told him, apologizing almost in the same breath for not being able to remain at Xurosh; he had sustained a broken leg while storming the fortress. Alemar had noticed his slight limp. "He has shared blood with the war-leader."

The youth went on to describe the battle, particularly the attack on the southern keep, where he had received his injury. Alemar sat with him and the few Po-no-pha present and listened patiently. He had heard the story of Xurosh several times. He knew of Shigmur's death, the poisoning of the well, and Lonal and Elenya's desperate stand. Nevertheless, he enjoyed it for the social aspect, which he often missed in his travels with Gast, and he was proud of his sister's new honor.

It was late before he excused himself and wandered to the edge of the camp. He stood at the edge of the jungle, bathed in the glow of Motherworld, enjoying the sensation of being surrounded by trees. He had never totally adjusted to the desert's overwhelmingly open spaces. Soon he realized he was being watched.

It was a woman. She was about Alemar's age, small, sturdy, and calm in her movements. She waited respectfully for him to acknowledge her, which he did.

"Would you look at my daughter? She is ill." Something in her tone told Alemar that if he should decline, she would accept that gracefully and retire, but with the same observation he realized that she was not the type to summon him without cause.

"Of course," he answered.

The girl, a four-year-old, was under a small awning, segregated from her family's tent for fear that her sickness was contagious. She was fierce with fever and had a rash across her chest and throat. Alemar frowned. He had not seen the symptoms before, but they matched one of Gast's descriptions. He could fetch the Hab-no-ken . . .

He decided against it, instead placing his palms around one of the little girl's hands. Within seconds he had entered a trance.

The girl's form seemed to become transparent. He could sense the functioning of each organ, the pulsing and coursing of her bloodstream, the amount of urine in her bladder. The source of her problem was immediately apparent. He could see the *wrongness* leaving the upper intestine and spreading throughout the rest of the body. He memorized the aura of the irritant, and ended the trance.

"What has she eaten in the past two days?" he asked the mother.

"Millet, cheese, dates . . ."

"Any milk?"

"Yes, of course."

He gestured out at the spot where the sheep and goats had been penned. "Fetch a bit of fresh milk for me."

When she returned, Alemar lifted the milk to his nose and sniffed. "Grass, water . . . yolo weed."

"There's a great deal of it growing nearby," she said. "The sheep won't touch it, but the goats don't care."

"Your daughter's body is sensitive to yolo weed," Alemar said. "Stop giving her milk, and she will recover." He rummaged in his pack. "I'll prepare something to help her fever."

Alemar tilted the bowl to the little girl's lips, supporting her upper back with his other hand. She sipped his concoction reluctantly, closing her eyes against the bitter aroma, but eventually she finished it. He laid her back down on the sweat-drenched mat.

"Good girl," he said.

She was near delirious, and did not answer.

"Be sure to give her plenty of liquid. If she's still hot tomorrow, give her another dose of the potion. You're sure you remember how to mix it?" He had thought it best to teach her, in the event the problem recurred in future seasons.

The mother nodded. He was impressed once more by the intelligence behind her young eyes.

"You're the brother of the warrior woman, the hero of Xurosh?" she asked.

"Yes." He was intrigued. The woman was a T'lil. She should have referred to Elenya as a man. "Why do you ask?"

"Yetem has changed the world," the woman said, stroking her little daughter's hair. "Perhaps this one will have it better, because a female has become *hai-Zyraii*."

"She is not called a female."

"The truth is known."

Abruptly the woman reached to her collar and pulled off the small rawhide necklace she wore, and handed it to Alemar. He saw then that it was decorated with a small bit of turquoise. No doubt it was the only thing of value she owned.

"For Yetem?" he asked.

"No, that is for you. For your help. My husband will give you nothing."

"I can't accept it."

She insisted. "It isn't that you healed her—it's that you bothered to try."

He understood. By accepting the gift, he was accepting her worthiness to give it. Though it barely fit, he managed to tug the necklace over his head. It settled inside the gold chain of the amulet.

The mother's smile was cut short by a sudden shudder from her daughter. The girl opened her eyes, wearing the fright of a fever dream, calming when she saw her parent beside her.

"Don't let the Dragon get me," the little girl begged.

Her mother scolded her. Childlike, she was asleep within seconds. Alemar, however, had been brought resoundingly alert.

"What did she mean?"

The mother looked embarrassed. "Her grandmother has been scaring her into obedience, saying that the Dragon will come to get her if she is bad, burning her up as he did the people of Elandris."

"What? The Dragon can't— When did you get this news?" Alemar asked urgently.

She seemed surprised at his tone. "Three weeks ago. Why?"

"Never mind," he said. "Just tell me all you know."

She seemed worried by his sudden agitation. "It is said that the Dragon has grown his wings and taken to the skies. He burns the boats that try to cross the great water, save the ones that belong to him. The cities that oppose him are cut off, and the old king is dead. The people are despairing."

Alemar stood up abruptly, nearly upsetting the awning. "I must find my master," he said, and left before the woman could respond.

He nearly bumped into a man who had just stepped out of the family's tent. It could only have been the girl's father. "She will be well?" the man asked.

"Yes," Alemar answered curtly, and strode on toward the guest tent where, sometime before, he had seen his teacher conversing with the clan's Ah-no-ken.

"Good," the father said as Alemar departed. "She'll be able to carry her load soon."

Gast was alone, taking tea. He nearly spilled his cup, so sudden was Alemar's entrance. "What is it, my son?" the Hab-no-ken asked.

"Have you heard the news from Elandris?"

Gast shook his head in wonder as Alemar finished his story, still not quite believing. "It was right that you kept your secret," he said finally. "If you are what you say, your actions may destroy the very magic that keeps Setan sacred. Zyraii would have made sure to be quickly rid of you."

"But you'll take me there?" Alemar asked again.

"Yes," Gast said slowly, "but as God is my witness, I do it only because you are a healer, not because you are an Elandri prince. I had hoped for a few more months before I took you to Setan."

"I can't delay."

Gast stared down guiltily. "You won't have to. You have been ready for some time now."

"Then—why have you waited?"

The healer sighed. "I have never taken an apprentice before. Since I was young, I have been alone in my travels. It was . . . good to have someone with me."

Alemar felt his eyes grow moist. Of all the teachers who had instructed him—from Obo to his grandfather to Lord Dran—Gast had become the nearest and most precious of them all. He, too, had hoped to make the apprenticeship last. It bothered him to have to ask the man to commit a sacrilege.

He drew out the amulet of Alemar Dragonslayer. Gast looked at him quizzically.

"My sister has to know."

Alemar regarded the talisman ambivalently. Once he used it, he would have turned his back on the life he had known for the past year. He was not eager to do that.

But a small voice whispered in his ear: *"Don't let the Dragon get me."*

He lifted the jewel to his forehead, his mind reaching out. . . .

XXXIX

Elenya strolled across the bridge of Xurosh, easing the languor of alcohol with a dose of desert night sky and cool air. The revelry within Xurosh was a soothing buzz. The sentries recognized her and let her go her way. She stopped in the middle of the span. The gorge yawned underneath her, its bottom lost in shadow as Motherworld headed for the horizon. The tradc route that caused so much conflict was completely hidden.

The fight was over. A month earlier, the mercenaries had given up the siege. Now, the first caravan of the season had arrived, offering a tribute greater than any given to the Zyraii in several generations. Soon, Lonal could feel safe leaving the maintenance of the fortress to capable, lesser hands, and would finally be free to make good on his promise to take Elenya to Setan.

So, in a way, she had double reason to celebrate. Yet here in the quiet, tired from the evening's merrymaking, she was wistful. The months at Xurosh had meant a long, sometimes frustrating vigil, but in another sense it had been an enjoyable interlude. She had a respected place within the community of defenders. It had been easy to know what was expected of her. Here, everyone had been a prisoner, exiled from their homes, united in camaraderie. That would end after tonight.

In the back of her head was an itch. She had felt it inside the fortress an hour before. It was stronger this time, as if the wall had muted it. She almost managed to ignore it, blaming it on the wine, until she felt a stirring from the jewel on her chest. She was aware of lifting the amulet to her forehead.

The signal came—brief, distant, but perfectly clear.

She had been gone from Xurosh only a few hours when she heard the sound of a single oeikani and rider rounding the bend.

She roused herself from her resting place at the edge of the road, and was on her feet as he appeared. The morning sun cast a halo around him, but she had no difficulty recognizing him. She placed herself in his path.

Lonal regarded her stiffly, his veil and cowl in place. When she didn't run, he dismounted and tethered his reins to a stone.

"Why?" he said.

"I'm sorry," she said. She gestured at the badlands behind her. "My brother has sent for me. I have to go to him."

"You couldn't tell me this?"

"When I find him, I am certain we will go to Setan."

Lonal drew away the coverings from his face. She could still see a small scar on his forehead from the battles of Xurosh. He was still as handsome as ever, but he was no longer the unmarked youth she had met on her arrival in the desert. He held out his right hand. He had another scar there, on his wrist. It matched the one on hers.

"You have come far among the Zyraii," he said. "Don't lose your honor now. I would have kept my promise, in no more than another few weeks."

"There's no time to waste. Something has happened. I can't risk the wait."

"By law, I am required to stop you."

She nodded. "I know that. Will you?"

"Yes," he whispered.

She sighed, and slid her rapier out of its sheath.

He drew his scimitar.

Elenya's head ached from the previous night's drinking. She hadn't slept all night. Lonal, however, was probably in the same state, and he wasn't as rested. She weighed each factor, one by one, trying to take each advantage and disadvantage into account. Too much thinking. She couldn't clear the complexities from her mind and concentrate on the task of defending herself.

They closed the gap slowly. They had both seen each other's mettle at Xurosh. They circled, just out of range, testing the ground. Elenya tucked back a stray lock of hair. She kept her rapier point out of reach of his weapon, peripherally aware of the roadway underneath her and the hills on either side. Her oeikani nibbled noisily at the feed she had set out for it.

They lunged.

She bit her lip, stifling the pain in her thigh. He jumped

back, transferring his scimitar effortlessly into the other hand. A small spot of blood stained the upper arm of his garment.

She should have died. She had left her lower body open. Just as he had exposed his heart.

He lowered his scimitar.

She sheathed her rapier.

"This is pointless," he said. "I'll give you a day's lead. When you reach the Ahloorm, ride upriver. When a large stream merges from the west, follow it to its source. You will come to Setan. I'll be behind you, with a party of Po-no-pha. They may be able to do what I cannot."

"Lonal?"

"Yes?"

"Thank you."

He met her gaze, pretending to be stern but failing. "I don't know why I put up with so much trouble from you. Bind that wound and get moving. I want to know myself what you've come so far to find."

So do I, she thought as he turned and rode back toward Xurosh.

XL

"She's riding hard," Gast said.

Alemar and the healer stood on the crest of a foothill, overlooking the upper Ahloorm Valley. A single rider had appeared out of the plain on a lathered oeikani. Alemar lifted the amulet out of his collar. The jewel was so bright it flickered visibly even in the sunlight.

An answering glint of emerald came from the rider's chest.

"She's pursued," Alemar said matter-of-factly, "but she has a good lead."

"It tells you all that?"

All activity from the amulet ceased. The jewel once more looked like a dull green, semiprecious stone of no great rarity. Alemar stuffed it back out of view. "She is telling me that. It never used to be so clear from a distance. Maybe now that we're older, or now that I've been trained as a Hab-no-ken . . ."

"Why did you stop?"

"It's been a long time, master. It's a bit overwhelming to communicate with her so strongly."

Gast caught the huskiness of his apprentice's voice. Abruptly he said, "I'll wait for you downslope. There's a spring there. We need water."

Alemar nodded, not bothering to watch the healer. He never shifted his sight from his sister's approach. It seemed like no time at all after his teacher's hoofbeats had faded away before he was smelling the dust of her arrival.

They listened to her oeikani wheeze. It was a proud, sleek animal, and had traveled near the limit of its endurance. She patted its neck, murmuring gratitude, and flipped back her cowl and dropped the veil. Alemar removed his hat.

"You look good in green," she said.

"You look good, period." Maturity had taken the severity from her features. Her breasts were fuller and her hips flared, a belated womanly blossoming that had dissolved the hints of tomboyishness she had still possessed two years earlier. She had a deep tan; her hair was unbound.

But such ferocity. No Zyraii had ever exuded it as strongly as she did. Perhaps he was overly sensitive to it, by virtue of their twinness, or the amulets, but there was no question that she had become the kind of warrior the desert itself would admire.

He didn't dwell on it. In the same instant, they had rolled out of their saddles and into each other's embrace.

They stayed that way for a long time. Finally Alemar said solemnly, "The Dragon flies."

She stiffened. "Tell me everything."

He told her what he knew. Her lips pursed tighter and tighter as he spoke. "I feared as much, when I felt your summons," she said.

Alemar became aware of a familiar sensation. "You're hurt," he said.

"It's only a scratch," she said. "It's old. I didn't think it showed."

"It didn't. Let's go down to the spring and I'll take a look."

The next day, Elenya removed the poultice and examined the slice along her vastus muscles. In slightly over twenty-four hours, all that remained of the damage was a section of pink tissue and a slight stiffness when she stretched.

"It's amazing," she said. "It doesn't even look like there will be a scar."

"There won't be," Alemar said.

"Obo would be proud. He could never prevent scars."

"Obo can still do things I can't. This was easy, because of our attunement."

He glanced up the slope they had been climbing. "Let's see what Gast has found out," he said.

They had ridden through the night, conversation filled with their lives of the past year, ending always with the topic of the Dragon. They left unsaid their worries that their effort now might be too late.

The final leg of their journey had been over jagged escarpments and grades not meant for travel. It had cost them time, but they agreed that it was worth avoiding being sighted by anyone from Setan. It would have been too easy to have established a guard around the citadel to thwart their objective. They had abandoned their oeikani a few minutes back, near a water hole.

The healer lay on a smooth rock slab at the ridgeline, lifting only cranium and eyes above the horizon. The twins wormed their way up to either side of him and peered over.

A circular valley opened up in front of them, totally unlike the desolate landscape to be found everywhere else in the eastern Ahrahikte. Steep hills ringed it on every side, the only easy way in being the narrow defile that carried a small tributary to the Ahloorm. The far wall was almost a sheer cliff, its lower face decorated with carved columns, gargoyles, and geometric designs, vestiges of herculean construction long past.

But the relic astonished them not half as much as the verdant orchards, vineyard, and hayfields. A small lake lay up against the cliff; it emptied via canals into furrows, ditches, and smaller reservoirs. The cultivated land formed a broad horseshoe around the relic, the ground immediately in front of the cliff swept bare. The road from the pass led ostensibly straight to the ruins, but the route showing the most wear veered off to the right, to a cluster of buildings.

The village bustled with activity, people standing in the avenues in conversation, individuals striding from door to door on various missions, boys being instructed by blue-robed Ah-no-ken, maintaining their neat rows and proper posture even out in the indolent shade of date palms. Young acolytes of the Zee-no-ken, Bo-no-ken, or Hab-no-ken could be distinguished by their colors as they engaged in menial tasks such as raking, sweeping, or harvesting dates. A few individuals were working out in the fields. A bent old man was carrying a bundle of scrolls from one building to another. The twins could see occasional tents, but for the most part the structures were substantial, of clay or of stone quarried from nearby slopes; and many remarkably fitted with doors or trim of actual wood.

The white garb of the Po-no-ken was absent, nor could a single woman be seen.

"Setan," Gast said reverently.

The twins absorbed the view, if for no other reason than the length of time since they had seen so much water in one place. Finally, distractions fell aside, and their glances settled on the citadel once more. At the very center of the cliff, though faint from the centuries, the twins were able to discern a symbol etched into the stone surface: a dragon in its death throes, an arrow jutting from its midsection.

"The emblem of Alemar," Alemar said. "It is no myth. He built this."

"The mountain is honeycombed with chambers," Gast said, "but the only way in is there." He pointed to a portal near the lake. Both the opening and the entire pool were surrounded by tile trim, some of it now cracked and moss-ridden, but obviously set by a master mason.

"I don't see any guards," Elenya said. Furthermore, there was no door, only an empty frame, thus nothing that could be locked.

"There seldom are any. There is nothing to seal inside. It contains only what you bring."

"What do you mean?"

"You'll see soon enough once you go in. I'll believe that there are physical relics inside only when you bring them out."

Not only was there no guard, but the village stood a good half mile away. An open pasture took up the center of the valley, the few dozen grazing animals it contained the only obstacles between the twins and their goal.

"Now we wait for sunset," Alemar said.

The doorway led into darkness, an ominous blackness impenetrable to Motherworld's brown glow. They had crossed the valley in silence, hugging the edges of the orchards for cover, and now, at last, Alemar and Elenya could reach out and touch the place Keron had sent them to find. The entire trek had lasted twenty-three months. To be certain it was no phantom, Alemar reached out and brushed one of the tiles with his fingers.

"You are sure?" Gast asked.

"It wouldn't make much sense after all this to turn back now," Alemar said. "Give us the layout once more in detail."

Gast sighed. "Immediately within is a small antechamber. You should each take a torch from the stack you will find there. Five corridors lead into the mountain. It doesn't matter which one you take. All will soon bring you to stairways. Take only those which go upward. If you continue straight or descend, you will be lost in mazes. In ages past, before the school was founded, men died within them, unable to find their way out.

"You will need to light your torches at the stairs. At the top, you will find another antechamber. Beyond it lie a series of large rooms. These are the chambers within which the ken are tested. To become a Bo-no-ken, one must enter the first and return. The Hab-no-ken must penetrate the second room, as I once did." For a moment, his voice quavered. "The Zee-no-ken must survive the third."

Gast searched their faces. "If what you seek is truly within the citadel, it must be past the third chamber. Some of the Zee-no-ken have reported seeing a portal at the end of that room. If any have entered, they have never emerged to tell the story."

Suddenly he reached out and clasped Alemer's hand. "I don't want to lose you, my son."

Alemar stepped forward and hugged the old man. "We have to try, master."

"I am not an old fool," Gast said as they separated. "The danger is literal. Only one out of every two who venture into the third room survive as whole human beings. Even the first claims victims. What guarantee have you that your quest is true?"

"Only the word of a ghost," Alemar said, his throat sore. "But you still haven't said what is *in* the rooms."

"All the fears you have ever felt," Gast said. "And nothing else. Remember that: Whatever happens inside, it is nothing more than fear."

"We have company," Elenya said.

They turned toward the mouth of the valley. They heard echoes of many hoofbeats and saw a night-lit shroud of dust.

Gast said, "If they are Po-no-pha, they must leave their weapons and wait for permission of the High Scholar to approach the citadel. But now the ken will know you are here. Go in now, or lose your chance. Take off your clothes."

The twins blinked.

"Take them off," Gast insisted. "You don't want clothes in there. Leave your weapons as well."

They stared at him skeptically.

"Trust me," he implored. "I have been inside. You haven't."

Elenya toyed with the fastenings at her collar. "You can't expect us to leave our weapons here. What happens when we come back out?"

Gast was adamant. "What good will two swordplayers do against many Po-no-pha? And in there, weapons will only be your ruin. You will be undone by your fears." He groaned. "I wish there were more time to prepare you."

The intensity of his plea eventually persuaded the twins to strip, but neither would disarm. They stood ready, naked except for their belts and the weapons hanging from them.

"I feel like an imbecile," Elenya said.

"You look like one, too," Alemar said.

Elenya shot him a backhand swipe. He ducked it. "I see you haven't changed a bit." She smiled.

They needed the humor. One look at Gast's expression was enough to dismay the stoutest heart.

"Choose separate routes," the healer said. "And God be with you." In Zyraii, the phrase mean a permanent farewell.

"And with you," Alemar said. The noises from the far side of the valley were stronger. They took deep breaths and stepped into the dark passageway.

Full of bitter thoughts, Gast gathered their clothing into neat piles and began to prepare the proper eulogies.

XLI

The corridor was lit with cerulean light. It seemed to come from the stone walls themselves, and though this should have dispelled any shadows, the impression was of shadows everywhere. Alemar peered ahead, half expecting something to come shambling toward him, but all that appeared were forks and curves, steps and intersections of halls long lost to sepulchral dust and the mephitis of ancient sorceries. The dread of the wight reawakened, an almost forgotten memory given an unwelcome resurrection.

The passageways contained no artifacts, no designs, and nothing to indicate that they may have served some purpose other than the one to which they were now being put. It awed them to think of the man-hours it must have taken to build this place. Who was this ancestor, that he should construct so laboriously a site he meant to abandon?

He turned a corner and saw a stairwell on his left, sinking into the depths of the citadel. Remembering Gast's instructions, he ignored it and soon found another ahead to his right. The path he had followed led up the steps, marked by channels in the dust. He paused at the base.

Laughter rebounded down the stair, deep baritone cackles that froze him where he stood.

Goose pimples rose on Elenya's flesh. No human voice had produced that laugh. She looked behind and farther down her corridor, and wished that she and Alemar had not separated. The source of the mirth lay upward, where, until a few moments before, she had planned to go.

She understood why searchers of ancient times had passed the climb up and found their fates deeper within the maze.

She struck her flint, igniting the torch. A cheerful glow

dispelled the somber blue of the werelight, momentarily buoying her spirits. The desert people knew how to make their lamps and torches. This one, from the stack in the anteroom, burned almost without smoke, consuming the brand very gradually.

She found it hard to think of herself as an Elandri princess, and of the relic as her ancestor's work. She was Po-no-pha. What was she doing intruding on chambers meant only for the ken?

"Elandri tu," she murmured, trying to convince herself the words were important to her. For Elandris, for the empire, for her father's people. For duty.

She placed her foot on the first step. The light of the corridor went out.

She turned, but found only darkness beyond the range of her torch. Like the laughter, it bothered her. The magics of this place were far from dead.

She took another step. Something boomed in the distance. A third pace, and the wind sputtered her light, almost extinguishing it. The fourth—

And nothing.

Somehow this frightened her more than the active manifestations. She climbed on into ominous silence.

Alemar felt the air close in with every step, thick with the odor of thaumaturgy. The torchlight never penetrated far enough or strongly enough; there was always something lurking just beyond his vision. He had to concentrate to keep breathing normally, his lungs by now aching from constriction. Doubts began to plague him. Gast was right; he should have waited until he was properly prepared.

The flight of steps, though it took forever to climb, was actually quite brief. At the top was an anteroom, just as Gast had described. Like the rest of the citadel, the chamber was empty, its only feature the portal leading into it at the top of the stairs and an identical opening in the opposite wall. As he stepped into it, the room seemed to shrink, pressing in from every side. The walls and ceiling, though he could see otherwise, felt as close as the sides of a coffin. He stopped in the center.

A sibilant hissing came from the darkness. Abruptly Alemar's saber was in his hand. He held the torch higher and approached. Something whispered to him. It spoke the High

Speech, with a Cilendri accent, but the words were indistinct. Surely he only imagined it?

As he started to walk again, his progress was halted by a stench so foul he almost choked. It smelled like death, like something rotting, maggot-ridden, bloated with gases until the guts had exploded and released the fumes to sear the lungs of those who came near. He shuddered. It seemed so real. Nervertheless, he proceeded. The manifestations disappeared as he reached the entrance to the first of the rooms of the Test, the one the Bo-no-ken were required to enter. He took a deep breath and crossed the threshold.

The first thing that happened was that his torch went out.

Elenya screamed aloud as the blackness fell, dropping the torch in her panic. She groped on the floor, but couldn't find it; not even a tiny ember remained to guide her. Instead, her fingers touched something soft, slimy, and living. She jerked away, only to back into a group of sticky, thin strands unmistakably like a spider's web. She felt the prickle of tiny feet on her face, her knees, her back. She brushed frantically, but they came on in greater waves. She felt a bulbous, furry body scurry up her thighs and poke at her womanhood. She squeezed involuntarily, and the creature burst with a sickening *splrrrt,* hot ooze splattering her labia and perineum. *Oh, rythni, it got inside.*

She tried to dig it out, almost nauseated from the scent, but had her footing swept out from beneath her by the slap of a huge, serpentine object. She hit ignominiously on the side of her hips, landing not on stone pavement, but in a wet and yielding mass. In an instant, she had sunk up to her armpits. It felt and smelled like a cesspool, but it clutched at her, dragging her lower. She went down to her chin, panting. When she did free an arm from the suction, it only made the rest of her sink. In another moment, she submerged entirely.

The morass closed over her head. She could feel its foul texture invade her outer ears. She held her breath, reaching up and failing to feel the open air. There was no solid footing beneath. She was trapped. There was no way out.

She cursed the father who had sent her here. She cursed Alemar for coming here. She cursed the ancestor who had made this place.

And gradually, her thinking became clearer. Her anger had given her the key. She had momentarily quelled a small part of her fear. What was it Gast had said? In a few more moments she would be out of air and perish. There was only one way out.

She opened her mouth and inhaled. Filth flowed down her throat. She let it. She let it fill her lungs. She swallowed it until her stomach threatened to burst. Let it kill her. She dared it.

Gone.

Alemar wept in relief. All gone. No more crawling things, no more walls that moved in, no more suffocation, no more sense of falling, no more voices, and no more darkness.

No more darkness. He gawked in surprise. On the floor nearby, his torch sputtered but maintained its flame. It had never gone out. Likewise, the room had been empty all along, merely another bare chamber, though much larger than the anteroom. It contained only a spell, from which all the other creatures and phenomena had sprung, nothing more.

Well, not quite nothing.

Now that he had retrieved the torch and held it up, Alemar could see the mummified remains of human beings at either end, dry skin stretched taut over brittle skeletons: other entrants who had not been so lucky at conquering the magical attack, denied even the token of a comrade who would dare the chamber to drag the corpse out to a decent grave. He grimaced.

He was sitting on the cold floor in a puddle made of his own feces and urine. Gast had advised him well; one should not challenge Setan's rooms of horror wearing clothes. Though it was a small consolation, Alemar was glad to know that he wasn't the first this had happened to, and forgave his master the undetailed warning. He climbed unsteadily to his feet. The terrors may have been phantoms, but his body had reacted to them as if real, and now he ached. He wondered how Elenya was faring, but quickly stifled his apprehension. The room might react to his worry and send him through another round of what it had just given him. Though he knew he could probably deal with it, he needed the energy for the next challenge. The second room, he was certain, would provide it.

He would have liked to rest, but thought better of it. This

was not the place. He would rather get it over with quickly—whatever that meant.

He stood up. One of the corpses, somewhat fresher than the others, lay out toward the middle of the room. He shoved it toward the others with his foot. It slid with a rasp. He tried not to look at the pile of bones beyond it. It was no time to be reminded of failure.

He crossed the threshold into the second room.

As soon as Elenya entered, the room blazed with light. Behind her, a stone barrier slammed to the floor, blocking off her exit. Her eyes had just enough time to adjust to identify the monstrosity before her.

The Dragon virtually filled the huge chamber. It loomed over her, balanced on its tail and rear legs, wings fanned out to either side. She saw the glitter of its scales, the flesh of fantastically long teeth, and worst of all, the intelligence behind its indigo pupils. It laughed, Elenya not hearing it but feeling it inside her mind. It knew her. She knew it. This was Gloroc, bane of her forefathers.

The Dragon waited only just long enough so that she would know the source of her doom. Then he lunged for her, jaws spread wide to swallow her whole, fearsome talons extended. There was no place to duck. She felt her skin pop and eyes melt in the blast of dragonflame, and the snapping of her bones as his teeth skewered her—

Then he was gone.

She sagged to her knees, her torch tumbling out of nerveless fingers. Somehow, uncertainly, her heart remembered how to beat. She was in a room identical to the first. There had been no stone wall dropped behind her; the portal was open. There had been no light, other than her torch. There had been no Gloroc, king of dragons, either.

Fast, so fast, she thought. *Just time enough to die.* That had been the spell's intention of course. Pick the thing whose sudden appearance would cause the greatest fear, and throw it at the victim so fast that there was no time to be rational. She again saw corpses lying toward the sides of the room, even more than in the previous one, a mummified expression of shock on the individual nearest the torchlight. If the spell had been one iota more intense, she would have joined them. But some part of her had realized in time that there was no sensible reason why Gloroc would be here, deep in a mountain in the Eastern Deserts, in a vault with no passageway through which something as large as a dragon could have entered. Still, it had been a terrible jolt. Had she been older or in poor condition, she wouldn't have survived regardless of how well her mind met the challenge.

She was worried by the sentience of the sorcery. This had been no random set of fears thrown at her, as in the first room. Gloroc was a very specific nightmare, and while being fried and swallowed by a dragon would terrify anyone, she was sure that the spell had concocted the image specifically for her. It knew what would scare her, as a unique individual. She wondered if Alemar would face the same trial; it would be logical.

She decided to gather her composure. Whatever the third room held, it was bound to be sinister.

When Alemar had recovered from the vision of Gloroc, he swallowed deeply and crossed into the third room.

No sudden darkness. No blazing menace.

The walls exuded the bluish glow once again. Though he had only seen the person who stood in the center of the room twice in his memory, he recognized him immediately. It was his father.

"You have failed me," Keron said.

The hair on the nape of Alemar's neck rose. "How have I failed? How did you get here?" he asked plaintively.

"I am dead," Keron said. He walked in front of the remains of men who had perished in the room over the ages. The pile was smaller than that of the second room; not many men had penetrated so far within. Alemar could see their dehydrated forms *through* the image of his father. He was a ghost.

"You killed me," Keron continued. "Elandris has fallen to the Dragon. I and all of our relatives have been obliterated. They took me to the torture chamber, where I lingered for days. You are too late. Your quest was our last hope, and now it is for naught."

"No," Alemar moaned. *Go away, go away!* The specter couldn't be real, but nevertheless each word cut like a razor. They had become more than words; they were weapons against which Alemar had no shield.

"It is true. You are the only one left."

"There is Elenya!" Alemar cried.

"Elenya is dead! She didn't survive the third room. It's your fault!"

"I . . . I . . ."

"Go ahead and babble! I wish you had never been born, you incompetent fool! Elandris is ruined. All the effort of my father and his father and his before that, dragged into the mud by the procrastination and indulgence of my own son. Why did you dally in this wasteland? What has it brought you? Have you found what you came for?"

"Leave me alone!"

"No. I shall haunt you. The only joy left me is that I could come here and confront you with your own ineptitude, with your unforgivable irresponsibility. I shall not leave you until you are twisted from your own guilt—until you beg for death!"

Alemar licked the sudor off his upper lip, burned by its saltiness. Something was happening. Something was crumbling inside. Keron was right. Every word was true. The blood of a nation had stained his hands. He could have acted months sooner. He could have returned to Elandris or Cilendrodel and at least contributed to the fight, even if he never found the wizard's talismans. Better yet, he could have tried to find Setan when he'd first arrived in Zyraii. Had he died, at least it would have been an honorable passing.

"Your mother could never have me," Keron hissed. "She had to settle for you. She had to love you in all your wretchedness. Was it enough for her? Did it satisfy her? Did she die content?"

Alemar groaned.

"How can you ever atone? What do you have that is worth the suffering you have caused?"

Alemar didn't remember drawing it, but his saber was in his grip, its steel echoing the color of the walls. *Take it. Slide it across my throat. End this shame. Make it up to my father. Free myself from this agony.*

Gradually, his hand lifted, and set the edge of the sword against his gullet. *Be quick. Cut deep.*

He paused, feeling the solid contact with the loops of the necklaces. One was the talisman that he and Elenya shared, the other the memento of the grateful mother whose child he had saved only a few days before. They would interfere with a good slice. He began to remove them.

He stalled, the paltry bit of turquoise dangling in front of his eyes. Modest as it was, he was proud to have it. He deserved it.

He had had good reasons for delaying the quest. He had been able to protect a fatherless family, had learned a beautiful and just art that would give his life meaning throughout his days, and he had saved a little girl scared of dragons. He had made his decision, and though in the end his duty to Elandris had called him back, he could be proud of the road he had followed in the meantime.

He sheathed his weapon. The phantom of Keron had already vanished. But it was not simply relief that Alemar felt; no, it was exultation. He had beaten a fear that had plagued him during his entire stay in Zyraii, and found in its place a new sense of self-worth. The sorcery of the room had actually helped him. He was a more complete being now than when he had entered. He understood why the ken had conceived of the tests. Those who survived the rooms could rightly provide the spiritual leadership for a nation.

He noted the green flicker of the jewel on his chest. The ghost had lied about everything, even Elenya's death. Alemar refrained from attempting contact. His sister might be struggling for her life at this very instant and need all her concentration.

Lies. Who could say whether or not his father was alive, or how the war was going? They might still have a chance; perhaps a good one. Furthermore, Alemar had not failed. He had thwarted the third room. Beyond, somewhere through the portal that now beckoned, the weapon left by Alemar Dragonslayer was waiting for one of the Blood to claim it. Excitement, not fear, drew him to the entrance of the fourth room.

He was waiting for her in the middle of the third room.

Elenya tensed, expecting the rush of menace or other psychological attack, but all she saw was the lone figure in the middle of a room identical to the previous two. The werelight was back, so she set her own torch in place of the charred remnant in a niche by the door, and moved forward.

He wore a gleaming set of leather armor, cut in the style of the Calinin Empire. The hide could turn or slow all but the best sword thrusts, yet it was light enough so as not to slow its wearer down appreciably. In one hand he bore an Aleoth longsword, as thin as her rapier but, she knew, far stronger, with an edge that allowed him to slash as well as parry and thrust. In his other hand he held a stiletto, an excellent balance to the longsword: he commanded both reach and infighting. The man himself was well over six feet tall, lithe and young. He was a member of the Shadow Corps of Xais, the elite assassins whose founding generations had played the vital role in winning the Old Kingdom for the Calinin.

She began to get worried.

"Draw your weapons," he said. "Or be cut down where you stand."

He had hardly spoken before he charged her. She drew her rapier and deflected his chop in one motion. Though she had almost stepped clear, avoiding most of the force, her arm almost went numb from the impact. She drew her dagger with her other hand and backed up.

He followed, the longsword prodding her like a stubborn oeikani, its length thwarting any counterattack she could think of. He denied her the luxury of time to gain her composure. It was all she could do to stay alive.

A trickle of blood ran down her dagger forearm. She hadn't even seen the jab that had nicked her. Casually, contemptuously, he pinked her on the underside of each breast.

Damn, he was good.

But she survived the first sixty seconds. Though bleeding from half a dozen small cuts, he had not wounded her critically yet. She had time to develop her defense.

She used classical strategies, to save her mind, to give her the time to originate better moves. First the Tiandra Block.

He sloughed it off with the Ezenean Offense, the maneuver Hoy of Orr had developed exactly to circumvent the Tiandra. The man knew his fencing. Not that she had doubted it.

She tried the Square next; and was nearly disembowelled. Likewise he mocked the Southern and the Rhidan Feints. By now she had backed up so far that her ankle came up against one of the dead men. She fell, making it appear that she had stumbled. He leaped forward. She thrust toward his groin. He sprang back, pinked her inner thigh, while she rolled and regained her feet.

Bones and old flesh lay underfoot everywhere in this part of the room. Good—Elenya liked obstacles. Small in stature, she could avoid them with greater ease than a large opponent. She hopped from spot to spot. The assassin imitated her, graceful and sure—but not quite as fast. She had gained the respite needed to take the offensive.

She had realized her earlier error. She had used strategies that were too classical; they all stemmed from the days of the empire and would be well known to one of the Shadow Corps. When she attacked, she used the unique Cilendri Maneuver that had made the original Lord Garthmorron famous.

She was jolted by a sharp pain in her ribs. Suddenly she was on the defensive again, blood pouring out of her side. He had skewered her well that time. She tasted bile deep in her gullet.

He had her now. Already it was hard to hold the dagger on that side. He didn't even have to press the attack now. If he simply held her at bay until the loss of blood sapped her strength, she would be putty in his hands.

He obviously realized this. He broke off and retreated to the center of the room, where the clear floor put the advantage squarely in his territory. He wasn't going to leave her the opportunity for tricks. He was making it plain—she was going to lose.

She was. She could tell. She had met the one. Lonal might have been able to beat her and maybe not, but there was no question with this man. He was a demon. She dropped her dagger and held a palm against her wound. The blood leaked through between her fingers, sticky, hot.

"Amateur," he taunted. "You should have left this art for men."

She tumbled forward, already finding it hard to walk a steady line.

"Such a dainty babe," he said. "You would have made a fine ornament for a harem." He snorted theatrically. "Look. You are so tiny, I could blow you over."

Her rapier began to twitch in her hand. She was still walking forward.

He only smiled. "Put down your toy and—"

She lunged, swallowing the last few paces between them. His point speared her heart, the pain blacking out her awareness. But nothing was going to stop her. She buried her rapier in him up to the hilt even as she fell.

The impact with the floor woke her up again. She ached

incredibly. She hadn't thought it could get much worse after the first two rooms. It took her several long, heavy breaths before she could lift her head up.

The room was empty.

Gradually she understood. She had ceased to care whether she lived or died. She was willing to sacrifice herself, as long as she could avoid defeat. In so doing, she had lost all fear.

Three times the spell had captured her. She should have felt like a fool; instead she laughed. She pitied the man who might challenge her with the sword in the future. After this, what could intimidate her?

Three rooms, three types of fear. In the first, primal terror—all the things that traditionally frighten human beings. In the second, the fear of the enemy, of sudden death at the hands of the Other whose greatest desire is to destroy you. In the third, fear of failure—self-doubt—not technically a fear at all, but just as threatening. What, Elenya wondered, would come next?

She stood up. Her knees were skinned, her jaw sore from banging it on the floor, but she had suffered no permanent damage. She was ready, full of an intoxicating sense of resolve, to enter the fourth room.

XLII

The fourth room was different, Elenya realized. It was smaller, and contained none of the human remains that had distinguished the others. But like its predecessors, it resembled a vault, hollow and barren. Only after a few seconds did she notice that the walls seemed smoother than in the other chambers. They were marble, polished slick and so perfectly seamed that the cracks between the sections barely showed. There was no door on the other side of the room; the way she had come was the only visible access. She took a few cautious steps forward.

Four things happened.

First, the by now familiar blue illumination increased to full, white light, painful to her pupils. While she blinked, a stone partition sealed off the portal through which she had come. Simultaneously, a section of the far wall slid away, revealing a niche that housed a large, sealed tank of water. The tank contained objects Elenya immediately recognized as Elandri airmakers. Finally, a crack appeared in the floor, splitting it down the middle across her path. Both halves of the floor began to fold downward, as if hinged at the walls. The widening crevice smelled dank and led to darkness.

She could hear mechanisms whirr within the structure. The floor dipped slowly, but inexorably. It took only a moment for her to ascertain that neither the walls nor the floor would provide any hand- or footholds. She was going to be dumped into whatever waited below.

All at once she identified the scent rising from the opening. It was water.

The gap spread to almost six feet across. The slope was now almost thirty degrees. Cursing, she sprinted to the edge and jumped. She landed on the balls of her feet and scurried up the other side.

The tank lid was not locked. She lifted it, grabbed the nearest airmaker, and quickly set it over her head, letting go of the lid. By the time she had adjusted the fit securely, the floor was listing sharply. She could stay there until the room dumped her, or she could face the pit immediately. She made her decision, sat down on the floor, legs flat in front, and slid down past the edge and into space.

She fell only a dozen feet before she struck the water. She scissor-kicked, halting her descent. She didn't bother to rise; she was already breathing through the airmaker. To her relief, she had only been down a few moments when the light increased. Soon she could make out her surroundings.

Above, the floor of the room continued to unfold. It didn't stop until both halves hung perpendicular to the surface of the water. The fourth room didn't like visitors, but its riddle was now plain to Elenya.

It was a physical trap, not one of sorcery. Small wonder that no one had ever returned from beyond the third room. If, as she suspected, most of those who had tried over the ages had been Zyraii, then they had endured the most unusual cause of death the desert people could imagine. Except for occasional flash flood victims, no one in the nation drowned.

The room wanted only individuals who knew what airmakers were to survive.

The smooth marble walls continued downward on all four sides. Somewhere far below Elenya detected the convoluted rock that must have been the original, natural walls of the spring that lay under Setan. On one side, however, she could see a large, square opening some twenty feet from the surface.

She descended, rediscovering how good it felt to have water around her body. The coolness invigorated her and rinsed the sweat of fright from her skin. She took a moment to wash herself more thoroughly, and felt better than she had since entering Setan.

Such a long period without swimming awakened vivid memories of her first use of the airmakers. She had finally reached an age when Obo, her grandfather, and Lord Dran had agreed that she and Alemar could be told their heritage, and one of the first fringe benefits took the form of training to use the ancient devices. The experience by itself would have been memorable enough, but coupled with the idling through the deeps and shallows was the chance to fantasize about being an Elandri princess. She was young enough for that to seem grand

and precious, and the airmakers had always thereafter represented the romantic visions that failed to come true once she neared adulthood. Thus far being an Elandri princess had meant little beyond hard training and personal sacrifice.

Armed with a little bit of feckless confidence of a more naive point in life, she passed through the opening tunnel. She saw no markings or side openings. The passageway tilted slightly upward, and at the far end the light seemed brighter.

The distance was greater than could be expected of a man holding a single breath. Finally the tunnel ended and her head popped up into clear air.

Alemar found himself in still another barren chamber. But this one, unlike the others, contained a living man.

Alemar pulled the airmaker off his head and jumped out of the pool. He knelt down beside the stranger and gently lifted his head. The man opened rheumy eyes. He was middle-aged, emaciated, and ripe with the odor of diarrhea and vomit. He wore a tattered robe similar to that of a Po-no-pha, but so soiled and worn that it was difficult to tell if it had ever been white. Only his sword seemed to be in good condition.

"Who are you?" Alemar asked in Zyraii. "How did you get here?" He saw no other entrances.

"Eehhhhh," the man said. Just to exhale seemed to cause him strain.

Alemar took the man's hand and concentrated. *What is wrong? Why do you suffer? How may I ease your pain?*

The voices of the man's body were faint. Alemar felt like a beginning apprentice, his attempt feeble when the man's condition required sure and tested talent. He heard hollow echoes. It was nothing like any other living human he had ever scanned before. It was almost as if the man were . . . empty.

"Help me," the stranger rasped.

But Alemar didn't know what to do. He couldn't tell if the man's intestines were inflamed, if his lungs were rotted, if he had been poisoned, or even if his heart were beating normally. The knowledge and the Sight had left him.

He had only one choice. He opened the man's collar and placed both hands firmly on the latter's chest. He called on his energies, and felt them begin to flow from his fingertips.

The man screamed.

Alemar broke contact, smoke rising from the spot he had

touched. Livid imprints of his hands still remained, seared into the man's skin. The man emitted a rasp and his eyes glazed over.

"No!" Alemar cried. He looked at his betraying palms.

The smoke increased. Hissing and popping, the man's hair, skin, and clothing began dissolving away. Alemar stepped back, horrified. Greasy pools formed beneath the body, themselves bubbling and evaporating away. The rib cage appeared, at first covered with red, brown and gray coatings of tissue, until these in turn fumed away, leaving only gleaming white bone. The eyes exploded. Foul gases burbled out of body cavities. Finally, every last bit of soft tissue had vanished. The floor contained only a skeleton, an ancient one at that.

All except the sword. Its belt and scabbard had melted along with everything else, but the blade sparkled in the artificial light.

The skeleton reached out and grasped the sword hilt.

Alemar retreated halfway to the pool. The skeleton clambered to its feet, joints rattling and creaking, but united as if tendons, muscles, and cartilage were still present. It advanced toward Alemar.

It's not real, Alemar told himself. *It is another spell. Another test of the mind.* Though filled with a preternatural dread, he planted his feet and waited for the creature to come.

It didn't hesitate a moment. When it came within range, it swung the sword like an axe at Alemar's neck.

Just in time, Alemar fell back. The sword tip nicked his throat, leaving a superficial but profusely flowing cut.

The skeleton laughed.

The blood convinced Alemar. The wound was real. This spell wasn't like the others. It had found a fear he could not conquer. He would always be a healer, and always hold inside the worry that one day his talent would fail him. The skeleton wouldn't go away. It could, and would, kill him. As the knowledge settled into his mind, the room shifted. The dust of the centuries appeared. Lying in molding piles were the remains of three previous visitors who had penetrated this far. To his shock, the freshest corpse wore the insignia of the Claw, Gloroc's prized cadre of assassins.

The skeleton waited patiently. It knew it had no need to rush. It had waited centuries for its few victims. It might wait many more before another breached the chamber. In the meantime, it would enjoy the diversion. Alemar felt the trickle from his neck pass his belt and start down his leg.

Tentatively he drew his weapon.

The hilt felt alien. He had not wielded it in actual conflict since the pass of Hattyre. But his childhood training had been exhaustive, and his general physical condition was as good or better than it had ever been, minus the ordeal of the past few hours. Perhaps he had a chance.

The skeleton, as if reading his thoughts, cackled again and began with a thrust.

Alemar avoided it and returned a riposte. The skeleton ignored it. The tip of the saber slipped between two ribs, inflicting no damage. The skeleton casually lapsed into the Ezenean Offense. Alemar parried and retreated. The classic move was not a potent one, but it was difficult to counter or redirect—a safe, time-consuming way for a superior player to wear out an unskilled challenger.

Alemar swore. This was a situation for armor and a battle axe. The only threat he could pose to his enemy were in hacking blows designed to break the bones. His saber wasn't meant for that.

Nevertheless, he had to try. The skeleton taunted him, left him openings, so he took one. He slashed toward the thing's ribs again. The edge of the weapon clattered against the target, creating sparks and leaving a numbing tingle in Alemar's wrist.

More sorcery. The skeleton was not only animate, it was invulnerable. At any point, whenever it tired of the fray, it could simply step in and butcher Alemar.

Alemar fenced for his life. He was far better than the thing. Its movements were mechanical; it was slow as well. Even out of practice, Alemar would have won in seconds if the contest had been against a mortal being. But each time he successfully jabbed or slashed, the only reward was a bell-like clang and more sparks. Once, he knocked a few grains out of the skeleton's collarbone, but the blow left Alemar's arm so nerveless that he had to transfer his weapon to the other hand.

Alemar had always been an ambidextrous swordplayer, and he continued now to fight with nearly equal skill, but it was increasingly hard to motivate himself. He adopted a strictly defensive strategy. But he was tired, and could only get more tired, while the thing never wore out.

Finally, the skeleton thrust more strongly. Alemar parried.

Another thrust, another parry. Five more, and Alemar met each one. Then the thing nicked him on a bicep. A few blows later, another scratch on the thigh. Within another two minutes, he was wounded superficially in several places, and droplets of blood splattered the floor. The time had come. The creature was through with its game.

Alemar wept. All these years and miles, just to be cut down like so much wheat. He clenched his teeth in rage.

The skeleton battered at him again. This time, he returned a savage cut to its neck.

The saber burst in two. Alemar jumped back, narrowly avoiding a stab at his chest. His feet landed on something slick, and he tumbled down.

He landed on his back, the shock to his kidneys knocking the wind out of him. He had slipped in a pool of his own blood. With one arm numb from the slash that had destroyed the saber, he could do no more than lift the remaining arm to ward off the killing cut.

The skeleton raised its weapon and stepped forward to finish its victim. Its foot stepped in the pool of blood.

And it paused.

It looked down at its foot. The bones smoked. Waiting a few seconds, it had dissolved up to the tarsals. The creature let out a plaintive whimper.

"The blood of Alemar!" it said.

The remainder of the skeleton dissolved rapidly, momentarily leaving a caldronish puddle; then this, too, boiled away. Only the sword remained.

The mountain trembled with the sound of a thunder crack. The wall opposite the pool vanished. A small pentagonal chamber was revealed. Another loud boom followed, and abruptly the side walls disappeared as well. The new chamber was now the center of a much larger pentagon, the increased area composed of Alemar's room and four other identical spaces, obviously the end points of the other routes into the citadel. In one of them, Elenya was lowering her rapier, amazement on her face. She spotted Alemar and gasped. Together they stared at the center of the room.

On a five-sided dais in the center of the area stood a short dark-haired man, clothed in wizard's robes. In his hands he held two jewel-studded mail gauntlets. He stared out at an indeterminate location, as if unable to see either of the twins.

"I am Alemar Dragonslayer," the wizard said.

The twins blinked. No, it wasn't their famous ancestor in the flesh. The figure was translucent. If they tried, they could see the far walls through him. Only the gauntlets seemed substantial.

"That you can see this image means that the blood of my blood has successfully unwrought the spell I laid upon this sanctuary. You can only have come because the child of Faroc and Triss has at last appeared, and that which I prepared to meet this eventuality is now needed." He raised the gauntlets. "These are my greatest creations. Wear these, and you cannot be dragon-touched. Their very proximity will cause any dragon great pain. You must have these if you are to successfully challenge this monster. Dragons can weave illusions on a grandiose scale—only the wearer of these gloves will be able to utterly thwart this power. But do not depend on these alone. I have left other things, as you no doubt know. I hope that there are those left among my family with the proper attunement to use any or all of my legacies. But have caution. These and all my talismans were designed for use by me or my sister. They will not work as well for any other. Put your trust not merely in my trinkets, but in your own abilities and courage."

The wizard dropped the gauntlets to the floor. They grew more solid than ever, while the man began to fade. "I can offer you only one other small bit of advice, and hope that not so much time has passed as to make it useless: Seek the followers of Struth, the Frog God. In my time, their temple was in Headwater, the capital of Serthe, my birthplace. They will know how to defeat a dragon."

And he was gone. But the gauntlets waited on the floor where he stood. Alemar walked forward and picked them up.

They were light, lighter in fact than if they had been made of leather or cloth, but the feel was that of cold metal and polished gems. Tiny jewels were strewn like sequins everywhere except the palms. A large gemstone, each of a different type and color, decorated the base knuckle of every finger and thumb. The mail seemed to be made of gold. Alemar tried one on.

The weight increased so suddenly he dropped involuntarily to his knees, his hand striking the floor with a thud. The impact dented the stone. At once, the world changed. He could see that the floor beneath him was actually the lid of a well. A few feet below him lay another branch of the pool that ran under Setan, a passage leading away toward what Alemar guessed was the outside. He could see waves of light around Elenya, each one exuding a particular character and intensity. Stretching his new perceptions, he could see the gossamer web of sorcery knit into every crack of the mountain. Even as he watched, its structure was dissipating. The purpose of the magic had been fulfilled; there was no longer any need for the energies to maintain their ancient cycles. It was so potent a work of thaumaturgy that it might take hours for it to entirely vanish. Setan, as Gast had feared, would never again serve the ken as it had for centuries.

He was so mesmerized that he only belatedly realized that he was standing, buoyed up by a strength greater than any he had ever felt. It flowed from the gauntlet, but he could sense that the source, as in the case of his father's belt, came from himself. The gauntlet took that power, magnified it, returned it to him, and then drew off of the increased amount, recirculating the same energy to ever-higher levels. Its principle was much the same as his and Elenya's necklaces, but instead of the strength being squared, it was limited only by what he could physically endure. Unlike his father's belt, it would not enable him to lift boulders. He sensed that it suited itself to its wearer's character. In his case, it multiplied his endurance.

"Here," he said, holding out the other gauntlet to Elenya. "No one person could wear both of these."

She came and took it. He watched her go through a similar period of orientation. When it was over, he noticed a phenomenal quickness to some of her movements. She tested it, sheathing her weapon and drawing it again, spinning, flipping, and simply running. She uttered a laugh of pure enjoyment.

"The Dragon doesn't stand a chance," she said.

He pursed his lips. That, unfortunately, was simply not true. "Come. Let's be on our way."

They retrieved their airmakers from where they had dropped them, found the handle in the dais that opened the hatch, and jumped into the water.

Gast set at the edge of the pool of Setan, slightly apart from the others who waited for the two who had gone into the citadel. He was almost forgotten now. A knot of several dozen members of the ken, as well as the Po-no-pha who had arrived with

Lonal, had surrounded the entrance. Gast could see their angry faces by the torches they held, and he wished for the return of the High Scholar and the latter's calming influence.

Gast wondered how long the vigil would last. When the twins failed to emerge, how many days would they wait? Would they send men inside to find them? He thought not.

The healer's eyes wandered to the mountain's face. Was it his imagination, or was the emblem—the sigil that his apprentice had assured him was that of Alemar Dragonslayer—actually glowing? Though the night was dark, he could clearly see the outline of the convulsing dragon. It seemed to be growing brighter, although curiously, the arrow in its belly remained dim, like the stone it had been carved in.

Suddenly the water of the pool bubbled. A moment later, two heads broke the surface. The Po-no-pha beside him jumped. Gast shouted with joy.

The twins clambered out onto the tile at the pool's edge, only a few yards from Gast. They stood naked, shivering, and marked by wounds, their skin pale in the starlight. They were alive! God had been merciful.

As the twins drew off the strange devices covering their heads and dropped them back into the water, the crowd of warriors and priests rushed to the site. But even as the twins turned to face the charge, all present stopped short and gasped.

The emblem in the mountain blazed. The figure of the dragon moved, became three-dimensional, a phantasmal bluish outline—abstract, obviously not real, but more terrifying by that fact. It spread wings wide and pounced toward Alemar and Elenya.

Both twins raised the strange gauntlets they wore. A nimbus of orange light surrounded them. The dragon veered off, uttering an angry cry. It circled three times, then streaked away into the northwestern sky. To Elandris.

"He knows," Alemar said.

All waited in surprise for a moment, then the Zyraii pressed forward, surrounding the twins on three sides. Angry voices murmured. Gast sighed. The westerners had come so far, and done so much. His countrymen had always been their greatest obstacle. Including himself.

"Stop!"

The voice sounded old and wavered, but it carried. At once, every Zyraii present halted in his tracks. They all knew the speaker, and when he spoke, all in the land listened.

The old man came forward, black robes rustling. He was the only member of the ken in the nation who wore black. He went straight to Alemar and Elenya, his stride bold and steady in spite of his advanced years.

"Give me your names," he told them. "Your true names."

"I am Alemar, of the dynasty of Alemar," came the reply. "My sister is Elenya."

Gast saw the old priest's shoulders shift, as if the burden of his entire life's work had been removed in one moment. He looked much older. He also looked relieved. Black cloth whirling, he turned to the crowd.

"Let them go."

Silence. Then all members of the ken backed swiftly away. The Po-no-pha hesitated.

"You heard High Scholar Esidio," Lonal said from the forefront. "His word is law." The warriors obeyed, some grudgingly, though in truth the priesthood had more reason to be offended at the violation of the sacred site.

"Let no one hinder their path from our land. If any should molest them, they and all their clan will be banished from Zyraii forever." In a softer, worried voice Esidio added, "They are the hope of all Tanagaran. Without them, the desert will be blackened, and our people killed or enslaved."

The crowd backed even farther away. The only ones left near the twins were Gast, Esidio, and Lonal. The latter produced the twins' clothing, which they gratefully put on. Esidio went to Alemar and Elenya and grasped them both firmly, as if to be sure they were real. "I have waited a long time for you."

"We owe you our lives," Alemar said.

"No. The debt is not to me," Esidio said somberly. He turned to Lonal. "I wish your father had lived to see this day." Without another word, he turned and walked back toward the community. The crowd parted quickly. Esidio had been one of the kindest, and most good-humored, high scholars within memory. He had never before threatened countrymen with banishment, the greatest punishment of all.

"God seems to let you get away with anything," Lonal told Elenya.

Alemar saw that it was time to look the other way. He helped Gast untie his bonds.

"I feared for your life, master."

"So did I. But blood is not spilled in Setan, and no Hab-no-ken in history has ever been put to death. It would have taken some time for them to decide what to do with me. And Esidio cooled their tempers. He seemed to be expecting all this."

"The aura around him was unlike anyone in the entire group," Alemar murmured.

"Eh?"

The young man held up his gauntlet. "I'll explain later. Whether God's on our side or not, the sooner we are away from here, the better." He nodded toward the still observant assemblage. "They are only part of it. Gloroc knows we are here. That was his spell that attacked us when we came out of the pool. He must have known about this relic for some time, and set an alarm. I found the body of one of his servitors inside."

He turned to his sister. She and Lonal finished a whispered conversation.

"Time to go," Alemar said.

Elenya nodded.

"We located your oeikani," Lonal said. "I will see that they are brought." He left to issue the command.

From deep within the mountain came the rumbles of falling rock. The Zyraii stirred uneasily. Gast shot a quizzical look at Alemar.

"Its job is done," he answered. "Not everything's going to hold together as well anymore." He stroked the gauntlet. "But what a work it was."

Alemar sighed as Gast tended his injuries. The healer and the twins were a few miles from Setan. Dawn teased the hills. Nearby the narrow tributary of the Ahloorm gurgled over cobbles, its lullaby taking Alemar to the other lands, where one never worried about getting enough to drink. Home. That would be their first goal. If the Dragon Sea were impassable, they couldn't deliver the gauntlets to Elandris. Keron would eventually look for them in Cilendrodel. Together they might pursue the lead concerning the temple of Struth.

"What will you do now, master?" Alemar asked, though his attention was on Elenya. She sat at the stream's edge, glancing frequently back the way they had come.

"Do not call me master," Gast said. "Your training is complete. You have been through the rooms of Setan. You are Hab-no-ken now."

Alemar assumed he would be glad when either his quest or his study of healing was fulfilled. Now both had culminated in one night, and he wasn't relieved. "I pray that I do the art justice."

"I rather think you will have more opportunity to practice than most of us. As for me, I have the implied protection of the High Scholar. I will make myself inobtrusive for a season or two, then return to my old haunts. Fear not for me."

They detected the clop of hooves. Elenya sprang to her feet. A single rider appeared around the last bend.

"I was wondering when he'd show up," Alemar said.

Lonal reined up nearby, but remained on his oeikani. They all looked at one another and hesitated, as if reluctant to disturb the dawn quiet.

"I came to say I'm sorry," Lonal said finally.

"For what?" Alemar asked.

"I put many obstacles in the way of your quest. If what Esidio says is true, your mission may mean more to Zyraii than my whole life's work."

"You couldn't have known that. Even we can't be sure it's true."

"Nevertheless it's a bit humbling. I wish that I had been able to give you something as worthy."

Alemar lifted the material of his green robes. Elenya, just as emphatically, held out her scarred wrist. Lonal raised his eyebrows, then laughed merrily. "You are kind. But then, Esidio did tell me that there were reasons why it was necessary for you to become a healer. I suppose we were all following God's plan."

"Or someone's," Alemar said.

Lonal looked at Elenya, and his eyes rested there for a long time. "You are taking my best war-second," he said mournfully, and paused. "Where will I ever find another like her?"

"You'll find many more," Elenya replied with conviction. "Xurosh has seen to that."

"I think you're wrong," he said in a husky voice. "It would take another miracle." He turned to Alemar. "Tell me, are all the women in Cilendrodel like her?"

"None."

"You see? Your brother understands." He urged his mount forward with a subtle pressure of his knees. He and Elenya touched wrists together, joining the scars of the *hai-Zyraii*. They parted slowly. Lonal headed back to Setan.

"I will not forget you," she called after him. He didn't answer.

"Last night Esidio told him he would become opsha," Gast said of the departing figure.

"I don't have any doubt," Elenya said. "I envy him, you know," she told Alemar.

"Why?"

"Because Lonal wants his destiny."

She looked at her gauntlet, which she wore on the left hand. She picked up a small cobblestone and squeezed. It broke. "I have a Fear," she said. "I think you will understand what I mean. I am afraid of a life where I am nothing but a warrior, fighting for causes not my own. Sooner or later I'd be left standing in the midst of open desert, and all the people I've known—friends, lovers, and even you, brother—would turn and run from the killer I've become, leaving me alone, with only myself to fight."

Alemar came forward and held her.

"If you hadn't defeated our ancestor's spell when you did," she said gravely, "I might have died of loneliness."

"I understand." Only after he had said it was he aware that he had bespoken her. The amulets took so little concentration now.

"I don't know what we're facing now," she replied in kind, *"but at least we'll be out of this mad country."* She pulled off the gauntlet and regarded it. "Let's see if we can put these to good use, after all."

Alemar nodded. They climbed into their saddles and began riding. The lands of the Dragon Sea were calling.

GLOSSARY

Achird The sun. The star around which Motherworld revolves.

Ahloorm "The River." The only major river traversing the Zyraii nation, source in the mountains north of Setan, outlet in the Gulf of Chrysajen.

Ah-no-ken Sect of the ken responsible for the daily religious affairs of the tribes, including teaching, counselling, and leading of religious rites such as prayer and the *pulstrall*. Blue robes.

Alemar Dragonslayer Founder of Elandris; slayer of the dragons Faroc and Triss. Also Alemar the Great, Alemar I.

Bo-no-ken Ruling sect of the ken, possessing the power to make laws, promote Ah-no-ken, exile individuals from or adopt them into the tribe. Red robes.

Bu "The Game of Life." In Zyraii religion, God provided souls to men in order that they might play out the great scheme of existence. The Bu is the development of character over many lifetimes.

Buyul A tribe of Zyraii bordering the T'lil on the south descended from Cadra's fourth son Yul.

Cadra Progenitor of the Zyraii.

Calinin 1. An ancient nation in the far west of the southern continent. 2. The empire that originated in Calinin, composed, at various times, of the countries of Calinin South, Aleoth, Cotan, Acalon, Tanjand, Agon, Neith, Tiandria, Serthe, Riannehn, Sirithrea, Numaron, Irigion, Rhida, Rhada, and Moin, as well as the motherland. 3. Those lands culturally and linguistically tied to the empire, including the countries above as well as Ranagara, Elandris, and Cilendrodel.

Dark Night A term applied to those rare occasions when Achird, the Sister, Motherworld, and all of the moons are below Tanagaran's horizon. Although traditionally celebrated only once a year, Dark Nights may happen as often as a month apart. Likewise, many Dark Nights are barely dark at all; total lack of suns, moons, and mother planet sometimes last as little as an hour. One of the major preoccupations of early Tanagaranese astronomers was the calculation of when Dark Night would occur.

drelb A dwarfish people inhabiting the countries of Transilia, Intralia, Cisilia, Drelbhaven, and the Drelbmarch.

Ena The second largest clan of the T'lil.

Faroc The male of the pair of dragons that once ruled the Dragon Sea, slain by Alemar the Great.

the Frog Royalist euphemism for Gloroc; a derogatory term.

Hab-no-ken Healing sect of the ken, possessing no rank within the priesthood but endowed with considerable prerogatives. Green robes.

hada A sect of the Zee-no-ken possessing the power of precognition, distinguished by their gray robes.

haiya Honor. A heightening of the reputation of a tribe or individual Po-no-pha by virtue of noble deeds.

hai-Zyraii A state conferred upon an individual Po-no-pha, through blood ritual, in recognition of deeds that greatly benefit the Zyraii nation.

Hattyre 1. An ancient Zyraii hero, killed in battle. 2. The hills dividing the western sections of the T'lil and Buyul from their eastern sections, where Hattyre was killed.

hoeanaou A tree found along the middle and lower reaches of the Ahloorm, ranging up to three hundred feet high and nine feet in diameter.

hussa A small, burrowing rodent, living communally in prominent mounds, found throughout the Eastern Deserts and the Ahirinar Steppes.

ju-moh-kai 1. Literally, the game of blades. 2. A duel fought with edged weapons.

ken The priesthood of the Zyraii, consisting of four castes: Zee-no-ken, Bo-no-ken, Ah-no-ken, Hab-no-ken.

Miranda Sister of Alemar Dragonslayer; inventor of the airmaker; cofounder of Elandris.

Motherworld The gas giant planet around which Tanagaran revolves.

Menhir of T'lil A stone monument, possibly a meteorite, at the Oasis of Shom. The most holy relic of the T'lil tribe.

niutap Adoption of a foreigner into a Zyraii tribe, in order to replace a slain member of the tribe.

oeikani (wah-kah-nee) A large, herbivorous mammal found throughout Tanagaran, used as a saddle and pack beast, and occasionally as a source of food. Plural: oeikani.

olom A stash of coffee selected by a trader as being the best of his lot. May be any of the different coffees he is transporting, or a blend, entirely dependent on his mood and the quality of that particular cargo.

opsha The military leader of all Zyraii.

opsib 1. Originally, the supreme religious leader of Zyraii. 2. Since the passing of Mhemet, great-grandson of Cadra, the term applies to the highest-ranked Bo-no-ken of each tribe.

Po-no-pha (Po-no-fa) The warrior class among the Zyraii. Any adult male of property, capable of bearing arms, is automatically a Po-no-pha, regardless of other professions he may have, unless he enters the priesthood.

rashemi A drug used to induce trance.

rythni The fairy people of Cilendrodel, a reclusive, intelligent race rich in sorcery and worshipping tranquillity. Adults range from ten to twelve inches high. Females are winged during their reproductive years.

sagecrawler A large, herbivorous lizard of the Eastern Deserts, prized for its highly edible flesh.

sand-runner A moderately large, bipedal lizard common to the Ahloorm Basin.

Serpent Moon A moon of Motherworld, original home of dragons and the serpent men.

the Sister Achird's orange companion star, visible from Tanagaran even in daylight.

So-de'es A great religious council called by Mhemet, great-grandson of Cadra, at which the holy laws of Zyraii were codified. Slightly appended to within the next few generations, the laws of the So-de'es became the inviolable moral canon for many centuries.

soul An aspect of Man that is entirely immaterial.

Tanagaran The world. Fifth moon of Motherworld.

T'krt Largest clan of the T'lil.

T'lan A minor clan of the T'lil.

T'lil The second largest tribe of modern Zyraii, descended from Cadra's seventh son, Lil.

torovet Raid. An attack by one Zyraii tribe upon another, governed by strict rules. Often used by Po-no-pha to increase their haiya.

Trance of the Listener An altered state of consciousness, in which the awareness of the practitioner is heightened in order to receive psychic messages. Often used in conjunction with the Trance of the Speaker.

Trance of the Searcher An altered state of consciousness, in which the awareness of the practitioner travels out of the body.

Trance of the Speaker An altered state of consciousness, which a practitioner may use to send messages to other beings, particularly those in the Trance of the Listener.

Triss The female of the pair of dragons that once ruled the Dragon Sea, slain by Polk (kill later credited to Alemar).

vartham A transparent, incredibly strong substance created by Miranda and Alemar the Great, used to form the great domes that enclose the underwater cities. Like the airmakers, the secret of its creation was lost with the two great sorcerers.

Zee-no-ken Monastic sect of the ken, uninvolved in political and social life, often hermits. Highest ranked of the ken, but possessing no secular authority. Most of the Zee-no-ken wear brown, the exceptions being the gray of the hada and the black of the High Scholar.

ANDREW OFFUTT'S

CORMAC MAC ART SERIES

Son of an Irish King, in bitter exile from the land of his birth and the woman of his heart, Cormac mac Art has made a life and a name for himself with his wits and his strength and his bright, deadly sword...

☐ 76354-5	**SIGN OF THE MOONBOW**	$2.50
☐ 79143-3	**SWORD OF THE GAEL**	$2.50
☐ 81925-7	**THE TOWER OF DEATH**	$2.50
☐ 84516-9	**THE UNDYING WIZARD**	$2.50

Prices may be slightly higher in Canada.

Available at your local bookstore or return this form to:

ACE FANTASY
Book Mailing Service
P.O. Box 690, Rockville Centre, NY 11571

Please send me the titles checked above. I enclose ______. Include 75¢ for postage and handling if one book is ordered; 25¢ per book for two or more not to exceed $1.75. California, Illinois, New York and Tennessee residents please add sales tax.

NAME______________________________

ADDRESS______________________________

CITY______________________ STATE/ZIP______________________

(allow six weeks for delivery) SF 7